The Daughter's Secret

The Daughter's Secret

EVA HOLLAND

First published in Great Britain in 2015
by Orion Books,
an imprint of The Orion Publishing Group Ltd
Carmelite House, 50 Victoria Embankment
London, EC4Y 0DZ

An Hachette UK Company

1 3 5 7 9 10 8 6 4 2

A CIP catalogue record for this book is
available from the British Library.

ISBN (Trade Paperback) 978 1 4091 5703 8
ISBN (Ebook) 978 1 4091 5705 2

Typeset by Born Group within Book Cloud

Printed in Great Britain by CPI Mackays

The Orion Publishing Group's policy is to use papers that
are natural, renewable and recyclable products and made
from wood grown in sustainable forests. The logging and
manufacturing processes are expected to conform to the
environmental regulations of the country of origin.

www.orionbooks.co.uk

For Rachael

ELEVEN DAYS

I was forty-two years old when I stopped worrying. I don't know why it happened then. Maybe it was the quietness of the almost-empty house or the way that one day melted into the next without Freddy to feed and argue with. Or maybe I had worried so much for so long that my neural pathways had been ground to dust and my brain could no longer make the leaps required to see the catastrophes waiting behind the acts of everyday life.

I noticed the change when I started to linger in sleep. Instead of waking before dawn, my eyes springing open to lock sights on the threats of the day, I would breach consciousness only with Dan's alarm. Sometimes I went back to sleep, slipping into that limbo state in which dreams link arms with reality and the sound of Dan in the shower became the lash of rain or the thrum of an aeroplane cabin. I started to be late for morning classes; I was no longer the woman outside the lecture theatre five minutes before it opened, a black coffee clenched in a tense claw. I was the one who slid into the back of the room at ten past nine with a smile and a nod, the woman I had always envied.

Like tuning into the picture on an old television set, another way of living came into view. It grew in clarity every day. I once read an interview with an obese woman who had spent decades trying to lose weight. Her greatest wish, she said, was to live for a day in the body of a thin woman. I was like that woman but my wish had come true: I was living in the skin of a normal person, seeing the world through eyes untainted by panic.

At the same time that my anxiety dwindled, things around me started to settle. It was as if some mighty cosmic force had whispered *shhhh* and the fretting and striving that drove motion and action had diminished then ceased. The cogs of life continued to whirr: sleep was slept, food was eaten, walks were taken, books were read, but nothing significant – nothing that could be classed as a happening, an event – took place. Other people didn't seem to have noticed. I asked some: Dan, Beatrice, Cam. I even asked Stephanie when she rang one evening, but she said she didn't understand what I meant. Now, of course, I wonder whether she knew that things were only slowing down to gather strength for what was to come.

I should have known it couldn't last.

It was at three o'clock in the afternoon on Thursday the twentieth of November when the beeping ring of the phone happened. I heard it as I shook off my coat and pushed the front door closed behind me, the smell of Cam still caught in the weave of my scarf. I knew it was Tanya before she had finished forming the first syllable of my name. Her voice had once been so welcome but on that afternoon, after years of silence – her silence – it was as unwanted as orange juice after toothpaste. It was the sound of the past, of things I had tried to forget.

'Ros, I wanted to call you as soon as I heard,' she said. She had never been one for small talk, which had seemed surprising for a police Family Liaison Officer. I remember waiting for her to come to the door the first time. I imagined cardigans, platitudes and coffee breath. I thought she would hold my cold, trembling hands with cold, trembling hands of her own. But that wasn't what she did at all. Sometimes she reminded me to get dressed in the mornings. Sometimes she made Freddy's sandwiches and took him to school. Sometimes she stood outside our door and snarled at the press pack until the clump of reporters and photographers retreated to the café at the end of the road, at least for a while. Was it any wonder that I had clung to her so tightly?

'What is it?' I said.

'He's getting out early. At the beginning of next month.'

'Which month?' Of course I knew what she meant but I couldn't think of anything else to say.

'December, Rosalind. Eleven days from now.' Her voice was calm and solid; I could have leant on it if I had let myself. I could picture her at her desk, her dark hair pulled back from her face, the pale scar that runs from her left ear to the corner of her mouth flexing as she spoke.

'But they said seven years. At least seven years,' I said. 'It's only been five and a half.'

'He's been a good boy and the prisons are bursting at the seams. There's nothing we can do about it, no right of appeal.' She sounded flat, resigned. Where had her anger gone? Her omnipotent bitterness? 'Do you think Stephanie knows?'

'No. I can't see how she would.'

'She doesn't see him, then? There's no contact at all? Letters? Visits? Phone calls?'

'No, of course not. She got over it all. She moved on.'

'I hope so, but you remember what she said back then, Ros. Where's she living now?'

'London. North, though. Near Finsbury Park.'

My ear was filled with the hiss of Tanya's exhaled breath. 'How far from the prison is that? Ten miles? Fifteen?'

Ten point three miles. I didn't say anything.

'Does she have a boyfriend?'

'I don't think she'd tell us if she did. That's what they're like, aren't they? Too grown-up to share everything with their parents. She's in her final year now and she's on track for a First.'

I was trying to make the conversation normal, a catch-up between long-separated acquaintances, but Tanya wouldn't let me.

'Do you want me to tell her? I'll ring her if you give me her number. There's still support available to her. She might benefit from counselling to help her get used to the idea. I've got better resources now than when I was with the police.' Tanya had left her old job to become Head of Victim Support for Hertfordshire. I glimpsed her on the local news from time to time. I always made myself change the channel.

'I'll tell her. It will be better coming from me. I'll go up to London and take her out to lunch.' I hadn't done that for a while, hadn't seen my daughter for nearly two months, I realised. She seldom came home, and since I had started letting the days and weeks flow over and around me instead of carefully measuring them out hour by hour, I had slipped out of the habit of going there. I had tried to arrange a family dinner for her twenty-first birthday earlier in the month but she had fobbed me off, telling me she was too busy and didn't want to celebrate until the end of term. I hadn't pushed it, had just sent a card and slipped an extra couple of hundred pounds into her bank account. 'It will be . . .' Was I really going to say that it would be nice? Of course it wouldn't be nice. 'It will be better for her,' I said instead.

'Well, do it soon. The press will get hold of this and she shouldn't have to find out like that.'

'Will they still care? Surely everyone's forgotten by now, what with the war and the riots and the floods and everything.' But how could they forget it? It was unforgettable.

'Oh, they'll still be interested all right. They chased that story for weeks and they won't have forgotten what she said. They'll want the big reunion or the big rejection and they won't mind which. Star-crossed lovers to marry or pervert teacher gets his comeuppance. It's all the same to them. It's a good story either way, Ros.'

'A story. Yes, I suppose it is. But there won't be any big reunion.' I wanted to end the phone call; I wanted it never to have started.

'Let's hope not. But tell her as soon as you can. The tabloids will be on the story the minute they get a sniff of his release and they have their sources too – better than mine most of the time – so that isn't going to be long. I'm not involved officially any more, but I'll be there for Stephanie if she needs me.'

What about me? I found myself wanting to say. *Will you be there for me too?* But she was already gone.

The telephone receiver slipped from my hand as I placed it back in its cradle. It clattered to the floor where I swore at it, angry words rising up to puncture the silence of the room. I fumbled with the Italian chrome coffee machine that squatted on the kitchen counter. It was Dan's obsession, an ageing man's toy. I suspected it of sneering at us behind our backs, mocking our provincial ways, our milky Americanos and china mugs. In that moment, its rank of shiny knobs irritated me so much that I pulled the emergency jar of instant granules from the cupboard under the sink.

I took my coffee into the empty cavern of the sitting room and started to prepare myself to ring Stephanie; I'm not sure when it had become something I had to gird myself to do. I imagined picking up the phone and dialling her number. I imagined her voice: as soon as she answered she would ask me how I was, what I was doing, how my course was going. In her bright, brittle telephone voice she would throw questions at me gently but insistently for ten minutes before I got a chance to ask her anything at all. Sometimes I would talk to her for half an hour and later, when Dan asked me whether she had any news, I could tell him almost nothing about her.

Once I had swallowed the last drops of cold coffee, I picked up the phone and dialled. It went straight to voicemail and I didn't leave a message. Tanya had said eleven days. That was nearly two weeks. With my newly calibrated brain I could see that there was nothing to gain by worrying about it yet. I would ring her again tomorrow.

I was flicking through the photos I had taken with Cam on my camera's tiny viewfinder when I heard the clatter of keys in the front door. I moved to stand beside the sink, turned the tap on full and stood there rinsing my mug as Dan passed through the house.

'You're back early. Everything OK?' I said as we moved towards each other, drawn into a shallow kiss by the magnetic force of habit or love.

'Everything's fine. I just thought I'd come home and see you. I'm sorry I didn't make it back last night.'

I shrugged. He had rung at half past nine the night before to tell me he had not yet left work and would stay in London rather than get the train home.

'That hotel's so bloody noisy,' he said. 'It was gone midnight by the time I left work and I was wide awake listening to the traffic by six this morning. Anyway, how are you?'

'Fine. I've only been in for half an hour. I went into university and worked in the studio.' I was wrapping a lie in a truth. I had been to the studio that morning, but I hadn't come straight home. My camera lay on the table, a smear of dust on its fabric strap the evidence of my dishonesty. I moved to stand in front of it and block it from his view.

'Did you get much done?'

'A bit. I'm still not sure about showing my Empty Rooms paintings at the exhibition. Sometimes I think they're clever and communicative and then I look at them again and they're like something a teenager who thinks her parents don't understand her might do for her art GCSE.'

'I'm sure they're great. You'll have to tell me all about this pop-up exhibition of yours.'

'I think "exhibition" might be too grand a term for a few art students' scribblings hanging in an empty shop for half a day.'

'Nonsense. It will be great. You just need a break from it. You know, to get some perspective. You need to, you know, let yourself breathe.'

He always said 'you know' a lot when he was nervous. What did he know? I felt Cam's fingers on my jawbone, remembered the heat of his breath on my lips. 'Yes. Maybe you're right. That's why I came home; I was just going round in circles. But you're here, so now I'm glad I did.'

'Let's go out,' he said. His words were fast, hard, rehearsed.

'Out?' We didn't go out.

'Yes. Out. Let's go and drink wine by the river then stumble into town for a pizza. I want to talk nonsense and eat olives like we used to. It will help with your work, I promise. You need to relax.' He stretched his arms out and pressed his fingers gently into the stiff muscles at the base of my neck, holding me still but distant. That was the moment to tell him about Temperley's release. But Dan's uncharacteristic nostalgia for what we had once been had infected me. Waiting another day couldn't hurt.

'It's a bit cold for al fresco drinking,' I said.

'Nothing a coat and a scarf won't fix. Come on.'

I ran upstairs to get my other scarf, the mauve one that I could wrap around myself three times; the one that didn't smell of Cam.

It was a good night, unusual and illicit, like a day stolen from work with a lie. We went to two bars then to Gino's for pizza. As I sat at our table rubbing the tarry bow of red wine from my lips with a napkin, I listened for the mumbling of familiar words almost out of earshot: 'the parents', 'I remember', 'prison', 'she loved him, silly girl', 'sorry for her', 'I remember', 'four-teen', 'fifteen', 'pervert', 'paedo', 'sicko', 'marry him, she said', 'I remember'. I heard nothing and wondered whether people had forgotten or whether Dan had been right and I really had been imagining it during those stilted dinners in the months and the years *after*. We had given up on eating out eventually and I started cooking elaborate dinners at home instead. Internet shopping saved me from the supermarket, another nest of words and stares. Most of the time, though, even at the weekends now that Freddy had turned eighteen and fled to university, Dan stayed late at work and I ate cheese and biscuits on the sofa.

We were almost drunk when we got home, almost drunk and saturated in each other. We didn't see the light on the answer-phone flashing as we shrugged off our coats and scarves and went up the stairs to bed.

TEN DAYS

W̲e̲ were woken by the chirping of the phone on Dan's bedside table. I felt him roll over and scoop it from its cradle. In my dream I had been with Cam again, chasing him through empty hallways and dusty rooms, slowing down every time I got too close. Reluctantly, I opened my eyes and listened.

'Sarah? Sarah? Shall I get Rosalind? Do you want to talk to her?' He put his hand over the receiver and spoke to me in a stage whisper: 'Ros. It's Sarah. She's upset. Can you . . .' He held the phone out towards me: *Take it, please, take it.*

I sat on the edge of the bed, facing the wall. Sarah's voice was damp with tears but hushed, as though she was afraid of being overheard: 'Oh, Ros. You need to come and get her.'

'What do you mean? What's wrong?'

'She's not well, Ros.'

'Does she need a doctor? A hospital? An ambulance?'

'She needs you. I can't look after her any more. You need to come. Now, before she starts again. Will you come?'

'Yes, Sarah. Of course. But before she starts what? What is it? Please tell me.'

'She's . . . she's drinking. A lot. Maybe other stuff too.'

'Stuff? You mean drugs?'

'I don't know. Maybe. She's a mess. Please just come.' Her words were swallowed up by the wetness of her sobbing.

'Sit tight and we'll be there as soon as we can.' My voice was calm, but under that voice, in my stomach and my lungs and my veins, something was rising, something old and familiar and frantic. I stood for a moment with the phone in my hands and my back to Dan, pushing the panic – my old companion – back into the past where I thought I had left it.

'What is it, Ros?'

I spoke to the wall: 'Sarah says Stephanie is drinking too much, that she's got herself into a state. She says we need to go and get her. I'm sure she's exaggerating but we should go anyway. Sarah's very worried.'

'Drinking?'

'Drinking and possibly drugs. Sarah isn't sure,' I said, forcing myself to turn and face him. He was half in and half out of bed, one leg on the floor, his knee still resting on the mattress and the edge of the duvet in his hands. Fear or shock had frozen him in place, leaning towards me like a tree in a gale. It was rare to see him so still.

'Did you know about this, Ros? I thought she was OK now.'

'Of course I didn't!' I snapped. 'She's your daughter too. Did *you* know?'

'No. Sorry. Of course you didn't.' He swayed away from me.

'Well, we need to get there as soon as we can. Forget showers. Let's just get in the car and go.'

'Maybe it would be better if I went.'

'No. We'll both go.' What good would he be to Stephanie? I tried to recall the last time he had spoken to her: probably at the surprise birthday lunch Beatrice had arranged for me back in August. He wouldn't have seen her since then.

'I just think it might upset you to see her in a state.'

'We'll both go,' I said again. This was how Tanya had dealt with us both in the days after Stephanie disappeared: instructions given as short statements of fact. We will both go, we will do the television appeal in spite of what your mother might think; later: we will give her space, we will sit on our hands in court.

'Yes, yes. OK. Yes. Right.' Then he stood there in his boxer shorts and T-shirt, motionless and frowning.

'Get dressed, Dan.'

I glimpsed Sarah's face at the upstairs window as we drew up outside the flat she shared with Stephanie. She launched herself at me as I stepped across the threshold, her bony hands clutched at my coat, pulling me into her and she stooped to press her wet face to my neck. I put my arms around her; she was so easy to love, my daughter's devoted friend.

'I'm sorry,' she said into my shoulder. 'I'm sorry I didn't ring you sooner.'

'Is she in her room?' asked Dan. When Sarah nodded he strode across the hallway, surging forwards like an iceberg. But he stopped short outside Stephanie's door and waited for me.

'Stephie? Stephanie?' There was no sound from the room. As soon as I cracked the door open, a smell seeped out: vomit, staleness, something chemical and corrupt. I covered my nose with my hand as I fumbled for the light switch.

At first the form on the bed was just a broken line of hair and skin and clothes, then it was Stephanie. The image of my daughter was juxtaposed with a scene of chaos: an ashtray dribbled butts across the floor and empty wine bottles huddled beside the bed. The rug squelched wet beneath my feet. I closed my fingers around her shoulder and felt the rise and fall of her breaths.

'She's been smoking,' Dan whispered behind me, as if that was the worst thing that had happened. 'She doesn't smoke.'

'Go outside. Go and ask Sarah what's been going on. I'll wake her up,' I said. 'And close the door behind you.'

He stood for a moment, looking between Stephanie and me. I thought he was about to speak but he said nothing before he tiptoed out of the room. When I turned back to the bed, Stephanie was looking at me. Her eyes were shining pink slivers between swollen lids. I wondered if she had been crying; I wondered if I should cry.

'Mum,' she said. She closed her eyes.

'Darling, we've come to look after you. We're going to take you home for a while.'

'Is Dad here?'

'Yes.'

She closed her eyes again, then drew a handful of hair across her face.

'I can't come home,' she said eventually from behind her hair.

'Yes, you can. You are.'

'I'm bad. You'll hate me.' Her words were slurred, her voice husky.

'I'll never hate you, Stephie. Whatever has happened we can fix it together. Your father and I can sort it out, whatever it is. There's nothing that we can't work out between us.'

'That's exactly what you said to me before. At the police station.'

'Then you know it's true, don't you?' I crossed to the window and pulled it open, flooding the room with cold November air.

After a long pause she said, 'OK, Mum. Let's go.' It was only later that I wondered at how meekly she agreed to come home with me, how readily she agreed to be my child again.

The two of us shuffled together to the bathroom, her leaning hard on my arm, her bony hip pressing into my flesh. When I let go of her to close the bathroom door, she swayed on her feet as though she was still slightly drunk. I ran her a bath and perched on the loo while she took off her filthy black jeans and the purple top that was ripped and spattered with vomit. I remembered her wearing that top at Easter for a night out in St Albans with Sarah. She had been so beautiful, seemed so untouchable with her pale skin and shining auburn hair; I had been jealous of the youth and possibility in her face.

'What has happened, sweetheart?' I asked as I rubbed conditioner into the wet tendrils of her hair, slowly and methodically, spinning out the task. I felt safe in the steamy confines of the bathroom with Stephanie contained in the bathtub. It was like bathing a child before bed, part of a comforting regime that ended with blankets tucked in and tiny eyelids fluttering over tired eyes.

'Happened?' she said. 'Oh, nothing has happened. Well, apart from you turning up.'

'Is this about Nathan Temperley?'

At the mention of his name she sat up straight in the bath and irritably pushed my hands away from her hair. 'Oh, please, Mum. That was years ago. Years ago! You can't blame Nathan Temperley for all the ills of the world. I bet you think he caused the tsunami and the earthquake and the war in Iraq. He's not omnipotent, you know.'

The sound of his name on her lips brought Tanya's phone call back to me. *How far is that from the prison?* Suddenly the bathroom didn't feel so safe after all. 'We need to go,' I said. 'Get out of the bath, Stephanie.' As I unfolded the towel Sarah had given me and held it out for her to take, I noticed that my hands were shaking.

Dan and I walked her to the car between us while Sarah watched from the window. I wanted to run back up the stairs and beg her to come with us but it wouldn't be fair. I slid into the back seat next to Stephanie. As soon as the doors were closed Dan clicked the heating on and turned the radio up so the car became too hot and too loud. I was grateful for that, for the fact that we could drive home in our individual bubbles of warmth and noise. Stephanie leant her head against the window, her eyes on the road as it slipped by. When we left the motorway and crossed the border into Hertfordshire, she sat up and pressed her open palm against the window. I reached across and held her other hand, the one that lay in her lap. It was freezing cold and each finger ended in a black crescent as though she had been digging in the garden without tools. I unbuckled my seat belt and shifted across the space between us to wrap myself around her. I thought she would pull away from me right until the moment she relaxed into my arms.

'Bloody hell, that hatchet-faced fantasist is the last thing we need right now,' said Dan as we approached the house, breaking the silence that had lasted the length of the journey. Pete from number four was standing at the bottom of our drive, sunlight flashing from his glasses. He must have seen us setting off and caught the whiff of something unusual.

'Hello!' he said as soon as we got out of the car. 'I saw you two haring off this morning and now here you are with the lovely Steph.'

'She's got the flu,' Dan said, stepping in front of us, shielding us. 'A nasty case. We've brought her home for some TLC.'

'Oh, the poor thing, she does look ill. It's that time of year, I suppose,' he said. 'You get better, love. And—'

'Let's get you inside,' Dan said to Stephanie, putting his arm around her and propelling her gently forwards. 'Bye, Pete.'

Pete backed out of the drive, probably formulating news angles, headlines, sound bites as he went. Speculative stories about Stephanie failing exams, having a breakdown or being dumped would soon be criss-crossing the street. When he stumbled on the kerb, part of me willed him to fall and bash his head on the concrete.

As I walked up the stairs with Stephanie shuffling in front of me I had already started to think in terms of *This time* and *Last time*. This was the second time my daughter had arrived home thin, blurred and packed tight with secrets.

* * *

When Stephanie and Nathan Temperley were discovered, they were both taken into custody – Stephanie's custody protective and his the normal type, whatever that meant: Pentonville, a cell, a bucket, bars, men with smudged tattoos on their hands. Stephanie had refused to come home to us at first.

'I can't go with them,' she said when Dan and I went to collect her from the police station, turning her whole body away from me and speaking only to Tanya. I had already hugged her. I had already cried into her hair – the strange hair, dyed from its natural red to an unconvincing platinum blonde since I had last seen her – as she stood there with her arms around me in a limp echo of my embrace.

'What do you mean, darling?' I said. 'Of course you can come home with us. We meant what we said on telly, you're not in any trouble. We aren't cross with you. You're not going to be punished. There's nothing that we can't work out between us.' I had rehearsed those words for days, knowing that they would be needed but not knowing when.

'I can't just go back there and pretend it never happened,' she said, turning towards us. 'That's what you want, isn't it? You want me to forget Nate even exists, to pretend it was all a big mistake. Tell me, Mum, Dad, is it just a phase I'm going through?' Her voice was a savage whisper, almost a snarl. Had this anger always been inside her? Had I lived alongside it unknowingly for fifteen years? Or was it something he had given her?

'We just want you safe at home with us, Stephie. We want to look after you. We love you,' I said. Dan nodded but said nothing. He was looking at me, at Tanya, anywhere except at Stephanie.

'And I love him,' she said. 'And when they let him out we will be together. Will you still love me then? Will you accept us? They will let him out so it's no good pretending that it isn't going to happen.'

'Of course we'll still love you. Nothing can change that.' I reached out and took her right hand in mine. After a second, she snatched it back.

'That's not what I asked you.' She looked me straight in the eye for the first time, her pale irises flashing in the strip-light's glare. 'Will you accept him? Us?'

'We can talk about that at home, Stephie,' Dan said. 'We've been so worried; it's been very difficult—'

She cut him off. 'Your answer is no. You won't. So I'm not coming home. You don't get me without him so it's us or nothing. Your choice.' She walked away from us and stood by the door, her hand already resting on the handle as she looked to Tanya for permission to pass through it. I felt a bitter burst of resentment. I thought Tanya was my ally, I thought she was on my side.

'Back in a moment,' Tanya mouthed to me over her shoulder as she left the room with Stephanie.

For the next three days we didn't know exactly where Stephanie was – just that she was safe. We didn't leave the house in that time; Dan, Freddy and I huddled behind closed curtains. We sat under blankets watching daytime television and eating tinned soup and toast from our laps as though we were all off work with colds.

I still don't know – even now that I know so much – what made her decide to come home. Did she miss us? Did she not like wherever it was she was staying? Had she started to forget him now that he was locked away? Or did she think things would go better for him if she could get her family on side and show the court that there had been no lasting damage? Tanya brought her home to us on a Saturday morning and left her with Dan and me in the hallway. There was a collection of long seconds when the three of us eyed each other, waiting for someone to speak. Then Freddy barrelled through the door from the sitting room and put his arms around her. She cried against his shoulder, and said, 'I'm sorry, Freddy. I'm sorry.'

In the hours that followed, I tore myself between never wanting to take my eyes off her again, not even when I knew she was safely in her bedroom, and Tanya's insistence that she needed space to grieve for her relationship with Temperley. I followed her to her bedroom door but went no further. I tried to work out what she was thinking and waited for her to talk to me.

* * *

This time I followed Stephanie into her old bedroom. I had a feeling that the bedding hadn't been changed since Beatrice had stayed a couple of weekends earlier. Stephanie returned to her old room so seldom that Beatrice had taken to using it when she came to stay. Bea said it was quieter up here in the attic but we both knew it was really so she could smoke cigarettes out of the bedroom window without Dan catching a whiff of menthol smoke.

'You should get some sleep, sweetheart,' I said, pulling back the duvet cover and scanning the sheet beneath for telltale hairs, patches of evidence.

I gave her one of Dan's T-shirts and put a glass of water on the bedside table. I drew the curtains but daylight seeped through them and the darkness was unconvincing. I hoped she would sleep. What would I do with her if she wouldn't? What would I say? She lay flat on her back and pulled the duvet up to her chin. I dropped a kiss on her forehead then turned to go.

'Stay for a bit,' she said. 'Please.' I lay down on the bed beside her, my left hand almost touching the mound of her right hand under the duvet. I couldn't remember the last time I had been so close to her. For years there had always been something between us: Freddy, Sarah, a café table, a painting, a cubic metre of empty space.

'Mum?' she said, just as I had thought she was falling asleep. 'Yes?'

'You've stopped chewing your lip. When did that happen?'

'I don't know. I just stopped.'

'Don't start again. Please.'

'I won't.' It had been months since I had tasted blood in my mouth. I had even started wearing lipstick now that it slid on smoothly rather than catching in the scabs and furrows of torn skin. Of course, I would never have lips like other people's: in bright light I could still see the thin white lines of scar tissue beneath the surface.

Dan would be downstairs, waiting for answers, but I delayed the moment of sliding soundlessly off the bed and away from Stephanie. I lay still, running my tongue over the smoothness of my lower lip, until I was sure she was asleep. I listened to her breathing and tried to ignore the sense of old forces stirring in a dark corner of my mind, waking from their slumber and wiping the sleep from their eyes.

Dan was sitting at the kitchen table, staring into the black hole of an empty iPad screen. For a moment he looked unfamiliar. He was unshaven due to our rush to leave the house, his chin rough with blond stubble and his dark blue eyes faded like old denim. Was that part of ageing? Would my green eyes fade too, from bright green to the wishy-washy shade of a lettuce leaf?

'I need to go and get her some things,' I said. He jumped up from his chair and moved towards me.

'What has she told you?'

'Nothing,' I said. 'You saw her. She was exhausted. She's fast asleep now.'

'Nothing?'

'Nothing.'

'Well, what did you ask her?'

'I haven't asked her anything. She needs sleep, not an interrogation.'

'I've been looking into things.' He tapped the iPad in his hand. 'There are places that can help but we'll need to get her in front of a GP. We need an initial diagnosis before we can get the ball rolling. Do you think Dr Bashir will do a home visit tomorrow morning?'

'What do you mean? What kind of places?'

'Places where they help them, you know, *dry out*.' He dropped his voice to a whisper. 'They're not just quick fixes, though, they get to the root of the problem.' His eyes sought mine, looking for approval. I took the iPad from his hand and stirred it into life. The screen lit up with smiling faces framed in shades of aqua. *The Elms: Tomorrow can be different.* I knew all about The Elms; it was where celebrities went, suffering with 'exhaustion' after months of tumbling loose-limbed and wide-eyed out of bars, or after messy divorces played out blow-by-blow over glossy pages.

'We can't outsource this,' I said. 'We can't just pay somewhere you've seen on the internet to take her away and fix her.'

'She's ill, Ros. Sarah said it had been going on for weeks, that she was drinking in the day last week. Spirits as well, not just wine. She could have damaged her liver. Are you telling me she doesn't need help?'

I thought of Stephanie lying in bed two floors above us, the damp tangles of her hair coiled across the pillow. I thought of Nathan Temperley pacing in his cell, counting backwards from ten. 'No. I'm telling you that you're not sending her away like an unwanted dog. We're her parents and we're going to take care of her.' I didn't usually speak to Dan like that; he didn't like to be told.

'Rosalind,' he started. But I was already on the move, slipping out of the house and away from him. I heard his fist hit the table top as I closed the front door.

I walked as fast as I could into town, so fast that sweat beaded on my upper lip and in spite of the November cold, I had to unbutton my coat and let it flap behind me like a cape. I went the long way round and when I had to stop at pedestrian crossings, I shifted my weight from one foot to the other and concentrated on taking deep breaths of chill air. Still I couldn't shake the sense of déjà vu, of Stephanie in her bedroom, full of mysteries, and Dan downstairs hatching a plan to send her away.

Direct approaches never worked with Stephanie. It had always been necessary to sidle up to her, to perch on the edge of an issue, to open a door, wait patiently and hope that she would step through it. Even as a child, asking her what was wrong yielded nothing more than a shake of the head or a slow retreat from the room.

I carried two mugs, a packet of pink jelly sweets in the shape of pigs and three offerings from the cheaper end of the magazine shelf up the stairs along with a bag of new underwear and pyjamas. When I realised that I was pinching my lower lip tight between my teeth, I stopped outside the door and forced myself to breathe.

'Hey,' I said, shouldering the door open.

'Hey to you too.' Her voice held the thrum of a moth trapped in a lampshade. She winced when she took a mug from my hand and the bruises and scrapes on her knuckles leapt out from her pale skin. Was that what a fist looked like after a fight? I wasn't sure; fights had never been a part of my world. For a moment I slipped out of my role of mother to a sick child and let my artist's eye take over. I imagined painting that horrible intriguing mess in scarlet, cerulean and ochre.

'Hot Ribena?' she said, sniffing the mug.

'What else? The sugar hit will do you good.' It was what I had always fed my children when they were ill or upset.

'I bought a bottle in London but it was never the same as when you make it. It didn't make me feel any better.'

'It only works if someone makes it for you. I used to make it for myself but I gave up eventually. Shove over.' I spilled the magazines onto the duvet on top of her then pulled open the packet of sweets and set them down on the cover between us. I sensed her weighing me up, trying to gauge my intentions. If she was surprised by what she found she didn't let on; but then Stephanie was good at keeping her thoughts and feelings to herself. With her dual talents for mathematics and inscrutability, it was a wonder she had never taken up poker. Perhaps she had. How would I know?

I picked up a magazine and she did the same. We both took sips of Ribena.

'My internet dreamboat was a cannibal love fiend,' she read aloud from the cover of the magazine in her hand.

'My belly exploded in Iceland,' I read from mine.

'Bun in the oven after brekkie at the bakery.'

'Santa's sack gave me a shock.'

I took a pig from the packet and she did the same. We each leafed through a magazine in silence for a while, sipping our drinks and chewing our way through the packet of sweets. I could sense the questions gathering within her, rubbing against the shell of her detachment.

'Are these magazines supposed to make me feel better? You know, things can't be that bad because I'm not appearing in *Break Time*?' she said, eventually.

'Goodness, no. I'm just using you as an excuse. If your dad catches us I can tell him that these are yours. A respectable woman like me can't be seen reading such trash.'

She almost smiled. 'Am I not respectable?'

'I'm not one to judge but you look like you've been in a bar brawl and you were sick in your hair last night.' I didn't look at her as I spoke. I wasn't sure if I had gone too far, pushed too soon for something that she would never be willing to give me. She let the magazine in her hands droop so she could look at the butcher's block smudge of her knuckles.

'It looks worse than it is, Mum.'

'Good.' I let the silence stretch, willing her to say more.

'The journalists on these magazines could certainly make a good headline out of me, though.'

'What would it be?' Perhaps it had finally arrived: the moment when she would drop her guard and show me what she was really thinking for the first time in all these years. A burst of anxiety so intense that I had to stifle a gasp ran through me like the pulse of white light before the roaring bang of an atomic bomb. I watched her run her left thumb over the broken skin of her right hand. I sensed her indecision. Then she looked away. 'It's probably best if we don't think about that right now. What would yours be?'

'Probably best if we don't think about that either.' *I went potty for my pottery class paramour*, I thought, but that wasn't quite right. I didn't have the magazine journalist's talent for juxtaposing the mundane and the ridiculous.

'It's a deal. How come you read these? I thought you only read your art books. I didn't think you were the type for this.' She gestured to a photo of a young woman I vaguely recognised from the television walking on a beach, a tiny ripple of fat at her waist highlighted by a bright red arrow.

'Because I'm nosy and voyeuristic and all my friends apart from Bea are too dull for gossip. Anyway, they're addictive. I keep telling myself that I'll stop reading them but I never do, or at least not for long. You've only been reading them for ten minutes and you're probably already hooked for life.'

'You're a dark horse,' she said. We swapped magazines and I pushed the urge to tell her about Tanya's phone call down deep and buried it. The pulse of white light had not yet been followed by the crash of the bomb. Now was not the time.

To an outsider it would seem strange that I lay next to my battered, bruised daughter and didn't insist that she told me everything: why she had turned from a diligent student into a wine-guzzling cigarette smoker, who or what she had punched and why she hadn't been wearing any underwear when I had helped her to strip for her bath. But it wasn't strange at all. For the past six years we had talked about books, plays, theatre, films, food, family, her studies and her friends, but talking about her – asking her about the details of her life, her thoughts, her feelings, why she made the choices she made – was off limits. Trespassing on forbidden territory resulted in a withdrawal that could last weeks or months. The fear that she would one day withdraw completely was what kept my most burning questions unasked.

Most of all, we didn't talk about Nathan Temperley and what happened when she went missing with him. The day that Stephanie would break down, cry in my arms and tell me how it happened and why she did what she did had always been tomorrow and never today. *Take it slowly*, Tanya and the family psychologist she arranged for us to see had said. *Don't push her and she'll come to you when she's ready to talk.* So that was what we did, even as days became weeks, became months and then years. Now I understand that not talking about it was like launching an object into a vacuum: once we started in that direction there was no reason ever to stop.

*   *   *

To begin with, in the first days after she came home, Stephanie was like a shy woodland creature creeping through the undergrowth to shield itself from predators. She answered questions in hushed monosyllables and never spoke unprompted. There was no sound from her room when she was inside it, and when she did emerge, she moved around the house noiselessly on bare feet. There was something about the sight of her feet that pressed the hair-trigger of my anxiety. They were so small and neat and young-looking that it was them more than her eyes or her face that slapped me with the wrongness of what had happened. *How could he?* I screamed silently over and over when I glimpsed the pearly crescents of her nails peeping out from beneath her pyjama bottoms. My heart would race and I would have to gulp down a dose of beta blockers and hide in the bathroom until my hands stopped shaking.

Sometimes, when I was watching television or ruining the pages of my sketchbook with ugly doodles, I would sense the pressure of being watched and turn to find her behind me. The first few times this happened I thought she had come to talk to me. 'Are you OK, love?' I would say, trying to project warmth and openness, just as Tanya had told me to do. 'Fine,' she would reply. Then she would fill a glass with water or pick up a book she had left on a table and disappear again.

One morning, just over a week after she had arrived home, she came downstairs in her school uniform. I was sitting in the kitchen listening to the roar of a jet passing overhead. I had caught a snippet of news coverage about a plane accidentally releasing its cargo of holidaymakers' luggage into the sea off Spain and hadn't been able to shake myself free of the fear that it could happen above St Albans. Could a suitcase of bikinis and sarongs smash through the roof if it fell from a thousand metres? Would it pierce slates, plough through plaster and find our fragile skulls in the rooms below? In the hushed, tense days since Stephanie had returned, this fear had grown to fill the silence. Later, when I had stopped worrying about escaped luggage, I started worrying about other accidents that could happen in the home. I turned the gas off at the mains at night and installed carbon monoxide monitors in every room. I bought ugly rubber strips to stop people slipping on the stairs. For a time, until Dan's patience snapped, I served all food blended into soup or cut up into tiny pieces, too small for anyone to choke on. But on the day that Stephanie went back to school, it was still the falling luggage that was bothering me.

I thought about Stephanie walking down the street, black suitcases hitting the ground and bursting open like poisoned flowers around her. Had I got her back only so I could lose her again? It felt possible, probable even. 'Stephie, I don't think school are expecting you back just yet,' I said, fighting to keep the panic out of my voice. The school had said she was welcome back whenever she felt ready, but the psychologist and social worker agreed that it could be weeks before that happened. Dan had other ideas and didn't want it to happen at all.

'I emailed Miss Yardley and told her I was coming back today.' She got herself a bowl and filled it with muesli, just as she always had.

'What did Miss Yardley say?' *Talk to her as though she is an adult,* Tanya had instructed. *You need to win her trust.*

'She hasn't replied yet.' She cut a banana into neat slices and added it to the muesli.

'When did you email her?'

'This morning. I used Dad's computer. She'll have checked her emails before I turn up. What is it you always say about forewarned being forearmed? Well, she'll have time to forearm herself, won't she?'

As she sat at the breakfast bar in her claret-coloured blazer and candy-stripe blouse with her hair caught in a messy bun, she looked like the photo we had given to the police on that very first day when she hadn't come home.

'Stephie?'

'Mum?'

'I know we've asked you this before but are you really sure you want to go back there? We thought you might want a fresh start at a new school. Maybe Hilltop. We talked to the head there and it's an option. Or there's another school a bit further away you might prefer.' A boarding school in Shropshire; Dan's big idea.

'No, thank you.' She chewed the last spoonful of her breakfast.

'Won't you even think about it? We could just go and look at them. There's no rush.'

'I have thought about it. I'll stay where I am. It's too close to my exams to move. And why should I have to move anyway? He's not there any more. He's in prison.' She put her bowl in the dishwasher.

'I'll drive you,' I said. Would a car roof offer any protection if holdalls and boxes, skis and bicycles fell from the sky? It was the best I could do.

'I'm meeting Sarah. I'll walk.' I clenched my fingers around the edge of the kitchen table and breathed deeply. *Give her space*, Tanya had said. *Let her come to you.* I wished Tanya was there with me, squeezing my hand and whispering words of encouragement into my ear.

She scooped an old canvas sports bag from the kitchen floor as she left. I couldn't remember exactly what had happened to her school bag; it was probably in an evidence box somewhere. At least I could no longer hear the plane.

Dan had gone back to work and I spent that day alone. I drove past the school three times. I finally got through to Miss Yardley at lunchtime, the fifth time I called. The receptionist had refused to pull her out of lessons to speak to me, had said it was against school policy. *Do you know who I am?* had been on the tip of my tongue, but, of course, she did. Miss Yardley hadn't expected Stephanie back so soon or even at all but she seemed pleased and her pleasure surprised me. What teacher would want to be responsible for Stephanie's pastoral care after what had happened? I had assumed Stephanie would refuse to go back to the school and that the school would breathe a sigh of relief. I had spent hours scouring the internet and ringing the heads of other schools; few had rung me back. Not one of the public schools in Hertfordshire would touch her in spite of her academic record. The best I had come up with was Hilltop, the comprehensive sinkhole on the other side of town. That was when Dan had showed his hand: the all-girls boarding school in deepest darkest Shropshire. We argued about it for days in hushed voices when Stephanie was in her room. 'She'll be safe there. She can have a new start,' he hissed as we cleared the table after dinner one evening. It had been three days and he still hadn't managed to look her in the eye. He was hyper-vigilant for the possibility of being left alone in a room with her, leaping to his feet to make tea or bolting for his study on the flimsiest of pretexts if I showed any signs of leaving him in her company. 'You're not banishing her to Shropshire. She'll think we're ashamed of her however you dress it up,' I hissed back. 'Don't accuse me of not loving my daughter,' he replied, even though I had accused him of nothing at all.

Now Stephanie had taken the decision out of our hands. 'She'll have Shelley Hart for geography,' said Miss Yardley on the telephone. 'She's a great teacher, really dedicated.' I knew what Miss Yardley meant: *Shelley Hart isn't a pervert, or even a man.*

That afternoon, I stood in the garden and watched six planes pass overhead. None of them flew in the direction of the school.

I was cutting carrots into precise slices when Stephanie got home at the end of that first, long day. I had had to retrieve the vegetable knife from the locked cabinet in the study where, on Tanya's advice, it had been bundled up with the paracetamol, Dan's razor blades, even the pizza wheel. I didn't know what I was going to do with two kilograms of sliced carrot but I had needed a way to fill the last half an hour of waiting. I had turned up the volume on the radio so I couldn't hear the planes. I couldn't hear the front door, either, and suddenly she was standing in front of me, her shadow falling on my hands. I jerked and raked the knife blade over the tip of my finger.

'Oh, Mum, what have you done to yourself?' she said, dropping her bag and moving around the kitchen table towards me.

'It's nothing, I was just being clumsy.' I put my finger in my mouth. It stung and I could feel my pulse as the salt of my blood covered my tongue.

'I'll get a plaster,' she said. 'Sit down, Mum.'

'How was your day? What did you do?' she said as she unwrapped the plaster and handed it to me.

I couldn't tell her that I rang her school five times, or that I drove past it every hour between ten o'clock and one o'clock. I couldn't tell her about researching flight paths on the internet or my two hours in the garden watching planes. 'Oh, you know, just caught up on a few things that don't get done when I'm at work.'

'When will you go back to work?'

'I'm not sure. Margaret said I could take as long as I needed. Or I might not go back at all.'

'But you love working in the gallery.'

'Yes. We'll see. Did—'

But it wasn't my turn to ask questions yet. 'How's Auntie Bea getting on?' Beatrice was my best friend not my sister but she has always been 'Auntie Bea' to the children. Never missing a birthday or a school play, she was more of an aunt to Stephanie and Freddy than Dan's sister had ever been.

'She's fine. I talked to her yesterday. She's looking forward to seeing you. How was school?' I said before she had the chance to fire another question at me.

'Good. I've missed a lot, though. Did you know that Mrs Reynolds in retiring at the end of the year?'

'No, I didn't know. Who—'

'She is. Sarah thinks Miss Yardley will go for the deputy job. Do you think she'll get it?'

'I hope so. Did you speak to her today?'

'Yes, she's given me some extra homework to help me catch up. I better go and make a start.'

I had always loved the offcut of time between my children getting home from school and their homework, computer games and television programmes claiming them. Without the formality of the dinner table they would chat to me about their friends, their lessons, the trivial fragments that brought their days to life for me. But Stephanie wouldn't do that any more. There was no more chatting. Instead, we had careful conversations in which she steered me like a tugboat steering a ship through a canal, edging and nudging me towards safe topics, then cutting the rope and speeding away when I tried to pull her in my own direction.

That evening, Dan came into the kitchen carefully, as if the fallout from Stephanie's day at school might be lying all over the floor.

'She's doing her homework upstairs.'

'Did she say how it went?'

'She said it was fine. We talked a bit when she got home.'

'About him?'

'No, just about school. But at least it's something. I talked to Tanya about it. She said we should support Stephanie's choices where we can and that it could be really positive for her to be back amongst her peers.'

'Huh.'

'Why don't you go up and say hello?'

'I don't want to bother her if she's doing her homework. She must have a lot to catch up on.'

At dinner that evening we followed Stephanie's lead. We pretended to be ourselves from the time before she had gone missing. Dan didn't look at Stephanie but he didn't look at me, either. We made conversation about the new bypass, the weather, the Christmas lights going up in town. We smiled small, polite smiles until our jaws ached. We played our parts well that evening and we have been playing them ever since.

NINE DAYS

When I stay in hotels or the homes of friends or family, it takes me a few seconds after waking to become conscious of where I am. Even when I am sure of where, I find myself wanting to know why. These first conscious thoughts are often the most honest of the day: I might realise I am at Dan's mother's house and know it is because I miss my own mother; I might realise I am in Bea's spare room and know it is because I am lonely in my empty nest; I might realise I am in a boutique hotel in Berlin and know it is because Dan missed the last train home from work six times in the past three months and feels the need to atone for his absences. I woke up in my own bed the day after we collected Stephanie from London. The knowledge that she was in the room above me was like a muscle memory, as innate as the ability to open my eyes. So the only question I had was why she was there. *Because of him*, came a whisper from that locked up part of my brain, the section surrounded by red NO ENTRY signs and yellow CRIME SCENE tape. It made me shiver. I was glad that I had kept the news of Temperley's release to myself. I couldn't delay telling her for long but I could give her another day at least.

Dan shifted into wakefulness beside me. It would be dishonest to pretend that I wasn't avoiding telling him too, but I was less willing to think about my motives for that. I had already used up my burst of honest thought for the day. It was Saturday, and Stephanie had a doctor's appointment booked for Monday morning. Dan had insisted on it, hoping no doubt that the doctor would support his plan to bundle her off to The Elms. The span of time between the present and the appointment hung as loose and formless as the slack string of a kite that has failed to catch the breeze.

'Do you think we should call Tanya?' Dan had asked as we slid into bed the night before.

I had clattered my glass of water onto my bedside cabinet in surprise.

'No, I don't think so. I don't think this is quite her remit.'

'She was a good friend to you. I know you haven't seen her for a while but I'm sure she'd want to help.'

'It might upset Stephie. Tanya would remind her of him, of that time. It could do more harm than good.' Tanya *had* been a good friend. She had put up with me for as long as she could, for far longer than anyone else would have done.

'I suppose so.'

'Let's see what the doctor says on Monday. And she might open up a bit more over the weekend. Maybe it's not as bad as it looks.'

He sat up in bed and leaned over me, his hair a glowing halo in the light from his reading lamp. 'Why aren't you more worried, Ros? I don't understand. I know you've been more calm lately.' *Less neurotic* was what he probably wanted to say. 'But this is Stephanie. She's got a drinking problem. And you're just taking it in your stride?'

If we had been talking about any topic other than Stephanie, I would have captured his words and preserved them like dried flowers so I could take them out and look at them whenever I chose. Here was my husband, the man who I had more than once heard describing me as 'less like Wonder Woman and more like Worry Woman', accusing me of being insufficiently anxious. 'I am worried and I'm trying to do what's best for her,' I said.

'Well, you almost seem relaxed about it. It's a serious situation we're in here, you know.'

'What good did me suffocating her with my anxiety ever do? It was part of the reason she—'

'It wasn't your fault,' he said. 'Let's not have that conversation again.'

Dan got out of bed, tucking the duvet back into the space where he had lain and unhitching his mobile phone from its charger. I lay still, my back to him. Saturday mornings had once meant coffee in bed and warm, lazy sex. For the past couple of months we had just had the coffee. I had missed the sex as I listened to him whistling while he shook out beans, adjusted nozzles and lined up mugs. I had wondered about his prostate; we were nearing that sort of age. I even left an article about it from the *Sunday Times* open on the kitchen table. A few nights later, he came home from work late. I was woken by the grip of his hand on my shoulder and his breath in my ear as he tugged my knickers halfway down my thighs and entered me without a word. His prostate wasn't the problem.

Our house was big, it had felt vertiginously big when we had first moved in, but its Victorian builders had constructed it for speed and profit not solidity or privacy. Sounds travelled through the walls and empty spaces as easily as birds between trees. I listened for any movement from Stephanie's room but what I heard was Dan's voice raised in the interrupted staccato of a phone call. The thought that he could be ringing Tanya snuck up on me but I shooed it away; he probably didn't even have her number.

The clock ground out seventeen slow minutes before he returned to the bedroom. 'Is everything all right?' I asked.

'Not really. Something's come up on the Shipson deal and I think I'm going to have to go in. I should be back for lunch.' He was already pulling off his boxer shorts and heading for the en suite bathroom.

'Really? Today? Can't you handle it from here?' It was Saturday. Even Dan didn't work on Saturdays, or at least not in the office. He often spent weekend afternoons half watching sport while replying to emails or writing presentations.

'No, it's a real mess. I need to be there. A lot of feathers have been ruffled and I don't trust anyone else to smooth them down.'

'Ruffled feathers? And you think I'm insufficiently worried about Stephanie?'

'I shouldn't have said that, I'm sorry. And I'm sorry to leave you like this but I missed a lot yesterday. You know it's hard for me to take days off like that. Will you be OK?'

'Yes,' I said. 'I will.' *I'm used to it*, I would once have added. But I had lost my appetite for that kind of thing. Besides, it wasn't me he was absenting himself from this time, it was Stephanie. Of that I was sure.

Stephanie was still in her room when he left. Twice I crept up the stairs to the attic and pressed my ear to her door, but heard nothing. I sat in the kitchen and thought about the directions in which the day could unfold until Stephanie made me jump. 'Where's Dad gone?' she said from the kitchen doorway which had been empty just a second before. She was wearing a pair of the pyjamas I had bought for her. Their purple polka dots matched the ripening bruises on her right hand and the shadows beneath her eyes.

'Work.' I got up and filled the kettle.

'Really? Is that what he does on a Saturday these days?'

'Not always.' *Only when you're here.* 'You look like death warmed up.'

'I feel like hell. I can't sleep but I can't stay awake either. I can't even read. It's so quiet here compared to London. It's eerie.'

'You'll feel better when the alcohol is out of your system.'

'Nope, 'fraid not. Why do you think I put it in my system in the first place?'

'Oh. Did it help?' I kept my tone casual, dug my fingernails into my wrist to stop myself from spinning away from the whistling kettle and demanding that she told me why she had been drinking herself into oblivion.

'Sometimes. A bit.'

'Not enough and not for long?'

'Right.'

I nodded. I knew. 'Well, there's only one thing for it.'

'More magazines and hot Ribena?'

'Maybe later. But we need to wear you out first. Wear out the body and the brain will follow. I know the perfect place.'

'No.' She shook her head, already starting to retreat from the room. 'I don't want to go out. I can't stand the thought of people. Even ones I don't know.'

'You'll feel worse if you're cooped up in here all day, and there aren't any people where we're going.'

'None at all?'

'Not a single soul. It will just be you and me and a flask of tea. And you can pretend I'm not there.'

That morning was my third real visit to Croome House but I had been dipping in and out of it in daydreams and sleep for weeks. It looks like a castle from a distance, but it isn't on the highest hill in the area, it doesn't have a moat and its walls could be easily swarmed with a stepladder. Up close, its true nature becomes clear. It is a Victorian folly, a banker's house with battlements – a man's vanity played out in stone. After being bought by the council and used for various things since the nineteen fifties, it had been left to stand empty for the past ten years. On my first visit, with my photography group, I had expected it to feel desolate and unwanted, but its emptiness felt like exclusivity, its abandonment like proof not of its worthlessness but of its tenacity: it had outlived those who built it, been strong where they had been weak. I am often drawn to objects and places, compelled to be near them, touch them, own them, but nothing had ever reeled me in like Croome.

It was with Cam, the day of Tanya's phone call, that I had squeezed through the fence and ignored the NO TRESPASSING and DANGER signs to come back. He had been leaning against his car when I parked beside him in the overgrown, not-quite-proper car park at the bottom of the hill. 'This is prime dogging territory,' he had said as he helped me out of the car and we had both laughed. I don't think he meant them to but his words let the shadow of sex, of lust and things that are not quite as they should be, fall across us. We had carried that shadow up the hill and into the house. It had been with us as we walked side by side through the dust-blurred rooms, talking without looking at each other.

If I was less impulsive and less taken with Croome, I might have decided that an abandoned house – once a shelter for orphaned children and, later, the mentally ill – a quarter of a mile's scramble up a windswept hill, was not the right place to take Stephanie. But she needed somewhere to go and I needed somewhere to take her and Croome was waiting for us both. Stephanie was wearing my thick down jacket but she shivered and pulled the hood up as we climbed the hill, the wind tearing at our jeans. She hesitated as we approached the perimeter fence, a solid wall of dull grey steel looping around my treasure, but she followed me as I slipped through the gap between the signs telling me not to. I took her silence as a vote of confidence. The house stood in front of us, offering up its dark stone bulk and blank windows beneath the steel of the November sky. My pulse quickened as I took in the crooked teeth of its battlements and the solid reaches of its towers.

The broken window was set in the building's left flank. I moved the rock with which Cam had wedged it shut and it opened with a rusty squeak. 'In we go,' I said. Stephanie's hood nodded back at me and she stepped over the low window sill and into the house. We emerged into a corridor, stony and dim, with its walls painted that shade of lemon only ever used in hospitals and schools. As I led Stephanie towards the main body of the house, we moved from light to dark and back again as we crossed the pools of daylight that seeped through the dirty windows. I took her to my favourite room first in case she wanted to leave. I think it was once the grand dining room. Later, it had been a canteen, perhaps when the house was a children's home. Later still, it became a day room for Croome's troubled residents. In the vast space, layers of what the building was and all the things that it had once been were at their most transparent: the ceiling was a portrait of white clouds in a blue sky blotted with a dirty yellow stain that blossomed from the wall; the grand stone fireplace with its marble columns and mighty grate was flanked by sagging chairs, their cushions covered in wipe-clean fabric impervious to damp and the passage of time. Everything, whether old or new, was coated in dust, nibbled by mice and journeyed over by spiders. Wind, rain and fallen leaves had found their way in through broken windows and the air was damp and frigid.

'See. No one here but us,' I said.

We didn't talk as we walked slowly around the rest of the building, we just let it soak us up and absorb us. I led and she followed. We climbed the sweeping staircase, bathed in green light from the cracked and leaf-strewn glass dome in the roof. I could just make out the shape of a bird lying on the glass above. It didn't move.

Unlike the rooms downstairs, those on Croome's first floor were mostly locked. Cam and I had tried them all, moving down the hallway rattling rusty handles until at last one gave way beneath my hand. That room has been the biggest surprise of all. It must once have been a sitting room or perhaps a master bedroom. Its three broad windows reached from floor to ceiling and gave way onto the battlement-topped balcony that spanned the front of the house. They had been boarded up, presumably to stop people from getting in, but the plywood boards at the top of the cracked central window had fallen away, flooding the room with winter light. It was as though less time had passed in this room than in any other in the building. Long grey velvet curtains, only slightly mildewed, still hung in the windows, the carpet still felt soft underfoot. In the corner stood a single metal bedframe, stripped of sheets but with its mattress still in place. A portable television rested on a chest of drawers at the bed's end. I sensed Stephanie's curiosity as we stood side by side and took in the room. She had pushed her hood down and she looked exhausted and grimly pale but somehow less desperate than she had. I sat down on a plastic chair by the window and took the thermos flask from my bag.

'How did you find this place?' she said as we drank our tea.

'My photography lecturer talked to the council and arranged a trip here. Then I came back afterwards and found the way to sneak in.'

'On your own?'

Part of me wanted to pretend that I had been brave enough to come here alone, part of me wanted to say Cam's name out loud and hear it echoing down the empty corridors. 'With a friend.'

'Did you get some good photos?'

'They were technically good but didn't do it justice. Other people were more pleased with them than I was.'

'I've not seen any of your work for ages.'

'I've got some paintings in a little exhibition on Tuesday. It's a pop-up thing that only lasts for a few hours. You can come to that if you want to, if you're up to it.'

'Maybe. I'll have to see how I feel.' She looked around the

room again, her gaze lingering on a shelf packed with paperback novels in the corner. 'How come this room's in such good condition when the rest of the building's a mess?'

'I don't know. I think a caretaker must have lived in here or something. But that must have been years ago. No one comes here now.' Except me. Me and Cam. We had spent longer in this room than any other.

'Maybe it wasn't a caretaker. I mean, you could live in here and no one would ever know, would they? It would be as if you'd just vanished off the face of the earth.'

We stopped at a petrol station on the way home. Stephanie waited in the car while I went inside and bought three pints of milk and a giant box of Maltesers. I felt her watching me as I walked back across the forecourt towards her.

'You got a text, Mum.'

I had left my mobile in the compartment between the front seats. 'It'll be your dad checking up on us.' I pulled away without reading it. 'You won't tell him where we went today, will you? Well, you can tell him where we went but not about going inside.'

'Oh, the trespassing bit? I won't tell him. He'd think it was really, really bad, wouldn't he?'

'He'd be horrified. He'd probably ground me or take me to the police station to confess.'

'That's quite funny when you think about it.' We shared a smile, the memory of Croome House binding us together just as I had hoped it would.

In the warmth of the house I realised how cold she was. She was shuddering violently and her hands were as damp and frigid as milk bottles delivered in a frost. I turned the heating up and shepherded her to bed. I dug two elderly hot water bottles out from the cupboard under the sink and hoped they would hold out as I filled them from the tap.

'Is this withdrawal from the alcohol, do you think?' I asked her as she swallowed paracetamol with another mug of hot Ribena.

'It's a hangover. I drank a lot of wine. And some gin. Then some more wine. No wonder I was sick.'

'Do you feel like you want a drink now?'

'God, no. I'd puke. I'm not a proper alky.'

'I didn't think you were.' There was something too extreme, too showy in her drinking for it to have run too deep. Didn't alcoholics drink vast amounts and still appear sober? Didn't they go to work with vodka hidden in bottles of orange juice, clinking and sloshing as they walked?

'Dad thinks I am, doesn't he? That's why the wine rack's empty. Your wine rack's never empty. And why he's making me see the doctor?'

'He's worried about you.'

'And he wants the doctor to tell him what's wrong with me? Well, he's always loved a label.'

I tried not to smile. I wondered whether normal mothers and daughters talked about their fathers and husbands like this. It was new for us. 'I suppose he has. It's just the way his brain works. It has to tidy things up and file them away. It's how he makes sense of the world.' He would like to file Stephanie away in The Elms but I wasn't going to let that happen. I thought of the labels he had applied to me over the years: lover, mother, anxious, neurotic, obsessive, artistic. There must be others that he used only in the privacy of his own mind: highly strung, needy, fantasist.

Uninvited, I lay down on the bed beside her. I mirrored her posture and closed my eyes; no one can sleep when they're being watched.

'I'd like to come to your exhibition, Mum,' she whispered just before she fell asleep.

I must have slept too, maybe just for a minute. I found myself crawling out of slumber, drugged by the desert heat of the room and the dim light seeping through the curtained window. The wrongness of being in bed during the day and the sensation of having been doped were menacingly familiar. Those memories in their boxes were rattling their chains again.

*   *   *

My lifelong fear of falling is very real but it isn't rational. Neither is my fear of drowning in the bath or of being killed in my bed by a suitcase tumbling out of an aeroplane and smashing through the roof. My fear of fireworks, which made me conspire to take Freddy and Stephanie out of the country over the fifth of November every year until they were both in their teens, wasn't rational, neither was my refusal to let them wear anything yellow after I saw a girl in a rainsuit the colour of sunshine dash into a road and be knocked down by a car. But my fear of losing a child was different; there was nothing irrational about it at all: children go missing every day in the wafers of time between one minute and the next.

'Missing child' is the most terrifying phrase in the English language. It is written in red, carved into us as children and etched into our cores as we become parents. It means shy smiles in photographs peeled from albums and printed on the front of newspapers; the stark fact about finding them in the first twenty-four hours or never finding them at all, at least not alive. It is the stab of self-loathing we feel when we read about a search party and shake our heads, already giving the child up for dead. Or, worse still, the thought that he or she is better off dead than in the clutches of a paedophile, a monster, the creatures from which our nightmares are made. Stephanie went missing when she was fifteen years and three days old. Technically, she was a teenager not a child. But teenagers were only invented in the 1950s – there were just children and adults before then – and in the eyes of the police and in my eyes, she was still a child.

The missing child scenarios I had always imagined were sudden. They split life into *Before* and *After* in a single brutal cut: I would go into the kitchen to make a cup of tea and come back to find the sofa empty, the television speaking to no one as the curtains flapped in the breeze from the open front door; I would lose a contact lens in the swimming pool and dig my glasses out of my bag to see only unfamiliar faces splashing and laughing as if nothing had happened; I would be walking down the street and realise that the hands which should be holding mine had vanished and I was walking alone. These imagined scenarios dogged my days and woke me in the night. Each time I imagined a new way in which my children could be taken from me, I would think it over and over, elaborating on the scenario until it felt as real to me as any memory. A therapist I saw for a while viewed my fear of losing my children as key to what he referred to as my 'anxious condition'. He pinned me into my chair with hungry blue eyes and urged me to confront my fears, explore my nightmare scenarios by pushing through the moment of loss and into what lay beyond. 'Gain control of your destructive fantasies, Rosalind. You invented them so you can control them,' he said. I can only assume that the man had no imagination. As soon as I let myself think about the moment after the moment in which Stephanie or Freddy went missing, I unleashed a whole new force of creative potential. I lay rigid in bed imagining not just the fact that they had gone but where they had gone to. The possibilities rose around me like a tide of floodwater, covering once-familiar rooms, roads, gardens and playgrounds with the wash of dread.

But in the end it didn't happen like that. It took me hours to realise that my daughter was missing. I was so wedded to the idea of the split-second, irreversible wrenching loose of normal life, that I failed to recognise it when it happened to me, just as catastrophic, but so very slow. They were clever, though. He was clever, I mean.

It was Thursday November the thirteenth. She didn't come home from school at the end of the day but that was OK because she went to orchestra practice on Thursdays and I didn't expect her until half past five. At quarter past five she rang from her mobile and told me she was going to Sarah's house to do homework and would have dinner there. Sarah's dad would drop her back on his way to work. Robert Lewis, Sarah's father, was a doctor in Accident and Emergency and dropping Stephanie home on his way to work was a regular arrangement when he had a night shift.

At nine forty, I sent Stephanie a text message. Robert was never late for work and he always dropped her off at nine thirty sharp, beeping his horn and waiting until she was safely through the front door before he drove off. Perhaps his car had broken down and they needed a lift. I put my shoes on ready to go and help. At nine forty-five I rang her but her phone went straight to voicemail. I rang again at nine forty-eight and nine fifty. Then I rang Sarah's house. I knew something was wrong when Robert answered the phone and started to chat about a book I had lent him a couple of weeks earlier. He didn't have a night shift and Stephanie wasn't there, hadn't been there for a couple of weeks, in fact. He had noticed her absence and asked Sarah whether they had fallen out, but Sarah told him Stephanie was worried about her exams and was staying in the library after school or holing up in her bedroom instead of at the home of her best friend.

'So where is she, Robert?' I asked.

'I don't know. Let me check with Sarah. I'm sure she can shed some light.' I realised with a jolt that he was talking to me in his smooth, calm, professional voice, the voice he must use to tell people that their leg or arm, their wife or daughter, couldn't be saved.

My voice was anything but calm. It drew Dan out of the living room and into the hallway as I waited for Robert to call me back. He had come home late and was chewing a mouthful of reheated lasagne. 'Stephanie's been lying to us,' I said. 'She hasn't been to Sarah's at all.'

'Well where is she?'

The phone rang. It had to be her. I would ground her for weeks, stop her allowance, take her computer away.

Only it wasn't Stephanie, it was a hesitant, mumbling Sarah. She thought I should know that Stephanie hadn't been to orchestra practice. She had told Sarah she had a headache and wanted to go home and Sarah hadn't heard from her since, in spite of texting to check up on her. 'Where do you think she is?' she asked. Even then I didn't realise what had happened. I focused on the fact that Stephanie had lied so I didn't see the fact that she was missing.

'She didn't go to orchestra,' I told Dan. 'She told me she had a good practice but she wasn't even there. It was another lie.' Grounding her wouldn't be enough. I had never had to punish Stephanie before. What would I do to really teach her a lesson, to make sure she never lied to me again? It worried me that I couldn't think of a single thing. It made me wonder whether I knew my self-contained daughter at all.

'OK, calm down. Calm down, Ros.' He was holding his arms out in front of him, hands palm downwards in a gesture as old as our relationship. He did it when I wound myself up about missing car keys or lost library books.

'I'm not making a fuss over nothing. She's been lying and I don't know where she is.'

'Do you think it's a boyfriend?'

'Oh, God. I didn't even think of that. But why wouldn't she tell us? We'd let her see him. We're not that strict. Why would she need to lie like this?'

'Maybe we wouldn't approve. Maybe he's a bit rough, covered in tattoos or something.'

'I don't care about his tattoos. She *lied* to me, Dan.' A new thought struck me like a blow. 'Maybe he's got a car. They could have been in an accident. He could be some seventeen-year-old yob who's just passed his test. He could have been drinking. Or taking drugs. Oh!' I remember the thought I had at that exact moment: *What if she's been hurt and Robert Lewis is at home instead of at the hospital? Who will look after her then?*

I rang Sarah back. She denied any knowledge of a boyfriend but I wasn't sure whether I believed her. If Stephanie could lie then Sarah could too. While Dan went to speak to Freddy I started ringing Stephanie's other friends. There weren't many, Sarah and she had always been too close to let others in, but there were a couple with whom they spent time every so often. I didn't have the girls' mobile phone numbers so it was the parents who I spoke to, apologising for ringing so late and failing to keep the panic out of my voice. Lucy and Maya were summoned from their rooms. Neither claimed to know where Stephanie was. But they would say that, wouldn't they? I wanted to reach through the phone line and shake them until I was sure that they were telling the truth. Their mothers were sympathetic: 'Ring us if there's anything we can do to help,' they said, 'anything at all.' Later, when I thought about those conversations, I wondered what they meant by help. Did they mean help to form a search party, to poke sticks into suspicious compost heaps and patches of disturbed earth?

'I'm ringing the police,' I told Dan when he reappeared in the hall.

'It's a bit early for that, isn't it? I mean, won't they think you're being a bit dramatic?'

'I don't care what they think. I want to know where Stephanie is and who she's with. Just because you think I overreact to every-thing doesn't mean that there's nothing to worry about now.'

'Ros. I just think it's a bit early to be calling in the cavalry.'

I turned my back on him and picked up the phone. I thought of everywhere that she could be, one scenario leading to the next in a fractal pattern of fears sprouting from fears. She was in a car driving too fast along a winding black road, the faceless driver laughing at her screams. She was sick with drink at a party, lying on her back and breathing hard, moments from choking. She was alone in a moonlit field, abandoned or left behind. She was upside down in a ditch, her seat belt cutting into her thighs. She was trapped in a car, river water rising around her. She was falling from a bridge, her fingers gripping the empty air. Worse still: she had been taken; she was in the boot of a car, scratching at the metal with her fingernails; she was bound and gagged in a lightless room.

Dan took the phone from me when I found myself unable to speak. He explained that it had now been eight hours since Stephanie was last seen. 'It's completely out of character,' he said. 'She's never lied to us before. She's never gone missing like this before, not even for five minutes. My wife is very worried.' He had expected the police to tell them he was being ridiculous, but they had not. His face paled as he listened to the voice on the other end of the phone. The unravelling of his calm made my heart pound. I pressed my hands hard against the wall, made myself focus on the sensation of the floor beneath my feet as he described her school uniform, her hair, her build.

'The police are sending someone round. We need to check her room, to see if there's anything missing. Clothes, money, that sort of thing,' he said when he put the phone down. There it was, that word: 'missing'. Stephanie was missing. My child was missing and I hadn't even realised.

I ran up the two flights of stairs to her room. I went in there every day to pick up her washing and make her bed but this felt different. I kept expecting her to appear in the door and tell me to leave her things alone. The room was as tidy as usual and full of Stephanie: books, clothes, photos, her computer, a row of shoes peeking out from under the bed, a huge canvas print of the Golden Gate Bridge filling almost an entire wall. Every time I saw that picture I imagined people falling from the bridge, their despair uncoiling behind them as they fell. I didn't know how Stephanie could sleep with it hanging over her, but she said it was beautiful.

Months before she would sit her first mock GCSE exam, there was a revision timetable pinned above her desk. I leaned towards it as though it might tell me where she was. This week she would study Module Eight Physics and *King Lear*. I had always been proud of her academic success but it had unnerved me, too. It was the way she studied with determination but without pride. She never gloated about coming top in her year, winning awards for maths and science. In fact, she told me these things reluctantly and only when asked and I suspected that she wanted to avoid making me – her underachieving mother, pregnant before she even finished university – feel inferior. I watched her study in the evenings and weekends and it felt as though she was carving a road to take her away from me, grinding out her escape hour by hour. What if she had been travelling faster than I had known? What if that determination had taken her not to Oxford or London or California in a few years' time but somewhere else much sooner?

Dan pulled open her wardrobe, framing himself in the bruised colours she liked to wear. He looked over his shoulder at me.

'Black skinny jeans,' I said. 'If she took anything, that's what she'd take.' I pushed him aside and started rifling through the neatly hung clothes. The question that ricocheted around my head, that caused my hands to pause in their efforts, was whether I wanted to find her favourite jeans there, where they should be, or not. What did it mean if they weren't there?

What did it mean if they were? She had bought the jeans in Topshop a month earlier. Their fit was slimmer, their effect sleeker than any others she owned. I had hated those jeans from the moment she brought them home. I had boiled them in the wash, muttering into the powder drawer like a witch casting a spell in a hedgerow, willing them to come out of the machine shrunken and ruined. I had given them the full force of my evil eye but they had just emerged skinnier, gripping her thighs more closely and skimming with even less deference over her teenaged bones. I hand washed them after that, stretching them with all my might before hanging them out to dry. I had thought often about sneaking them from her room and posting them into the clothing recycling box in the Waitrose car park.

I went through her chest of drawers then upended her washing basket just to be sure. The jeans weren't there. The black ballet pumps she insisted on wearing even in the winter and her favourite purple cardigan had vanished too. I couldn't bear to think of her in those flimsy shoes in the cold of the winter night.

'She took her clothes. She planned this,' said Dan.

'Maybe.' I had sat down on the floor to look at the shoes lined up under her bed. My knees were drawn up under my chin, my hands covering my mouth. I looked back to the revision timetable pinned above the desk. Stephanie had always been a planner.

'Why else would she take her clothes to school? She went off this morning in her uniform, yes?'

'Maybe she didn't take them to school. They're not here but she might have left them at Sarah's at the weekend or—'

'Robert said she hasn't been there lately.'

I squeezed my eyes shut and tried to think when I had last seen those wretched jeans. She had helped me to cook lunch on Sunday. I remembered her tying my pink Cath Kidston apron around herself before she peeled the potatoes. We had laughed about how twee the floral pattern looked against the black denim of her jeans. She had been nowhere but school and home since then. 'She must have taken them today.'

'What if she's run away?' said Dan.

'No! She wouldn't! Maybe she just wanted to look nice for an hour before she came home. She hates that silly school uniform. Maybe she was meeting her boyfriend and he was driving her home but they crashed. A car crash.' I pressed my hands harder over my mouth to stop them from shaking. I saw the pitch-black road, the bridge, the speeding car turning over and over, the river rushing by. Dan's face had gone slack. In us both the ghastliness of not knowing was taking root, planting little engines of insidious horror to thrum in our cores, to churn out fumes that would taint our every thought. We both jumped when Freddy spoke. He was meant to be asleep, not standing in the doorway watching us unravel.

'Why are you in here? Where's Stephie?'

The doorbell rang.

'Who's that?'

'Go back to bed,' I said, my voice a strange, twisting thing that must have sounded even worse to him than it did to me because he did as I asked without question. Or maybe the sixth sense of the child told him that something bad was afoot and sent him back to his room where everything was as it should be.

I ran down the stairs and pulled the front door open. Perhaps she had lost her key. But there were two police officers rather than Stephanie standing on the doorstep.

Dan recovered himself on the way down the stairs. He had a talent for doing this: packing his emotions away and putting on a show when he had an audience other than me. I used to worry that it was a sign of a dishonest nature, of some deep-rooted ability to dissociate, but as he calmly invited the officers inside and started to recount the events of Stephanie's disappearance, I was just envious of it.

The female officer introduced herself as Inspector Fiona Haskins. Next to her sat Sergeant King who couldn't have been more than twenty-two years old. Perched on the edge of my white velvet sofa in their navy uniforms, they looked like misplaced extras from a television show. I would have done anything to be able to shepherd them back into *The Bill*, to go upstairs and stroke Stephanie's hair away from her sleeping face.

Inspector Haskins asked the questions and Sergeant King wrote down our answers, nodding every time we established a fact: where she was, where she wasn't, when she wasn't where she should have been. There was a hurried hunt for a recent photograph, the easing of one from its frame. In the picture she was wearing her school uniform, her head tilted to one side, her eyes made unreadable by the glare of the photographer's flash. She had hated me displaying it on the mantelpiece and I had often come into the room to find it turned to face the wall. I wondered whether she would still be here if I had just let her take it down.

There were phone calls and hissing bouts of handheld-radio talk as the navy-clad strangers set in motion the cogs and wheels that looked for the hiding, the lost, the mislaid. Still I dredged my mind for a harmless explanation. I dug my nails deep into my palms and urged myself to remember a sleepover, a school trip, a party. But there was nowhere she could legitimately be at one o'clock in the morning on a school night.

There was more back and forth on the radios. More questions, a slow unpeeling of Stephanie's life, a probing so thorough, so petty in its detail, so far-reaching in its scope that it seemed impossible that it could all relate to her.

'No, we don't let her have Facebook or anything like that. She just has her school email address and that's monitored by the teachers,' I said when the questions honed in on Stephanie's computer.

'But she has her own computer and access to the internet?' said the inspector.

'Yes, but not at night. The modem is in our room and we unplug the router at eight o'clock. She can't use it after that. And she has to leave her door open when she's on the internet anyway. I read the BBC's advice about it all last year.'

'We'll need to see her computer.'

'You won't find anything. She only uses it for school work,' I said as I started the silver computer on Stephanie's desk. The screen blinked into life. I typed her login details and the password – *KingsofLeon123* – she had written down for me as part of the agreement we had for her being allowed the computer in her room.

Error. Please enter valid login details and password.

I must have mistyped it. My hands were shaking as Dan and the two officers peered over my shoulders. I tried again, pressing each key so slowly that the inspector had to muffle a sigh of frustration.

Error. Please enter valid login details and password.

I went to the hall stand and collected the address book in which Stephanie had written the password. I handed it to Dan and he tried.

Error. Please enter valid login details and password.

'I'm going to take this straight down to the station for processing,' said Inspector Haskins, already unplugging the silver box from the monitor and hefting it onto her hip. 'Wait here, King. I'll be in touch.'

Sergeant King led us to the kitchen and boiled the kettle, opening and shutting cupboard doors until he found tea bags, milk and sugar. The tea was strong and sweet. I couldn't touch it.

'What do you think has happened? Really? Do you think . . . do you think she's been taken?' Dan asked. I hadn't noticed the silence until he broke it.

'I'm sorry but I don't know what's happened. I wish I did. But it's much more likely that she has either run away or . . .' He paused, took a breath. 'Or got herself in some kind of trouble. For her age group any sort of abduction is much less likely than running away. Abduction is really incredibly rare when you look at the statistics.'

'Jesus! You think she's killed herself, don't you?' said Dan.

'No, I didn't say that. We look into everything. We wouldn't be doing our jobs if we left any stone unturned. I know it must be hard for you to believe right now but this happens all the time. Let me assure you that in ninety-eight per cent of cases with teenagers they're back within twenty-four hours, forty-eight at the most. Right now that's exactly what we expect to happen here.' With his senior officer out of the house he was confident and well spoken. I wondered if he was one of the new graduate police offers I had read about in the paper. How was the fact that he had a degree in English literature or geography, or whatever policemen study at university, going to help Stephanie?

'What about the others? The two per cent? Where are they?'

'Ros, please,' Dan said. 'Listen to the policeman.'

'We'll find her, Mrs Simm. Stay positive, for her sake. She hasn't been missing for long. Not long at all.'

At some point it stopped being night and started to become morning. There was a long period of time when we were alone and it felt as though nothing was happening. At intervals the house filled up with people then emptied again. Beatrice arrived and took charge of Freddy. There were updates every hour, sometimes more frequently. But they were always about where Stephanie wasn't and not where she was. The computer had been hacked into but revealed 'nothing of immediate concern,' Sergeant King said.

Just after eleven o'clock in the morning, Inspector Haskins arrived with news. The school's CCTV cameras had caught Stephanie leaving the modern languages block after her last lesson. We watched on the inspector's laptop as the flickering grey image stood next to Sarah, pressing her hands to her head, hugging her friend then slipping away. The school's web of cameras passed a grey and black charcoal sketch of my daughter from lens to lens between themselves as she crossed the court-yard at the centre of the school, walked through the reception area and out of the main gates. A camera outside an off-licence she passed every day on her way home had caught sight of her fifteen minutes later, walking so fast that she was almost running. Once she had left that last camera's shaky field of vision she had disappeared. It should only have taken her five minutes to walk from the school to the shop, but the time stamps on the footage didn't lie.

Inspector Haskins blew the lurching image up so Stephanie filled the screen of her laptop. In the ten missing minutes, she had changed out of her school uniform and put on those wretched jeans. I couldn't help myself: I reached for the screen and pressed my fingers into the last image of her until the inspector took my wrist and gently moved my hand away.

'Wherever she is we now think she went willingly and planned it carefully. The change of clothes and the way she lied about where she was suggest that she's run away.'

The kitchen was unbearably hot. The three people gathered around the laptop were a crushing, tightly packed crowd. There wasn't enough air to go around. I wanted to get up and open a window but my legs were shaking so hard that my knees were bumping the underside of the table top and I didn't trust myself to stand. I squeezed my eyes closed but all I could see was the Golden Gate Bridge soaring above me, a tiny figure standing on its edge, right in the middle, neither here nor there. I felt her falling, reaching for thin air as the ground hurtled towards her and her stomach leapt high up in her chest.

* * *

Downstairs, I shook the memory card out of my camera and hitched it to my laptop. The pictures of Croome House I had taken with Cam appeared on the screen one by one: the stained blue-sky ceiling in the dining room, an empty corridor winding into the distance, a tatty noticeboard hanging above an elegant marble fireplace. The light had been better than on my first visit and rays of winter sun broke through the windows and lit paths through the dust motes. As I flicked from image to image I began to see traces of Cam. A shadow fell across the floor in one shot, a smudge of shoe crept into the corner of another. The last photo was of the dome at the top of the grand staircase. It was blurred with motion and framed at an angle as though the camera had been falling from my hand. The shutter had snapped shut at the same instant that Cam had reached for me. The text message I had received in the car had been from him, not Dan. On Monday afternoon he wanted me to come down to the empty shop in Hatfield where our pop-up exhibition would be held to hang my pictures and help with the finishing touches. Of course I wouldn't go, not when Stephanie needed me at home. I deleted the telltale blurred photo, wiped the memory card and snapped my laptop shut.

'Mum, can I put the TV on?'

She was standing in the sitting room doorway. Evening had arrived and the room was dark. 'Sorry. I didn't mean to creep up on you. There's a programme about sloths that I like.'

'*Sloth Sanctuary*? I never miss it. I didn't know you were a fan.' I started closing the curtains, wrapping us in a heavy velvet shroud.

'Where's Dad?' She had folded herself up at the end of one of the long powder-blue sofas, her polka dot pyjama-covered knees drawn up beneath her chin. I had ordered the sofas in the summer, choosing the fabric because I knew how beautiful her hair would look against it. Of course, she had barely been here to sit on it since.

'Still at work.'

'Really?' Was she feigning the surprise in her voice? The answer to 'Where's Dad?' has always been 'At work'. We had had that exchange – Stephanie and I, Freddy and I – over and over again since each had learned to talk. 'Where's Daddy?' had become 'Where's Dad?' then 'Is Dad at work?' then 'Is he working?' At some point they had stopped asking.

I nodded.

'Why? It's Saturday.'

Because of you coming home, I thought. *Because this time feels too much like last time, and it's exactly what he did then.* 'There's some sort of crisis, apparently,' I said.

'Don't you mind that he's always working?'

'It's just the way things are. I keep myself busy with my course and my friends.' I was used to defending Dan's absences to other people. I would talk about his commitment and dedication and try to forget how, in the early days of his career, he would invent doctor's appointments and sneak out of work to surprise me on Friday afternoons with toys for the children or cakes bursting with cream from the patisserie behind his office, or a plan to get up at dawn and have breakfast on the beach in Suffolk. I would try not to remember those long-gone mornings when he would miss his train to work because he had crawled back into our bed after his shower, how his hot damp skin would cling to mine and the taste of soap would fill my mouth and he would whisper into my ear that he wanted to take the smell of me to work and breathe me in all day.

'I used to wish he'd get made redundant,' said Stephanie. 'Do you remember when Ashworth relocated and all those people were laid off? The Shipley twins' dad lost his job. They used to whisper about it in the playground as if someone had died, but their dad used to come and collect them at the end of the day and he made their sandwiches. He used to put little jokes and drawings in their lunch boxes. I was so jealous.'

'Oh, Stephie, I'm sorry.'

'It's not your fault. I was only seven. I didn't understand things then.'

'I wonder what happened to him, the Shipleys' father.'

'I can't remember. It's funny that I remember what their lunch boxes looked like when we were seven years old and how envious I was of their matching yellow cardigans, but I have no idea where they are now.'

'Aren't they on Facebook?'

She shook her head and shifted further back into the sofa cushions. 'I don't use it. I hate the idea of my personal information being plastered all over the internet.'

'Me too.' I hated the idea of her personal information being anywhere that *he* could find it. Dealing with Stephanie's immediate problems had let me push Temperley's release to the back of my mind for the afternoon. But the sudden thought of him Googling her, seeking the breadcrumb trail of photographs, thoughts and feelings that most twenty-one-year-olds left online, brought it back to me. If Stephanie's eyes hadn't been fixed on the television screen she would have seen it on my face; I wouldn't have been able to lie to her, to protect her from the knowledge for another second, let alone another few days.

I closed my eyes and took deep breaths as the opening music for *Sloth Sanctuary* started.

The fearless woman who ran the sanctuary in Suriname had received a tip-off about a tract of sloth habitat that was about to be cleared to make way for sugar beet and beef cattle. She led her staff on a frantic mission to run behind the clearance crew and scoop the newly homeless sloths from the razed earth and bundle them into sacks. With no room left at the sanctuary, she took the new arrivals into her home where they snuggled into laundry baskets and hung happily from curtain rails. The sloths looked at her with trusting black eyes and rested their savage-looking claws on her wrists when she picked them up to weigh them.

Dan arrived home at the worst possible moment: Kiki, one of the orphans, was critically ill. The sanctuary volunteers were working in shifts around the clock to feed and care for her. Kiki's last hope, a visiting vet from Brazil, was examining the creature, peering into her enormous eyes and feeling for her pulse. Stephanie had drawn her knees up under her chin and clenched her hands in front of her.

'Sorry about that. I really had no idea it would take so long.'

'All sorted?' I asked, my eyes darting between him and Kiki's tiny body. *Be quiet and leave us alone.*

'Well, not exactly, but things shouldn't get any worse over-night at least. All OK here? What have you been up to?'

Stephanie looked from him to me. 'We went for a walk.'

'Oh, where did you go?'

I was about to answer when Stephanie did it for me. 'Just near the reservoir,' she said. 'It was nice. You should have come.'

EIGHT DAYS

On the kitchen table an empty coffee cup and a discarded iPad were the only traces of Dan. Part of me hoped that he had slipped out of bed and gone to work again. I wanted another long day to unravel Stephanie's secrets without him.

I refilled the coffee cup and clicked the iPad into life. Usually a mass of browser windows would be open. There would be *The Times*, Wikipedia, the timetable for trains to London, the chat forum about bluegrass that Dan lurked on. But this time there were no windows open at all. Even the search history had been erased. I was still staring into the iPad's blank face when my phone buzzed from my dressing gown pocket. I had taken to carrying it around the house with me since Cam started sending me messages.

The message was from Freddy, not Cam: **I hope you're doing a roast today Mum – will be home by 2.** He was only six weeks into his first term at Bristol University but he had spent the summer at a football camp in California, returning just three days before the start of term, so it felt as though he had been gone for months. He had vaguely mentioned coming home for a couple of days in November but I hadn't heard any more about it and had given up hope. I texted back with a promise of roast lamb. In a few hours' time I would have both my children home for the first time in more than half a year. Everything else receded from view.

Dan came in from outside on a gust of frost-scented air. 'Morning. I got breakfast.' He waved a paper bag speckled with croissant grease. 'Stephie's favourite.'

'Freddy's coming home for a couple of nights. Isn't it lovely? I really didn't expect to see him until Christmas. I'm going to do roast lamb.' The rush of my joy ceased at the sight of his frown.

'Is that a good idea?' He put the bag of croissants on the table and shrugged off his coat.

'What do you mean?'

'It's not very good timing, is it? Ring him back and put him off for a few days.'

'It's Freddy. This is his home and he's always welcome here. I'm not telling him he can't come.'

'I'm just thinking of Stephie. We need to get her sorted. That's our priority.' By sorted he meant sent away, packaged off: out of sight, out of mind.

'What's that, Dad?' Stephanie had done her trick of appearing soundlessly in the doorway and standing there unnoticed.

Dan flinched. I smiled at her around his shoulder. She looked so much better than she had the day before. The only sign of the state we had found her in were the bruises on her hand.

'Freddy's coming for a couple of days,' I said. 'That's OK with you, isn't it?'

'Yes! I've really missed Fred. I've been meaning to go down to Bristol, but . . . well, I haven't yet.' She turned from me to Dan and the smile left her face, the warmth evaporated from her eyes. 'So, what's the problem, Dad?'

'I was worried that you might not be up to seeing other people. That's all.'

'Freddy isn't other people.' There was something teenage in the way she spoke to him, except she had never been like that as a teenager. 'When's he getting here?' she asked me.

'By two. I promised him roast lamb so I'll have to go to the supermarket.'

'I'll help you cook. I expect Dad has work to do.' She spun on the tiptoe of her right foot – just as she used to as a child – and left the room.

I drove to the big Waitrose on the edge of the city. As I passed the flashes of red, black and white in the newspaper aisle, the memory of Tanya's phone call forced itself upon me: *It's a good story either way, Ros.* My heart started to race as old memories stirred, dark tendrils of panic reaching out from the past. I put my head down and rushed to the end of the aisle, weaving between other shoppers until the newspapers were safely out of sight. This was a day for family, for Stephanie and Freddy, and I wouldn't let Temperley in however hard he knocked.

As I filled my basket with racks of lamb, mangetout and dusky red potatoes, I reached for other memories. I had always loved feeding my children. Even when they were grasping with their fat hands and the black caves of their mouths for my cracked nipples at three o'clock in the morning, it felt right to me. In the first months of Stephanie's life, while Dan was finishing his degree, feeding her was how I measured out the endless hours in our poky basement flat where the dim brown light barely changed from night to day. Her need for my milk, the way her body went rigid with shock and tears when her hunger struck, then relaxed and curled into me as soon as my milk found her mouth, was proof that she belonged to me. I think of that time as liquid: the air in the flat was damp, time swirled around me in ripples and I remembered the spark of resentment, bordering on loathing, that would pulse through me every time Dan swept in after a lecture and lifted Stephanie away from me. He would spin around with her in his arms, standing with his back to me and holding her high so her face was level with his. She would look at me over his shoulder; I would wave at her and she would smile.

'You look so much better, darling,' I said to Stephanie when she walked into the kitchen and started helping me to unpack the shopping. 'How do you feel?'

'Right now I feel OK. But I know it won't last. This is what it's always like. I'll be fine for an hour or a day or even a week and then I'll start thinking about it all again. You know people say life is like a roller-coaster? Well, mine is like a merry-go-round, except it isn't merry. It's more of a misery-go-round. That's what it feels like to me, anyway.'

I froze in the act of unwrapping the lamb shoulder. My hands were perfectly still on the slab of cold meat. I had expected her to say that she was OK, to fob me off with a head shake or a weak smile and a change of subject as she always had before. 'Tell me about it, please.'

'Oh, Mum.' She sank into the patchwork armchair by the Aga. She was wearing the jeans and jumper I had lent her the day before, the pale blue cashmere making her look even younger than she was. Her hair hung in wet snakes around her face and the scent of my shampoo filled the room. 'We don't really do this sort of thing, do we?'

'Maybe we should try.'

'Where would we even start?'

Let's start with the day you decided to run away with your geography teacher, I wanted to say. 'Why don't you tell me what happened in London? We could start with that and see how we get on.'

She leaned her elbows on her knees and pressed her fingers to her temples. I pretended to concentrate on the lamb, shredding rosemary and peeling cloves of garlic with clumsy, shaking fingers.

'Nothing happened, exactly. Not really. Everything just started to slip away from me.' For a moment I thought that she wasn't going to say any more. I held my breath. 'I stopped being able to block out what I did. What an idiot I was. All of it. It was like an endless loop of everything I had ever done wrong playing on and on in my head.'

'When did this start?' I said, when her silence threatened to last.

'The summer.' She had stayed on in London over the summer to assist on a research project about modelling the spread of neglected tropical diseases. It was the time I had started to let her slide out of my thoughts, had stopped phoning or going to London. It was the time I had stopped worrying. 'I loved doing the research. I loved being in the lab all day. I loved how committed everyone was. But Sarah and my other friends had all gone away for the summer so when I wasn't at work I was on my own. I stayed at the lab for as long as I could, but Alex – Professor Aldridge – would lock up when he left and I would have no choice but to go. I hated going back to that empty flat. I tried bringing work home with me but I couldn't concentrate. I read books, watched films, went running, but nothing was enough to stop it.'

I pulled the skin from another clove of garlic. She had let her wet hair fall over her face.

'All I can remember are the bad things, the ugly things. I try to find happy memories but it's as if they've all been erased or they were never there to begin with. It's as though there hasn't been a single moment of joy in my life because when I look back at the last twenty-one years, all I see is what happened with Nate.' I flinched at Temperley's nickname. It reminded me of the television appeal his father did once we knew that they were together. *Come back, Nate. Come back, son.* Bile rose in my throat. 'I remember things about that time and I don't understand them. I don't understand myself. I don't trust myself. If I did that then, what might I do now?'

She raised her head and looked up at me, her eyes running with tears. There were dark spots of pressure where she had dug her fingers into her temples and they made me want to shrink myself down, become microscopic and crawl inside her head. I would run through her neural pathways picking out memories of him, of *it*, and painting over them with picnics on beaches and warm hugs from friends, of triumphs and joys and her in the paddling pool with her brother. I wanted to erase Temperley's existence, not tell her that he was about to be set free.

'Oh, Stephie.' I knelt in front of her and took her hands in mine. She pulled them free and wiped her eyes.

'I may as well tell you the rest. At the end of August I went to a party with Sophie, a girl from my course who was back at uni for a retake. She's not even really a friend but it was something to do, someone to talk to. It was her brother's party. I met a couple of guys and I drank a lot. We all drank a lot. When I woke up the next day I didn't know where I was. I felt vile. I loathed myself, but not for anything I had done when I was fourteen or fifteen. It was like a holiday from my brain. One of the guys, Jake, lives near me and we started hanging around together. He was always willing to go out for a drink, always had something or somewhere to take my mind off myself. I'm sure you can join the dots between there and here.'

'Oh, that bastard Temperley,' I said. It slipped out before I could catch it.

'No! I knew that's what you'd think. It's me! *Me*, not him. Me! It's what I did, not what he did. It's what I did that I can't live with. I don't want to be the girl who ran away with the teacher any more.'

'That's not who you are. It never was and most people have forgotten about it, Stephie. People have short memories for things that don't involve them.'

'But I remember. How can I ever trust myself to make a decision again when I know what I did? When I know it was me all day every day, all night? Me, me, me. I did it. I did it. And you know. And Dad certainly does. He'll never forget it.' She balled her hands into fists and knocked them into her forehead again and again until I wrenched them away and pressed them to my chest. 'I just want it to stop. I want the thoughts to stop. I don't want to think about it any more. I don't want to be inside my head any more,' she said into my T-shirt.

'It can stop. We'll stop it. I promise.'

It took a long time for Stephanie to stop crying. I squeezed her to me and let my own tears fall on her damp hair. At some point I heard Dan's footsteps in the hallway, moving away from us, and I wondered for how long he had been listening. For the second time that day I thought about Stephanie as a baby. In the weeks after she was born, the air in that little flat was close and ripe with the brine of my sweat, my milk and the tang of the blood that still flowed out of me. Sometimes, when sleep deprivation, hunger and loneliness combined, while Stephanie lay asleep beside me and I listened with hypersensitive attention to every breath she took, I would slip into a state between sleeping and waking in which I half dreamt, half imagined myself to be at the bottom of a rock pool, stranded there by the going out of the tide. People – sometimes vague and faceless, sometimes Dan – looked down at me through the water and I knew with instinctive terror that they were planning to scoop Stephanie up in a net and take her away from me. I would jolt into wakefulness, pulling her towards me and holding her close. I felt that fear again in the kitchen. For a moment I wished she was still a baby so I could pick her up and run with her, away from the house, away from it all. But, an hour before we expected him, Freddy was there, filling the house with his smile, his loud voice and his familiar hair gel smell. Stephanie wiped the last of her tears from her face and hugged her brother. Our home had always been a brighter place with Freddy in it.

After lunch, Dan and Freddy walked up the road to pick up the papers then we sprawled in the sitting room with cups of tea. I closed the curtains against the gathering darkness, chose a shiny Sunday supplement and curled up on the corner of the sofa where I could see them all: Stephanie, Freddy and Dan. I had closed the door when I brought the tea in. Now I wished I could lock it, or, better still, seal it shut with an enchantment so no one could enter and no one could leave. The world would carry on outside this room, but we would be frozen in a moment of safety and harmony without the nagging expectation of Freddy announcing he was off to watch a match or meet a friend, or Stephanie getting softly to her feet and drifting out of the room. Without Nathan Temperley creeping closer day by day.

As safe as it felt, even the sitting room wasn't free of the perils of remembering. I had redecorated it twice in the past six years, changed the furniture, painted new pictures to hang on the walls. Yet still the sight of dust motes swarming in a winter sunbeam or the path traced across the ceiling by headlamps when a car pulled into the drive could snatch me back to the time when Stephanie was missing. I wanted to move after it happened. I spent weeks looking at houses on the internet and even went to see one. It was brand new, an executive home in an 'exclusive gated community' built on the edge of a country estate north of the city. It was perfect: a big, blank box, bereft of history. Better still, it was the last house available and had been the site's show home so the developers would throw in all the furniture, the curtains, the bland ornaments and the paintings chosen to match the colours of the house's many 'feature' walls. Even the bedding, the crockery and the books on the shelves would be included in the sale. We could have just packed a bag of clothes each, locked up our home on Crispin Avenue and left everything behind. We could have shaken ourselves free, slotted into show-home lives in our new show home and never looked

you, Stephanie, and you're not in any trouble. Freddy misses you too, Stephie – you know how much he loves his big sister.' On the television screen I saw myself lean closer to Tanya. I was silent and hunched, my eyes wide and wet. The plan had not been for me to speak. We had tried it during a rehearsal but I had been unable to form the words, even when they were written on cards in front of me. And yet I watched myself lean across the table quite suddenly and put my mouth too close to the microphone standing between Dan and me, so close that my lips must have been touching its spongy top. I watched myself pull my hands from Tanya's and Dan's and splay them on the table top. 'Tell us where she is. Please,' I heard myself say. My voice was barely audible, the microphone giving a squealing buzz as I spoke. Then I let out a wet gasp of snot and tears and fell silent as Dan's hands came into view, reaching either for me or for the microphone. The camera cut quickly to Inspector Haskins.

I couldn't remember much about filming the appeal, but I could remember what happened afterwards. As soon as the cameras had stopped and the film crews melted away, Dan took me by the arm and pulled me into an alcove at the side of the police's media liaison room. He stood over me, his hands gripping my arms above the elbows.

'Why did you say that?' His voice was hushed but I knew he would be shouting at me if we weren't in a police station, if Tanya wasn't watching us from across the room. 'We were meant to be talking to her. To Stephanie. No one else. Who were you talking to?'

'I'm not sure.'

'Do you know something? Are you hiding something from me?' He stepped even closer to me, blocking the rest of the room from view.

'No! Of course not. But what if they're wrong? What if someone has her?'

'And what if you just did what the police told you to do, Rosalind? What about that?' He shook his head and let go of my arms and suddenly my back was against the wall and there was no air in my lungs. I was doused in heat and my heart was stopping and starting in my chest. The room was shifting away from me, the floor rising up behind me, beside me, on top of me. Then I was falling through empty air, a flat expanse of nothingness hurtling up to meet me. I wanted to scream but there was no air to carry the sound.

'Breathe, Rosalind. Just breathe. In through your mouth. Breathe with me. Open your eyes. Look at me. Just me. Inhale. Exhale. Slowly. That's right.'

Inhale. A cool hand cupping my face, light but firm. Another squeezing my shoulder.

Exhale. Brown eyes looking into mine, eclipsing everything else.

Inhale. The floor solid beneath me, my back against the wall. My knees under my chin.

Exhale. Dan's voice nearby, saying my name.

Inhale. Tears. Hundreds and hundreds of tears waiting to be shed.

Exhale. My head on Tanya's shoulder. Her words in my ear, tethering me to the ground. 'You did really well. Really well.' A glance to her left where Dan must have been. 'Both of you did really well.'

It was a panic attack; just a panic attack. It was not my first.

I used to watch those television appeals and wonder about the parents – about the secrets behind their quavering voices, the pauses between their words and the rings around their eyes. It never crossed my mind that I would be one of them one day, that people across the nation would watch a tear roll down Dan's cheek and hang from his chin, or see me wipe my nose on the back of my hand. Once upon a time I had cried along with those parents while knowing that my children were safely at school or in bed. Why did I watch them? It wasn't so I could help. The disappearance of a child in Doncaster or Walthamstow, Aberdeen or Penge could have nothing to do with me. I didn't scrawl down the hotline numbers or memorise the faces of the missing so I could search the streets for them. There was a part of me, a hidden part that I was careful not to examine, that enjoyed the rawness of emotion, the frisson of voyeurism. There was confluence between my reasons for going to the theatre and for hissing at Dan to be quiet when an appeal came on the news. Whether I was in front of a stage or a television, I sat in a place of safety watching a story of sorrow and love unfold.

A couple of years before I found myself on the other side of the camera, there was a case in which a man who wept and shook and begged for the safe return of his teenage stepdaughter one day was arrested for her murder the next. Again and again the news played a montage of clips. There he was, weeping as he appealed for the girl he had already raped and murdered to phone home, his arms around her mother; there he was, leading a candlelit vigil outside the girl's school, standing shoulder to shoulder with her friends; there he was, being led into a police station, cuffed to an officer, launching a phlegmy ball of spittle at a camera lens as a crowd booed and jeered. He had cried real tears for all of us to see when he knew she was stuffed into a suitcase in the corner of a cellar, her eyes blackened and his belt still cinched tight around her neck. I followed the case through court, poring over newspapers and collecting layers of detail as they emerged. It was revealed that the police suspected the step-father from the start but had been unable to penetrate his alibi, the lack of a body and the shield of the girl's mother's implacable faith in him. The detectives leading the inquiry pushed him into doing the appeal to see whether he would crack. It was routine practice to use these appeals as an opportunity to scrutinise the family – the husband, the father, the uncle, the friend. They looked for a sign that all was not as it seemed: a glance to the left which told of a lie, an inability to say the victim's name or an insincerity of voice or gesture. Sometimes the threat of the press conference, the process of rehearsing key messages and arriving at the police station to face the cameras, was enough to make the guilty party confess. For days after I read a *Sunday Times Magazine* article about the case – complete with pictures of the stepfather, his thick, tattooed neck red against the white nylon of his court-case shirt – I became hyperaware of people's body language and the way they moved their eyes. I didn't think of any of these things when I was in front of the cameras, but afterwards I wondered whether specialist detectives were sitting in darkened rooms, freezing Dan and me frame by frame. Did they zoom in on our hands, our eyes, the angles between our bodies? Did they listen to our voices and that wretched wet sniff, rewinding and replaying and listening for something that wasn't there to hear?

As I sat on the sitting room floor watching myself and my husband on television – remembering the moment in which he had accused me of knowing something that I didn't know – the police tip-line was ringing with sightings. There were nineteen in total, in St Albans, Brighton, Greenwich, Glasgow, Prague and everywhere in between. There was only one that the police gave any credence to: a girl seen buying a packet of sanitary towels in Woolley Edge services on the M1 just past Barnsley shortly before midnight on the Friday. The shop assistant who served the girl swore it was Stephanie. She said she remembered it clearly because a lone teenager wasn't the usual type of customer she saw at that time of night, when it was all truckers buying cigarettes or travelling salesmen seeking KitKats and paracetamol. She remembered the hat too. It was a thick, black woollen beanie that had looked too big for the girl's head and she had thought it a shame that such a pretty girl would wear such a horrible hat.

CCTV footage from the service station was infuriatingly patchy, the camera in the shop was not working at all and the one pointing at the forecourt was knocked out of alignment so all that it showed was a lurching procession of people's legs. At forty-eight minutes past eleven, a pair of slim black-clad legs moved past the camera, visible from calf to mid-thigh. Twelve minutes later, the legs left again.

Sergeant King came to the house. He told us the facts then paused.

'Mrs Simm, perhaps you know whether it would be likely that Stephanie would need to stop off for supplies,' he said eventually, examining the tips of the fingers on his left hand. 'You know. For her time of the month.'

'Would Stephanie have her period, you mean?'

'Yes. Exactly. And would she choose that type of product if she did? Not a . . . not the other kind?'

'She prefers towels. But her periods aren't regular yet. They only started when she was fourteen and they've never settled down.' Dan's mouth was a circle of discomfort. He was squeamish about my periods, let alone those of his missing fifteen-year-old daughter. 'She . . .' I was going to add that she gets terrible period pains, that she would need a hot water bottle and a packet of aspirin, someone to make her a mug of Ribena and remind her that the pain would pass. In slow motion, by tiny increments, I realised the full horror of her disappearance all over again. This was something that happened three or four times a day while she was missing. It was as though my brain collapsed under the burden of knowledge and had to shake itself free by making me forget from time to time. But forgetting meant remembering again, counting the hours she had been missing again, trying to picture the exact expression on her face the last time I had seen her and scanning my empty, feeble brain for a clue as to where she could be.

The last traces of whatever tranquilliser the doctor had given me after my panic attack evaporated. 'Wait here,' I said. Stephanie hated the fact that her periods arrived with little warning and not at the twenty-eight-day intervals biology classes had led her to expect. Mine were the same at her age and it had been my suggestion that she mark their arrival and departure on her calendar so we could see if a pattern existed. I ran up to her room and combed the month of November then flicked back through the pages until I spotted the tiny red stars popping up here and there. I counted thirty-five days since the last one. It was entirely possible – probable, even – that Stephanie had needed sanitary towels. I was so hungry for any scrap of proof that she had continued to exist after she had walked past the off-licence's CCTV camera and disappeared, that I instantly swallowed the service station sighting as truth and hung onto it with the ragged, chewed tips of my fingers.

'I knew she was in a car,' I said, bursting back into the kitchen. 'Come on, we need to go and get her. I can't believe she's in Yorkshire. It's so far away.'

But three days had already passed since a girl in black jeans walked into a service station. It was everything we had to go on but it was also nothing at all.

*   *   *

'Anyone want another cup of tea?'

Freddy was on his feet, his hand on the door handle ready to break the spell. *Don't open it. Just another minute, another hour,* I wanted to shout. But how could I? How could I tell them that it was only while they sat still and quiet, the curtains drawn tight against the outside world, that I could keep my creeping sense of panic at bay and pretend that everything was going to be OK? I took a last look around the room to imprint the scene on my memory before they had a chance to move.

'Me, please,' said Dan.

'Me too.' Stephanie was lying on the sheepskin rug, her hair glowing in the light from the fire, a fan of magazines and newspapers surrounding her. Tanya's words about the media came back to me once again: *They'll want their story, either way.*

'Mum? What's wrong? You look all weird.' Freddy was standing in the doorway with the teapot in his hand.

'Nothing, darling. I just realised I'd forgotten to take a library book back. I'll have a fine.'

'Scandalous!' he said.

'It's not a big deal. Everyone forgets a library book now and then.'

'I know, Mum. I'm joking. You should see the state of my library account at uni and I've only been there six weeks.'

'It's not like you, Ros,' said Dan. He put his tea down and shifted forwards in his seat. I felt his eyes on my face.

'It hardly matters, does it? I'll take it back tomorrow.'

'You—' he started.

But Stephanie cut him off. 'Give her a break, Dad. It's only a library book, for God's sake.' It was the first time I had heard anger in her voice since she had been a child of nine, bitter with the injustice of a lost game of Monopoly.

Dan blinked in shock. 'It's just not like your mother to forget things, that's all. You know how much she worries.'

'And you never forget anything, do you? You never make a mistake?' She had sat up and let the magazine slide off her lap. She was staring straight at him, her eyes locked onto his. When he looked away, she flicked her hair from her face and turned back to her magazine.

Dan stood up and stretched his arms above his head slowly as though nothing had happened. An old tennis injury caused his right elbow to click. 'I've got a couple of emails to send. Next week's going to be a tough one.'

'But, Dad, the Formula One starts in ten minutes. Don't you want to watch it?' said Freddy.

'I won't be long. You get watching and I'll come and join you. Someone's got to earn the wherewithal to fund this house full of students, haven't they?'

'I'm sure we'd manage without you,' said Stephanie. Then she was gone, the door swinging closed behind her. I hadn't even noticed her getting to her feet.

If Dan thought my late return of a library book was out of character it was nothing compared to him bringing money up in front of our children. His father – who had been far from poor – had resented every penny that slid out of his tightly fastened wallet. Wherever a conversation with David Simm started it always came back to the price of this or that. The first time I visited for Sunday lunch, as we drank sweet sherry in the sitting room and the rich scent of roast beef swirled through the house, he had asked me to guess how much his wife had spent on the joint. I tried to brush his question off with a vague comment about food prices and how nice it was of them to cook for us, but he wouldn't let me. He pushed until I guessed: seven pounds fifty. I had never cooked a roast dinner, never bought a joint of meat. 'Mary!' He called out to his wife, a glint of triumph in his eyes. 'This girl thinks you can get a beef joint for seven pounds fifty! She's got a nasty shock coming when she grows up and has a house to run.' He turned back to me: 'Eleven pounds seventy-five. That's how much she spent.' *You'd better be worth it* was the unspoken threat. We hadn't gone back there again until after Stephanie was born.

Dan's comment and Stephanie's strange burst of anger unnerved me. In that moment, more than any other in the past six years, I felt the wearing thin of the layers of politeness and quiet denial with which we insulated ourselves from each other and from the past. What would happen if those layers weren't there any more? What would we become?

I should have followed Dan up to his study. I should have smoothed over Stephanie's cross words by rubbing his shoulders and reminding him that she wasn't herself and that he shouldn't be upset by what she had said. Instead, I went into the kitchen, away from them all, where it was quiet and still.

I hadn't been lying about the library book. There was a beautifully illustrated biography of Antoni Gaudi languishing forgotten on the back seat of my car. I had been on the way to return it on Wednesday when I had bumped into Cam, or he had bumped into me, and we had gone for a coffee. We bumped into each other a lot. He would make casual enquiries about my plans for the week – the days I would be on campus and the times I had booked space in the studio – and he would turn up, bearing a book, a flyer for an exhibition, or sometimes just a smile. The number of hours we spent together had multiplied slowly and the tentative friendships I had with the young women on my course had started to slip. Sometimes I wouldn't be where I had told him I would be. I would stay at home, smudging sketches and snapping the points off pencils instead, to prove to myself that I wasn't arranging these 'dates'.

'You changed your studio time yesterday?' he would ask the next time I saw him at a lecture or tutorial.

'Something came up so I worked from home,' I would say and watch his expression change. Moods passed across his face like clouds across a landscape, turning it from light to dark then light again. It was so different from Dan's face to which happiness and sorrow clung for days. Being able to transform Cam's face with a word or a gesture was like being granted the powers of a weather god; it was one of the things that made him so addictive to me.

'We can go for coffee after this,' he would say. 'I want to ask you about where to stay in Barcelona. I need a hotel that's equidistant between the Park Güell and the best churros in town.' These rationales for our coffees, drinks and lunches were one of the rules of our game.

I had always wondered how people took the decision to commit adultery, to step across that line. I had been aware of plenty of opportunities over the years. There had been fathers at the children's schools, two of Dan's colleagues and even one of Freddy's teachers. I had sensed their interest in me but their eagerness to prise me free of my marital vows had been as erotic as having my head plunged into a bucket of iced water.

'Wouldn't you, if you had the chance? Not even with Javier Bardem?' Beatrice asked me once, as we picked over the bones of her neighbours' marriage, which had ended when the wife finally figured out her husband's iPad password and laid bare the evidence of his affair.

'No. Not Javier or anyone. I couldn't live with the guilt and the fear of getting caught. People like me just don't do cheating – we're not built for it. And I've told Dan it's a deal-breaker. He knows it's game over if he ever cheats on me.' But not long after I first saw Cam, when I arrived late for my first seminar of the autumn term in the second year of my degree and sat in the last available seat, the one next to him, I started to understand how people like me cheated. We did it in tiny increments, sliding passively towards it like rivers towards the ocean. We pretended it wasn't happening – we just had coffee, just had lunch, just chatted, just texted – until it already was. People like me didn't decide to have an affair at all, we just didn't decide not to until it was too late. It wasn't too late for me yet, but nearly. Our kiss at Croome House had been the last stop before the point of no return. I vowed not to let myself be alone with him like that again.

It had been innocent enough until I let him make plaster casts of my hands. He had been creating a collection he called The Lost Ones. He scoured the streets of Hatfield for things people had dropped: a button, a baby's shoe, a set of keys, a toy dinosaur, even an iPod. Week after week he pressed these things into tablets of wet clay and used the impressions they left as moulds to make plaster facsimiles of the originals. When the plaster models were dry he painted them with the wing markings of butterflies extinct from the British Isles, before trapping them in small Perspex boxes. He wanted to make people question the value they placed on objects and the nature of possession, he said; did we care more for the iPod carelessly dropped in the street and easily replaced or for the butterfly species lost to us for ever? I tried to ponder these questions when I looked at his work, but the brightly painted models with their smooth edges and blurred lines made me think of marzipan fruit perched on top of a Christmas cake. I had to fight the urge to nibble them.

'You're really getting the hang of the moulds,' I said one afternoon, as he painted a plaster watch with the monochrome wing markings of a black-veined white. His first efforts had been crude and misshapen, but the watch was almost perfect – the buckle on its strap and its tiny winding knob clearly formed. 'What are you doing next?'

He looked up and smiled his lazy smile, the one that made me want to run my fingers over his lips, probe his mouth and see whether his teeth were as smooth as they looked. 'This.' He slid his hand across the table towards me, something small concealed beneath his palm.

I picked up the lipstick in its familiar black and gold case, turned it over and read the words *Ripe Plum* on its base. 'This is mine! I lost it last week.' I had puzzled over where the lipstick could be, turning out my handbag and make-up bag and searching the car. I wasn't in the habit of losing things, but then I hadn't been in the habit of wearing lipstick until recently either. 'Where did you find it?'

'Oh, I can't remember. I've been picking so much stuff up. Maybe in the car park? Or the coffee shop?'

Inside its case the lipstick was a shapeless mass of dark purple gloss, as though someone had pressed a finger hard onto the surface I had grown used to running over my lips. 'Yuck. You can keep it. I've already got a new one.'

'I might not use it. I want to try something bigger. Something with a bit more flexibility.'

'Like what?'

'A hand. Well, two hands.'

'Hands?' I laughed.

'A pair of hands would look great done as a blue mazarine or an almond-eyed ringlet.' I was sitting opposite him at a narrow workbench in the busy pottery studio. As he spoke he reached out and took my right hand in his. He turned it over and traced the outline of a butterfly's wing across my palm. 'Besides, I think I need something human to tether the collection together. It was human hands that made all The Lost Ones, and human hands that dropped them.'

Did I realise how physical it would be? How close he would lean to press my hands into the soft, yielding coolness of the clay? How gently he would bend my fingers and position my wrists to create the shapes he wanted? It took less than twenty minutes for him to make his moulds, but days later I could still feel the warmth of his body behind mine, the pressure of his fingers on my arm; I could still remember the way the hum of the studio and the hiss of the kiln had receded until the only sound was the squelch of the clay and the rush of his breath in my ear. It was different after that. We were different. All my life I had been so careful to do everything right, to be above reproach, especially from Dan. I had been like a cautious child with a colouring book who is terrified of choosing the wrong crayon or straying outside the lines, who makes every stroke with infinite care. Then I met Cam and he made me want to colour outside the lines; he made me want to scribble all over the page. I wouldn't though, I couldn't.

The phone rang in the hall, dragging me back to the house, to the presence of my family. I picked it up, feeling a sudden spike of guilt at the thought that it might be Tanya.

'Hi, Ros. How is she?'

'Oh, Sarah. It's good to hear from you. Sorry, we should have rung you and let you know how we were getting on.' I lowered my voice. 'She's doing OK. We're taking her to the doctor's tomorrow and we'll see what he says, but she hasn't been drinking.'

There was a pause before she spoke: 'Well that's a start.'

'Has she talked to you about it? About what went on over the summer?'

'No, not really. She's got new friends. She spends a lot of time with them.'

'Jake?'

'Yes. Jake.'

'You don't like him?'

'Does it matter? Can I speak to her, please?'

I set the receiver down on the hall stand and started up the stairs to fetch Stephanie, but she was already there, standing on the landing above me. I wondered how much of my conversation with Sarah she had heard. She wanted to take the call on the extension in our bedroom as she had in the days before she had a mobile phone. Her mobile had been nowhere to be found in London. At her behest I had picked through the bedsheets and turned her handbag inside out to no avail, so Dan had reported it lost when we got home.

I waited with my ear pressed to the receiver as Stephanie made her way into our bedroom. I heard the crackle of her picking up the receiver.

'Hanging up now. Bye, Sarah, love,' I said. I scratched my nails across the dimpled plastic of the receiver's microphone before giving it a single firm tap while pressing the mute button. It had been a long time since I had eavesdropped like this, and it was Dan whose calls I had invaded then, not Stephanie's. I held my breath for a moment, unsure whether they would notice me hanging silently on the line.

'Hi. How are you?' said Stephanie.

'I'm fine. Are you OK?' The warmth Sarah had had when she spoke to me was gone.

'Yes. Better. I won't be back for a few days though.'

'That's probably a good idea.' Sarah paused. 'I'm ringing because Jake's been round here looking for you. He came today and yesterday.'

'Oh. You didn't tell him where I was, did you?'

'No. I just said you'd gone away for a bit.'

'Don't tell him where I am. Please. And don't give him this number.'

'OK. But I don't think he'll give up. He seemed desperate. He said you just ran off and left him on Thursday and he was worried that you'd do something stupid.'

'Oh. I'll email him. I'll tell him to leave you alone.'

'OK.'

'Look, Sarah, I'm sorry for this. I'm sorry you had to call my mum and talk to Jake. And I'm sorry I've been avoiding you. I—'

'You're sorry. I know. Just get better, Stephie. Stay there until you're better, please.' I bit my lip to stop myself from speaking. I almost wished I hadn't listened. These girls had loved each other for so many years and now Sarah was retreating when Stephanie needed her most.

'OK.'

There was a pause and then Sarah spoke again, her voice a hushed whisper. 'Have you talked to her yet?'

'No. I've told him he has to do it but he's putting it off. Maybe it's for the best. I don't know. What should I do? I can't decide. What would you do?'

Sarah seemed to soften with those words. 'I can't make that decision for you. I don't know. I really, really don't know what you should do. Toss a coin?'

'Toss a coin? Seriously?'

'No.' Sarah sighed. 'Give him some more time, I suppose. I'll call you again, OK. I miss you.'

'Miss you too.'

Sarah hung up. I waited for Stephanie to do the same. But a couple of minutes passed before she stopped crying and put the receiver back in its cradle.

As I stood alone in the hallway and listened to Stephanie pad back up the stairs to her room, I caught a glimpse of my face reflected in the darkness of the window by the front door. My eyes were wide and bright. I looked away quickly, before I could ask myself why I had let another day pass without telling anyone about Temperley's release.

SEVEN DAYS

'How do you think you'll play this doctor's appointment?' It was just after seven o'clock and Dan had brought me a cup of coffee in bed.

'Play it?'

'Are you going to go in with her?'

'Only if she wants me to.'

'She might not tell him what's really been going on. She might minimise the state she was in and tell him she's only there because she had a couple of drinks and we made a fuss.'

'I don't think she would *minimise* it.' This wasn't his language. He must have been on the internet again. I wondered what search terms he had used. How did one Google a problem like Stephanie? 'She wants help. We talked yesterday and she's really starting to open up to me,' I said.

'Really? What did she say?' He sat on the edge of the bed so his face was level with mine.

'She's having a hard time coming to terms with her past. She was on her own a lot over the summer and things got tough for her. She couldn't stop thinking about it all, about him. She hates herself for what she did.' It was as much as I was prepared to give him.

He nodded. 'I think it's post-traumatic stress disorder. PTSD. Is she having flashbacks?' This was definitely the work of Dr Google. Is that what he had been doing when he had slipped off to 'answer emails'?

'Sort of, I suppose. She says she doesn't have any happy memories any more. That it's like everything that happened has blotted them out so only the bad stuff is left. That's why she was drinking. She was trying to forget.'

'I knew it was that bastard's fault. I knew he was at the root of it. Go in with her, Ros, and ask the doctor about PTSD. There's medicine and therapy – cognitive behavioural therapy – for it. They're getting really good results, even in soldiers who have had limbs blown off. She'll need a referral to a specialist for a proper diagnosis but it should all be covered by our insurance.' I could see some of the tension lifting from him, the pulse of his natural optimism starting to beat again. He was foreseeing a referral, a specialist, a diagnosis, a treatment plan; the solving of a problem.

'You don't know that's what's wrong with her. Isn't it just part of being human, to go over your mistakes and beat yourself up about them? Don't you do that?'

'It wasn't her mistake. It was his mistake, remember.'

Then why do you blame her? I thought, but he was already stooping to kiss me on the forehead. He took the stairs two at a time and the front door clattered closed behind him. He would make the seven-twenty train if he hurried.

Maybe I had been hard on him for the way he had buried himself in work since Stephanie's return. He had pored over diagnoses and treatments on the internet while I had tried to worm my way beneath her protective shell. Perhaps that was the best he could do. After all, it had taken months after her last return for him to be comfortable having a conversation with her again, years before he could give her a hug or a kiss on the cheek. But then I remembered him coming home early on Thursday afternoon, his desire to go out, the sense that he was trying to recapture something we had lost. And then there was Sarah's phone call: *Have you talked to her yet?* Did she mean me? My heart started to beat faster, my fingers clenched around the cooling coffee cup. My breaths came sharp and shallow. Everything that had happened since Sarah had rung us on that Friday morning galloped through my mind, my brain twisting half-forgotten comments into vicious nooses to set around my neck. Then, as I always did, I thought of him, of Nathan Temperley smiling in his cell. He was why Stephanie was here, fragile and haunted in the room upstairs. He was why Dan was fleeing his family and struggling to meet my eye. The thought of his impending release slammed into me, knocking the breath from my lungs. I felt myself falling into panic until the sudden iron tang of blood snapped me back into the moment. I had sunk my sharp front teeth so deeply into my lip that I had broken the skin. I pressed a fingertip to my mouth and it came away red.

'Pull yourself together,' I said out loud. 'For Stephanie's sake.' Then I dug my painting clothes out of the wardrobe – indigo jeans worn to velvet softness and an old shirt of Dan's. But before I could go upstairs to my studio, I found myself going through an old, almost-forgotten routine: checking the locks on doors and windows then checking them again, looking in cupboards, switching on lights in empty rooms; drawing curtains tight across the downstairs windows after scanning the garden for anything out of place.

The room I call my studio is the half of the attic not taken up by Stephanie's bedroom and bathroom. It is a light trap, pulling in every one of the sun's rays through its full-length dormer window which looks out over the garden. Last year the ash trees I planted when we moved in had finally filled out with leaves like banks of cloud, blurring the boundary between our garden and the acres of parkland beyond. I loved being up there alone when the house was empty and the rain had chased the dog walkers and joggers from the park so that from the window I could see nothing but a green expanse broken up only by the different textures of leaves and grass. In my studio, there wasn't a trace of my family to be found and I had always been able to leave Dan, Stephanie and Freddy downstairs as soon as I ducked beneath the awkward low beam behind the door.

With Stephanie sleeping in her old bedroom next door, it was different. The remnants of deep reds and blues on my unwashed palette reminded me of her bruised knuckles. The thought of her hands led to the thought of Temperley's hands, those short thick fingers that had scuttled through my dreams for so long. I had to shake my head to rid myself of him. *Think of Stephanie,* I whispered, *don't let him in.*

There was more paper than I could possibly use in a year stacked inside the low cupboard that spanned the back of the room. I knelt down and ran my hands across the sheets, leafing through bundles ordered online or bought from the dusty little art shops I drove miles to find. I found the package at the back: ten sheets of hand-moulded Himalayan Washi in the grey of a pre-dawn sky, its imperfect surface textured like the shell of an egg. I had bought it months ago but it had always seemed too precious to use. Every few weeks I would take out a sheet and let its chalky smell fill the room. I would hover over it with a pen or pencil, urging myself to commit to a stroke. Then I would put it away again, unmarked. With the paper in my hand I moved quickly to my desk in front of the dormer, knowing that to pause would be to lose my nerve.

The subject of the first drawing was easy to choose. It is the morning of her fourth birthday and we have filled her bedroom full – floor to ceiling – with helium balloons. She stands at the door, her face raised in wonder, the light from the window pouring through the balloons and mottling her white nightie with bright spots of colour. Dan and I spent hours filling those balloons with helium, hiding them in our walk-in wardrobe until Beatrice distracted Stephanie with pancakes and we herded them into her room, giggling like children when they slipped through our hands and bounced on the ceiling above us.

I drew with charcoal, quick strokes that left no time for thought. I picked out details in coloured pastels: the pink of her cheeks, the red of her hair, the sheen of the big blue balloon that was her favourite. When it was finished, I set it quickly on top of the cupboard, careful not to let my critical eye fall upon it.

The next one was easy to choose, too. It is December and she is six years old. She is Mary in the Christmas play with a plastic Baby Jesus wrapped in the yellow towel from the downstairs cloakroom in her arms. In the background stands Sarah, her dark head topped with a tinsel halo. Stephanie wore her Mary costume everywhere – at home, to the supermarket, to friends' houses. There was a crisis when Baby Jesus was left on a train after a trip to London to see the Christmas lights the weekend before the performance. I still remember the physical sensation of relief when I found an identical doll in Toys R Us and the sound of her joy when she found the second Baby Jesus wrapped in a new towel and sitting on the end of her bed.

In the third sketch she is eight years old. She is standing over a square chocolate cake with a number five written on it in blue Smarties. It is Freddy's fifth birthday and she has made this cake for him. He stands beside her, looking not at the cake but at her.

'Mum? What are you doing? What are those?' I didn't know for how long she had been standing behind me.

I got up and laid the third picture alongside the other two. She bent over them one by one, touching the tips of her fingers to the edges of the paper, her hair falling across her shoulders to hide her face. I held my breath.

'My memories,' she said. 'You're drawing my memories for me. My happy memories. Is that it?'

'Yes. So you can keep them until you don't need the pieces of paper any more. There are seven more to come.'

'Mum, they're beautiful.'

'They're beautiful memories.' It was only then that I realised I had painted my own happy memories rather than hers. But perhaps we could share them and they would help to bind us together. Soon I would have to tell her that the man who had ruined her life was about to walk free. I needed her to cling to me when that happened, not to spin away back into the dark place I had scooped her up from three days earlier.

She paused over the picture of the birthday cake, picked it up and angled it to catch the light. Slowly, starting behind her eyes, the sun of a smile began to transform her face.

'I was so proud of that cake. I made you buy all those tubes of Smarties so I could pick out the blue ones. Freddy loved it, didn't he?'

'Yes,' I laughed, remembering. 'I don't think he thought such a wonder of the world could possibly exist. He was only little but I bet he remembers that.'

'I hope he does.' She looked at each picture again. A strand of her hair fell onto the paper, its colour almost an exact match for the pastel I had used to depict it. 'What are the others going to be?'

'You'll have to wait and see. I'll do some more when we get back from the doctor's. We better get a move on, actually.'

'I can come in with you if you'd like me to,' I said in the car.

'Thanks. I better go on my own.'

I was relieved; the idea of sitting beside Stephanie as she told our GP why she was there was uncomfortable to me. So much of what I had whispered to the doctor in that very same surgery over the years would have gone unsaid if Stephanie or Dan had been sitting beside me. 'I'm not at all sure that I agree with him but your father thinks you have post-traumatic stress disorder. PTSD. He wants you to get referred to a specialist.'

'Really? That sounds a bit . . . dramatic.' She didn't sound surprised. I wondered if Dan had been more right than I had given him credit for, whether father and daughter had both used Google to come to the same conclusion.

'You could mention it to the doctor, just to keep your dad happy if nothing else.' She stayed silent. 'But it's up to you.'

'Did he ask you to tell me this?'

'He thought I would go and talk to the doctor with you.'

'He didn't volunteer to come though, did he?'

'Would you have wanted him to?' I had an image of Dan and Stephanie in the doctor's office, him leaning across the desk, brandishing wads of pages printed out from the internet.

'No. I want to go in on my own. I'm twenty-one, for goodness' sake. It just doesn't seem fair of him to lumber you with all this while he skips off to work.'

'I don't feel lumbered in the slightest.'

'But you've got your exhibition tomorrow. You must have things you need to do.'

'Oh, that doesn't matter. It's only a silly little thing. I'd completely forgotten about it, to be honest.'

'I saw the flyer on the fridge. It sounds really cool. Pop-ups are all the rage these days.'

'I'm sure we'll have another one soon. It really doesn't matter.'

'Are your pictures already there?'

'No. Cam, one of the other students, is meant to be taking them over this afternoon for hanging. I'll tell him not to worry, though. They've got more than enough stuff without my little efforts and I'd have to go over and help out.'

'You should go this afternoon, Mum. I'll be fine with Fred.'

'Let's see how you get on with the doctor.' While I drove Stephanie through the morning traffic jams of St Albans, Cam would be at the university with the other students who had work in Going, going, gone! They would ferry my pictures to the empty shop that would be our makeshift gallery. It would only take me twenty minutes to drive over and meet them there. I could help get the place ready for half an hour then come straight home. But I wouldn't. Not if Stephanie needed me.

We sat side by side in the waiting room. Stephanie shifted in her plastic seat, fraying the corners of her magazine and flinching every time the gunshot cough of the elderly woman opposite us cracked through the air. No one spoke. A boy wearing only a nappy and a T-shirt bashed a wooden toy onto the floor over and over again. His tired-looking mother turned her head away.

When Stephanie's name was called I watched her walk across the room. She turned back to look at me over her shoulder as she knocked on the doctor's door. I gave her one of the discreet thumbs up I used to do as she walked away from me at the school gate. Then there was nothing I could do but wait.

Minutes stretched. I tried magazine after magazine but nothing could hold my attention. My thoughts were a coiling mass of memories from the past few days mixed with moments from longer ago: Stephanie lying drunk and broken on her bed; her face on the front of the newspaper; the silence of her empty bedroom in the days she was missing; and him – Temperley – smiling at me across the courtroom. I was trying to chase the memories away, to stay in the present where Stephanie needed me to be, when the surgery's front door banged open and a man walked in. He wore a black coat with a hood pulled low over his face. Instantly, I was tense, poised to spring. I looked between him and the door behind which Stephanie sat with Dr Bashir. Without thinking, I got to my feet, my hand reaching into my bag for my phone. He pulled the hood back. It wasn't him, of course it wasn't him. I sank back into my chair, my heart already slowing and the black cloud of panic receding. Eyeing me suspiciously, the mother of the boy in the nappy got up and scooped him onto her lap.

For a long time I had seen Temperley everywhere. A pair of shoulders glimpsed through a shop window or the fall of dark hair across the forehead of a passer-by was enough to make me follow strangers down streets, breaking into a run and calling out his name until I saw their faces and could be sure. Twice I had been so certain I had seen him that I had rushed to Stephanie's school, weeping on the receptionist, pulling Stephanie out of class then bundling her home until phone calls to Tanya had reassured me that Nathan Temperley was still locked up in Wandsworth. But it had been two years since I had last mistaken an innocent stranger for Temperley and I couldn't let myself start doing that again. I forced myself to think about Cam. I would use him like a beta blocker and feed myself thoughts of him when my brain threatened me with things I had worked so hard to forget. I tried to picture Cam's hands – the tapering muscled fingers, the pearlescent crescents beneath the nails – but I saw *his* hands instead.

'Mum. Let's get out of here.' Stephanie was standing in front of me at last, tucking a fold of paper into her bag. Her eyes were glassy with tears. As I stood up they started to spill down her cheeks and she choked back a sob. Heads turned. The receptionist craned her neck to see what was going on. I swept the room with a scowl then put my arm around Stephanie's shoulders and walked her out of the surgery like a bodyguard hustling a celebrity through a crowd.

It had started to snow. Feathery flakes the size of oak leaves tumbled down in slow motion, resting on the tarmac for a second before melting into invisibility. Stephanie stopped and stretched out her hand to catch one as it fell. She watched it collapse in on itself in her palm.

'Do you think it will settle?' she said, rubbing her nose with her sleeve and tipping her face towards the falling flakes. I did the same, feeling them catch in my eyelashes and glance off my cheeks.

'I hope so. Come on.' She followed me to the car and we both got in. I started the engine and turned the heaters on full. We sat and watched the snowflakes bouncing off the windscreen.

'You'd better read this.' She passed me the piece of paper she had carried out of the doctor's room. It was a sick note for her university, signing her off for two weeks and citing the reason as stress.

'And this. He's given me a prescription. It's only a low dose. I have to go back and see him on Friday and he'll up it if he thinks I need it. He said we'd talk about some counselling then. He knows someone good in London.' The prescription was for fluoxetine, twenty milligrams a day. Prozac. I remembered having a prescription like that; the little white tablets had given me a headache but nothing more. They hadn't 'taken the edge off' in the run up to the court case as Dr Bashir had hoped.

'I asked him not to put depression on the sick note. Stress doesn't sound as bad, does it?' I shook my head as she continued. 'He'll extend the sick leave if I want him to.'

'Did you ask him about PTSD?'

'No. He's the doctor, not Dad.' I nodded. Dr Bashir had been our doctor for twelve years; he knew as much about what had happened to Stephanie as I did and I trusted him to come to his own conclusions.

'Do you mind being off uni for two weeks?' She had always hated to miss school. But maybe this had changed in the past few months. Perhaps she had stayed in bed with hangovers, missing lectures and skipping tutorials.

'It's a relief.'

'Because of Jake? Because you don't want to see him?'

She looked at me sharply. 'Jake?'

I shouldn't have said that. I couldn't let her know I had listened in on Sarah's phone call. 'You said you drank a lot with him. I thought you wouldn't want to see him now you're having a break from all that,' I said.

'Oh, yes. Partly that I suppose.' I waited for her to say what else it was that made her reluctant to return to London, but she had fallen silent. There was a week to go until Temperley's release. Was St Albans the worst place for her to be when that happened, or the best? If she was here he would know exactly where to find her but he would have to get past me first. I had a sudden, horrifying image of her leaving her flat in London and heading for the tube station, a figure moving unseen a few paces behind her. In my imagination he was a thinner, grizzled version of the smirking cockerel he had been in court. He wore the shapeless grey tracksuit and laceless trainers (why take his laces? Why not give him every possible opportunity to hang himself?) of his incarceration and held a brown paper parcel under one arm even though I knew that probably only happened in old American films. London, St Albans – neither was safe.

'We could go away somewhere. You and me. For two weeks,' I said, trying to shake myself free of the image and turning down the car's heaters to let the windows mist up again with the steam of our breath.

'Where?'

'Wherever you want to go. France, Italy. No, somewhere warm. Thailand maybe. I've always fancied going there.'

'Thailand? Really?'

'I'm serious, Stephie. We can do whatever you need to do. Maybe we could go on a yoga retreat to help with your stress.' I had seen a yoga break at a spa hotel on Koh Samui advertised in the *Sunday Times*. The pictures showed a thin rind of sand the colour of moonlight running for miles between the glittering turquoise sea and the lush greenness of the island. There were two of everything in the pictures: two sun loungers beside a private pool, two exotic salads on a table by the sea, two serene women sitting in perfect harmony closed-eyed and cross-legged on the beach, their hands placed palms up on their knees. We could leave in the night and tell no one where we were going. We could check in under false names and wear headscarves and dark glasses. Dan would wake up in an empty house, Cam would stalk the campus in search of me. Nathan Temperley wouldn't know where to begin to look.

'You think we should run away?'

As fast and as far as we can. If she agreed to the holiday I would have more time before I had to tell her. The thought of burdening her with the knowledge as she sat beside me limp and tearful, a prescription for antidepressants in her hand, was unbearable. I waved the sick note at her. 'I think we should go on holiday. It doesn't say anything on here about where you have to be sick. It just says you won't be at uni. You might find it easier to relax somewhere fresh where you don't have all these memories.' She looked away from me and out of the window. The snow was falling more heavily, feathery flakes hitting the windscreen and settling on the bonnet. Her face was framed in the wing mirror. Twice she leant forward and started to speak only to stop herself. 'I'm too tired to think about it now. I'm so tired all the time. Dr Bashir said the pills will help with that,' she said eventually.

'Sorry, I'm rushing you. It's an option, that's all I'm saying.' I let the windscreen wipers work for a few moments before I pulled out into the road.

Freddy was lying on the sofa, a textbook forgotten on his chest as the television blared. I closed my eyes for a second and visualised the snow falling harder, sealing shut the doors and trapping the three of us here, safe inside the house.

'Hi, Mum. All right, sis?'

'The doctor gave me mad pills and two weeks off uni.' Freddy blinked and looked to me. For a second he was twelve again, caught up in a world of adult conversations and missing sisters.

'They're not mad pills. They're just to help with the stress.'

'It's OK, Mum. I'm joking. Anyway, Fred, you're lumbered with me this afternoon. Mum's got to go and get ready for her exhibition.'

'I don't have to go. I can stay here. I told you it's not important.' Stephanie and Freddy had always loved each other deeply; they didn't bicker like other siblings and had always been a team. I had forgotten the way the two of them smiling at each other could fill me with warmth and gratitude and I wanted to stay and warm myself in their glow.

'You should go. We'll be fine,' said Stephanie.

'Yeah, go, Mum,' Freddy said. 'Don't worry about us.'

'I need to grill Fred about what he's really been up to at uni,' Stephanie said.

'Yeah, right. Like I'd tell you. We're watching the football at half four,' Freddy said. Stephanie shrugged, kicked off her shoes and sat down on the sofa opposite the one on which Freddy was slouched. 'Oh, this came for you, sis.' He reached down and picked something up from the floor beside him. It was a package, a little smaller than a shoebox, wrapped in white plastic. There was a printed label stuck wonkily on one side.

'My new phone. I didn't think it would come that quickly.' She was already tearing into the bag, stretching the tough plastic wrapper with her thumbs as Freddy turned back to the television. I stood by the door, redundant. I tried not to let it sting.

In our bedroom, with my wardrobe open in front of me, I wondered when Stephanie had ordered a new mobile. She had seemed so ragged and helpless since she arrived that I couldn't imagine her picking up the phone, speaking to someone in a call centre and making all those tiny decisions that these tasks require. Perhaps she had used Dan's iPad to do it online. I remembered the way its browser history had been wiped clean and felt a rush of relief. The thought of her having traced Dan's journey around the web as he looked for places to send his 'alcoholic' daughter sickened me.

When I went back downstairs they were each lying on a sofa facing the television. A cold blue light winked on and off on the sleek white phone at Stephanie's feet, the wire of its charger snaking back towards the wall.

'You look nice, Mum. I might borrow that top.'

I pulled my cardigan around my shoulders. Perhaps the deep purple top with its low-cut scalloped neckline had been a mistake. 'I'm hoping the others will have done the dirty work before I get there. Anyway, I suppose I better be off.'

'See you later, Mum,' said Freddy.

'See you, Mum.'

I moved towards the door then stopped and turned back. 'Are you sure you'll be OK? There will probably be far too many of us there. I'll just get in the way. I really can just stay here.'

'Go. We'll be fine,' Stephanie said.

'Ring me if you need anything. Anything at all. I'll have my phone on and it only takes me twenty minutes to get back. I won't stay long. Just long enough to make sure they don't hang my pictures upside down or anything. And, Stephanie, make sure you get some rest, please, sweetheart.'

'I am resting. Look.' She smiled at me and pulled the beetle-green blanket covering her legs up under her chin.

'We'll be fine. Stop worrying about us,' said Freddy when I made no move.

'Mum, go,' Stephanie said.

For weeks, each time I had driven to the university campus in Hatfield I had let myself sink into the fantasy I had built around my flirtation with Cam. When he filled my thoughts at home I chased him away, feeling the wrongness of harbouring him in the house I shared with Dan, but in the car I allowed my imagination free rein. I invented trysts in country pubs, pottery studios and foreign cities. I gave us languorous, teasing hours in mysterious, locationless rooms or frantic seconds in the hallways we walked together in real life. Always in these fantasies he was chasing me, wooing me and I was allowing him the crumb of a kiss, the touch of a hand. After twenty minutes of these imaginings, I would walk into the lecture theatre or classroom to the seat he had saved for me. Sitting hip to hip in those dimly lit places, it was almost impossible to think that he wasn't aware of the time he had spent in my head. But this journey was different. Thoughts of Cam held no allure when every metre of road took me further from where I wanted to be.

I had been perched next to Cam on the edge of the group in the Students' Union bar when Karen and Tom – a pair of twenty-year-olds who even I could tell were the coolest kids in the class – had announced they were going to curate a pop-up exhibition, just like one they had visited in a disused public toilet in Dalston. They had big ideas for a week-long show at the top of a condemned council tower block, or a month-long takeover of an old air raid shelter on the edge of the town. A few weeks later, it had boiled down to this: a twelve-hour exhibition in an empty shop in Hatfield. An uncle of Karen's had taken a short lease on the shop. Once we had packed away our pictures, our sculptures and our installations, it would become Jimmy's Famous 99p Christmas Wonderland, offering 'everything for Christmas for under a pound'.

I had been surprised to be asked to take part in the exhibition, but Karen had cornered me in the studio one day and gushed about my Empty Rooms paintings. 'Their message just, like, really chimes with our venue and what we're all about,' she said. I wasn't sure whether the paintings had a message, but I agreed to be part of Going, going, gone!, as Karen had decided the pop-up would be called. I helped Tom to write a press release and took photos of the empty shop for the flyers. I worked side by side with Cam as we pushed ourselves to get our work ready in time, the fast-approaching date of the exhibition was the perfect justification for all the extra time in the studio, the extra hours with him. I took a flyer home and stuck it to the fridge door. After that, I spent a lot of time thinking about Cam and Dan being in the same room. Would Dan notice? Would he care? Would he take one look around the shabby empty shop space and draw the right corner of his mouth upwards like he used to when one of the children showed him a mess of crayon scribbles and explained that it was a picture of him? Would the rest of the students look at this man in a suit with his shiny black shoes – my husband, with his clean-shaven face and threads of grey in his hair – and mutter 'OMG' and 'LOL' behind my back? Would Dan even turn up, or would another late night at work mean no one would have the chance to mutter anything to anyone? But those weren't the worries that crackled like bonfire-night sparklers as I parked the car and made my way down the high street. How could I think of anything so trivial with Stephanie at home and Nathan Temperley pacing the floor of his cell, counting down the hours until he would walk free?

The sight of the shop took me by surprise. The sheets of newspaper that had covered the plate-glass window when the shop was empty had been peeled away. Instead, the windows were alive with light. *Going, going, gone!* was scrawled across the glass in swirling letters formed by bright yellow points of LED encased in transparent plastic tubing. In the dreary greyness of the street's cracked concrete bollards, empty benches and broken litter bins, the glowing shop front could have been the portal to another world. I pushed open the door and made my way inside.

'It's great, isn't it?' Cam appeared from the storeroom at the back of the shop, making me jump as I stood alone, absorbing the transformation that had been wrought on the space. He was wearing a jumper-electric blue wool, the sleeves pushed up to his elbows and the thin fabric gripping the contours of his chest.

'It's fantastic. It looks like a proper gallery. I didn't think it would be like this.'

'I know. I didn't want to be negative but I always thought it would end up being a bit, well, amateur and crap. But I'm glad I was wrong. Turns out Karen has a real flair for this kind of thing.'

'More than she has for painting, I'd say.' Realising how unkind my words were I put my hand to my mouth and peered through the door into the storeroom. But no one was there. 'Where's everyone else? I thought the whole gang would be here by now.'

'You just missed them. They're out dropping flyers round the shops. Or, more likely, the pub. I suspect there are a lot of flyers in the Junction Arms by now. There's not really anything left to do here except have a good look at your amazing pictures and pat yourself on the back for having the best work in the room. Look at them, Ros.'

The front of the shop was all window, so there were only three walls on which to display our work. Rather than imitate the sleek minimalism of a typical modern art gallery, Karen had played to the shop space's strengths, clustering paintings, sketches and pieces of sculpture around the old fittings, cramming smaller items between shelves and choosing pieces that came to life against the ugly mustard-yellow paint on the walls. She had evoked the atmosphere of a curiosity shop bursting with possibility. But the wall at the far end was different. It had been painted white and there was nothing hanging on its wide plane except my three Empty Rooms pictures. On each square canvas I had used glossy black oil to sketch an image of the same room. It was the room I lived in in the alternative reality of my daydreams, the dreams in which I had no husband, no family, no ties. There was a bed covered in rumpled sheets, an easel and a shelf crowded with books. I had used colour to add detail to each room: one was called *Joy*, one *Fear* and the other *Envy*. In *Joy* there were traces of other people in the room – bright teacups on the desk, a pile of coats on the bed; sunlight pooled on the floor in front of the easel. *Envy* was littered with indistinct shapes in acid yellow and green. *Fear* was darker still: the room was empty but for a violent orange light seeping out from beneath the bed and creeping in through the open window. As I had told Dan, sometimes I loved these paintings and at other times they seemed teenage to the point of pity. But surrounded by the rest of Going, going, gone! they worked. They were lit from below in the crossed beams of two anglepoise lamps and the yellow light brought them to life, gave them an extra dimension and allowed the moods they contained to shine out of the canvas. They seemed to rise above the jostling chaos of the rest of the room and demand to be looked at.

'What do you think? Are you pleased?' Cam said. I had been so lost in my pictures that I had forgotten he was in the room. Now I was acutely aware of him in the empty space behind me.

'Yes. Very pleased.' I wanted to say more, to share my bubble of pride with someone, with him. 'I feel like I've created something that can really talk, can really express itself. I know this exhibition doesn't mean anything in the big wide world but it does to me. I'm actually proud of what I've done.' I couldn't remember being proud of anything before, apart from Stephanie and Freddy, of course, but that was different.

'You should be damn proud. I'm damn proud and I didn't even paint them.' I laughed and he laughed with me, more from relief than humour. It felt so easy, so simple to stand there between him and my pictures and let the moment of pride and happiness fill me up so there was no room for anything else. 'Where are your Lost Ones?' I said when we stopped laughing.

'I made some last-minute changes. I'm going to have to bring them in tomorrow.' He had moved closer to me. His mouth was inches from my ear. I folded my hands in front of me. In the pottery studio and in the dark corner at the back of the lecture theatre I had discovered that my hands were subject to strange forces when Cam was nearby. They were drawn to him, drifting towards him before I even realised they were on the move.

'What did you change?' I said. If I turned my head a fraction his lips would meet my cheek.

'You'll have to wait and see,' he whispered.

He shifted behind me. The toes of his shoes came to rest against the heels of mine. The warmth of his skin penetrated the denim of my jeans and made me shiver in the unheated air of the shop. His breath, hotter still, was on my neck, seeping down the collar of my jacket until it lit a blush that raced up my chest and made my cheeks burn. If I leant back a millimetre – shifted the weight from the balls of my feet to my heels – I would be leaning on him, the length of my body pressed to his; nothing between us but a few scraps of cotton and lace.

'Ros,' he murmured.

'Not here,' I whispered back. We were standing in front of the window, lit up by the lights of Going, going, gone!

He took my hand and led me towards the storeroom but it was me who pushed the door closed behind us. A fluorescent light cast flickering shadows on boxes overflowing with stock of blue tinsel and bright-purple plastic baubles. Shelves were piled with inflatable snowmen and pottery elves waiting to take their places in Jimmy's Famous 99p Christmas Wonderland. I leant my back against the closed door. He stood two steps in front of me, his hands loose at his sides. In my fantasies he had always chased me, reached for me as I turned away. And yet here I was reaching for him, putting my hands on his neck, pressing my fingers into the heat of his skin, running my thumbs over the curve of his lips as he held his breath. Here I was leaning into him, moving closer when he slid his hands onto my hips; closer still when I felt his thumbs slide down to rest for a second on the waistband of my jeans before moving down to the lace of my knickers, then down further still. It was me who leant in and kissed him. It was his tongue sliding against my teeth, into my mouth, snatching from me the power to think, to breathe. I opened my eyes and met his. They were smiling, hungry. I knew I wasn't going to stop.

Then my phone rang, the ringtone growing louder and louder in the main shop space.

'Leave it,' he whispered, his lips still touching mine.

'Stephanie. It might be Stephanie.' I pulled open the storeroom door and scooped my bag up from where I had dropped it on the floor in front of my paintings and rummaged with clumsy fingers for the phone. On its ringtone trilled as I rifled through pockets until I found it, pulling it free just as it stopped ringing and a local number I didn't recognise was replaced with *1 Missed Call*.

Cam was leaning on the frame of the door between the shop and storeroom. He was smiling, his lips bright with the sheen of my plum lipstick. I flinched when I noticed that a smudge of it had found its way onto one of his teeth. In the cold air of the shop, three metres away from him, I was struck by the stupidity of what I had almost done. My children were at home. Stephanie needed me. Temperley was almost on the loose.

'I have to go. I'm sorry,' I said, turning away from Cam so I didn't have to see the effect of my words on his face.

'Stay, Ros. Just for a bit. I've got coffee and pistachio macarons back here. We can just talk. Or we can go and catch up with the others for a drink. Don't go.'

I was already at the door. 'I'm sorry. It's my daughter. She's not well. I have to go. I'll call you tomorrow.'

My phone beeped to alert me to a new voicemail as I hurried back towards the car. It was my hairdresser ringing to remind me of an appointment the following morning. Stephanie hadn't rung me at all. But I didn't turn back. I quickened my pace as my car came into sight, all the time wondering when I had told Cam that I loved pistachio macarons.

The snow was falling hard on St Albans, gathering on top of walls and in the branches of trees. The front lawns and driveways of Crispin Avenue were already covered in downy blankets. I felt the house's emptiness as soon as I opened the door. The television was cold and silent, the sofas strewn with coiled blankets and books. I ran up the stairs two at a time calling their names but knowing I would find their bedrooms empty. Back downstairs I dug in my bag for my phone and it was then that I saw the note scribbled on the pad on the hall stand: We've gone to watch the match with Matt. Back for dinner – F and S. I ripped the sheet from the pad and held it in my hand, relief tinged with irritation. Matt's house was only a five-minute walk away and he had been Freddy's friend since infant school. He was an only child and the three of them had played together for years until Stephanie outgrew the boys. A bit of company would do her good, I told myself firmly. And give me time to work on her memories.

As I reached for my pastels on the shelf next to my studio's dormer window, a glimpse of movement in the garden caught my eye. I paused and looked out. The leafless trees stood still. Nothing moved. Yet I was sure I had seen something: a flash of blue against the glistening white carpet over by the potting shed which crouched in the furthest corner of the garden. Perhaps I had caught a glimpse of a bird, its feathers a blue flare in the last of the winter light, or the memory of the blue of Cam's sweater. But as my eyes adjusted to the glare of the snow, I was sure that there was something different about the quality of the snowfall over by the shed, the tufts of grass showed through the white blanket there but nowhere else. I leant on the window with my open palms, pressing my face to the glass and straining to see more clearly in the day's failing light. My breath painted roses of mist on the glass and my reflection looked back at me. A woman in a long black coat walked a Dalmatian across the park beyond the garden, its black spots jumping out from the snow, but nothing else moved as I stood watching.

There was a sudden bang and I was falling, hurtling forwards towards the ground, the cold of the outside air slapping my face. I screamed and then yelped in pain as I crashed to my knees on the Juliet balcony, my left wrist landing hard on the low railing, my right hand grabbing the balcony's edge. The floor-to-ceiling window must not have been locked. My weight on the glass had caused the latch to slip and let the door fly open, throwing me to my knees but no further. I was looking down at the patio below, gasping for breath and shivering as a new shower of snowflakes began to fall. I imagined myself lying down there on my back, my arms thrown wide and my legs twisted beneath me. The snow would cover me and darkness would fall. Stephanie, Freddy and Dan would arrive home, switch on the lights and draw the curtains. They would wonder where I had gone as I lay still a few metres away, cold and silent beneath my blanket of snow.

I crawled back into the room on my knees and struggled against a gust of wind to pull the door closed. The breeze had scattered my beautiful paper across the floor. As I bent to retrieve it I was struck by the bulk of the empty house beneath me. What if I hadn't locked the front door? What if someone was in the house, creeping slowly up the stairs towards me, trapping me in my eyrie? Dropping the paper, I ran down both flights of stairs. The front door was locked, as was the back. I walked slowly through the rest of the house, checking each room, each window, each door. I took the torch from its drawer in the hall table and looked in wardrobes and under beds, growing calmer with each step of my old routine. There had been a time when I had done this every day.

*   *   *

IS THIS VANISHED STEPHIE? the front of *The Sun* screamed on the Monday, four days after she had disappeared. Below the headline was a picture of the disembodied legs grabbed from the service station CCTV footage. I hated the way they had appropriated our pet name for her. It felt even more intrusive than them printing the photo of her in her school uniform, or the one of her eating an ice cream on holiday. We had provided those pictures to the police Media Liaison Unit, knowing that they would be given to the press. With the papers in front of me, I felt uneasy about the picture with the ice cream. I hated seeing photos of myself eating and I worried that Stephanie would feel the same. What if she loathed the image so much that it became the thing that stopped her from coming home?

'I know it's hard for you to look at, but this level of exposure is excellent,' said Tanya. She had arrived with the day's newspapers, spreading them out on the kitchen table. 'Millions of people across the country will see these pictures today. Say what you want about the tabloid press but in cases like this they're our best bet.'

Cases like this was a phrase the police repeated to us over and over again. I supposed it was meant to be reassuring, to imply that they knew what they were dealing with, but it sounded ridiculous to me. There had never been a case like this because Stephanie had never gone missing before. There was no precedent for what had carved deep grooves in Dan's forehead and made his hands shake, or caused Freddy to wake screaming for me in the night.

Dan had been silently leafing through the broadsheets. He let the *Guardian* fall from his hands and turned to Tanya. 'The gutter press are our best bet because you lot don't have a clue, is that what you're telling me?'

'Dan,' I hissed, nodding to the ceiling in the direction of Freddy's room.

He lowered his voice. 'But it's true, isn't it? We've got nothing apart from the service station lead that has led us absolutely nowhere and might not even be her.'

'It was her,' I said. 'I know it was.'

'No, you don't. You just want to believe it. You haven't got a clue, Rosalind.' I had known Dan for more than half my life and Tanya had met him for the first time only the day before, but it was she who realised what was happening, that his self-control hadn't just slipped but shattered. Who could blame him, sitting opposite the quaking wretch his wife had become, his kitchen table covered in countless fuzzy images of what might or might not be his daughter's legs?

'This won't help, Dan.' She was already up from her seat and moving around the table towards him when he started to shout.

'You should know where she is, Rosalind. You should know where she's gone and who she's with. It's your job to be her mother. It's the only bloody thing you have to worry about! You must know something. Think, damn you! Think!' He was leaning across the table towards me, pinning me in place with his anger.

We both flinched when Tanya's fist hit the table. 'If it was that bloody easy we would have figured it out by now. We're throwing everything we have at this.' She glared at Dan. She was a foot shorter than him, petite to his muscular, but for a moment she made him seem small.

'I'm sorry,' he said. He was apologising to Tanya not to me.

'She's a teenager. If anyone knows anything it will be her friends, not your wife. We're speaking to them again today. All of them. OK?' He nodded. Her phone rang and she answered it as she left the room. I wanted to follow her. I wanted her to wrap her arms around me, stroke my hair and tell me that everything would be all right. But I knew she wouldn't say that unless she knew it to be true. So instead of running after Tanya I sat opposite Dan in silence.

I could tell that Tanya had news – bad news – as soon as she walked back into the kitchen.

'No!' I heard myself say as my chair fell backwards and clattered onto the floor behind me.

'No, no, no. Not that. Not that,' she said. 'Rosalind, not that.' She was holding my arm, lowering me back into my chair. 'We've had a tip-off on who she might be with.'

The call had come in to the school secretary, Mrs Brindle, at twenty to nine that morning. She had answered the phone expecting the usual explanations for absences she dealt with every Monday. The voice on the phone was a woman's, or perhaps a girl's. It had been difficult to tell because she was whispering.

'Stephanie Simm is with Mr Temperley,' the voice said before the line was disconnected. The call had lasted less than ten seconds. It could have been a prank – a cruel joke played by a pupil who had seen the story in the newspapers and had a grudge against the teacher – but Mrs Brindle had only just read an email from Nathan Temperley explaining that the stomach pains which had caused him to ring in sick on the previous Friday had grown more severe and that he had been admitted to hospital with appendicitis.

'He's not at home and he's not in City Hospital. No one at the school has seen him since his last class on Thursday,' said Tanya. 'We checked as soon as the head called us.'

'You think she's with this teacher?' Dan said.

'We're looking into it as a matter of urgency. We're checking other hospitals now. He could have been taken sick elsewhere or rushed straight to Watford or Hemel Hempstead. We can't jump to conclusions yet.' A 'but' hung in the air.

It took Dan much longer than it took me to realise what Tanya's words meant. How many reasons did he think there were for a teacher to run away with a girl three days after her fifteenth birthday? I could only think of one, but there was a long moment during which he failed to join the dots between what was obvious and our daughter. 'But why on earth would she be with him?' he said.

I tried to answer but my mouth had filled with bile. Cold tea churned in my stomach as Nathan Temperley's face flickered in my mind. I said something or made a noise. I can't remember which but it was enough to turn Dan's thoughts down the path on which mine were already racing. I watched the realisation hit him, turning bafflement to awareness to horror.

'Look, we don't know that she's with him. Not for sure,' said Tanya. But it was too late to take it back. I was already sure. I think she was too.

'Is he some sort of fucking pervert? With Stephanie?' said Dan at last.

'He's her geography teacher,' I said.

'Well, what the hell is he doing teaching geography to little girls when he's a kiddie-fiddler?' The word 'fiddler' made me think of Temperley's fingers. My mouth was flooded with hot saliva and I retched into my teacup, my eyes streaming. My ears were ringing but not quite loudly enough to block out what Dan was saying. 'She's fifteen. She was only fourteen a week ago.'

'Sit down! Your son is upstairs. You need to keep it together right now. Inspector Haskins is on her way here and she'll have more questions for you.'

I swallowed hard, wiping a slime of tea and vomit from my chin. I had stopped shaking, the clouds of unreality that had blurred my thoughts since the moment the police had arrived three days ago parted. It was like the moment when you find a key in your pocket after having turned the whole house upside down searching for it. 'You have to find him, now. Right now,' I said. 'He's too much for her. She won't stand a chance.'

*   *   *

My phone buzzed beside me, snatching me back into the empty house. It was a message from Dan: **Snow causing train chaos. Going to cut my losses and stay in town tonight. Will be back early tomorrow. Love to S and F xxx.** He had been disappointed that the doctor hadn't referred Stephanie to a specialist, but reassured by her diagnosis of stress and the clear time frame of her two-week sick note. 'See? I knew it was stress,' he had said when I told him on the phone at lunchtime. In his mind she would be fine again in two weeks' time and we would all put it behind us and move on. His version of reality carefully overlooked the depression, the uncertainty about dose and effect, not to mention the fact that nothing had really changed since the day we brought her home. And Temperley's release, of course. But it wasn't his fault that he had overlooked that. At least he hadn't mentioned The Elms. At least he seemed to be letting go of the possibility of sending her away. Maybe he would stay away himself, claim work stress and travel problems until she was safely back in London and he could return home. All the more reason for Stephanie and me to go on holiday; that way she wouldn't have to witness her father's ill-disguised rejection.

The afternoon had slipped away and night had arrived, as thick and dark at six thirty as it would be at midnight. Stephanie and Freddy would be home soon. Without consciously deciding to, I checked the house again, moving from room to room, switching on every light and leaving all the internal doors wide open. As I double-checked that the porch light was on I glimpsed the brightness of the snow through the round windows set into each half of the double front doors. I pulled the doors open and looked out at the thick carpet that blurred the lines between the octagon of lawn, the beds of plants and the path which wound its way from the gate to the door. A street light peered over the tall box hedge that edged the garden, shedding its orange light across the seamless blanket of snow. At first I thought the footprints were mine, that a quirk of the snowfall had covered some of them so it looked as though I had stopped halfway up the path. But then I noticed the second set facing in the opposite direction. Someone had walked halfway up the path then turned around and walked back again as though they had changed their mind.

'Mum, you nutter. What are you doing?' said Freddy. I had been so lost in the clunk and scrape of the spade on the gravel path that I hadn't noticed their approach.

'I didn't want you falling over.' I sunk the spade into the last remaining footprint and hefted the snow onto the lawn.

'You haven't even got a coat on. It's bloody freezing.' He exchanged a look with Stephanie. It was a look I had seen many times before, passed between the two of them and Dan. *Here she goes again*, it said. I had been planning to ask Freddy to go and look in the back garden to check for anything strange over in the corner by the shed, but that look made me reconsider.

'I thought it would only take a moment.' I was still wearing the purple top and flimsy cardigan I had put on before I went to Hatfield. My hands were numb with cold.

'Come on, Mum. Let's get inside,' said Stephanie. She put her arm around my shoulders and shepherded me through the front door.

'Where's Dad?' asked Freddy.

'He's staying in town. The trains are all in chaos because of the snow.'

'Really? Jack managed to get back half an hour ago.' Jack was a friend of Freddy's. Instead of heading to university he had talked his way into a back-room job in the City. He was still living with his parents but swore he would be a millionaire before he turned twenty-one.

'Well he must have been on the last one that got through. And you know what your dad's like. He'll have waited at King's Cross for half an hour and then given up. He hates twiddling his thumbs.'

'So where's he staying?' said Stephanie.

'The Thistle on Euston Road, I expect. They have a deal with them so he always stays there.'

'You didn't ask him?' There was doubt in Freddy's voice.

'No. It's not the first time he's got stuck because of the trains.' The way they were questioning me was unsettling; it was as though they thought I was hiding something from them. I changed the subject as we trooped through the hallway to the kitchen. 'Did Jack pop round to Matt's too?'

'We went to the pub,' said Freddy. 'To watch the football.' Their note had said that they were with Matt, not at Matt's house. While I had imagined them safely closeted in the basement room Matt's family called the 'entertainment space', they had actually been out in a pub where anyone could have seen them. *He's still in prison*, I reminded myself, *locked up*. He couldn't touch her. Yet.

'Don't worry, Mum. I stuck to lemonade. No booze for me.'

'Oh, right,' I said. 'I didn't think you wanted to see people, that's all.'

'We went to the Albion. No one goes in there. It's just old people, isn't it?' said Freddy. The Albion, our local pub, was oddly down at heel given the affluence of the street it sat on. I hadn't been in there since a power cut a few years ago had sent me out in search of warmth and light. I walked past it often though, wincing at the smell of yeast and unwashed urinals that wafted from the door every time it opened. It wasn't the kind of place people we knew spent their evenings.

'We only saw Matt and Jack,' said Stephanie. 'It was fine. Stop worrying.'

'Mum, is your lip bleeding?' said Freddy.

I ran my tongue over my lip and tasted blood, thought of my lipstick on Cam's teeth. 'Oh. They're just a bit chapped.'

'Mum, what's wrong? What were you doing out there in the snow?' said Stephanie.

I should never have gone to the gallery. I should have stayed here with her, stopped her from leaving the house; stopped myself from kissing Cam. Had Freddy locked the front door when we came in? I needed to check. What about the garage? I hadn't looked in there. I had parked my car on the drive. Someone could be hiding under it. They could have watched me digging in the snow, watched Stephanie and Freddy come home.

'Mum?' Stephanie took my arm and pulled me round to face her.

'I'm OK. I was just worried about you slipping over out there. And I haven't done anything about dinner. You must be starving.' They were both watching my face, green eyes and blue eyes, wary. I couldn't let them see the unspooling of my calm. I turned my back to them and knelt down to rummage in the freezer, letting the ice-cold air tumble over me, inhaling it deeply and counting to ten. I could fight this. I had to. My fears were all irrational, at least for the next seven days.

'Let's order pizza,' said Freddy. 'Dad isn't here so we can do what we want.' Dan hated takeaway food. Fish and chips could be eaten by the seaside but ordering food to be eaten at home was, to him, beyond the pale. I had never been sure why, but I suspected it was a belief passed down from father to son. Dan's father would hate to pay someone to cook a meal when he had a wife at home to do it for free.

'That was quick,' Freddy said when the doorbell rang twenty minutes after we had phoned in our order. 'Stay there, you two.

I'll go.' I heard him open the front door. I made a mental note to check the deadlock and fasten the bolts before I went to bed.

'False alarm. It must have been someone dropping this off.' Freddy came back into the sitting room, carrying a single post-card rather than the boxes of pizza I had expected. I took it from him. It was a picture of a bustling, sun-soaked street lined with trees and pavement cafés. I recognised the scene from my last trip to Barcelona, the trip I had taken with Bea. It had been brutally hot and we had spent our afternoons strolling beneath La Rambla's trees and sipping coffee under parasols. I turned the card over slowly. *Wish ~~you~~ we were here! C x*

'Who's it from?' said Stephanie.

'I don't know.'

'Who's C?'

'Oh, it must be Charlotte from my course. She's been away.' Cam. It was from Cam. For weeks we had been sharing a wistful pretence that we would one day visit Barcelona together.

'Weird that she didn't post it.'

'I always forget to post postcards until I'm home. I guess she was just passing.'

The doorbell rang. It was the pizza delivery man, saving me from further lies and, at least for a while, from wondering why Cam had put the postcard through the door.

We flopped the lids of the greasy cardboard boxes open across the coffee table and ate in a ring of quiet complicity. I would wrap up the boxes and hide them in the boot of my car so Dan would never know. The hot food chased the chill from my bones and the sight of Stephanie and Freddy cocooned in flickering light from the television wore away the fear that had ambushed me in my studio and dogged me ever since. I had just been imagining things, hadn't I? It wasn't as though it was the first time. And the postcard was just a joke, a silly joke. I would ask Cam not to do anything like that again.

Stephanie's phone rang as we were eating, the pocket of her jeans vibrating with a tinny imitation of the rotary phones of my childhood. She frowned into its screen, pressing a button before pushing it down the gap between two sofa cushions. A few seconds later the sofa began to vibrate as it rang again. She frowned before scrabbling it out of its hiding place and scowling at it.

'What's wrong, love? Is someone bothering you?' Could Temperley have found her phone number somehow? Bribed someone or hired a private detective from the confines of his prison cell?

'It doesn't matter. I've switched it off now. Anyway, Mum, what time are we going to your pop-up thing tomorrow?'

A few days earlier I had been looking forward to the exhibition. It would have been a day spent with Cam, chatting and flirting gently – harmlessly. I had thought about going for a drink with everyone afterwards, maybe even leaving my car in Hatfield and getting a taxi home when the pub shut. I had never imagined arriving there with Stephanie at my side. But then I hadn't imagined the guilt of kissing Cam like that either.

'Actually, it's looking pretty shoddy. I don't think we should go at all. I think I'll just leave the young ones to get on with it.'

'Don't be like that, Mum! I bet your stuff looks great. We have to go.'

'You're supposed to be resting,' I said. 'You need to recuperate.'

'I'll rest all day. And Dr Bashir said I should try to get out the house at least once a day.'

'We're definitely going, Mum,' said Freddy. 'Stephie showed me the flyer and it sounds fun.'

'Yeah. Fred and I will go without you,' said Stephanie, smiling. 'It's a public exhibition so you can't stop us. I'm going to go there and be proud of you whether you like it or not.' Her words took me back to the time before Nathan Temperley. She had never gone in for flinging her arms around me and telling me she loved me the way some children did, but every so often she would sneak up behind me and disarm me completely with a handful of words of love or admiration. 'You're the prettiest mum of any child in the whole school,' she had told me as I stood looking for crow's feet in the mirror the day before my thirtieth birthday. 'I'm lucky that you're my mum,' she had said in the car on the way back from buying her first school uniform, just as I was busy comparing myself unfavourably to Candice Lewis – Sarah's mother, who we had bumped into in the street – and wondering how much Stephanie wished she was Candice's daughter rather than mine.

How could I say no? 'Well, there's a sort of drinks reception at six o'clock. We could just pop in for that, I suppose. Just for half an hour.' It would be busy at six. There were seven crates of cheap white wine stowed in the back room next to the snowmen and the elves. Students would pile in on the promise of free booze and we could get lost in the crowd. And there was no way that Dan would get there by six.

'OK. It's a deal. Dad's not coming, is he?'

'He knows about it but I doubt he'll be back in time.'

She nodded and turned back to the television.

When Stephanie went up to bed, I boiled the kettle and made her a hot water bottle. I listened at the bottom of the narrow stairs that reached between the main landing and the floor that housed her bedroom and my studio. When I heard the running of a tap in her bathroom I sprinted up the stairs two at a time. I tapped as gently as I could on the door then eased it open. She was in the bathroom with the door closed. 'Just popping a hotty in your bed,' I called out.

The wretched little phone was on the bedside table, tethered to the wall by its charger cable. I wanted to snatch it up and throw it out of the skylight to shatter on the patio below. Instead, I ran my fingers over its touch screen until it sparked into life. My phone was an ancient relic compared to Stephanie's and, for a moment, I couldn't figure out how to operate it. But with a pulse of relief I realised that it worked in the same way as the iPad. After a few false starts and with the seconds before Stephanie emerged from the bathroom racing by, I found what I was looking for: the list of calls made and received. There were two numbers in her missed calls list. One was saved as *Don't Answer*. That number had rung her three times since three o'clock that afternoon. But the last two unanswered calls were from a different number. They had come while we were eating pizza downstairs from a number saved as *Dad Mob*. Dan's number. Skipping back to the menu screen I started searching for a text message icon; Stephanie had always preferred messages to phone calls, at least for communicating with me. I tried icon after icon until the flush of the loo forced me to give up. By the time Stephanie came into the room the phone was back where she had left it and I was turning down the bed.

SIX DAYS

I woke in the space between night and morning. With Dan's travel schedule, I was used to being alone in bed, but in the moment that I jolted awake I was overwhelmed by the emptiness of the room. The grey light that snuck between the curtains cast a host of sullen shadows across the carpet and I snapped the bedside lamp on to chase them away.

I had lain awake until the early hours pursuing the puzzle of Stephanie's missed-calls list around my mind. Why had Dan rung her and not me, and why hadn't she told me? I had looked at it from every angle without finding an answer.

When I had rung Dan to tell him about Stephanie's doctor's appointment, he had been out for lunch somewhere noisy with the roar of car engines and the bustle of a crowd. I used to know where he went for lunch and even what he ate every day: usually a sandwich from a deli called Carlo's. Often his PA would pick it up for him and he would eat at his desk, filling his keyboard with so many crumbs that it had to be replaced every year. When had I stopped knowing where he went and what he ate each day? It bothered me that he hadn't answered my call straight away. He had rung me back after I had left him a message. Perhaps he had seen my name flash up on his phone and rushed out of a restaurant to stand on a busy street corner while his dining companion waited at the table. Or maybe he had been walking back to his office from wherever it was he bought his lunch these days and just missed my call because his hands were full of paper bags. Then, later, he had texted me to tell me that he wouldn't be coming home but had rung Stephanie twice. Maybe he wanted to hear her account of the doctor's appointment in her own words, or to know why she had been so hostile to him since we had picked her up from London. If he was worried about that, though, why hadn't he just come home?

Then there was *Don't Answer*. The number saved under that name started with zero-seven, so it was definitely a mobile. Mobile phones were banned in prisons, but I had watched enough documentaries about incarceration over the past few years to know there are ways to smuggle them inside: in the pockets of corrupt prison guards, concealed in packets of crisps or wedged into the cracks where prison visitor pat-downs didn't reach. But surely Stephanie would do more than frown and switch the phone to silent if Temperley was ringing her? It had to be this Jake, or someone else from the dark months she had spent losing herself in drink and strangers. Whoever Don't Answer was, his calls were clearly unwelcome. If she would confide in me I could answer her phone and threaten to report him to the police or blow the whistle I kept in the drawer next to the phone into the receiver to scare him away. I had bought that whistle years ago, just in case Temperley tried to reach Stephanie by ringing the house. It was still in the hall-stand drawer but it was no use unless she asked for my help. I couldn't risk shredding the fragile fronds of her confidence in me by admitting I had snooped.

It was twenty past five and I was wide awake. I lay cold and rigid in my bed, piling the questions one on top of the other until the heap of unknowns collapsed and I had to start all over again. The problem was that I couldn't think clearly; I couldn't follow a rational process of examining evidence and deducing motives because every thought led back to Nathan Temperley.

Every road led back to the fact that he was about to be released. That knowledge was like a black hole; it distorted time and space, it dragged everything towards itself and swallowed it up. Nothing could avoid it and nothing could escape.

A noise from downstairs cut through the snowstorm swirl of my thoughts. It could have been the jolting open of the back door or the scrape of a chair on the kitchen's flagstone floor. Dan must have taken the first train home, arriving into St Albans before the dawn and creeping through the house towards me even as I lay in bed doubting him. Perhaps I had woken because part of me had sensed him approaching. Then I remembered the flash of blue in the garden on the previous afternoon and the fear that had gripped me. And Temperley, I thought of Temperley, too. I imagined him sliding between the bars of his cage, crawling down walls and leaving no tracks in the snow-covered streets.

I crept to the door and crouched there listening. For a long time there was only silence. If Dan had arrived home I would have heard the telltale clump of his leather messenger bag being dumped on the parquet hall floor, then the tread of his feet on the stairs, which squeaked beneath him however quiet he tried to be. But none of those sounds reached me. The house's silence was so thick that I could hear the blood rushing through my ears. I shivered in the cold draught blowing in from under the door and clenched my teeth to stop them from chattering. Somewhere outside, a car engine clamoured to start in the cold. It heaved and wheezed until, coughing like the bronchial woman in the doctor's waiting room, it finally revved into life. There was silence again and then another sound: a tiny indistinct noise travelling up the stairs from below. Someone was downstairs. Stephanie was above. I was in between.

I pulled my dressing gown on over the T-shirt and knickers I had worn to bed and eased my keys and phone out of my handbag. I considered taking one of Dan's heavy-soled shoes or a belt with a thick brass buckle to lash out with, but both seemed inadequate. Didn't some men use their time in prison to work out, growing more muscular and bulky with every year they spent behind bars? The keys would have to do. The self-defence lesson I had taken decades ago had taught that keys jabbed into eyes and feet rammed into crotches were the best weapons a woman had. As I opened the door, I slid the long key that fastened the bottom lock on the front door between my forefinger and thumb and held it out in front of me like a wand. I barely breathed as I crept forward step by step then stair by stair, my way lit by the grey of dawn and the orange wash of a street light seeping through the big, round uncurtained window at the top of the stairs.

From halfway down the stairs I could see that the front door was closed as usual. The security chain was on, the bolts fastened. No one had come in that way. I ducked down below the level of the banister to descend the last few steps which coiled in a gentle spiral towards the hall floor. On the final step I held my breath and listened to the silence before taking a single swift leap across the hallway to crouch behind the hall stand, a thick layer of winter coats providing cover while affording me a view of the five doors that led off the hall to the sitting room, the dining room, the cellar, the cloakroom and the kitchen. The sitting-room door stood ajar. It was pitch black inside and there was no sign of movement. Looking back into the hallway I realised something was wrong. The kitchen door, which always stood wide open – held in place with a smooth oval-shaped stone which Stephanie had chosen on Chesil Beach – was shut tight. I hadn't closed it for months.

Gripping my keys in my right fist and thinking of Stephanie asleep upstairs, I crept down the hall to stand in front of the kitchen door. Light bled out beneath the door and onto my bare toes but there was no sound from within. I gripped the handle in my left hand and twisted it slowly and silently. Then I drew a sharp breath and threw the door open, screaming in fright at myself.

Stephanie stood up, her chair clattering onto the floor behind her.

'Mum! You scared the life out of me.' Her eyes were enormous in her pale face. She was wearing the purple polka dot pyjamas with my blue jumper pulled on over the top. Around her the kitchen was bright and warm. There were no shadows here, let alone any creeping creatures hiding within them.

The keys fell from my hand, landing on the slate floor with a ringing clang and I lost Stephanie in the sudden blur of tears. I stood there, mute and unmoving until I felt her hands on my shoulders, cold through the silk of my dressing gown.

'Who did you think was down here?' Still I didn't speak. 'Mum, who did you think was in here?'

'Temperley,' I said at last, forcing the three hated syllables out one by one.

'He's in prison. He's not here.' The way she looked at me was familiar. There was pity in it and a measure of frustration too. It was the *Here she goes again* face. It was the *My neurotic mother is losing it again* face.

I wasn't going to tell her, and then, quite suddenly, I was. I forced myself to. I gathered my fragile will in the balls of my fists and pressed it to my chest. It was like the dreams in which I was falling and I wanted to scream in terror but couldn't make a sound. I had to fight to open my mouth, to move my tongue, to make my lips form the words one by one: 'He's getting out of prison,' I said, 'at the beginning of next month.'

'Oh my God! How do you know?' Her hand flew to her mouth. She took a step away from me.

'Tanya told me.'

'When?'

'On the first of December. Six days' time.'

'When did she tell you? When did Tanya tell you?'

I looked away from her. 'Yesterday afternoon. She rang my mobile.' The lie came from a strange place of wanting to protect the new honesty between us. 'I wanted to tell you yesterday but I just couldn't bear to. You seemed so much better, so much calmer. I'm so sorry, Stephie.'

'I wouldn't have wanted to tell me either.' She laughed the bitter new laugh I had first heard when we went to pick her up from London.

'I just wanted to choose the right time. I wanted to give you more time.'

'Or less time. Less time to worry about it before he gets out. I think I'd prefer that.' She walked slowly back around the table and picked her chair up from where it had fallen over when I had burst into the room. I was waiting for tears or questions. I was waiting for something, but she just sat back down, letting her shoulders slump. There was a twenty pence piece on the table in front of her and she slid it across the table top, flicking it from one hand to the other and back again.

Back in the days when I thought that understanding the human brain might help me to find a button I could press to recalibrate myself to normal, I read about an experiment in which psychologists repeatedly electrocuted pairs of dogs. While one half of each pair could stop the shocks by pressing a lever, the other half had no means of controlling the shocks at all. Their pain would end only when their canine partners lifted their paws and pressed the levers. Later, the psychologists – white coats, the glint of wire-framed spectacles, justifications repeated over glasses of whisky night after night – put the dogs into boxes and gave them electric shocks through the floor. This time, each dog could escape the shocks by jumping over a low barrier to the un-electrocuted floor beyond. The dogs which had been able to stop the shocks with the lever hopped over the barrier without hesitation, but the other dogs – the ones who had had no escape from the abuse – just lay down and whined, waiting for the next shock to come. I had a sickening vision of Stephanie laying her head on the table, refusing to move, just waiting for him to scuttle through the house and tap her on the shoulder. I would lose her all over again. Maybe I already had.

'Stephanie,' I started when the silence between us had grown so thick that the room hummed with it. 'Talk to me. Please. Tell me what you're thinking.'

She let the coin she had been playing with fall out of her hand and hit the table top with a rattle. She looked up at me once through her lashes – a long assessing look – before she started to speak. 'There was a letter. I didn't tell you because I knew how much you'd worry. I got it at the end of the summer term. It was sent to uni and addressed to Professor Stephanie Simm. I guess that's how he managed to get it past the people who vet their letters. No one sends me letters to uni so I never bother to check at the office. But one of my tutors left a book there for me to pick up and when I went to get it the office manager gave me the letter, too. It had been sitting in a pigeon-hole waiting for me for months. I must have walked past it hundreds of times without even knowing it was there.'

'Please tell me it wasn't from him,' I said. I had always feared this letter. Until she left home I had waited by the letter box each morning to make sure I got to it first.

I wasn't sure if she had heard me. 'I knew it was from him as soon as I saw the postmark on the envelope. I stuffed it inside the book in case anyone else saw. No one at uni knows about me, or at least they pretend they don't know. I locked myself in the disabled loo next to the office. I hadn't opened it by the time someone knocked on the door. I had been in there for half an hour and there was a man in a wheelchair outside waiting to use the loo.' She didn't look up as she spoke. I held my breath.

In the telling of this story about the letter, I felt the edge of the thread that I needed to catch hold of to unravel the whole tightly woven, closely guarded story of her and Temperley.

'I put the letter back in my bag and went to my lecture. I couldn't concentrate. I kept looking at the people sitting around me and all I could think about was that none of them had that letter in their bag. There was a boy from my tutor group who looked as though he had been crying, Kim who was failing and about to get thrown out, the man with no arms who comes to lectures with an assistant to take his notes. I would have swapped places with any one of them in a heartbeat just for the chance not to be the one with that letter in my bag.'

'Did you open it?'

'I carried it around for a few days. I zipped it into an inside pocket and I kept looking to check it was still there, hoping it would have vanished. I felt as though I was in one of those plastic hamster balls, going through the motions of my life but sealed away from everyone else. Even from Sarah. I knew the only way to escape was to open it and read it but I couldn't bring myself to. I just carried it around with me and every day it grew heavier, dragging me further away from my life.' I took her hand as she started to cry, her tears rolling down the sharp angles of her cheekbones and painting dark spots on the blue woollen jumper.

'You could have burnt it,' I said. 'Or ripped it up.'

'I tried but I couldn't. I decided to ask Sarah to read it. But one day ran into another without me giving it to her. I sat opposite her every day with it in my bag in the next room and I didn't say a word. Then term ended and Sarah was gone and you know what happened next.'

'I could have opened it for you.' I had been picturing her alone, dragging her burden behind her: a sealed envelope of pale blue paper, rank with the scent of prison, trailing the broken silk of its author's web.

She took a deep breath and wiped her eyes. She spoke fast, as though her patience for the story had run out. 'I opened it with Jake. We were outside the pub at Alexandra Palace. It's beautiful up there and I could see the whole city spread out below me – all those millions and millions of people – to remind me of how tiny and anonymous I am in London. But as I waited for Jake to come back with our drinks I realised that the wind was blowing towards us from the south. The air I was breathing could have passed through his cell or his exercise yard. It could be his air. I told Jake that it wasn't the right place but he talked me into it. He said we should just rip the letter into tiny shreds and throw it off the top of hill. We did, but I read it first.'

'What, Stephanie? What did it say?'

'That he was waiting for me and he knew I was waiting for him.'

'Bastard!'

She shrugged her shoulders, whether in agreement or to dismiss me, I couldn't tell. 'As soon as I read it I realised I had always known what it would say. I had dragged it around with me, making it the centre of my world for all those weeks, and I could have just read it. Or flushed it down the loo. It wouldn't have mattered. What had stopped me was the hope that it would say something different. How does that saying go? It's the hope that kills you? Well, it is.'

'What did you want it to say?' I could feel the end of the thread. I was so close to grasping it, to being able to untie the riddle of my daughter.

'Something honest,' she said, raising her eyes to mine. 'I just wanted him to be honest about what we did. But anything honest would have done.'

'Honesty is the last thing I'd expect from him.'

'Or anyone around here, apparently.'

Just like that the thread was snatched out of my hand and I had lost her again. 'I'm sorry I didn't tell you as soon as I knew.

Really, I am. I just . . . I was trying to protect you. I got it wrong.'
I held my hands up, palms flat in front of me.

She shook her head and sighed. 'It's OK. I didn't mean that. It
doesn't matter really, does it? Who told who what when? It all
comes out sooner or later, one way or another.' She picked the
coin up from the table top and tossed it in the air, catching it
neatly between her palms as it fell. She looked at it for a second
then tossed it again, then again. She was slipping away from me
as surely as if she was falling through the empty air. In a few
moments she would be as distant and unknowable as she had
ever been.

I shifted forwards in my chair and stretched a hand towards
her tensed wrist, not quite daring to make contact. 'I haven't
told your father yet.'

It surprised her, stopped her midway through the process of
locking me out. 'When are you going to tell him?'

'Tonight, I suppose. If that's OK with you?'

'Whatever. I don't care.'

I thought of the websites Dan had been looking at: The Elms
with its high walls and smiling doctors. I wondered what it
was like to turn oneself over to a place like that. I imagined
muted voices and shatterproof vases of cut flowers; narrow beds
with tightly tucked sheets; a day room where people sat very
still, books lying unread in their laps. Could you leave your life
outside when you checked in or did you have to take it with
you? 'I won't let him bulldoze you. I know you need to do this
your way.'

'Do this? You're talking about it like it's a thing that people
do. Like eating those meatballs at Ikea or queuing up outside
shops to buy new iPhones. Those are things people do.'

Like Dan, she had always had the ability to twist my words
to make me sound stupid. I swallowed and forced myself not to
think about the tone of her voice or the deadly accuracy with

which she threw her barbed arrows. 'Confront this, then. Deal with it. You need to deal with it your way.'

'Do I? What actually is it? What is the thing I have to deal with? A man I used to know is going to be living on a different side of a wall. That's all it is if I choose not to let it be anything else.'

'Don't kid yourself, Stephanie. It will be in the papers again. You know how much they love this type of story. At least one of them will get hold of it.'

'Yes. I realise that. But there's nothing I can do about it, is there? I'm not talking to any scummy journalists.'

'And he'll want to see you, won't he? He'll come looking for you?' I didn't quite believe that I was having to spell this out to her, to lead her step by step through the horrors that were about to unfold. Whatever we had thought and felt moment to moment, day to day, hadn't our lives always been converging on this single dark point?

'You don't know what he'll want. You don't know him.' It was her old refrain from the days between her return to us and the point at which she fell silent and refused to discuss him at all.

I balled my hands into fists to quell the urge to put them on her shoulders and shake her until it all spilled out: the twisting coils of the truth. 'You don't know him either. Not after he's spent all this time in prison. You might think you do but you don't.'

She flinched. I didn't think she had ever understood how much I was holding back or how carefully I rolled on my kid gloves to talk to her. I glimpsed a different world: one where she feared me, where I screamed and wailed and begged and she folded in on herself layer after layer until there was nothing left to hide. I mastered my voice. 'I will support you in whatever you want to do. Whatever you need, we'll do it.'

'*Whatever* I want to do? I don't think you mean that.' It was impossible to ignore the echo of her words six years earlier – the day after they were found – when she had refused to come home with us and told us how it would be: accept them as a couple or lose her altogether. Her feelings had changed, though. After the sentencing, in the days in which her love for Temperley crumbled away from her like bark from the trunk of a dead tree, I tried to believe we were free of him, but I couldn't. Even as the years went by with no sign of him, no stumbles or falls on her path away from him, I knew that we were not yet free. When Dan begged me to put the past behind me and move on, I couldn't, because it wasn't the past at all.

There were so many things I wanted to ask her. For twenty-one years her life had been at the centre of my own and yet out of bounds to me. I wanted to know why she cut off her fringe when she was seven and why she was inconsolable with grief at the idea of turning ten. I wanted to know why she has only ever had one close friend and whether she minded looking so much like me. There were countless things I wanted to know about her and Temperley: how it started, why she did it, whether she ever really thought they would live happily ever after, whether it had been hard to ring me up and lie to me on the day she went missing. I wanted to know whether it hurt, how much and where. But, at that moment, there was only one question that mattered. 'Do you want to see him?' I said. 'When he gets out?'

She tossed the coin up in the air again, caught it between her palms but didn't look at it. She paused and exhaled, placing me in suspended animation for the time it took her lungs to squeeze themselves empty of air, for her breath to pass across her tongue, between her teeth, over her lips and out of her mouth. 'No.'

'Really?'

'I don't want anything to do with him. Him getting out won't matter. He doesn't matter.' She drew herself up as she said these words, pushing her shoulders back and setting her hands neatly on the table in front of her, as though a piece of business had been concluded.

'Oh, thank God. Thank God. Thank God.' I wrapped my arms around her and pressed my face into her hair. I squeezed my eyes closed and tried to believe that a resolution made in the space between one breath and another could be firm enough to hold.

* * *

Before Nathan Temperley hovered over my every waking thought, he was just Stephanie's geography teacher. I met him at parents' evening six weeks before she went missing. I always found those evenings stressful. Hearing about Stephanie was never the problem, it was the peck and scratch of the other parents that set me on edge, the way that Julian and Caroline Reid lay in wait for me to compare their daughter's performance in mathematics to mine, referring to Stephanie and Charlotte as 'our two little geniuses in the making'. It was the shades of envy and triumph that passed over the face of Julia Wall – mother to tedious little Clara Wall with her debating society and gymnastics medals – as she clawed from me the details of predicted grades in history and physics. Their anxiety fuelled my anxiety, but mine was stronger and more tenacious; while I was sure they left theirs behind when the evening ended, mine deepened and grew. In the days that followed I would have flashbacks to the heat of the packed reception area, the dust and disinfectant smell of the school's corridors, the hard-set jaws and the press of hot hands on my wrists. I would have to lean against walls and take deep breaths to stem the tide of panic.

It wasn't just the pressure to tell and be told that unnerved me. Every parent was issued with a schedule of ten-minute appointments to discuss their child with each teacher, but they never ran to time. The inevitable spiralling of one late start into the next made me dig my nails into my palms and blurred the teachers' words as the seconds and minutes spun away from me. The printout of my timetable became damp in my hands and I left a trail of torn-off corners behind me as I moved from room to room.

And every year there was the knowledge that Dan would only appear halfway through the evening in spite of his promises that this time would be different.

On the evening I met Nathan Temperley I sat in the car for ten minutes before my first appointment, sunk low into my seat. I held my mobile in my hand ready to pretend that I was making a call if anyone saw me and wanted to talk. By the time I dashed across the car park and into the building, there were just two minutes to go before my appointment with Stephanie's maths teacher. 'Sorry, I'm running late! Traffic! Catch up later!' I called to Julia Wall who was lurking by the reception desk, waiting to ensnare me.

I was doing well for time until I got to English. There was a queue outside the teacher's office and I had to wait for fifteen minutes next to Gloria McCarry with her mute ex-husband and unnerving level of knowledge about the school curriculum. She had very strong views on our daughters studying *King Lear* rather than *Othello* and a grasping need for opinions about the English teacher who I had not yet met. I had started to wonder whether she was some kind of test, an experiment being run by the school to collect candid opinion of the teachers, like the mystery shoppers sent into department stores. Or perhaps it was me she was testing, gathering information to judge whether I was suitably engaged with my daughter's education. It was a sweet relief to be released from her company.

Temperley, Mr Temperley, was my fourth appointment. I was fifteen minutes late to see him when I rounded a corner and found his office tucked away at the end of a corridor. But there was no anxious parent outside Temperley's room, just me alone in the cool emptiness of the corridor. I would make this meeting short and win back some of the minutes I had lost. Geography, I was sure, was one of those subjects that would disappear without a trace as soon as Stephanie's GCSEs were over. I gave myself thirty seconds to breathe, to imagine Dan appearing beside me, then I listened at the office door. There was no murmur of voices. I don't know why I didn't just knock. Instead, I pressed my eye to the gap between the door and its frame and peered inside. There were the blue and white stripes of a man's shirt, the pink skin of a neck. I stepped backwards just as he opened the door, the heat of a blush already climbing my chest.

'Mrs Simm? Are you OK?' He stood in the doorway, his hand still resting on the handle. *He looks like the boys at university*, I thought, remembering Dan and his friends as they had once been, their unlined skin, sharp cheekbones and narrow waists. His dark curly hair fell loosely around his face, a strand of it catching in his eyebrow as if daring me to brush it away. His black tie lay at an angle, the top button of his shirt undone. He had nothing in common with the grey-haired, paunched man – my own geography teacher of twenty-five years ago – I had been expecting.

'Yes, thank you. Just a bit warm.' I fanned myself with the tattered remains of my appointment timetable.

'We haven't met before. I'm Nathan Temperley.' He offered a hand and I shook it. His grip was firm and so warm that it threatened to ignite the fire of my blush all over again.

'Rosalind Simm. Stephanie's mother.'

'Of course. Come in, please,' he said, motioning for me to walk past him and into the room. His manner, the handshake and the way he stood back to let me enter, made him seem older than I had first thought him to be. As I passed him I looked up and glimpsed the early beginnings of wrinkles at the corners of his eyes and a heavy shadow where a beard would grow in a few hours' time. 'Please do sit down. I'm afraid it's a bit cosy in here. There's a shortage of offices at the moment so I'm having to make do with this.'

The room was tiny, little more than a cupboard crammed with a narrow desk and a couple of bookshelves. The only window was a narrow oblong, positioned high above our heads.

'It's like a prison cell,' I said as he squeezed his way between the end of the desk and an overloaded set of shelves to sit opposite me. 'I hope they let you out at home time, Mr Temperley.'

'I hope so too.' He laughed more than my weak joke deserved. 'Please, call me Nathan.'

The table between us was so narrow that I could sense how close his knees were to mine and feel the heat of his skin through my linen trousers. I could have shuffled backwards, put some distance between us, but I didn't.

'It's rather hot in here. You won't mind if I take off my tie, will you?' he said.

'No, of course not.' He didn't look away from me as he pulled the tie from around his neck and undid another button, revealing a dark curl of hair. He was taller than me so I was forced to look upwards to meet his eyes.

'That's better. Mr Simm not with you tonight?'

'He's been held up at work. He should be here any moment. Well, he should have been here an hour ago, of course, but I expect he'll be here any moment. He so wanted to come but he's got an awful lot on. It's difficult for him, and then the trains are forever getting delayed. I expect that's what has happened tonight.' I was gabbling, my pulse racing as fast as my words. The routine stresses of parents' evening and the unexpectedness of this man had unpicked my fragile grip on myself. The room was oppressively hot. I felt the urge to get up, to run out of there, out of the school and away into the cool evening air. Instead, I slipped my cardigan from my shoulders and twisted its sleeves between my hands. Perhaps I would have kept it on if I had remembered the skimpiness of the camisole I was wearing underneath. I felt Temperley's eyes glance off my bare shoulders.

'I'm sorry not to meet him. I do enjoy meeting my pupils' parents. It gives me a better idea of who they are. These evenings are always so interesting from this side of the desk.' He rested his elbows on the table and moved his hands as he talked, extending and flexing his fingers in time with his words. Temperley's fingers were short and thick yet there was a supple elegance in the way they moved. The hair on his arms gave way to a fuzz that dusted the backs of his fingers. His hands seemed more grown-up than him: if I saw them anywhere other than attached to his arms I would never have guessed they were his.

'We're not very interesting, I'm afraid,' I said, forcing my attention back to his face.

'I'm sure you are. With such a bright daughter, you must be.'

'She gets her brains from her father.' I hadn't decided to flirt with him and yet there I was using my tried and tested technique, the one I had learned as a teenager and never completely given up: putting myself down to invite him to compliment me. A charge of guilt passed through my stomach, but then I remembered I was only alone in a room with this man because Dan wasn't there, even though he had said he would be. I relaxed a little.

'But she gets her looks from you. I mean, she looks like you. I knew you were her mother as soon as I saw you.'

'Yes, people say we look alike. Much to Stephanie's chagrin, I'm sure.'

'Well, she's a wonderful student. You should be very proud of her.' He hadn't taken the bait this time and it stung. Instead, he talked about Stephanie's course work, igneous rock and a field trip to Cheddar Gorge. But I couldn't concentrate. I was distracted by him: his hands, his lips, the rise and fall of his voice. Was he married? Did he have a girlfriend? I wanted to know how old he was and what a man like him was doing in this old matron of a girls' school with its layers of rules and frumpy uniforms. He said something that I missed.

'What was that, sorry?'

'Would you like Stephanie to study geography at A level?'

'We're all for it if that's what she chooses. I know she enjoys it,' I lied. 'We'll let her make up her own mind, though.'

'That's the best attitude, in my experience. Let them follow their interests. She's very passionate about geography. I'm always delighted by how keen she is to learn.' He said these things to me, to the mother of the child he was reeling in. And I just listened, thinking about myself and what he might think of me, what I looked like to him with my skimpy top and my absent husband. It didn't occur to me for a moment that it was Stephanie's shoulders he wanted to look at, her teenage skin on which he wanted to lay those hands.

'Good. I'm so glad you're pleased with her.'

'She could take geography further. Much further. She has a real . . . affinity for the subject.'

'An affinity?'

'Yes. I always feel that she understands exactly what I'm saying. She gets me – it, geography – Mrs Simm.'

'Good,' I said again. There was a moment of silence and I wondered if the meeting was at an end. 'How long have you been here at the high school?' I said.

'Two years now. But where are my manners? May I offer you a small plastic cup of lukewarm water? It's all I have but it must be thirsty work trudging around to all these meetings.'

'Yes, please.'

'We can pretend it's a nice cold Pinot Grigio.'

'Or a Chablis.'

'Chablis it is.' I hadn't noticed the jug and pile of plastic cups squeezed onto the shelf beside him. He put two cups on the table and sloshed water into them. 'For you, madam,' he said, holding one out towards me. I stretched out my hand but as soon as the tips of my fingers connected with the cup Temperley let go and it fell onto the table with a crack, its contents lurching out across the pieces of Stephanie's course work that lay between us. 'Don't drop it!' he laughed.

'You let it go!'

'No, I didn't. You're a butterfingers. I hope Stephanie hasn't inherited that from you too.'

I was sure he had dropped the cup but it seemed childish to sit there protesting as he mopped the table dry with tissues from his pocket. 'Sorry about that. Lucky it was just water after all,' I said. He gave me half a smile. Perhaps it was me who had dropped it. Only the other day I had let Stephanie's favourite mug slip out of my damp hand and shatter on the kitchen floor.

There was a tapping at the open door.

'That must be my next victim.' He stood, dismissing me. I got up quickly and pulled on my cardigan, mumbling a thank you.

As I hurried down the corridor I almost ran into Dan. The rest of the evening was uneventful: Stephanie was a joy to teach, Dan was sorry he was late. In the car on the way home he held the ragged appointment timetable and asked me about the sessions he had missed.

'The geography teacher was a bit odd,' I said. 'Young, youngish anyway, and a bit full of himself. But he thinks Stephanie is wonderful. He seems to be under the impression that she's mad keen for geography, wants to do it for A level.'

'Really? She never mentions it, does she?'

'No. And, well, geography? Who studies geography?'

Dan laughed. 'Do you remember fat Sam Rylance from uni?'

'Of course I do! How could I forget? We called him Pie Boy, didn't we?'

'He was doing geography. I heard he is teaching it now.'

'Maybe they're all a bit odd.' I felt better then, as though by slighting him to Dan I had got Temperley back for whatever it was he had done, or not done, to me.

I was in that tiny room with Temperley for less than ten minutes, but I have relived each second so many times that they have expanded to fill years in the timespan of my life. The question, of course, the one Dan asked me and the one I asked myself, over and over again, was whether he did or said anything that could have alerted me to the danger that Stephanie was in. I don't think he did, not really, but how good was my memory of that evening, and how blinkered was I by the sense that he was flirting with me? Missing something that could have saved Stephanie isn't how I failed her. What I did wrong was to show him how weak I was. He was testing me, testing us, and what did he find? A father who couldn't even make it to parents' evening and a mother too anxious and vain to stick up for herself, who apologised even when she had done nothing wrong. He preyed on Stephanie not because she was weak or stupid but because we were. If I had been a different person in those ten minutes he would have turned his attentions to someone else's daughter and left mine – my precious Stephanie – alone. Every time I think back to that evening and the way he pulled my strings, toyed with me and shepherded me into self-doubt, I am reminded that Stephanie didn't stand a chance. What fifteen-year-old would?

The other thought I have about that evening always comes involuntarily, late at night or early in the morning. I am sitting opposite him again, my handbag open on my lap. 'She gets her looks from you,' he says. I reach into my bag and touch the cold heft of my steel artist's pencil. I feel the tearing of fabric, the parting of flesh and the splatter of warm blood on my face as I drive it through his striped shirt, his hair-covered skin and into the twisted, pulsing coil of his heart.

*   *   *

The day that followed Stephanie's early morning promise was a long, airless corridor of false starts and closed doors. Freddy was restless, uncertain of what to do with himself in St Albans without his friends to distract him. I cancelled my hairdressing appointment and tried to watch a game of ice hockey with him but the smack and slap of the faceless men in their padded outfits shunting each other around the ice made me flinch and I didn't understand the rules. Time wore on and snowflakes pattered against the windows, blurring the lines of lawns, hedges, trees and buildings until the scene outside resembled clumsily carved marble. Stepping out into that white expanse became unthinkable, as did climbing the stairs to my studio and looking out of that big, cold window with its memories of yesterday's fear. I dug an old sketchbook out of a drawer and let it lie open on my lap. But the snow had fallen inside my skull and blanketed my mind, blurring the lines between thoughts, and I drew clumsy, indeterminate objects with soft edges.

'Bloody hell! We'll be buried alive in the snow at this rate,' said Freddy, looking up from his book at the egg-sized snowflakes bouncing off the window.

'Do you think?' Would being buried in snow be like drowning? Would you die of asphyxiation or of cold? Or both? Or was the weight of the snow the problem? Would it get heavier and heavier, flake by flake, until your chest collapsed under the strain?

'No, Mum. It'll be fine. It's meant to stop by this afternoon. Don't worry about it.'

But I was worried. I was worried about Stephanie in her attic room. How much snow could the roof take before the slates cracked and the beams started to groan and squeal? The house was over a hundred years old; what if the roof beams were rotten, riddled with woodworm or gnawed to twigs by mice? One flake too many on the roof's weakest point could fracture a tile, which would crack a beam, which would send the whole lot crashing through the thin plaster ceiling and into her room.

I ran up to the first floor landing but came to a halt at the foot of the curving stairs leading up to the attic. It was the memory of the trip to Stratford-upon-Avon that stopped me. I had driven Stephanie to the school early on a Saturday morning to board the coach that would take a group from her year to Stratford for a matinée of *A Midsummer Night's Dream* and a theatre tour. It was the beginning of the school year, a couple of months before she would disappear with Temperley. It was raining so I parked alongside the coach. Other parents did the same and by the time Stephanie had boarded the coach with Sarah I was caught up in a knot of boxed-in cars and apologetic waves. As I waited for my turn to wiggle out of the car park, my attention was caught by the coach's front tyres. Were they bald? Should they be that smooth? Were coach tyres different to car tyres? The rain was growing heavier. The roads would be slippery. Spray would fly up from the motorway's surface, cars would skid and swerve. Somewhere from deep in my memory came words from old news reports: *school trip, tragedy, coach, crash, young lives.* More parents had arrived and the queue to get out of the car park had grown increasingly chaotic. I got out of the car and went to look at the tyres. 'They look OK to me,' said Mrs Harris, Stephanie's English teacher, when I asked her to look. 'Only been on two months. Good as new,' said the driver. But they weren't good enough for me. Stephanie looked worried when I asked her to get off the coach and into the car with me. A few minutes later, when she found out why, she was furious. She didn't speak a word to me as we followed the coach all the way to Stratford-upon-Avon then all the way back. Days passed before her anger faded into something more like piteous contempt. I couldn't afford to lose her like that again. Not now.

'Stephie, come down if you want a cup of tea,' I called up the stairs. Then I went back down, forcing myself to inhale and exhale on every step.

'Mind if I shut the curtains? I can see that snow swirling around even when I have my eyes closed,' said Stephanie a few minutes later when she appeared, blinking in the sitting room.

'You sit down, love. You must be tired.' As I pulled the curtains closed I caught brief glimpses of the world outside. With its fences and flowerbeds blanketed in white, the garden looked huge and alien, as though the house had been picked up as we slept and dropped into a snowy wilderness. I wondered whether Dan would come home that night or whether the snow would hold him fast. Perhaps he would board a train only for it to get frozen to the tracks somewhere between there and here, snow settling on the carriage until it disappeared into the landscape. I was going to tell him about Temperley when – if – he got here, 'But don't make a big thing of it, Mum,' Stephanie had said in the kitchen that morning. 'Try to have some perspective.' That phrase was one Dan had repeated to me so many times that I had found myself on the brink of weeping and had had to turn away from her.

But it was a big thing. What had Dan's word been? 'Minimising.' I didn't think I would be capable of minimising it even if that was what Stephanie wanted. I was already trying out words and phrases in my mind, looking for the right way to tell Dan. Once upon a time I would have known with certainty that his views and mine were exactly aligned when it came to Nathan Temperley. But as the years passed, that had changed. He had stopped comforting me when I came home panicking after another imagined sighting, and started telling me to pull myself together. The burden of hating and fearing the man and what he had done became mine to carry alone. Eventually, it became too heavy and I started to put it down from time to time, locking those memories and fears away and wrapping them in chains. At first I couldn't keep them locked up for long, but it became easier as time went on. Before Tanya's phone call, a whole day could pass without a single stirring, a week without the dream in which Temperley and I were falling and he was pulling Stephanie down behind us. I guess that was when I stopped worrying.

I heated up soup and baguettes. When I carried the tray of bowls and plates back into the sitting room I found that Stephanie had picked up my sketch pad. She had turned the vague shapes I had scribbled that morning into strange creatures with glassy eyes and downturned mouths. They moved across the page, melting slowly under individual clouds of rain.

'Sorry, Mum,' she said when I looked down at what she had done.

'That's OK. It's better than anything I've managed to do today.'

'I like these,' she said. She had flicked back a few pages to some older sketches. I leant over her shoulder to see what they were. A gust of heat ran up my spine and burst over my chest. I had done them with Cam as we sat round a tiny table in the coffee shop on campus. I had been explaining why I loved Barcelona so much, drawing silly little pictures to illustrate my favourite things: the beach, the sunshine, the Sagrada Família, Gaudí's lizard, tapas on La Rambla. In my mind I hovered above the scene in the café. There was the top of Cam's caramel head. There I was smiling at him, leaning back in my chair and laughing, letting him take in the curve of a breast beneath my T-shirt.

'They're just silly doodles,' I said. **I'll be there at 6 with my son and daughter x** I had texted to Cam in response to his two messages asking when I would arrive. I had thought about adding something about the postcard but I couldn't work out what to write. Then I had tried to talk Stephanie and Freddy out of coming to the exhibition, but they wouldn't be swayed.

Stephanie was pale and her eyes were pink with tiredness but she refused to stay at home. It was as though they had decided that I needed them to be there. Perhaps I did.

'Mum, this actually looks quite cool,' said Stephanie as we crossed the road and approached the glowing window of Going, going, gone! She had had a nap before we left then appeared in the kitchen looking rested and calm and wearing one of my tops. It was a petrol blue camisole dotted with sparkling black beads the size of poppy seeds. I had told her she looked beautiful and should keep the top and she had hugged me. She had forgiven me, I thought, for keeping the news of Temperley's release from her.

The 'gallery' *did* look quite cool. The LED words in the window threw light across the dark pavement. The glass had steamed up with the heat and breath of the people inside, and the fud fud fud of a bass beat and the sound of laughter reached us before we opened the door.

'Are you sure this is the right place?' said Freddy. I was wound so tightly that I nearly answered before I realised he was teasing me.

The free drinks and promise of a party had certainly brought the students out. The shop space was packed with them – some I recognised from around the campus but other faces were new to me. In amongst the groups of laughing twenty-year-olds was a couple my age making their way slowly around the edge of the room, looking at each piece and whispering to each other. The woman had Karen's high cheekbones and gloss of black hair and I realised they were her parents.

'Where are your pictures?' said Stephanie, raising her voice over the music and chatter. We skirted the crowd clustered in the middle of the room and came to a halt in front of Empty Rooms. I had spent so much time worrying about Cam and Dan and my children being in the same place at the same time that I hadn't thought about Stephanie and Freddy seeing the pictures. Would they guess that the room I had sketched over and over again to produce these three paintings was the place I had always fantasised about escaping to? There was no space for them in the rooms, no trace of them in the paintings at all. With them beside me, my pride evaporated. I loathed those pictures, regretted every stroke of my brush. When I came to pick them up I would kick my toes through the canvas then fling them in a wheelie bin in the supermarket car park across the road.

'They're great, Mum,' said Stephanie. I wished she would stop looking at them. I cast my eyes around for something with which to distract her. But all I saw was Cam.

'Ros! There you are.' Before I could stop him he had gripped my arms in his hands, planted theatrical kisses on each of my cheeks. His lips were hot and wet with wine. Hidden by the crush of the crowd, he let his right hand trail down my side and rest for a second on my hip.

'Stephie, Freddy, this is Cameron from my tutor group,' I said, taking a step away from him. 'Cam, these are my children.'

'Hi, guys. Don't you think Ros's stuff is the best?' said Cam. He looked from Stephanie to Freddy then back to Stephanie. I sensed something pass between them: the mutual recognition of youth and beauty, perhaps. I pictured them together, his arm draped loosely around her as they walked down the street, passers-by – unable to stop themselves from looking – would form a tunnel of envy around them. Well-meaning old men would wink and wish them well. Traffic would stop. Planes would stand still in the sky.

'Of course it is,' said Stephanie. 'We never doubted it. Do you have a picture here?'

'Not a picture. I'll show you. Ros hasn't even seen these yet. Come on, Ros.' Stephanie followed him and I followed her. She had slipped off her coat and was wearing only my skimpy top and a pair of my jeans. I caught Billy and Toby from my tutor group admiring her.

Maybe if I had been less worried about seeing Cam I would have noticed the plaster shapes in the corner earlier. They weren't presented in Cam's usual style – there were no Perspex boxes. Instead, the plaster hands were suspended from the ceiling on nylon fishing line so they appeared to be floating in the air. A right hand and a left hand – my right hand and my left hand – were posed as a pair, palms inwards and about thirty centimetres apart with the left slightly higher than the right, echoing the shape of Cam's hands on my waist the day before. The third hand was alone, its fingers pointing upwards and its palm facing out from the wall as though it was stopping traffic. They were hanging at shoulder height, swaying slightly in the breeze created by the passage of people around the room. Their palms were painted in the graduated dark and bright blues of a mazarine butterfly, their backs with the lace pattern of a black-veined white. The label tacked to wall the beneath them read *I'm In Your Hands by Cameron Hawe.*

'What do you think?' said Cam. He was smiling his easy smile, his teeth wiped free of my lipstick. But his eyes were locked onto mine so firmly that I couldn't look away.

'What happened to your found objects in boxes?' I managed. My cheeks were burning. The heat and noise in the shop were pressing in on me, making the ground tilt beneath my feet. My hands – the unpainted ones, the ones attached to my wrists – shook.

'Whose hands are they?' asked Stephanie. She had been examining them closely, had reached out to run her fingers over them. She held her left hand up to the lone right hand, palm to palm. 'They could almost be mine.'

Cam laughed. 'Just another student's,' he said. 'Ros, I was about to go and haul some more plonk out of the back room. The bar needs stocking up. Can you give me a hand?' The 'bar' was a trestle table borrowed from someone's dad. It was spattered with paint and dotted with plastic cups.

'I'll help,' said Freddy.

'No, no. We can't have our visitors doing all the hard work. Have a look round and get yourselves a drink. There's some orange juice left if you hurry.'

I had no choice but to follow him into the back room. I left the door ajar, but he reached around me to close it.

'Cam! What are you doing? My children are in there,' I whispered.

'Just a second. I've done nothing but think about you since yesterday. I just want a second with these.' He took my cold hands in his. He must have felt them trembling. 'The real things.'

I should have snatched back my hands but the heat of his fingers on my wrists travelled through me and pushed away my fear, chased away every thought that wasn't of him. His eyes clung to mine as he kissed my fingers, ran his tongue over my palms, slid my right thumb into his mouth.

I don't know when I would have stopped him if Toby hadn't opened the door, letting in the roar of voices from the shop space and making me snatch my hands from Cam's grip.

'Oh. Sorry,' Toby said, his eyes wide with shock or amusement. 'Just want to grab some wine. Bar's dry.'

'We'll bring it out, mate,' Cam said. Toby winked at him – actually *winked at him* – and shut the door.

'I have to go,' I said, wrapping my arms around myself. How long had we been in the storeroom? Had Stephanie and Freddy noticed the closed door? Had Toby whispered about what he had seen to Billy, who had whispered to Karen who had whispered to everyone else as she made her way around the room?

'When can I see you properly?'

'I don't know. It's . . .' I took a step away from him and reached for the door handle. I needed to get out of that room, back to Stephanie and Freddy. But Cameron had his hand on the door, holding it closed.

'Ros, please. I need to see you.' The familiar summer breeze warmth had gone from his voice. The plaintive neediness that had taken its place made me want to push my way out of the door and keep going. 'When? Ros?'

'After our tutorial on Friday,' I said.

'Friday.' The clouds lifted and he smiled his afternoon sunshine smile. He handed me three bottles of wine and followed me out.

I scanned the room for Stephanie and Freddy. They were with Karen and a girl I didn't recognise. I couldn't remember ever seeing Stephanie looking so relaxed, not even when I had snuck into her bedroom to watch her sleeping. Maybe that was what she was like when I wasn't around. As I set the bottles of wine on the bar a sudden gust of cold wind made me shiver. I looked up to see Dan standing just inside the door, the shoulders of his grey wool coat dusted with snow. He must have left work early and taken the train straight to Hatfield. In the moment before he saw me he looked tired and flat. Then his eyes found me and he smiled the smile he used at parties, the one that was big enough for everyone in the room. I should have walked towards him, away from Cam who was beside me at the bar, but I was too stunned by his arrival to think of that. In a few long strides Dan was in front of me and it was too late.

'I know people give actresses flowers but I wasn't sure about artists.' He held a vast bunch of long-stemmed roses towards me. There were at least forty flowers, each one the colour of clotted blood, of scabs on lips.

'Thank you. They're beautiful.' I moved to kiss him on the cheek but he pressed his hand to the back of my head and kissed me on the lips. The roses were heavy in my arms between us.

Behind me, from the end of the bar where Cam was standing, came the sound of a bottle being dropped.

As I shuffled around the gallery with Dan, Freddy and Stephanie, delivering hushed critiques of my fellow students' work and counting the seconds until we could leave, I felt Cam watching me. Twice I turned around to find him chatting to Stephanie but I couldn't hear what they were saying.

'Cam seems nice,' said Stephanie in the car on the way home. 'His hand sculptures are weird, though. Kind of beautiful but creepy at the same time.'

'Yes, I suppose they are,' I said, lowering my face into the bunch of roses on my lap.

'Is he a mature student?'

'Yes. There are a few of us.'

'He's not very mature though, is he? I mean, he can't be that much older than me.'

'He's older than he looks,' I said into the roses. 'Besides, I had two children in school by the time I was his age. I think I'd have called myself mature.' I wasn't sure if Stephanie had heard me. It wasn't something I had said out loud before; I had only whispered it silently inside my own head. It had sounded better in there.

Stephanie and I told Dan about Temperley together after dinner that night. It was how she had wanted to do it. We sat at the kitchen table while he stood over us.

'For fuck's sake. That's all we need,' he said. Stephanie and I flinched in unison. He turned away from us to face the wall, digging the fingers of both hands into the back of his head.

'Dan—' I started.

He turned back, holding his palm up to my face as though I was just a person in a crowd. 'How long have you known about this for, Stephanie?'

'I told her this morning.'

'You're saying that you didn't know before your mother told you?'

'No, Dad, I didn't.'

'Dan!'

She stood up and looked at Dan and then at me. 'Both of you need to stop bending yourselves out of shape about this. I told Mum earlier that Nate coming out isn't going to make any difference to me. I'm not going to let it.'

'What does that even mean, Stephanie? What the hell do you mean by that? You refuse to talk about this man – this pervert who ruined our lives – for *six years* and then you expect us not to worry when he's set free? You tell us not to "bend ourselves out of shape"? And Rosalind, is her telling you it won't make any difference good enough? After the thousands of hours you've spent imagining that you've seen him in the street, trying to convince me that he's just waiting to get his fangs into her again? After everything you put us through?'

I could sense Stephanie beside me, poised for flight. It had been a mistake to deliver the news to Dan like this: two against one. There was nothing he hated more than knowing less than everyone else in the room.

I took a step forwards to put myself between them. 'That's not what I said. But we've gone over this before. We always knew it would happen and we always knew we couldn't let it drag us down. We can get through this together. Can't we? Both of you? Can't we?'

'Yes.' Stephanie nodded. 'I've already said I'm not going to see him.'

'Dan, perhaps you should tell Stephanie what we know about the legal side of things. She should know her rights.' I was coaxing him onto solid ground. He had always dealt with Arthur Summers, the solicitor who advised us about Stephanie's situation. In the months after Temperley started his sentence, when we still feared some form of appeal, some wriggling out of the longer-than-expected time he had been ordered to serve, we had set about discovering what happened when a prisoner is released, what rights the victim has. I had not been reassured. Of course Temperley would be forbidden to harass his victim, but when had he ever cared about the law? It would just be another challenge to him.

Dan's anger subsided as he talked. He swiftly covered the possibilities of restraining orders. Most importantly of all, he said, Stephanie's right to anonymity in the media remained in place. If anyone threatened it, he would come down on them hard and they wouldn't know what had hit them. 'It would be best if you stayed here for the time being,' finished Dan. 'You can commute to university once the doctor says you're well enough.' Journalists staked out places like The Elms in the hope of catching a glimpse of a celebrity patient, a whiff of scandal. Dan must have weighed the discomfort of having Stephanie at home against the humiliation of exposure and abandoned his plan to send her away.

But Stephanie shook her head. 'I'm not going into hiding. I want to go back to London.'

'No.' Irritation pulsed in his voice. 'You saw some of the stuff they printed after the court case. Those journalists will come looking for you and it could get nasty.'

'So I'll deal with them. I'm not a child.'

'You don't understand. They're real scum. They'll do anything to get your story.'

'I won't talk to them.'

'Stephanie, I'm telling you they'll pressurise you and bully you until you give them what they want. You'll stay here until we know how the land lies.'

'Pressurise me and bully me? Gee, I can't imagine what that would be like, Dad.' She sat back in her chair and glared at him from beneath raised eyebrows. 'I'm not stupid, you know. You're not the only one here with a brain.'

'Yeah, well, you've done some pretty stupid things,' he said. I don't think he meant to say it. There was a tiny moment after the words left his mouth when his eyes widened in shock, but he didn't take it back immediately and then it was too late. The air between us thickened, crackled. The hairs on my arms stood up. A cloud was forming in the silence. It was a cumulonimbus, the type that brings lightning, blizzards and flash floods; weather that destroys houses and leaves people dead.

'And you haven't?' Stephanie said, leaning across the table towards him. She spoke slowly, letting each word land before throwing down the next one. 'You can't make me stay here. You can't make me do anything.'

Dan sat back in his chair. 'Stephanie. This is for your own good. You saw what the *Globe* did to Kitty Marks. You don't want to end up like her, do you?'

I didn't want Stephanie to return to London but I didn't want her here either: *he* knew where here was and that gave him power. He would be able to imagine her even if he couldn't see her. Perhaps he had even been in our house once, back then. Maybe they had sneaked in here at lunchtimes while Dan and I were at work and Freddy was at school. Maybe they had lain in her bed or our bed or both.

'I think we should go away,' I blurted. 'Me and Stephie. Not hiding, just a holiday. We could both do with a rest. And then the papers won't be a problem.'

Dan's head snapped round in surprise. 'Rosalind?'

'Stephanie's been through a lot and some sunshine could be just what she needs. I've seen a lovely place in the paper. And it would keep her out of the way of any journalists until they lose interest.' Out of the way of him and you and all of this. Out of the way of Cam and of this house where ripping off the wallpaper and replacing all of the furniture every two years did nothing to erase what lay beneath. 'If you wanted to, sweetheart?' I added, looking at Stephanie. 'It's up to you.'

'All right, gang?' Freddy said, banging through the door. 'Why's this door shut?' Stephanie and I had cornered Dan in the kitchen while Freddy watched a film next door. He pushed the pebble that wedged the door open back into place.

Dan stood up. 'Freddy, we're just discussing something with Stephanie. Could you give us a few minutes, please?'

'Oh, yeah. Don't mind me. I don't live here or anything.' He took two long steps backwards out of the room, pushed aside the pebble and let the door swing shut behind him.

'You didn't have to be like that with him, Dad,' said Stephanie.

'We're talking. This is important.'

'And Freddy's not a part of this?'

'No. Well, yes, of course. But—'

She stood up, her chair banging back into place on the flag-stones. Her eyes were bright, her skin as pale as the snow that beat against the window. I was so unused to seeing extremes of emotion on her face that it took me a moment to realise that she was furious. 'I think we've said all there is to say. Nate's coming out. I'm not going to see him. I won't talk to any jour-nalists. End of.'

'And you'll stay here for the next few weeks!' Dan called after her as she made for the door. She didn't even turn back to look at him. I realised that he was going to follow her, keep steam-rolling her until she agreed.

'Leave her, Dan. For God's sake, leave her.' He was a burning rush, lighting things around him. I needed to quell him before he burnt our house to the ground. I wanted to push him out of the back door and into the cold, wet snow.

'You saw the state she was in in London. She can't go back there with this hanging over her. I can just see the headlines now if they get wind of her drinking like that. I know they can't reveal her identity but everyone will know it's her.'

'Maybe. But shouting at her isn't the way. It never has been. You know what she's like.'

'I don't know what she's like and neither do you. She's a law unto herself. Have you ever known what she was thinking? Honestly?'

I thought of her as a baby, of the way I had always woken up half a minute before she had cried for me in the night, of the perfect stillness and warmth in the seconds between my eyes opening and her calling me to her side, and how Dan always slept through her cries. 'She doesn't respond to being bullied or treated like a child. I've spent days trying to reach out to her and she'll just go further into herself if you speak to her like that. She needs to know that we're on her side. That's the only chance we have to protect her from him. Her trust is the only thing we have.'

'If she even needs protecting from him. Surely she's too old for someone with his tastes now.'

'He's not the type to move on. Don't you see that? He won't give up.'

'What? You still think he's going to come after her, proposing marriage to save his reputation? That's ridiculous. Utterly ridiculous.'

'I just know he'll come after her. And I don't want him anywhere near her.'

'You don't know that. Really, Ros. You can't. What is certain is that the press will get hold of it and that will be rough for her.'

And for you, I thought. It had taken me years of marriage to realise the extent to which Dan's behaviour was driven by the way he saw himself in the eyes of others. Perhaps I loved him too much to see it at first. The way love lights a person up can do that: they become the brightest thing in the world, but that brightness can dazzle us so the harder we look the less we see.

It was when he insisted that we bought this house that I realised how important our status to the outside world had become
to him. While I was buried in my world of nappy changes and
rattles, soft hands and the drip, drip, drip of tiny anxieties about
unlocked doors and bath-time drownings, he had been propelling us down the path first to respectability then enviability.
Sometimes it felt as though I had closed my eyes in that dank
flat in Durham, my pregnant belly pinning me to the brown
Draylon sofa, and opened them again on a stage set playing the
part of the wife of a successful man. The cottage we had bought
when we moved from our flat in Finchley to St Albans had been
cripplingly expensive for us at the time. I loved that little house
with its wonky staircase and inglenook fireplace, its low front
door and Narnia lamp-post in the garden. We extended it to add
a third bedroom and I relaxed in the knowledge that we would
never need to move again. But after four years, when Dan's
salary had tripled and the bonuses had started to come in, he
decided it was too small and on the wrong side of the city. We
followed estate agents around a series of ever more expensive
houses. Month after month they grew bigger and grander and
closer to Crispin Avenue. One Saturday afternoon we stood with
an estate agent in the kitchen of what would become our home,
its rooms still thick with a dead man's possessions. Dan thought
it was perfect and wanted to snap it up straight away, whereas
I struggled to find anything to admire in its aggressively square
rooms and gloomy garden. I realised we were seeing the house
from different perspectives. He was looking not for a family
home but for a shopfront in which to display himself and us.
He loved the house for its size and its address. Later, I unpicked
the trail that led from me kissing Dan's cider-wet mouth at the
back of a pub in Durham when I was nineteen years old to me
standing next to him in that house on a fashionable street in
St Albans. I saw old memories with new eyes. I understood for

in case he accused me of fanning its flames. 'Try not shouting at her. Try looking her in the eye and remembering that she's twenty-one years old.'

'I do try. But she's so bloody stubborn. And we wouldn't be in this situation if she just hadn't done what she did. No one else's daughter had to run off with her damn teacher, did they?'

I rested my head on his shoulder so I didn't have to look at him. 'It wasn't her fault. You have to remember that. You have to forgive her.' Over the years people asked me again and again whether I would ever be able to forgive Temperley for what he had done. They asked Dan the same question. But no one ever asked us whether we would be able to forgive Stephanie.

* * *

Tanya told us that the police would complete their process of checks to confirm that Nathan Temperley was not innocent and afflicted in a hospital bed before they acted on the assumption that Stephanie was with him. 'It won't take long,' she said. 'They're throwing everything at it and you just need to sit tight for now. Inspector Haskins will be here soon.' I could tell that Tanya, like me, had already condemned Temperley; it was clear from the way she spat out his name and the fury stitched into her frown.

It felt as though we had been trapped in the sitting room for weeks. We kept the curtains drawn so the yellow light was unchanging from dawn to dusk. Dan had slept on the sofa the night before. I had left him there and crept upstairs to lie on the floor of Freddy's room, listening to him breathe and trying not to wake him. Beatrice had gone to the spare room once Freddy was asleep, but the drifting hint of tobacco on the landing as I crept past at three o'clock in the morning had told me that she was smoking out of the bedroom window.

At some stage during the previous day, in the time in which the police presence was slackest, the updates fewest and furthest between, I had discovered that I could no longer bear to be alone with Dan. When we were the only people in a room, I felt myself teetering on the edge of the abyss and knew that I was only seconds from falling in. In his face I saw an unspoken plea: *This is family stuff, your domain – fix it, Rosalind, fix it, please.* He sought me out whenever he could, drawing me into corners and taking my hand in his, following me ceaselessly from room to room as though he needed me in order to breathe. All the time he looked at me, begged me with his eyes.

'I'm going to have a quick shower,' I said. He started to pull himself up from the sofa. 'Wait here in case the inspector arrives.'

I turned the shower on full blast then pulled the door closed as I left our bathroom. I crept up the second flight of stairs to Stephanie's attic room. Inspector Haskins's team would do exactly what I was about to do but I needed to be the first.

Her computer was still at the police station and her desk was almost empty without it. There was a silver mesh pot of pens and pencils. In a Perspex box was the silver Mont Blanc pen Dan had given her as a reward for passing her maths GCSE a year early. He had come home with it on the day she got the result. 'Did you choose it?' she had asked him and cried when he told her that he had. Next to the pen was a pink heart-shaped eraser the size of my palm. I picked it up and felt the smoothness of its unused edges, smelled its artificial strawberry smell. I dropped it when I realised that I didn't know where it had come from, that it could be a gift from *him*. Memories pulled me back to that little room, the heat of his body beneath the table. I shook them from me; I didn't have much time.

Above the desk was a shelf carrying a rank of A4 ring binders. They were blue, grey, maroon, purple – all the colours that Stephanie loved, and each bore a neatly printed label. They were a world away from the tatty exercise books covered in wrapping paper that had carried my academic efforts, but then my efforts were a world away from Stephanie's. She typed her homework and coursework on the computer and handed in hard copies to be marked. Sometimes – only if I asked – she showed me an essay, the lines of black text glowing with red ticks, a neat dose of praise at the end: *Excellent work, Stephanie. Well written and thorough, Stephanie. Very good, Stephanie. Well done, Stephanie . . . You silly fool, Stephanie. How could you, Stephanie? Where are you, Stephanie? Did you do it because of me, Stephanie?*

The folder labelled *Geography – Year 11* was purple, her favourite colour of all. I heard his voice in my mind as clearly as if he was standing behind me, whispering in my ear – *She gets her looks from you.* My hands shook as I reached up to the shelf and pulled the folder towards me. As I lay it on the desk I knocked over the pot of pens, sending its contents clattering across the floor. I froze and listened for a moment but there was still no sound of Dan's tread on the stair.

The year's work in geography started with *Module 9.1: Tectonic Plates.* There were two typed essays interwoven with sheets of lined paper on which Stephanie had made her notes in class. I had never before noticed how similar her handwriting was to Dan's: the same angular scratching, lower case letters cramped into the bottom third of each line dwarfed by capital letters which spilled outwards, bursting free of their cages. In Stephanie's purple ink her writing would not have looked out of place in a book of spells.

She had always doodled. It was a tiny trait – perhaps the only one – we shared. Sheets of paper, old envelopes and shopping lists left within her reach were quickly reefed with flowers, stars, eyes, trees and the logo of Kings of Leon, her favourite band. Finishing exercises quickly, she often found time to doodle in class and it had been one of the few things her teachers had complained about. But the doodles in her geography folder were different. From the first page they were littered with nothing but sketches of facial features. The same eyes, nose and mouth were repeated over and over again. There was the fall of a dark lock of hair across a brow, a jawbone shaded with stubble. There were bits of him everywhere. There were hearts too, but I couldn't bear to look at those. *Bad work, Stephanie.*

The first assignment was about plate margins. Destructive margins, constructive margins and collision zones were mysteries to me, but not to my daughter, it seemed. This splitting of the earth into jigsaw pieces was not what had passed for geography when I was at school. A few red ticks peppered the two pages of text and diagrams. At the end Temperley had written *A+ Very good. Excellent diagrams.* Beneath this he had added a picture of a smiling face scrawled without a fraction of the care that Stephanie had taken in sketching his features. His writing was looping and feminine. I pictured a red biro gripped in the blunt fingers of his right hand. I turned the pages carefully to avoid touching any of his ink.

The second assignment was a case study about tectonic activity and the formation of fold mountains in the Alps. Four pages long, it was slathered in inky red praise. He liked the colours she had used in her diagrams and her use of the word 'contorted'. *Room for improvement B+. Let's have a quick chat about this after class.* Stephanie never got a B, considered an A minus to be an abject failure, and where was the room for improvement to be found between all the points he had highlighted to admire? The assignment was dated the twentieth of September.

September was always a bad month for me. I found the transition from school holidays to term time unsettling, and that September had been worse than most. Dan was away a lot, either working abroad or in London, it hardly made any difference. When he was at home he was quiet and unengaged, gliding over the surface of family life like a pond skater. We had argued about it during the first week of term. I remembered the day he called me a neurotic shrew and I heard a door slam upstairs and realised too late that Stephanie and Freddy had been perching on the landing listening to us. Later, Beatrice and I called that time the Autumn of Discontent.

When I looked back at the page, Temperley's ink was wet and running like blood, the pigment unpicked from the paper by my tears.

In the first week of October, Stephanie studied *Module 9.2: Volcanoes and Earthquakes*. Her notes on volcanoes were covered in squiggled trees with heart-shaped leaves. She drew fireworks exploding in pencil-shaded skies. The police had searched her room. How had they failed to see this? How had they not known? She received an A+ for her essay on the processes involved in volcanic eruption. He had added two ticks to the sentence *Volcanoes occur where weaknesses in the Earth's crust allow magma, ash, gas and water to erupt onto the land.* He had highlighted the sentence *Build-up of pressure over time is finally released in a volcanic eruption.* Next to a paragraph about dormant volcanoes he had added a note and yet another smiley face: *Dormant volcanoes always pose a risk to the people living nearby.* I began to crave the sound of Dan's footsteps, the touch of Tanya's cool hands on my arm, Inspector Haskins and her evidence bags, but I couldn't stop reading.

Stephanie's notes on earthquakes were different. The pages were topped with a thick bank of grey clouds. There was a lone tree on a mountain, its last heart-shaped leaf twirling towards the ground. The next week there was nothing but spirals, their ever-decreasing circles carving deep grooves into the paper. Stephanie received an A+ for her essay on predicting and responding to earthquakes. He had given her a tick for her diagram of fault lines and added a single note: *The intensity of shock waves decreases with distance from the epicentre*. It was dated the week before the October half-term. We had spent the break in Sicily, Dan dropping out at the last minute when work made it impossible for him to travel. Stephanie had been irritable and distant and I thought it was because of Dan's absence. She had obsessively read a series of books about vampires and squabbled with Freddy in the car as we wound our way up Etna's side in the driving rain.

Module 10.1 was *The Movement of Population*. Here again on the first page of notes were his features, separated and scrawled in margins. There was a nose, an eye, three pairs of all-too-familiar lips. A sun ray shot out from a page edge and spread across an entire sheet. I held my breath as I leafed through Stephanie's scrawl about the plight of ageing populations, tourism and refugees sprinkled with hearts shed from tiny clouds. I went back to the beginning and read what she had written again. I moved on to an assignment covered in his red pen.

'Ros, I didn't know where you'd gone. You left the shower on. What are you doing in here? Inspector Haskins needs to ask you some questions.' Dan was standing in the door, his feet jigging with impatience. For a moment I was trapped in silence, unable to take my hands off Stephanie's geography folder and powerless to put into words what I had found. I thought of the pretty girl in the ugly woollen hat alone in a service station in the middle of the night. I looked at the poster of the bridge above Stephanie's cold, empty bed. I felt myself teetering on the edge of that bridge, I felt myself starting to fall.

'Get Inspector Haskins up here. And Sarah, get Sarah.' He was still moving towards me, unwilling to leave the room without me at his side. 'Dan! Right now! Bring her up here!'

It was all there in black and white, in Temperley's red and Stephanie's purple. It was an assignment on Urban to Rural Migration. Under the subtitle *Advantages and Disadvantages of*

Urban to Rural Migration, Stephanie had created a neat table. There were many advantages typed within it: *Lower housing costs, fresh air, wide open spaces, rural pursuits and new opportunities.* To this he had added in his red, girlish font: *Freedom from oppression, distance from family = less stressful lifestyle and opportunity to start again.* Under disadvantages Stephanie had typed just one thing: *People left behind may suffer.* Beneath this he had added *Move must be permanent, there can be no going back.* Below his scrawl she had added three purple kisses.

FIVE DAYS

'Ros! Ros! Come and look at this.' Dan's hissed whisper dragged me into wakefulness. Our bedroom door was open and I could see him on the landing peering into the round window that overlooked the front garden. We had stayed up after Stephanie and Freddy had gone to bed. We had drunk a bottle of wine with grim determination as I tried once again to make him understand my fear of Temperley. He listened, or at least he let me talk. I told him about the letter. I nearly told him about my visit to the prison but realised just in time that the fact I had sneaked off to Wandsworth and failed to mention it for three years wouldn't help my cause. Dan was torn, I knew, between believing what I told him – believing in my fear for Stephanie – and knowing how many times my fear had been misplaced. However reasoned my arguments were, they couldn't erase his memory of the trip to Palma I had ruined by refusing to get on the plane because I was convinced that a woman glimpsed in the queue to board was a terrorist. He couldn't forget the time he had arrived home from a week-long work trip to New York to discover that I had kept Stephanie and Freddy off school for four days because of a classroom shooting in Texas, or the fallout from the trip to Stratford-Upon-Avon. He couldn't forget the times I had pulled Stephanie out of school because I was sure I had seen Temperley in the street, or the day I crashed my car into a bollard with Freddy in the back because a dark-haired road worker had looked so familiar. So Dan listened and he nodded, but I don't know what he heard. Before we went to bed I made my case for whisking Stephanie away on holiday. The more I thought about it the more I was sure it was the right thing to do.

I felt the wine running thickly through my veins as I got out of bed and pulled on my dressing gown. The air was frigid and I walked through clouds of my own breath on my way to join Dan.

'Look!' He tapped the window. 'What the hell is that? And what's it doing on my lawn?'

I pressed my forehead to the window and let my eyes adjust to the gloom. A long, low shape had been carved out of a heap of snow in the front garden. Bathed in the orange light of the street lamp, it curved across the octagonal lawn, a head clearly visible at one end and a tail at the other. Four short legs spread from the body, giving the impression that the creature was frozen in the act of scuttling across the ground. It was Gaudí's lizard scooped up from beneath the blazing sun of Barcelona and shrouded with snow in my garden. It was Cam, painted across the front lawn.

'Oh! Why is that there?' I said. In the flickering orange light I thought I saw a leg move, the twitch of a tail. I took a step back from the window. I shivered.

'I have no idea. Some idiot has strolled into our front garden and built a dragon out of snow on the lawn. Why would anyone do that?'

'Has anyone been in the house? Is anything missing?' Cam wouldn't have broken in but I needed Dan to leave me for a moment so I could gather my thoughts. Did he know? Could he? Had he arrived at Going, going, gone! earlier than I had realised and stood at the window unnoticed as I disappeared into the storeroom with Cam? I heard him opening and closing doors, testing handles and moving curtains before he ran back up the stairs to my side. I peered out of the window. The street beyond the garden was perfectly still.

'There's no sign that they came anywhere near the house. Nothing's missing and no one's been round the back.'

I stepped away from the window, worried that he would read the truth in the reflection of my face. 'I think I heard something about this a few years ago. There's a bunch of people who go around making snow sculptures in unexpected places. They call it snowbombing. They do it with knitting too – they knit covers for telephone boxes and giant tea cosies to put over buildings. It's a kind of guerrilla art thing.'

'Really? So why do it in my garden instead of the park?'

'Well, I guess it wouldn't be very guerrilla to do it in a public space. And look at the way they've positioned it right under the street light for maximum dramatic effect. I wonder if they've done any more on the avenue.' Of course 'they' hadn't.

He was leaning forwards to take another look, already losing a degree of tension from his forehead. That was what made Dan and me different: if someone handed us both a nice, convenient solution to a problem he accepted it gratefully while I donned protective gloves and picked it apart bit by bit, looking for the nasty little catch hidden inside.

'It's actually pretty good but the last thing we need right now is a bunch of weirdoes creeping around the garden at night,' he said.

'You don't need to tell me that.'

'It's probably someone from your exhibition.'

The shock was like a handful of snow being plunged down the back of my dressing gown. Had he seen the text messages? Found my sketches of Cam's hands and noticed the extra time I was spending at university? 'Why do you say that?'

'It's the type of thing you art students are meant to do, isn't it? And they were all sloshed by the time we left.'

'Oh. Yes. But I don't think they'd have come all the way over here. None of them live in St Albans.' I dragged my face into a smile. Of course he didn't know. What was there *to* know? Some coffees and text messages fuelling hours of daydreaming; an empty-nester with too much time on her hands and too much caffeine in her veins letting her imagination run away with her. And a kiss. And fingers sliding over skin, and heat, so much heat passing from one to the other and back again.

I flinched when Dan put his hands on my shoulders. He stooped to put his face level with mine. 'Hey, don't worry about it, Ros. It's just a silly prank. It's nothing to do with Temperley. We've still got nearly a week until we need to worry about him sneaking around the garden, if we need to worry about it at all.' He pulled me towards him, pressing me into his chest. The bright scent of the lavender linen water that our cleaner, Marie, used on his shirts filled my nose and fizzed on my tongue. For years it had been my job to iron those shirts, to spray the water from its blue glass bottle onto the wrinkled whiteness then pass the iron over the droplets to fill the room with the ghost of sun-baked lavender. Ironing my husband's shirts for work felt like a grown-up thing to do back when we were still playing at having the lives of adults. Dan had started his job as a trainee management consultant with its paltry wage and promise of better things to come. We were living in the flat in grimy Finchley, Stephanie becoming less of a baby and more of a toddler every day. There had been pinches of shame during my unresisting slide into the closeted life of a nineteen fifties housewife. It wasn't what my mother had wanted for me, wasn't what a generation of women had fought for. At first I made a joke of it to friends from university whose fledgling careers were already carrying them away from me. I talked about how I would return to university when Stephanie started school. Then I had Freddy. Eventually, I picked up the sketchbooks and pencils that had lain unused since I met Dan. I took classes in life drawing and portraiture in the afternoons and called myself an art student instead of a housewife. I filled my sketchbooks with snapshots of Stephanie and Freddy, the laundry baskets, saucepans and supermarket aisles that were the landscape of my days. I made vague noises about doing a degree in illustration and going into advertising once the children were older. In the meantime I had Stephanie and Freddy all day and Dan all night and a hundred little domestic chores with which to pad my cell. I wouldn't have admitted it to anyone but I enjoyed ironing Dan's shirts. For years, whenever I had to do anything I was anxious about – a PTA meeting, a driving test, a mums and babies group – I would iron the lavender water into the sleeve of my cardigan so I could fortify myself with his smell.

'Yes, you're right. I'm just tense.' Tense with the knowledge that my almost-lover had serenaded me with snow as I slept obliviously in Dan's warmth.

His chin tapped the top of my head as he nodded. 'Maybe you should go away with Stephie for a while,' he said, as though it was his idea. 'I don't know about Thailand but I think a holiday for the two of you would be good.'

'I'll see if I can convince her.' We would go somewhere with no snow, where our feet would leave no prints.

'OK. Good.' He was already detaching himself from me. Mentally he was halfway to the station, checking email on his BlackBerry as he walked. 'Ring me if you need anything. I'll have my phone on and I won't let it out of my sight.'

I stayed at the window as he walked down the path. He didn't tread tentatively across the snow as most people would, but forged onwards confidently with long strides, as though his leather-soled shoes allowed him to hover two inches above the slippery ground. I held my breath when he paused by the snow sculpture. He bowed closer then shook his head, straightened up and carried on. As soon as he closed the garden gate, I went back to our room and pulled on jeans and a jumper. At the door I shoved my feet into wellies and zipped my down coat up to my chin.

The cold hit me like a gale, the frigid air stinging my cheeks and crackling like popping candy in my mouth. It was too extreme, too elemental for the suburbs, as though I had been dropped onto the Arctic tundra or the hostile surface of an alien planet. I went back into the house to wrap a scarf around my face.

Up close, Cam's sculpture was even more impressive than it had looked from the window. It was beautiful, glittering in the weak winter light. Four feet long, it wound sinuously across the lawn, its skin dotted with triangular scales stamped into the surface of the tightly packed snow. I knelt beside it and traced the scales on its tail, ran my hands over the rise and fall of its arched back. How had he done this without waking us up? We must have slept deeply, washed far from the shores of conscious-ness on tides of wine and worry. An image kept presenting itself to me: Dan in his boxer shorts confronting Cam, fury etched into the wrinkles of his face, white hairs mixed with the blond ones on his chest and the recently forged paunch of his stomach rising above his waistband as he shouted. I imagined Cam kneeling in the snow, laughing as he shaped claws and scales with his ungloved hands.

I shuffled round to the head of the lizard, my knees aching with cold where the wet snow had bled through my jeans as I knelt. Its head was less well-formed than its tail. Perhaps he had started to lose his nerve. Or maybe his fingers were numbed to clumsiness by the chill of the snow and the air. The only spots of colour on the creature's body were two bright green discs placed where its eyes would be. I leant forwards to examine them but still it took me a moment to understand what I was looking at: two pistachio macarons grown soggy in the snow, their colour leaching away from them. *Stay, Ros. Just for a bit. I've got coffee and pistachio macarons back here. We can just talk.* The realisation made me stumble. I put my hands out to steady myself and landed heavily on the lizard, my gloved hand punching a hole in the ridge of its back. I slipped again, the compacted snow glass-like beneath my feet, and crushed a delicate clawed leg with my elbow.

Back on my feet, I looked up to see Stephanie at the landing window where Dan and I had stood, her forehead pressed against the glass. She wasn't looking at me, but past me and into the road beyond. Quickly, I bent over and scooped the green biscuits from the ruins of the sculpture's head and threw them into a clump of ferns beside the path. When I turned around Stephanie was shivering in the open front door.

'Mum. What's that? Did you make it?'

'No. We think it was some kind of prankster.' I turned away from her as I spoke the lie, scanning the garden for anything I had missed.

'Someone built a snow dragon in our garden in the night for a joke?'

'I guess so. I heard about them once. People who build snow sculptures in random places.' It sounded weaker every time I said it. I forced myself to look at her and registered the panic in her eyes.

'But there was someone there. Over by the postbox. They were watching the house.'

'Are you sure?'

'I think so. Yes.'

'Go inside. I'll be in in a sec.' Had Cam been there, watching as Dan and I looked out of the window? Perhaps we had been so focused on ourselves and each other that I had failed to notice him as we embraced. But the night before, in the gallery, I had been so aware of his eyes lying heavily on me as I showed Dan around, the roses weighing down my every step. I would have felt Cam's presence, I would have known if he was there. I walked out of the gate and stood in the street. Four houses down, a man dug snow from the drive of number seven. Nothing else moved. It was unnaturally quiet and still for half past eight in the morning.

'Morning, Rosalind. How's poor Stephanie today?' It was Pete from number four. He was wearing a bright yellow ski jacket, his gold-rimmed spectacles glinting from beneath its hood.

'She's still down with the flu,' I said. 'It's a nasty case. It's awfully quiet out here. Where is everyone?'

'The schools are closed because of the snow so there's no school run. It's health and safety gone mad, if you ask me, not that anyone does. I've done my usual morning circuit twice and haven't bumped into a soul apart from you and David at number seven.'

On the way back up the path, I picked up a handful of snow and smoothed over the lizard's eye sockets, rubbing away any trace of the macarons' green dye.

Inside, I peeled off my coat and scarf and hung them on the hall stand. Stephanie was in the kitchen with her back against the Aga, lifting one bare foot and then the other to press against the warm metal doors. She was running the nails of her right hand up and down her left wrist, leaving bright trails across her skin.

'Did you see anyone?'

'No one. Are you sure someone was watching the house? They weren't just waiting for a lift or something?'

'He was just standing there. I'm sure he was looking at the house. Then I think he must have seen me because he walked off.'

'What did he look like?' *Tall with caramel hair and long fingers? Twenty-five years old with the ghosts of crow's feet around his deep blue eyes? Did he smell of sandalwood and summer?*

'I couldn't see his face. He had a hood pulled up.'

'It was probably our snowbomber wanting to see what we made of his handiwork. Or one of their mates coming by for a look.' Or no one at all. Pete hadn't seen anyone. Seeing a strange man watching our house would have made his day. It would have been enough to bring him to our door to ring the bell and angle for coffee.

'Nate's about to come out and there are suddenly people messing around in our garden and watching our house? What if Dad's right and it was a journalist, Mum? What if they already know he's getting out?'

'A journalist would have knocked on the door. They're not exactly shy.'

But she wasn't reassured. 'I should call Sarah and see if anyone's been there looking for me.' I only had to tell her about Cam to take away her anxiety. *Darling, it probably wasn't a journalist, it was probably the man you met last night, the one who made plaster casts of my hands. Yes, those were my hands. I've been flirting with him for weeks. I've kissed him twice. If you hadn't come home I might have done a lot more.*

I had taken her place at the Aga. I shuffled along to let her lean beside me when she came back with her phone in her hand.

'Sarah says no one's been there. Even Jake has given up going round looking for me. Thank God.' But she didn't look relieved. She looked sad and empty, small and broken.

'It couldn't have been Jake outside, could it? He seems very keen on you.'

She leant back, shaking her head and letting her hair fall over her face. 'He wouldn't have made that snow dragon.'

'But watching the house? Could that have been Jake?' Maybe it didn't make sense for Cam to have lingered in the road. Why go to all the trouble of making the lizard appear from nowhere in the middle of the night only to stand in the street like a peeping Tom and spoil the mystery? It would be like a conjuror making cards disappear while wearing see-through sleeves. Maybe.

'No, he wouldn't do that. He doesn't even know where we live. I never had any reason to tell him.' I wondered what Jake looked like and what he wanted from Stephanie. I almost felt sorry for him until I remembered the way she had shuffled towards the bathroom in London, bruised and scraped, swaying as she leant on my arm. It would have been easy enough for Jake to find our address. Besides, who knew what she had slurred at him over a glass of wine or a bottle of vodka?

As I leant against the Aga next to her, my fingers prickling with the rapid return of warmth, I felt them all gathering around me, watching with questioning eyes: Cam, Jake, Dan. Most of all I felt Temperley drawing nearer. I didn't believe Stephanie when she said she wouldn't see him. She meant it when she said it but it wouldn't be up to her. I saw in that instant how it would happen: he wouldn't jump out of bushes and surprise her or harass her at home, he would reel her in gently, chip away slowly so that when he pushed he would find her yielding. There would be statements to newspapers of love and remorse. There would be a subtle shift in the wind and Stephanie would be blown by it too. She was like a castle with towering walls, its battlements thick with archers, its moat full of sharks – impenetrable until she lowered the drawbridge and threw open the doors so he could walk right in. She had tried to tell me that his release was insignificant but I could see now that she was more panicked even than me. Perhaps it was what Dan had said about journalists tracking her down that had worried her, but perhaps it was worse than that: perhaps it was the thought of Temperley himself and what he might do. Worse still, of course, perhaps it was the thought of Temperley and what *she* might do.

I swallowed. 'I'm going to call Tanya. Just in case. I'm going to ask her what she thinks about us going away.'

Stephanie pulled her dressing gown around herself and nodded.

I remember reading in a magazine that relationships, romantic and friendly, forged in extreme circumstances – amongst fellow hostages, on ships lost at sea – never last. Once the highs of fear and adrenalin that drove two people together are replaced by the mundane rhythms of everyday life, they drift apart. But that wasn't how it happened with Tanya and me. There was no drifting. I clung to her until she prised herself free of my grip. Even then I didn't give up. I couldn't. Tanya was the only person who understood that it wasn't over, that there were no walls thick enough, no prison sentence long enough to let me consign Nathan Temperley to the past. Tanya's official role had been to support us while Stephanie was missing and keep us abreast of the case against Temperley once he was caught, but she had done more than that. She had barged her way through doors and wriggled into gaps until she knew everything about him, and she had shared it all with me. She warned us to be on our guard, to be vigilant and never to underestimate him. Dan called her a man-hater but I knew the story of the long scar that ran down her face and knew that she had good reason to hate men, but that she didn't hate them at all. She feared them, and that was a very different thing. Even after the court case, when her official involvement had come to an end, she was there for me, meeting me for coffees and the occasional drink. She was always there on the phone when I needed to talk, and I needed to talk a lot. As the months lurched onwards and Stephanie settled back into school, what had happened began to fade into the past for other people – even for Dan – but not for me. People stopped asking me whether Stephanie was OK. When I brought up Temperley, Dan and – later – even ever-loyal Bea would change the subject. But Tanya wouldn't. When Dan asked me to stop spending time with Tanya, said that it was stopping all of us from moving on, I doubted his motives. He just wanted Tanya out of the way to make our pretence that none of it had ever happened complete, just as he had wanted to ship Stephanie off to school in Shropshire. But it wasn't long after that that I had noticed Tanya starting to detach herself from me. She took longer to reply to text messages, stopped returning my calls. She was always busy when I invited her round for coffee or out for a drink. One day she rang and told me she was so bogged down with work that she thought I should find someone else to talk to. I should have taken the hint, but I didn't. It was when I waited outside the police station and tried to talk to her as she arrived for work one morning that she finally laid it on the line for me: *Stop ringing me, Rosalind, you're not my job any more. I can't help you.* Her words were blunt and hard, but there was sadness in her face. I wanted to know whether Dan had forced her hand or whether our friendship running beyond the court case was in some way improper, had perhaps caused her trouble at work. But I didn't have the chance to ask. The police station door swung shut between us and I had not seen her since. I missed her. At first it was the same jolting sense of loss repeated over and over again that I had felt when my mother died. Countless times a day I would think of something I wanted to tell her only to realise that I couldn't. It faded, eventually, but it never went away.

She picked up on the second ring. Half an hour later she was at the front door in the same sleek black suit and flat shoes-that-are-almost-trainers she had worn on her first visit to the house six years earlier. She was coatless but un-shivering, untouched by the bitter cold. The highlights in her long hair were brighter than I remembered, her brown eyes more kohled and her lips a deeper shade of red. Her scar seemed to have retreated into her skin. We eyed each other for a moment. A blink, a tiny movement of her head, told me that she was surprised by what she saw.

'Ros, I don't have long. You've probably seen the situation with the girl over in Kings Langley?' I shook my head. I hadn't watched the news or even checked the headlines on my phone for days. 'It's a nasty case and she's one of mine.' A pang of jealousy. Familiar jealousy. *I need you more.*

I took her into the kitchen where we had spent so many hours together. As she looked around, I realised the room was unrecognisable to her. The sleek modern units, copper saucepans and Italian industrial steel table that had all stood witness to Stephanie's disappearance had been erased, like everything else from that time. Half of the back wall had been knocked out and bi-folding doors and the huge red Aga installed in its place.

Stephanie hovered by the kettle, fussing with boxes of tea. She turned and smiled when she saw Tanya and for a moment I thought she would reach out to her, extend her arms for a hug, but then she froze.

'Stephanie. You look well,' Tanya said. 'Shall we all sit down?' She pulled out a chair at the head of the table, folded her hands in front of her to wait for us. I breathed. I wasn't the responsible adult in the room any more. 'So. Just a few days to go until Nathan Temperley comes out. How do you feel about that, Stephanie?' She always sped towards the kernel of an issue, never wasting time on pleasantries.

Stephanie shrugged. She was fifteen again, sinking down in her chair, avoiding our eyes. She took a coin out of her pocket – a twenty pence piece – and slid it from hand to hand across the table, just as she had done the morning before. Tanya continued to stare at her. I looked at the table. Eventually, Stephanie spoke. 'I just don't want any trouble. I don't want anyone bothering me or my family. I just want to be left alone.'

'OK,' said Tanya. 'And what about Nathan? Ros says he wrote to you?'

'What about him? He's nothing to do with me. He can look after himself.' She wound her arms around herself, looked into her tea and then out of the window. The silence rolled on. Tanya was good at waiting. Better than me. I cracked.

'She doesn't want to see him,' I said. 'But there's something else. Stephanie thought she saw someone watching the house today.'

'Well it can't have been him. It could be a journalist. They'd be over the moon if you waived your right to anonymity and sold your story, Stephanie. But you're not going to do that, are you?'

She shook her head. 'Never. That's the last thing I want.'

'Good girl. I didn't think you would. And it's not as though you need the money.'

'I think we should go away. I wondered what you thought about that? I could take Stephanie abroad for a couple of weeks.' I held my breath, hoping that my instinct had been right.

The lines of tension around Tanya's mouth softened slightly. 'I think that's the best thing you can do. If he does anything stupid it's likely to be as soon as he gets out and it'll give the papers time to find something else to write about. Take yourselves away for a couple of weeks and give people time to forget about him again. I'll keep my ear to the ground and see if he shows up around here.'

'Thank you, Tanya. Thank you so much.' Her approval was a prize, her answer a gift. We would go, Stephanie and I, and leave them all behind us. Why should we come back after two weeks, or even three? Maybe we could just keep going, bouncing around the world from port to port until we forgot what it was that we had left behind.

Tanya was already standing up and preparing to leave. 'You've got my number. Call me if you need to.' She reached into a pocket and pulled out a small white card. 'Here, Stephanie. Take this. Just in case you want to get hold of me. I'm here if you want to talk or if there's anything you need help with.'

'Thank you.' She placed the card in front of her and studied it until Tanya left the room.

'Thank you for coming,' I said on the doorstep. 'I know you didn't have to. You probably didn't want to.'

'Have you had official notification of his release yet?'

'Nothing.'

'The prison service is a bloody shambles. Between the system's incompetence, these ever-decreasing sentences and the rights of the bastards themselves, victims are just trampled underfoot. I see it every day and it makes me sick. If it wasn't for a few good souls still in the forces, none of us would have known about this. That's why I got in touch with you. I just don't trust them. Someone has to think of the victim.'

'Tanya.' I wanted to pull her and her anger back inside the house. I wanted to bind her to me, to tell her everything: Stephanie, Cam, Jake, Dan. I wanted to purge myself of secrets and unspool myself at her feet.

'I'm glad you're taking this seriously, Ros. How's Dan?'

'Much as ever. He thinks I'm overreacting.'

'I don't think you are. There's unfinished business between those two. I'm not sure he'll be prepared to let it lie.' For a second her hand was on my arm, as cool as I remembered it. 'You're doing the right thing, Ros. I've got to go.' I watched her hurrying down the path, quick steps planted confidently on the treacherous rink of snow. She paused for a second and took in the crushed churn of lizard on the front lawn but didn't look back.

I texted Dan: **Spoke to Tanya. She thinks getting away with Stephanie a good idea. Looking into options now. Love you xxx**

His reply came within seconds: **Sounds like the best plan then. Let me know if you need anything. Love to all xxx**

I wished we could leave immediately, just get in the car, drive to Heathrow and look at the departures board until something took our fancy: Miami, Rhodes, Marrakesh. Or one of those unknown places: St John's, Dalaman, Astana. We would take no luggage. I would stop at the bank on the way, drain our current account and fill a suitcase with fifty-pound notes. We would send goodbye text messages from the airport then grind our mobile phones into powder beneath the heels of our shoes.

Of course it couldn't work like that. Stephanie had to see the doctor again and the only appointment available was at five past ten on Thursday, the next day. I hoped we could get away on Thursday evening on a late flight that would whisk us through the darkness and deliver us into sunshine as we slept.

When I asked her where she would like to go she said she didn't mind. She was restless, squirming in her chair as I showed her pictures of hotels, beaches, cities and mountains on the iPad. Glittering seas and marble-white beaches began to blur into each other, their iridescent blues and improbable jades flashing before my eyes even when I looked away from the screen. She picked her phone up every few minutes and turned it over in her hands.

'Short haul would be better with my tablets,' she said. 'I don't want to get all out of whack with the time while I'm still getting used to them.' I couldn't argue with that. Thailand disappeared behind a cloud.

'Rome,' I said. 'There's a beautiful hotel up in the hills above the city. It's pretty warm there for this time of year and it's only an hour's time difference.'

'Sounds good. Perfect.'

'Or Corsica. They're having a heatwave. Look, Stephie – this place looks amazing.' It was a luxury hotel in Calvi, on the north-east of the island. Twenty 'guest bungalows' nestling beneath the mountains, overlooking the azure sea and sparkling yachts in the port. 'They only have the Queen Suite available but I'm sure we'll manage.' It was the second most expensive suite in a five-star hotel. It had its own plunge pool and hot tub. Even the bathroom had two chandeliers. She barely glanced at the pictures.

'Cool. Let's go there.'

I booked it. There were only two direct flights to Calvi a week and the next left Heathrow at nine o'clock on Friday morning. By the time Temperley took his first breath of fresh air we would be racing away from him, the Corsican sun already warming our faces.

* * *

People often liken a great shock to being hit by a train, but the realisation that Stephanie had run away with Nathan Temperley was more like being caught in a crocodile's death roll. It grabbed me by the throat, pulled me under the thick green waters of its swamp and held me down until I wished for oblivion. Then it relaxed its grip and let me surface to fill my lungs with hope before pulling me back down, its teeth finding new flesh to puncture with every roll.

My strength was leaving me minute by minute. I was sandwiched between Inspector Haskins and Tanya on the sofa, their shoulders the only thing holding me up. We had gone over it again and again, the inspector scribbling in her leather-bound notebook, angling it away from me so I couldn't see what was written there. Did she mention liking Temperley? Did she talk about him a lot? Had he ever come to the house? Had he ever rung the house? Had I ever suspected anything?

I answered no. No. No. No. No and no.

Dan was sitting opposite me, his fingers bunching his woollen jumper, teasing at his hair. I could feel his ability to contain his anguish being chipped away with every question from the police and every denial from me.

'She didn't know, for Christ's sake,' he snapped, making me jump. 'She didn't know anything. She didn't notice anything. Can't you understand that?'

'Well, did you, Mr Simm? Did you notice anything unusual about your daughter and her teacher?' Tanya said. I had started to get up, to go to Dan, but she seized my wrist and held me in place.

Inspector Haskins coughed.

'Sorry,' said Tanya. She pressed her fingers to her lips as if to remind herself not to step out of her role again. She was there to support us. Both of us.

'No, I didn't. I never even met the man,' he said. 'Rosalind did, though.'

I didn't want to talk about the ten minutes spent in that hot little room, Temperley's eyes on my bare shoulders, the strength in his hands, the way I had let him beckon me forwards then push me back. I felt the pull of his dark eyes and recalled the way that they never left mine as he loosened his tie. But they all looked at me expectantly until I started to speak. 'Only once. At parents' evening. He said she was a very good student. He hoped she would go on and do A level geography.'

'Bastard,' Tanya whispered under her breath for only me to hear.

'You didn't like him though, did you?' said Dan.

I cursed the power of his memory. 'He seemed arrogant. And he made a remark about Stephanie and me looking alike.'

'You didn't tell me that,' said Dan.

'People say it all the time. You know they do.'

'So you weren't suspicious?' said Inspector Haskins.

'No.' I closed my eyes. The crocodile turned again, biting harder and drawing me deeper beneath the water than ever before. In that moment, I pictured them: they lay side by side, Stephanie curled into his arms, strands of her hair spilling across the skin of his chest. His lips were at her ear, telling her the tale of when he met her mother. Then I felt the press of a hand on my shoulder, pulling me back. Tanya. 'Don't think about him. Think of Stephanie, Rosalind. Only think of her.'

The tone of the police investigation shifted immediately. They wouldn't state publicly that Stephanie was with Temperley but, on the morning of the fifth day after she went missing, they launched a campaign to find 'twenty-nine-year-old Nathan Alan Temperley for urgent questioning in relation to the disappearance of fifteen-year-old Stephanie Simm, a pupil at the school where he teaches.' Everyone knew what that meant. Behind closed doors, Inspector Haskins stopped entertaining any doubt. Her professional caution evaporated and her statements of 'if she is with him' and 'assuming they're together' were dropped. He stopped being 'Nathan Temperley' and became 'Temperley'. When she thought we were out of earshot, he was 'that bastard'. A flood of things happened at once: the pupils and teachers at the school were interviewed, Sarah was questioned, his flat was searched. We stayed in the house. We waited.

'There's some stuff on her computer that we think you should see,' said Sergeant King, arriving later that afternoon. 'Inspector Haskins will meet us at the station.'

'What is it?' said Dan.

My mind raced through possibilities: photos of him, of her, of them. A diary full of the gory details – today he kissed me, he touched me *here*. I shuddered.

'We're not exactly sure. Graphs we think you might understand. We don't know what they mean.' Tanya offered to stay with Freddy and I was grateful but jealous; I wanted her with me.

The sergeant drove, whisking us down Victoria Street and into a car park in front of the station. Dan and I didn't speak during the journey. I had sketched the police station once for a project on urban landscapes. I had been amused by the contrast between the grey concrete of the blocky seventies building and the moat of bright spring flowers planted at its base. *The attempt to separate the ugly reality of the police station and all that it represents from the pretty 'ye olde' atmosphere of the rest of the city perfectly illustrates the spirit of St Albans*, I had written in the reflective statement I had submitted to my art foundation course tutor. But now it was November and the flowers were dead. The building's walls were the same colour as the sky.

I had never been inside a police station before. From television shows I expected a rough, cacophonous place with officers sheltering behind bulletproof glass, shrieks and screams and a stream of criminals being dragged through the hallways with their arms twisted high behind their backs. But this was Hertfordshire, not the Bronx. In a waiting area a lone woman in a green parka read a magazine. We passed a circular reception desk behind which a single officer sat, unshielded from potential trouble. He nodded to Sergeant King and slid a clipboard towards him. He was young; younger than Temperley and his blue eyes were kind. I wished Stephanie has chosen him instead.

Inspector Haskins joined us and we followed her down corridors and through heavy doors with clunky locks which surrendered with a beep at the sight of her security pass. The police station was hot and dusty, the corridors windowless. The harsh glare of the strip lighting fed my sense of dread as I walked. The room we stopped in contained a single desk adrift on an ocean of carpet the colour of spilt tea. The window blinds were closed, the shelves that lined the walls bare. A vending machine wedged into a corner held a single, forgotten bag of crisps.

I didn't notice the pale man hunched behind the desk until Inspector Haskins introduced him. 'Mrs Simm, Mr Simm, this is Patrick Hyde who's with our technical analysis team.' We shook hands with him, Dan first and then me. He was thin and twitchy, seemingly incapable of stillness. The silver computer tower on the desk beside him was Stephanie's. We had had to order it and a matching monitor online because she refused to have the standard beige that the local computer store offered.

'Please show us what you found,' said Inspector Haskins.

He cleared his throat. 'Comms – communications – wise, there's nothing to see. It's as clean as a whistle. We've checked her school email and her Hotmail and instant messenger.'

'She doesn't have Hotmail. She's only allowed her school email,' I said.

Hyde looked at the inspector and she nodded. 'I have to tell you that she does have a Hotmail account. But there's nothing out of the ordinary. She emails her friends on it – all names we know from her school. She emailed a kid called Oliver Mathews a couple of times but he never replied. We've checked him out and he's a fifteen-year-old from Plymouth who she met in Cornwall in the summer. Seems as though she was more keen on him than he was on her.' He coughed and dropped his eyes to the floor. 'Sorry,' he mumbled, blushing.

'Local forces have interviewed Oliver Mathews and his parents and we're confident he hasn't seen her since then,' said Inspector Haskins. 'Sarah Lewis has corroborated his story.'

'Did he break her heart? This Oliver?' I said. 'That could be the reason why she's run away, couldn't it?'

'Well, she obviously liked him. It sounds as though they shared a kiss. But I guess it was a classic holiday romance and he lost interest when he got home.'

'Bastard!' I said. She had emailed him twice. I thought of her agonising over the first email, waiting for a response, writing another email when it didn't come.

'We're confident he has nothing to do with Stephanie's disappearance,' said the inspector again. 'Please go on, Hyde.'

'She uses the instant-messenger function.' He had to explain instant messenger to me.

'So she could have been up in her room messaging him?' said Dan.

'She could have been but she wasn't. She messaged her friends, Sarah Lewis mostly. We're going through Temperley's computer but we think he's too tech-savvy to have left a trail.'

'So what is it that you want us to see?'

'These.' He closed the web applications and opened a folder on the desktop called *My Life*. 'The folder was hidden and password protected. We only found it on our second scan of the computer.' Inside were two Excel documents. Hyde zoomed in so we could read the titles: *Home Sweet Home* and *Final Countdown*.

Haskins leant over my shoulder. 'They're graphs. The team think she created them to keep some kind of record of her life. If you can confirm that it might help us.'

'She liked graphs,' I said, so quietly that only Haskins heard me at first. 'She said they made everything clear. She said that however complicated the information you're dealing with is, it will all make sense if you can work out how to capture it in a graph.'

I pressed my fingers into my ears to block out Hyde's voice. It took me a few minutes to realise what I was looking at. The x axis was a list of dates starting in the summer, just after we had returned from Florida. The ten-day holiday had been a bad idea from the start. July was always a busy time for Dan. The dial-up internet connection in our villa was painfully slow so he had spent hours at a time in an internet café three blocks away trying to get a handle on the work he was supposed to have left behind. In the mornings he cursed the time difference between Miami and London and the fact that the café didn't open until eight. That left me to lead expeditions to malls, theme parks and beaches. I hated driving on freeways in the enormous SUV he had insisted on hiring, being jostled and honked at and with the rental company's warnings about carjackers targeting tourists playing on an endless loop in my head.

The y axis of the graph captured two things: my anxiety levels on a daily basis, ranking them from one to ten, and the number of hours Dan spent at home. They were inversely proportional.

Stephanie had quantified the relationship between Dan's absence and my anxiety.

'I don't see how this is going to help us find her,' Dan said.

When Hyde hovered over the icon for the other file I was gripped by an urge to smash the mouse out of his hand or shove the computer off the desk and into his lap to stop him. Then perhaps Sergeant King would lead me away to a snug little cell where I could hide until this was over. Before we left the house I had taken one of the tablets the doctor had given me to use on particularly bad days. It wasn't enough. I slipped my hand into my jeans pocket where I had stashed a beta blocker. I coughed and slipped it into my mouth, swallowing it dry.

It was another graph, of course. Dan and I leaned over Hyde's shoulders. The y axis plotted Stephanie's happiness each day on a scale of one to ten. The x axis recorded the number of days remaining until she would leave home. It stretched back to the first of January when she had recorded more than a thousand days to go before her escape. She meant the two years and nine months before she would leave for university. I had done the same equation on New Year's Day. I had woken with a hangover's edge of nameless despair and found Stephanie sitting in the kitchen and looking at university prospectuses. I felt the time I had left with her rushing past me, ebbing away in minutes and seconds. A thousand days was nothing at all.

On Stephanie's graph, her levels of happiness scudded between three and five with occasional peaks and troughs. She had been miserable in Florida and for most of the summer – twos and threes. But the week she had spent in Cornwall with Sarah and her family and the days that followed were nines and tens, before a crash to one when Oliver from Plymouth had failed to live up to her hopes. After the misery of the first two weeks of September came a sharp spike of joy. I knew that every nine and ten of happiness she had plotted on the graph had sprung from him; each one was an open sore: *I saw him in class today. He looked at me. He smiled at me. He gave me an A+. He asked me to stay behind. He invited me into his office. He closed the door. It was hot. He took off his tie. He kissed me. He touched me. He stole me away.*

'What we noticed was the point at which Stephanie starts using a new timeline for the day she'll leave home.' On the fifteenth of November there were 1,011 days left. On the next day there were only 15. 'They were planning this for at least two weeks,' said Inspector Haskins. 'It wasn't a spur of the moment thing.'

'Since just after half-term,' I said. I thought about Stephanie's doodles, about the way that black clouds and rainstorms had given way to rays of sunshine and flocks of birds. That must have been when they – he – decided.

'Stephanie is a very singular girl, isn't she?' Inspector Haskins said as we prepared to leave. 'Most fifteen-year-olds wouldn't do this.' She gestured towards the computer as though she meant the graphs and not the running away, the teacher, the whole unquantifiable mess. 'It helps us to know that.'

Sergeant King was tasked with driving us home. He walked us to a squad car and asked us to sit tight while he signed the vehicle out. 'It's our fault,' I said into the silence between Dan and me. 'It's all our fault.' My head hit the car window with a crack as he grabbed me by the shoulders and turned me to face him, gripping me hard.

'Don't ever say that. Don't ever say that again. It's his fault. He's a pervert and she's his victim. Listen to me, Rosalind.'

'You saw the graph. You saw how unhappy she was,' I said. He tightened his grip on my arms, pressed me harder into the window.

'I won't let you blame yourself for this, Ros. It's not your fault. Do you hear me? If you start blaming yourself you'll never stop and I won't let you do it. Say it. Say you know it's not your fault.'

'It's not my fault,' I managed, feeling the cushion of the bad-day tablet beneath me. He turned his grip into a hug as Sergeant King returned to the car.

'We need to tell Freddy what's going on,' I said later that afternoon.

It was Tanya, not Dan, who followed me up the stairs to Freddy's room. 'You're doing really well, Ros. Just keep going. Keep being strong. He needs you,' she said when we reached the landing. I wasn't sure whether she meant Freddy or Dan, decided it didn't matter enough to ask.

In Freddy's room the curtains were closed in spite of the daylight and he lay in a horizontal sprawl across his double bed. His face was aglow with shifting light – now pink, now green, now grey – from a handheld console. We had told him to stay in his room so many times since Stephanie disappeared that he had stopped leaving it at all. I couldn't remember deciding that he wouldn't go to school, or telling him that he didn't have to go. I wondered if anyone had told his teacher and had a vague sense that Tanya probably had.

He glanced at me briefly then went back to his game.

'Freddy. We've had some news about Stephanie.'

He dropped the game and pulled himself up on the bed. 'She's safe?'

'We think she's with . . .' My throat constricted, unwilling to provide me with the air I needed to say the words. Tanya placed her hand on the small of my back. 'We think she's with her geography teacher. Mr Temperley.'

'That's good, isn't it? That she's with a teacher? Mum?' I didn't know what to say. It was like a twisted version of one of those quizzes in women's magazines: would you rather that your beloved daughter, your first-born child, the person for whom your heart has beaten for fifteen years, is:

a. Alone and sleeping rough on the streets of London;
b. Nowhere, absolutely nowhere at all;
c. With her male teacher, twice her age, in an unknown location, the heat of his naked skin next to hers.

Tanya sat on the corner of the bed. 'The thing is, Freddy, that it's not right for a teacher to go away with one of his pupils like that.'

'Has he kidnapped her? Is he holding her for ransom? We've got money, haven't we, Mum? You can have the money in my bank account and my Premium Bonds. And Grandpa has lots of money. Maybe he'd let us have it for Stephie.'

'It's not about money. It's not her fault but we think he may have convinced her that she should go away with him,' said Tanya. I watched Freddy realise what this meant. He was old enough – just – to understand what a grown man might want with a teenage girl. He blushed. His eyes filled with tears. I tried to put my arms around him but he shrugged me off and shuffled away to sit with his back against the wall, his knees drawn up under his chin and his console held in front of him like a shield.

'I know it's difficult to understand,' said Tanya. 'But now we know who she is with we hope it will be easier to find her.'

'Maybe not. He's a geography teacher so he'll know all the best places to hide. Caves and mountains and places like that.'

*   *   *

There was a twenty-three-car pile-up on the M4, the road Freddy would have to drive down to return to Bristol. News footage shot from a helicopter showed a nest of jewel-coloured chassis jumbled together like toys in a toy box. Images shot from the ground showed handbags and tyres, wing mirrors and shoes flung onto the snowy verge. A bruised survivor stood by the twisted remains of her car and talked about the moment she thought she was going to die while another motorist complained about the four-hour tailback snaking away into the distance.

Freddy had called me into the sitting room to watch the news. 'You'll worry yourself into oblivion if I go back to Bristol today, won't you, Mum?'

'Yes. That's my job.'

He grinned. 'In that case, I'll stay an extra day. It's meant to thaw tonight so I'll go tomorrow. Tom's back so I might see him later.'

'I'm glad you're staying a bit longer. I feel like I've hardly seen you, what with everything that's been going on.' With the images of the crashed cars flickering on his face he sat still and let me talk to him. I kept it light. He told me about his new friends and his new rugby team and about a girl called Emma who seemed to want to do his laundry for him. I had always known there would be Emmas for tall, handsome Freddy with his blue eyes and easy laugh, but I felt a twist of guilt when he told me that he had handed over his laundry bag 'because it seemed to make her happy'.

'Why don't I make us lasagne and garlic bread for lunch?' I said when his restlessness started to build and he slipped his phone out of his pocket. Lasagne had always been a favourite of his.

'Actually, Mum, I'm going over to see Tom now. We're going to watch the F1 highlights.' He was already getting to his feet. He stretched his arms above his head just as Dan did. The resemblance between father and son was so strong that I often wondered whether I had really had any role in Freddy's creation. He certainly hadn't got his easygoing streak from me. 'I'll stay here if you want, though. Are you worried about the lizard thing and the journo Stephie saw?'

I shook my head. 'We'll be fine. But, Freddy, don't talk to anyone about Stephanie and me going to Corsica. I think it best if no one knows. Just in case.'

'I won't.' He walked to the door then turned around. He took a breath. 'Stephie says she's not worried about Temperley getting out, apart from the thing about the journalists and being in the paper. But you're worried about it, aren't you? About him and her?'

I nodded. 'I can't forget what kind of man he is.'

'But if Stephanie doesn't want to see him she doesn't have to, does she? So it will be OK, won't it? You don't need to start worrying again.'

He bent over me where I sat and gathered me in an awkward hug then, all too quickly, he was gone.

I could deal with journalists. What I didn't know was how to deal with Cam. Twenty-four hours earlier I had used thoughts of him to soothe my ragged nerves, but now the echo of his name in my mind made me nervous and sent my thoughts spiralling away from me. I wanted to believe that the lizard was nothing more than a playful prank, but what if there was more to come? More postcards, more lizards, something worse? I wanted to ring him up – or better still, send him a sternly worded letter – and tell him never, ever to set foot in my garden again. But what if that made him angry, brought him striding around here and knocking on the door? I had promised to see him on Friday, but I would be gone by then, speeding through the clouds at five hundred miles an hour even as he waited for me to arrive. I only had to hold him off until then. **El Draco is beautiful but he gave us quite a fright. No more surprises please :-) See you on Friday x** I texted. Then I held my breath, willing my phone not to ring, the doorbell not to chime. **I don't know what you're talking about ;-) Can't wait for Friday x** he sent back. I exhaled. By the time I got back perhaps I would find him sitting next to Karen or one of the other young women in our tutor group. I didn't let myself think about how that would feel.

Stephanie was still and quiet in her room. I climbed the stairs to my studio, to open the door and gather up the sheets of paper from where I had dropped them. The sky was already falling to night, grey clouds heavy with another tumble of snow were sucked one by one into the blackness. I dragged my two old photographer's lamps into the middle of the room and set them to shine pools of light onto my desk, but they only seemed to make the shadows that climbed the walls longer and more animated. I stared at the piece of paper in front of me and tried to conjure another happy memory for Stephanie, but I had caught her amnesia for joy. I recalled birthday parties and remembered only tears, absences, failures. I pictured holidays and found them veiled in a sticky film of sadness and resentment, of dissatisfaction with sandy sand- wiches and arguments over toys. I thought of her running into my arms after winning the sack race at her junior school sports day, but I couldn't forget how soon her laughter had turned to tears when she had lost in the egg and spoon race. I remembered her riding a bike without stabilisers for the first time but couldn't let go of the sense of fear that had gripped me on that day or the way I had locked her bike away at night through some unacknowledged fear that she might use her new-found skill to leave me.

Three, four, five times I heard her phone beep in her room next door as the hours passed. Then the crash of the front door and Freddy's feet on the stairs. I rubbed the salt from my cheeks.

'I'm in here,' I called.

His head appeared around the door. 'Hi, Mum. You all right?'

'I'm OK. Nothing to report here.' I made my voice bright and forced myself to smile. I felt the scab on my lower lip peel open and covered my mouth with my hand.

'Stephie still moping in her room?'

I nodded. 'She says she tired. See if you can get her downstairs. We could watch a film or something.' I had knocked on her door with tea and toast but she had taken it from me without inviting me in.

Freddy went into Stephanie's room and closed the door behind him. I heard them talking, laughing. I wanted to slide across the landing on my belly, press my ear to the door and hear their words.

'We're going out for a bit,' said Freddy, sticking his head around the door. 'Jack's back and we're all going round there.' They were both smiling. Stephanie was wearing one of my cardigans, a swipe of my lipstick lighting up her face. When had she lifted it from my make-up bag?

'I thought you were tired, Stephie?' I said, like a jealous friend trying to catch her out in a lie.

'I had a little sleep. It'll be good to get out and I won't see Freddy for ages after tomorrow. Probably not until Christmas.'

'What about—'

'We're going straight to Jack's and I'll deal with anyone who tries to bother us. I had a good look round on my way in and there's no one hanging about the street.'

I had no right to lock her up. If I started ordering her around she might refuse to come away with me and I couldn't risk that. 'Don't tell anyone we're off to Corsica. And be back for dinner,' I said. In the silence they left behind I forced myself to picture Temperley in his cell: he was pale, thin, folded into a bunk bed like a spider in its hole. I built walls around him, thick and topped with spikes. I dug a moat around him and filled it with savage, scaled creatures, their sharp teeth grey with shreds of rotting flesh.

Dan and I were eating salmon steaks and baked potatoes, dry from spending too long waiting at the bottom of the oven. I had shown him the pictures of our hotel in Corsica. He had breathed through his teeth when I told him how much it would cost but I knew that he didn't really mind; it wasn't the cost that was bothering him.

'Is this necessary, do you think?' he said.

'Yes. Tanya agrees. You were all for it this morning.'

'It's just a long time for you two to be away together.' He was creeping around the edges of something. In the past I would have burrowed into his words, dug through them for meaning or scratched at him to tell me what exactly he meant. But now I didn't care. All that mattered was getting Stephanie on the plane and away from here.

'You don't think that's a good thing?'

'Yes, yes, of course it is. But I still wonder whether she wouldn't be better off with some professional help.'

'She's doing really well. She's not drinking and she's handling the news about Temperley OK. She's going to see the counsellor Dr Bashir recommended when we get back. It's the idea of being in the papers that bothers her and hiding away in Corsica will help with that.'

'I suppose.'

Dan was tapping and swiping at his iPad in front of the news when I heard the crunch of snow underfoot and the scrabble of a key in a lock. I sprang into the hallway and opened the front door to find Freddy there. He had been struggling to open the door and hold Stephanie up at the same time. She was leaning into him, swaying slightly. Trails of mascara hung from her eyes like black icicles. The beery warmth of their breath formed clouds between us.

'Shit! Mum,' said Freddy. 'She's a bit drunk. Dad's not here, is he?'

As he spoke, Stephanie lifted her head and looked at me. Her face crumpled into a sob and she launched herself across the doorstep. I caught her weight and pulled her to me.

'He's a buggering bastard, Mum,' she slurred into my ear. 'But we won't leave you alone. We won't.'

'I know he is. And I won't leave you. We'll stay together and I won't let him hurt you. Not ever.' I rocked her in my arms, smoothed her hair back from her face. 'Let's get you up to bed. We'll be gone soon. Far away from him.'

'Sorry, Mum. I didn't realise how much she'd had. She was fine one minute and then she was like this,' said Freddy. All his usual energy had ebbed away. In the light from the porch I was sure that he had been crying too.

I was halfway up the stairs, my arm around Stephanie's waist and Freddy following behind me, his hands outstretched to catch us if we fell, when Dan came into the hallway.

'What's going on? You two should have been back an hour ago,' he said. He had stepped forwards to frame himself in the dark oblong of the dining room door. 'Your mother made you dinner.'

'Not now, Dan,' I said. I could feel something coming, the air was tinged with threat. I had to get Stephanie away, up the stairs and safe. I continued to propel her forwards with Freddy behind me. But I had already glimpsed the twitch of Dan's nose.

'I can smell beer. Is she drunk?'

'She's upset. She needs to go to bed.' What if he stopped us from going away? He had obviously cooled on the idea and this setback could be the excuse he needed to put her into one of those places. She would be taken away, not by me but from me, sealed into The Elms or somewhere like it, processed and changed. 'I'll be back in a minute,' I told him. I nodded my head towards the sitting room, gesturing for him to retreat and raising my eyebrows in the old *I'll explain later* sign we had used when the children were young and we wanted something to go over their heads. But he stood firm.

'Oh, just leave us alone, Dad,' said Stephanie. She stepped away from me and dragged the sleeve of her coat over her wet cheeks. 'Just bugger off back to London and leave us alone.'

'What did you say?'

'I said leave us alone.'

'How much have you had to drink?'

'That's none of your business. None at all! You might be Mr Big Cheese at work but you're not in charge here. You don't get to write our objectives and boss us around.'

He stepped backwards as if she had slapped him. 'I'm just worried about you.' He was almost pleading, looking up at her through the banister as though she held something fragile and precious in her hands and was threatening to drop it onto the hard floor below.

She laughed a quick bitter laugh and started to climb the stairs ahead of me. I held my hands behind her, not touching her but poised to catch her if she fell. Halfway up, she turned back towards Dan. 'You're not worried about me. You're worried about yourself. You, you, you, Dad. It's always you, you, you. Poor you with your scandalous daughter. Poor you who has to live with the shame of what I did. Poor you having me turn up here like this. Poor you with your train stuck in the snow and your bit on the side in London and all your bloody lies and—'

'Enough! Be quiet, Stephanie.' The volume of Dan's voice shocked us all, even him. We were frozen in the sudden silence that came after his words. We didn't breathe. We didn't blink. A tear stopped in its tracks part way down my cheek. Then Stephanie ran up the remaining steps and up the second flight of stairs to her room and we all came back to life.

Dan turned to Freddy, his voice a sour stage whisper. 'What were you thinking, letting her drink? She's ill and we trusted you.'

'Oh, just back off, Dad. Leave us alone.'

'Your sister has a drinking problem. She went out with you and now look at the state of her – she's plastered. She doesn't know what she's saying.'

'None of this is my fault. I'm going to bed and I'm going home tomorrow morning. Back to Bristol. I'll walk there if I have to. I wish I'd never come back here.' Freddy pushed past me where I stood halfway up the stairs. The slam of his bedroom door made me flinch. Ours had never been a house of raised voices and slammed doors. Maybe that was where we had gone wrong. Perhaps Stephanie knew exactly what she was saying and the words she had thrown at Dan before she fled up the stairs had been the most honest to be spoken in the house for years.

'Ros, she's drunk and she's upset. Come downstairs. Please. It's not what you think.' He raised his hands towards me as if he expected me to jump into his arms. I turned away.

'I need to make sure she's OK,' I said with my back to him. *Bit on the side, trains in chaos, late nights, strange phone calls. Have you talked to her yet?*

Stephanie was already asleep, or pretending to be, curled on her side with her face to the wall. She had dropped her coat beside the bed but still wore my cardigan. I lay beside her, shifting forwards until I felt the tickle of her hair against my forehead. I lay there, rigid with waiting. At some point I heard Dan creep up the stairs and whisper my name through the gap between the door and its frame. I closed my eyes more tightly and willed him to go away. The door creaked open and I sensed him standing over us. 'I'm sorry, Ros,' he whispered. 'I made a mistake. Just one mistake.' And then he was gone.

I must have slept eventually because in the depths of night I was pinched awake by a noise. Stephanie slept on beside me, her breathing even. Beneath us the house was silent, the rush of wind in the trees the only sound. I lay back down, thinking that I had dreamt whatever had woken me, until a blue light leapt up the wall beside the door and a beep broke the silence. Stephanie shifted but didn't wake. I slid out of bed and crept towards the light. Her phone was lying face up on the floor as though she had thrown it there. The phone's screen lit up under my touch and revealed the red flash of the low battery warning and two text messages waiting to be read, both from the number saved as *Don't Answer*. The most recent said only **I miss you x**. The one before said **Please just tell me U R OK. Worried about you x**. I tried to imagine Temperley crouched in a secret corner, an illicit mobile in his hands. I could ring the prison to tell them he had a phone and let an anonymous tip-off be his undoing again. But I couldn't marry up the concern and kisses of the messages with the predator in the cell. They had to be from Jake. Just as I started to probe more deeply into the phone's library of secrets it blinked a final low battery warning then shut itself down. I grunted with frustration then froze when Stephanie shifted on the bed. I waited until she was still again before lying down beside her and closing my eyes.

I dreamt I was in the flat where we had lived when Stephanie was born. The air was damp around me and the taut drum of my pregnant belly rested on my thighs. I held a pair of knitting needles from which hung a half-knitted baby's blanket. A ball of white wool lay on the floor at my feet. As I moved the needles, the blanket un-knitted itself stitch by stitch and the ball of wool beside me grew, spinning on the spot and growing fat as it swallowed up the wool from the needles. I moved the needles faster and faster until the blanket was dancing in front of me as it shrivelled away. With a final click of the needles the blanket was gone and I was left staring down at my flat stomach, my baby bump nowhere to be seen.

Later, I dreamt Stephanie was crying.

FOUR DAYS

'If I tell the doctor about last night he might say that I shouldn't go on holiday. He made a big point about how I'm not meant to drink on the tablets.' We were in the car on the way to Stephanie's appointment. I was tired and thick-headed, my throat dry as though I had breathed her hangover in as I slept. Saying goodbye to Freddy, letting my hand fall away from his arm and listening to the clunk of his car door closing had left me exhausted. 'Come and visit me in Bristol, Mum,' he said before he got in the car, the wobble in his voice making my throat ache with sadness. 'Bring Stephie and Auntie Bea. I'll show you the sights.'

'Mum?' said Stephanie.

'You should tell him, I suppose.'

'I didn't drink that much. I mean, I know I was a bit drunk but I hadn't eaten anything so it went to my head.'

I hoped she didn't believe what she was telling me; it sounded like something an alcoholic might tell a police officer or his wife. *Don't screw it up*, I wanted to say. *We need to get out of here, I have to get you out of here.* 'He'll just want to check how you are. Tell him what you think is important.' She wouldn't screw it up; she knew how to show people what she wanted them to see. The doctor would probably mistake the violet smudges beneath her hung-over eyes for tiredness.

'OK.' She caught my eye in the rear-view mirror. 'Mum, are you OK? I'm sorry about last night. I saw Dad in London and—'

'Can we just not talk about it? Please?' I cut her off. This was the second time she had tried to explain what she had said on the stairs. But I couldn't see how it needed any explanation. It seemed quite clear to me: all the extra overnight stays in the last few weeks, the lack of sex, the way he had disappeared to work the day after we brought Stephanie home, the phone calls to her rather than to me. I had always expected something like this, waited for it, considered it a matter not of *if* but of *when*. But where I had anticipated pain I was surprised to find I felt nothing at all. It was as though the snow and ice had bled through my clothes and numbed my heart. But it wasn't numb to fear. When I closed my eyes it wasn't Dan's face that I saw, or even Cam's, it was Nathan Temperley's and it was smiling.

The surgery waiting room was packed and noisy with the clamour of winter colds and fractious children. Every wall bore a sign warning that mobile phones were strictly prohibited. When Stephanie was called in to see the doctor I eased mine out of my handbag just enough to see the screen. I had waited for the noises of Dan's departure before I left Stephanie's room. It hadn't crossed my mind that he would not go to work. He had sent me a message from the train: **Early start. Didn't want to wake you. Let's talk later x** I had replied: **OK. Don't forget Stephie's passport.**

Stephanie returned after less than five minutes with the doctor. 'Signed and sealed,' she said, waving a piece of paper. 'He thinks our holiday will do me good. He's recommended a book about mindfulness for me to take.'

It probably wasn't appropriate to celebrate a sick note and a repeat prescription for antidepressants but I smiled as we walked back to the car. She didn't want to go back to her flat or to put Sarah to the trouble of rummaging through her wardrobe and dragging a suitcase across town, so we were going to buy her new clothes for our trip. Dan would meet Sarah at lunchtime to collect Stephanie's passport and then we would be ready to go.

It was only ten thirty in the morning and bitterly cold, yet the streets of St Albans were already packed with Christmas shoppers, their arms full of bags, their scarves wrapped tightly around their faces. We ran up against a tide of them as we made our way down London Road, a canopy of grinning plastic snowmen hanging above our heads. As we approached the cathedral, the tide became a torrent as coachloads of people made their ways to the Christmas market in the Vintry Garden. I have always been fond of Christmas markets with their huts of tat and hot, sweet *glühwein*. Beatrice was planning to come the following weekend and stay the night so we could visit the market. We had done the same the previous year and ended the evening light-headed with sugar and wine, our toes numb and our stomachs aching from gossip and laughter. She would be back from her trip to New York in a few hours' time. I would have to ring her and cancel. I longed to see her, to sit in her flat in Islington and tell her everything, to let her help me find a way out. But there was no time for that.

The snow in the town centre had been cleared away, leaving only a tidemark of dirty slush in the crevices between kerb and road. Stephanie pulled up her hood and tucked her scarf across her face as we approached the high street and I did the same. St Albans is a city in name but a village in scope; anyone who knew Stephanie knew me, so if she wanted to go unnoticed, un-gossiped about, then I must too. We pushed our way into the department store, the hot pollen scent of the perfume counters by the entrance welcoming us in. The shop felt empty – spacious, even – after the crush of the street outside. Stephanie and I hadn't been shopping together for years. As a child she was so difficult to buy clothes for that I had dreaded it, putting it off until inches of sock peeped out from the bottom of trousers and wrists poked twig-like from cardigan sleeves. When I eventually steeled myself to take her shopping she would creep up to the racks, poking cautiously at the clothes and rejecting almost everything without so much as trying it on. We would tramp from shop to shop – my head aching under artificial lights, my throat dry from the stale air – until she found a pair of trousers or a dress that, for some inscrutable reason, she deemed acceptable. I would buy as many as the shop had in her size and collapse back into the car. Giving her a clothing allowance and letting her go off into town with Sarah and choose things for herself had been a relief. But then she had bought those jeans; the black jeans that clung, the jeans she ran away in.

I let Stephanie lead me through the women's wear concessions. She touched each item cautiously, snapping her hand away from anything made of nylon, anything itchy or rough. Grey was the colour of the season and she picked out jeans and jumpers, cardigans and tops in shades of dove's feather, cobweb, wood smoke and morning mist. She would look like a winter sprite with her white skin, red hair and winter cloud outfits. I imagined us both clad in grey, walking together on a deserted Corsican beach, the sun shining weakly in a pale blue sky.

We had picked up the book about mindfulness and were heading to M&S to buy underwear, our arms full of bags, when I heard someone calling my name. The crowds had found their way into the Christmas market and the street was less busy than it had been. I shuffled my bags into my left hand and pulled my hood back into place. I bowed my head and wove through the shoppers, glancing back to check that Stephanie was still following me. We were only ten metres from the doors of M&S. We were almost there.

Five metres.

Three metres.

Two metres.

Stephanie grabbed my arm. 'Mum. It's Cameron from the exhibition.'

He was jogging towards us, his smile lighting up the street and flakes of snow settling in his hair. He was wearing a black down jacket which flapped open to reveal a tight jumper the colour of a rain cloud. I felt a sudden, unwilling flash of desire for him. Then I remembered the snow salamander and I wanted nothing more than to get Stephanie as far away from him as I possibly could.

'Fancy meeting you here,' he said when he reached us. Wasn't that what people who were entirely unsurprised to bump into each other said? I glanced at Stephanie but couldn't see past her hood. He was slightly breathless, clouds of vapour hanging white in the air in front of him.

'Cameron. What are you doing here?' My face burnt. I couldn't look him in the eyes. I forced myself to focus on his cheek instead.

'Christmas shopping. The shops are much better here than Hertford.'

He glanced away from me to Stephanie, tilted his head to see beneath her hood.

'Hi, Cam,' she said.

'What are you two up to?'

'Holiday shopping for me,' said Stephanie. 'I haven't got a thing to wear and we're off tomorrow.' She laughed and a cloud of air, exhaled from her lungs, passed over her lips and floated towards his face.

'Stephanie and I are off on holiday for a couple of weeks,' I said.

'Holiday? Since when?' He swallowed hard, his Adam's apple bobbing, the sunshine of his face replaced by clouds.

'Since yesterday,' said Stephanie. 'We need to get away for a while.'

'Where are you off to?'

'Corsica,' I said.

'Calvi,' added Stephanie.

'Oh, I hear it's very nice. I thought you'd have wanted to go to Barcelona though, Ros.'

'I've never been,' said Stephanie. 'Why didn't we think of that, Mum?'

'Never? Oh you have to go. Park Güell is just amazing. You should take her, Ros. Although I guess not everyone appreciates the sculptures.' Had he seen me crush his snow salamander's back, squash its claw beneath my hand?

'The weather's lovely in Corsica at the moment,' I said before Stephanie could answer. 'They're having a heatwave and it's only a short flight.'

He reached out and touched my shoulder so I was forced to look at him. 'What about your work? Our project? Friday?' Out of the corner of my eye I sensed Stephanie watching us. I hoped she had missed the plaintive note in his voice.

'My work will still be here when I get back.' Our 'project' was over. When had it ended? Maybe the moment Toby winked at us in the storeroom at Going, going, gone! Maybe the moment Cam broke our unspoken rules and sneaked into my garden. Maybe the moment Stephanie spat the words 'bit on the side' at Dan. 'Anyway, we'd better get going. Stephanie needs a new bikini.' I said this to punish myself, to leave him with the image of my beautiful twenty-one-year-old daughter dressed in a wisp of Lycra.

'So Cam has a bit of a schoolboy crush on you then, Mum?' Stephanie said as we sailed up the escalator in M&S. She was two steps below me, her hood still pulled over her head.

'Don't be ridiculous.'

'He does. I'm very perceptive about things like that. And he looks at you like he wants to lick you so it's not hard to figure it out,' she said. I glimpsed her smile beneath her hood.

'Stephie! Don't say that.' I pretended to look for something in my bag. My cheeks were burning and I was afraid I was going to cry. I should be relieved it was a joke to her, I reminded myself. Stephanie discovering what had happened – nearly happened – between Cam and me could be a disaster: in her eyes I'd be no better than Dan.

'He looked like the world was about to end when you said you were going away. Poor Cam.'

'Well, there's no shortage of young lovelies at uni to mop up his tears, not that he'll be shedding any.' I made myself smile at her as though I was in on the joke.

'We should have told him about the snow lizard in the garden. He might have known who made it,' she said.

I jumped off the escalator a split second before the tip of my boot would have been swallowed up in the gnashing metal teeth at the top. I shivered at the thought of the blood, the tearing of flesh.

On the way back to the car we were caught up again in the crowd for the Christmas market. The stiff cardboard shopping bags were heavy in my hands, their corners forever snagging on people's coats and bags, dragging me off course. I felt trapped in my coat, hemmed in by the crowds, weighed down by the responsibility of getting Stephanie home safely. Hangover and fatigue had hit her in M&S and she had grown silent as we waited in the queue, shuffling from foot to foot with impatience and checking her phone's screen every few minutes. As I twisted and turned to keep her in my field of vision, I remembered how much I had hated being in crowds with my children when they were young. It was dizzyingly easy to imagine a hand slipping out of mine, a child carried away in plain sight, a criminal moving unseen in a sea of unsuspecting innocents.

All the time I was watching out for Cam. It was with an itch of fear that I looked for his face in the crowd, but with sadness, too. He had been such a sweet dream.

The crowd thickened around Christopher Place. A section of railing was lined with Christmas trees wrapped in tight chrysalises of white netting. The smallest came up to my knees, the largest towered over me. A short man with a blue woollen hat pulled low on his brow was barking out prices to a man in a tweed coat and deerstalker while the crowd looked on. I changed course to go around them, looking back to check that Stephanie was still behind me. *Nearly there,* I mouthed over the noise as the Christmas tree vendor's negotiations reached a crescendo. In five minutes we would be back in the car. In ten minutes we would be home with the doors locked and the curtains drawn. Tomorrow we would be hundreds of miles away.

But as I stepped off the kerb someone grabbed my right shoulder hard and hauled me savagely backwards. I cried out and struggled to stay on my feet, my boots sliding in the dirty slush that filled the gutter. The grip on my shoulder tightened like a band of iron, wrenching my arm in its socket and pulling me head-first into the rough plastic wrapping of a Christmas tree so its needles scratched my cheek and the plastic mesh dug into my nose.

'Stephanie!' I screamed, the sharp tang of pine catching in my throat. But the crowd had already closed around her, a wall of down and nylon, anoraks and hats. I fought with the bulk of the Christmas tree and clawed at the netting, but the pressure on my shoulder was relentless. I had to shuffle forwards to avoid losing my footing and being dragged along the ground. Harder and harder the force on my shoulder pulled and faster and faster I shuffled to keep up. *Temperley,* I thought, *he's got me and now he'll go after Stephanie.* I screamed.

'Stop! She's caught! Stop!' someone shouted. Suddenly the grip on my arm eased, my feet stopped moving.

'It's OK, it's OK,' said a voice in my ear. I peeled my face from the plastic-wrapped tree and turned to see a plump woman in her thirties reaching into the confusion of bags at my side. 'Shhhh. It's OK. You're just caught up.'

She was right. I had caught the silly, over-engineered buckle of my Burberry handbag in the web of netting around the huge tree now being carried in the arms of the man in the deerstalker. 'Shhhh. I'm untangling you now,' the woman said. 'Just hold still.'

I forced myself to breathe slowly, to smile at the woman whose fingers were freeing me. Temperley was still in prison. Stephanie would wait for me by the car. She was twenty-one years old. No one was missing. I hadn't lost my child. She would laugh when I told her that I had been attacked by a Christmas tree. We would be gone soon. Just a few more hours and we would be gone.

And then I saw it. His face. Temperley's face. Watching. Smiling. Waiting. My foot slipped in the slushy gutter, jerking my eyes away from him for a fraction of a second. When I looked back there was nothing but a muddle of hats and coats, a hundred faces glimpsed as fractions: eyes, hair, chins, lips. He was gone.

I grabbed the strap of my handbag and freed it from the tree with a vicious wrench. Pushing past the woman who had been helping me I lurched into the crowd calling Stephanie's name and scanning every face for another glimpse of him.

'Mum? Mum?' Stephanie was there, gripping my arm to arrest my plunge into the crowd. 'Mum, what's wrong?'

'I thought . . . I thought I saw someone.'

She surprised me by giving my wrist a hard, almost savage pull and leaning so close to me that I saw the flash of anger in her eyes. 'He's still in prison. You know that. You're imagining things again. Come on, let's get out of here.' She kept her arm in mine, pulling me through the throng so I had to take awkward, quick steps to keep up. She kept her head down, looking nowhere but at her feet.

'I'm sorry,' I said as I pulled the car door closed behind me. 'It was so crowded. My handbag got caught in someone's Christmas tree.' I shoved my hands between my knees to stop them from shaking. *He's still in prison. He's still in prison. He's still in prison.*

'Shall I drive?' I was tempted to let her. I wanted to crawl into the footwell, curl myself around like a fox in its burrow and cover my head with my tail. Then I remembered how much she had drunk the night before and how little she had eaten. I started the engine.

* * *

'I'm confident this will flush them out,' said Chief Inspector Francis Marwell on the day that he took leadership of the investigation. He was Inspector Haskins's boss, a grey-haired man with a soft stomach and a hard face. He was older than the idea of political correctness and didn't baulk at referring to Temperley as 'that dirty swine' in front of me, although he dropped the volume of his voice a couple of notches to do it. I liked him for this. The other reason I liked him might have worried me if I had analysed it. It was my suspicion that he had little time for a suspect's rights when it came to men who messed around with girls. When I imagined Temperley being interrogated by Marwell I saw fists connecting with kidneys, feet with groins.

For the second television appeal, we were asked to appear alongside Nathan Temperley's father. I was calmer this time; the tranquilliser I had swallowed a couple of hours earlier was doing its work. Each of us had a script and we stuck to it. Dan and I had the easier job. We only had to tell the truth about wanting Stephanie to come home and her not being in any trouble. Christopher Temperley had to pretend that he wanted his son back, too. He had to ask him to do the 'right thing' and tell him that he loved him. But how could he love his son, really? If Nathan Temperley had been my son I would have wanted the shame to kill me. I would have lain down and wept at the feet of his victim's parents, not shuffled past them with an awkward nod.

'Good work, you two. That's going far and wide. They'll get your message wherever they are,' said Inspector Marwell when the cameras had stopped rolling and Dan and I were sealed in his office.

'I know you want to hear progress and I'm sure we'll have some soon. But right now I'm going to tell you what we're doing. We're throwing everything at this. Every pair of eyes we have is looking for your daughter right now. We've got some new data from his financials which is being analysed as I speak. It seems Mr Temperley had taken to gambling. Luck was on his side for a time but he took a big loss a month ago and he's in debt up to his eyeballs with the banks and probably with the loan sharks too.'

'You said the appeal would flush them out,' said Dan. 'What if it has the opposite effect? I mean, he's got nothing to lose, has he? What if he knows his game is up so he decides to take her with him?'

'Dan!' It was an avenue of thought so unthinkably dark that I had not let myself travel down it. I had pretended that it wasn't even there.

'We think that's very, very unlikely and we've taken precautions against it. The message we're giving him right now is that if he brings her home it will all be OK. That's why we got you on screen next to his father – we wouldn't have done that in any other circumstances. The most likely scenario is that he'll leave her behind and keep running on his own.'

'Why do you think that?' said Dan.

'We've had a top psychological profiler drafted in from London to go over what we know about the creep with a fine-toothed comb. She says he's selfish, he's cunning, he's egotistical and he likes to take risks, but he's not a murderer and he's certainly not about to top himself. Hurting Stephanie wouldn't fit the story. Stephanie thinks he loves her. He might even think he loves her – that's what they convince themselves, you see. Love is his only line of defence so he won't do anything to undermine the love story. And he certainly won't do anything to hurt himself.'

'So what now?' said Dan. 'We just wait?'

'You wait. We keep looking. He may be clever but he will have left something behind, some trace. People don't just disappear.'

But what if it wasn't Temperley who had left a trace? What if it was Stephanie? What if there was a tiny part of her that wanted me to find her if only I looked hard enough? 'We need to go home,' I said. 'Now.' I had work to do.

It was early evening by the time we reached the house. Freddy was watching a film with Beatrice. I hugged him tightly then went up to Stephanie's room. My watch beeped to tell me it was time for another dose of the tranquilliser the doctor had given me but I ignored it. If anything could help me now it was my overactive, hypersensitive, paranoid brain that saw sinister intent where others saw innocence, and sensed potential catastrophe where others felt safe.

I was methodical and determined. I split her room into areas: wardrobe and chest of drawers, desk, bookshelves, bed, and worked through them one by one. Whenever Dan or Tanya told me to stop – told me that the police had already done what I was doing, that it wouldn't do any good – I pretended to listen, went downstairs to check on Freddy or eat. Then I made an excuse to slip back upstairs and continue my work.

By the end of the first evening I had emptied the wardrobe and chest of drawers onto the floor and examined every item for clues. I asked myself where every top, every skirt every pair of jeans had come from. I peeled up the insoles of shoes, turned pockets inside out and unpicked hems until my nails split and my fingers bled. Tanya left. Beatrice put Freddy to bed. I found nothing.

When my eyes grew too tired for me to trust them, I lay in her bed beneath the glow-in-the-dark stars that spread across the ceiling. I wondered when Stephanie had stuck the stars up there, whether she had stood on a wobbling chair to reach up and put them in place. I didn't remember noticing them before, but it had been a long time since I had been into her bedroom in the dark to kiss her on the forehead and wish her goodnight. Why had I ever stopped? I should have crept in every night and watched her sleeping. I should have fixed her image in my mind so firmly that she could never disappear.

I started on the desk the next morning. There had been fifty-three tip-offs from the public following the appeal. Temperley had been spotted everywhere from Portsmouth to Aberdeen. There were sightings in Birmingham, London, Goole, Gloucester and Norwich. A caller had sighted them arguing outside a bar on Tenerife, another had seen them eating ice cream and laughing on Miami Beach. Stephanie's passport was still in Dan's desk drawer along with mine and Freddy's, so the police dismissed the possibility that they had left the country. I had never been further than six hundred miles from Stephanie. She had spent a week in the Alps on a school skiing trip and I had felt the distance as a physical pressure in my stomach, growing more intense as the coach pulled out of the school car park and becoming more like pain with every mile she travelled. I would know if she was in Miami; some innate sense of distance would sound an alarm.

Inspector Marwell came to the house and told us how each 'credible tip' was being followed up. 'We're closing in,' he kept saying, although I didn't see how.

'Have you found any clues at his flat?' I asked.

'Nothing yet. But we've found his car so we know he's not using his own vehicle. We're looking at rental cars and recent purchases on his credit cards.' That sounded like the opposite of progress to me. They were only finding out what they didn't know.

Tanya had arrived with the chief inspector, bringing an armful of newspapers with her. Dan spent the rest of the day poring over them, reading about floods, bombs, fires and house prices when he ran out of articles about Stephanie. A tabloid newspaper had lifted photographs of Temperley from his Facebook page. In one he had his arms around a woman whose face had been blurred out. They were standing on the face of a steep hill, a bright blue sky and a set of mountain peaks just visible behind them. If I didn't know who – what – he was, I could think it was a picture of a handsome man. If I didn't know what he was I wouldn't have noticed how he gripped the woman's arm so tightly that his thick fingers sank into the turquoise nylon of her jacket. In another photo he was rock climbing, hanging precariously from an outcrop on a thin blue rope. I took that picture into the downstairs cloakroom and knelt on the floor as I used the nail scissors to slice through the image of his rope. I imagined him falling, his glee turning to fear, his hands grasping empty air, as he raced towards the ground.

Later, Tanya found me emptying the drawer that ran the length of Stephanie's desk. She sat on the bed which was still unmade from where I had slept in it. 'What are you going to do when you've looked everywhere?' she said eventually.

'Look again.' I sensed her nodding behind me. She didn't move from the bed. After a while I forgot she was there.

I thought I had found it when I discovered a post-it note scrawled with a series of train times. But the journey time was too familiar: the twenty minutes it took to travel from St Albans to London King's Cross. Sarah and Stephanie had gone to the huge branch of Topshop on Oxford Street in the summer holidays, their first unaccompanied trip to the city. I pulled the empty drawer out and turned it upside down. Its blank under-belly yielded nothing.

I went through all her school work. Her favourite subjects – mathematics, chemistry, physics – were each the same: pages of her neat notes, barely doodled on. Assignments and tests were splattered with ticks and *A* grades. On the rare occasion she got an equation or exercise wrong she repeated it on the other side of the page over and over again until she got the answer she was looking for. For a fleeting moment I forgot why I was burrowing through her books, lost in the way she formed numbers and set them free across her pages to tell stories in a language that was a mystery to me. Her notes pages for English, history and music were framed with her fluid doodles, the mirrors of her moods. I pored through them looking for something, anything. At some point Tanya left. Freddy came into the room and lay on the bed with his handheld game until its beeping broke my concentration, letting dark thoughts through the cracks, and I had to send him away. Tanya came back with a sandwich cut into triangles and an apple sliced into chunks so I could eat them with one hand as I worked. The afternoon light started to fade.

Then there was geography. I forced myself to save it until last. I had had to beg for the A4 folder to be left in her room, promising the police that it would remain untampered with. I twisted their arms with my big wet eyes and my shaking hands. At first I wondered what they suspected I might do with it until I remembered Temperley's girlish writing and the way it wove in and out of the black-on-white lines of Stephanie's thoughts. I would have ripped it to shreds if I dared. Last time I had read the contents of the folder all I had seen was Nathan Temperley spread over every page. I would look at it again and make myself see past him to seek any hint of where Stephanie could be, any tiny clue missed by the police or overlooked by me. Phrases leapt out at me, twisting with ambiguity as I read: *Spheres of influence, fringing reef, human impact, intrusive rocks, transpiration, infiltration, rip-rap, ventifacts, yardangs.* I didn't let myself focus on her doodles of his eyes, his smiley faces and bursts of ticks. I couldn't bring myself to look at *Advantages and Disadvantages of Urban to Rural Migration* again, but I scanned every other page. I didn't even know what I was looking for. A map with an *X* marking the spot would have done nicely. There were sketches of maps aplenty, of Montserrat, Death Valley and the Atacama Desert, but they were only marked with population density, contour lines and urban centres. There was a bullet-point list of the challenges of building roads in the Lake District. There was a case study about tourism in Oban and a neatly drawn map of the town littered with his smiley faces, his ticks, his stars.

'Why the hell did she need to know this stuff?' I flung the folder back onto the desk.

'She didn't,' said Tanya. 'He's taught her all sorts of things she didn't need to know. Come downstairs and take a break.' But I didn't want a break. If I stopped looking I would start thinking again. I loaded the folders and textbooks back onto the desk and turned to the bookshelf built into the corner of the room in the awkward triangle of space between the attic's sloping ceiling and the chimney breast. The bottom shelf was nearly a metre wide, the top shelf a tiny nook. I started at the bottom and worked my way up, moving from left to right. I picked each book up, held it by its spine and shook it, then turned the pages one by one.

I slowed down by the time I reached the third shelf. I was running out of places to look. I started to pay more attention to the books' titles and to try to remember where they came from and when Stephanie had read them. But they were just the books of a teenage girl, the phases she had been through in the last year or two played out in paper and ink. There were all of the Brontës, the Austens, a run of Georgette Heyers. There was a novel about a girl dying in the aftermath of a nuclear war that she had chosen in a bookshop with some tokens she received for her eleventh birthday. For weeks after she read it she had appeared at the breakfast table with rings beneath her eyes and endless questions about how we would survive if the bomb dropped. I read the book too, hoping that being able to discuss it with her would help to calm her fear, but instead found myself sharing that fear, expanding on it and merging it with grains of knowledge about the fragile situation in Iran, the state of play with North Korea. I told Dan the stockpile of water and canned food, the chemical toilet and the bedding rolls in the cellar were for Stephanie's benefit, but it wasn't true. At least I would know where she was if we were all down there sheltering from the fallout. At least she wouldn't be with him.

There was the series of books about vampires that had obsessed her at the beginning of the new school year. I had worried about how much she had loved the books, convincing myself that she would be drawn into some gothic subculture steeped in drugs and underage sex. She had told me not to be silly and quickly moved on from vampires to werewolves, from werewolves to stories about twins.

Between the vampires and the werewolves was a book that didn't fit. It was a guidebook to Scotland, the type a retired couple going on a long-awaited trip in their new caravan might buy. Why would she have a book about Scotland? I was still puzzling over it when Dan crashed into the room.

'For God's sake, Rosalind, it's time to stop this. There's nothing here.' His anger must have bubbled within him for hours until the pressure grew so great that he was propelled up the stairs and into me.

'This. Why would she have this?' I held the book in front of me.

'Who knows? It's not important, is it? Why the hell she would run off with that pervert is what I want to know. They keep showing his face on TV and every time I see him I want to punch the screen. Is he good-looking, Ros? Is that it? Is he so bloody beautiful that she couldn't help herself? What is it about him that made her do this?'

'She didn't do this, Dan. He did this.' I threw his own words back at him, remembering the jolt of my head hitting the car window.

'It's not fair,' he said. 'We don't deserve this.'

'Neither does she.'

'I meant all of us. This family.' He sank back on the bed to stare at the ceiling. 'What if they can't find her? What if he's spirited her away and there's no way to track her down? That's what I keep thinking. What if we look for her everywhere, for ever, but never find her? We'll become nothing but the family whose daughter disappeared.'

His pain called to me across the metre of book-strewn carpet between us. He had picked up the only soft toy she still kept on her bed. It was a bright red lobster with big blue cartoon eyes and drooping whiskers that he had brought back from a business trip to Boston when she was nine years old. He held it on his chest, squeezing a furry claw in each hand. I forced myself to sit next to him, to lean over and take his arm.

'The police will find her. They will. It's just a matter of when.' I sank my incisors into the tip of my tongue – an old trick to keep me in the moment, to tether my mind to the here and now. I repeated what Chief Inspector Marwell had said to me. 'He can't hide for ever and as soon as he comes out of his hole he'll be spotted. His picture is everywhere. There can't be a single person in the country who doesn't know what he's done.'

Dan sat up, dragged his sleeve across his face. I watched his spine straighten as my words took effect. 'You're right. We have to stay positive, don't we? But this, Ros . . .' He gestured to the mess around me, the books sprawling across the floor. 'This has to stop. You're just making a mess and wearing yourself out.'

'Can you give me one possible reason why she would have this book?' I waved it at him again. 'I can't think of a single thing that would make her go out and buy a book about Scotland. She has no interest in Scotland. She's never even been there.'

'You're being irrational. There could be any number of reasons for her to have that book.'

'Such as?'

'I don't know. Maybe someone gave it to her. Maybe she picked it up by mistake. Perhaps she wanted to go there.'

'There are a lot of places she wants to go and she doesn't have books about all of them.' I remembered the wrench of finding her reading *A Guide to Studying in the USA* a few months earlier. I could see its loathsome red spine jutting from the top shelf. 'And look – here.' I pulled open the geography folder and spread the case study about tourism in Oban before him. 'Oban's in Scotland. Look. There's a map and everything.'

'Oh, for God's sake. You don't seriously think he figured out where to take her to from a geography assignment?'

'Maybe.' What was it that Freddy had said? *He'll know all the places to hide.*

'He would hardly stand up in front of a class and teach them about the place he was about to take an underage girl to.'

I thought about the cup of water hitting the desk, splattering Stephanie's work, smudging her ink. I remembered the way my fingertips had made contact with the cup for long enough only to let a sliver of doubt enter my mind. I didn't think he would have been able to help himself. 'I'm going to ring Tanya. This could be something. It could be a clue.' Tanya would believe me. Tanya would understand.

'Well I'm going to make our son some dinner.' *There's a first time for everything*, I nearly said, managing to bite back the words only at the last moment. Perhaps the mathematics was different now: maybe a single plate of tinned spaghetti on toast cooked in a crisis trumped twelve years' worth of lovingly roasted chicken and handmade pasta.

Later that night, Chief Inspector Marwell came to the house to tell us that two sightings reported after the television appeal were deemed to be 'very credible'. Both had taken place in Scotland. A woman swore that she had seen Temperley on a quiet stretch of road north of Dumfries the afternoon after Stephanie had disappeared. She had been driving back from visiting her mother in Locharbriggs, taking the road slowly in case of black ice. The man in blue jeans and a black coat appeared from behind a hedge, startling her so much that she beeped her horn. He got into a small silver car parked on the verge but she hadn't noticed the number plate or whether there was a passenger in the car. The second sighting had been at a petrol station in Irvine later that day. A man with a black beanie hat pulled low on his forehead had filled the tank of a small silver car and bought five large bags of Maltesers. The cashier had made a joke about the quantity of chocolate but the man had just scooped up his change and walked out.

'Maltesers are her favourite,' I said. 'When she thinks no one's looking she throws them up in the air and catches them in her mouth. She never misses.' I imagined Stephanie in the passenger seat catching Maltesers one by one while Temperley drove, his hand resting on her thigh. It was as if he was taunting us, playing the role of the dirty old man buying sweets for a child.

I showed Marwell the book about Scotland, explained that I couldn't understand what it was doing in Stephanie's room unless she had left it there for me to find. I put Stephanie's geography folder into his hands so he could pore over the case study of tourism in Oban. I saw him and Tanya exchange a glance and for the first time I wondered whether she was humouring me, whether she had really rung the team at the station and alerted them to my 'discoveries' or whether she had just shut herself in the sitting room alone, sat on the sofa and raised her eyes to the ceiling, muttering 'give me strength' through her teeth. But then she leant forward and squeezed my knee. She believed me.

'So are you releasing the sightings to the media?' said Dan.

'No. Our best chance of finding them quickly is if they stay still. We want them – him – to think they're safe where they are so they stay put. Then we can close in.' I pictured him tracking game across the Serengeti, moving silently on khaki-clad feet. Up ahead, two lions lounged beneath a tree, the larger one keeping its paw pressed firmly onto the smaller one's tail.

'You can't close in if you don't know where he is,' said Dan.

'Oban,' I said. 'Look for them in Oban, for God's sake.'

Dan shook his head.

'Dan, look.' I pushed the glossy A4-size map at the back of the guidebook onto his lap and traced the line from Dumfries to Irvine and on up the coast to Oban. 'They're heading north-west. Don't you see?'

'We're looking everywhere, Mrs Simm, including Oban. It's just a matter of time until we get him, wherever he is.' The chief inspector put a hand on my arm. 'Stay here. Let us bring her home,' he said to me as he left, as though he had read my mind, seen me racing up the motorway in my little four-by-four, skipping red lights and driving over roundabouts, my swerving path lit by the flash of a hundred speed cameras.

Dan and I argued that night. I wanted to go to Oban. He said I was being ridiculous, that I was in no fit state to drive and that we had to think of Freddy. He said I was having one of my irrational episodes; I hadn't known he had a name for them. We screamed foul words at each other, the point of the argument soon buried beneath strings of insults. We only stopped when Freddy appeared in the hall, wet-eyed and ragged. We apologised and shuffled to bed together. Even as sleep claimed me I was planning the journey I would make the next day.

When I padded down the stairs at four o'clock in the morning, I discovered that all the car keys – mine and Dan's, both spare sets – were gone. Tanya? Or Dan? It didn't matter. I lay down on Stephanie's bed and remembered her face lit by a fleeting smile on the Sunday before she went missing. I had caused that smile by sliding a page of the *Sunday Times Style* magazine across the kitchen table towards her. It was a feature on Christmas party dresses and there was a red-haired model wearing a long gown in purple silk, a gossamer wrap the colour of dried lavender around her shoulders. She had an array of jet necklaces looped around her neck and wrists as though she had ransacked a cabinet of Victorian mourning jewellery. 'It's amazing. It could be my wedding dress,' Stephanie had said.

*   *   *

It was Stephanie's idea to go to Heathrow that evening instead of waiting until the morning. She said she was worried about the snow making the traffic bad, but I thought she was just as anxious to get away as I was. I went online and booked a room in the Sofitel linked to Heathrow Terminal Five. We were waiting in the hallway with our suitcases packed and our coats on when Dan arrived home.

'Have you got my passport?' Stephanie said, as soon as he opened the door.

He stood half in and half out of the hall, flakes of snow clinging to his shoes. I felt his eyes reach for mine but I turned away.

'You're not going now, are you?'

'Looks like it,' said Stephanie. There was a bitter edge of triumph in her voice. She put on her scarf and gripped the handle of her suitcase.

'Ros, you don't need to go yet. Stay here tonight. Or wait an hour at least. We need to talk.' He took a step towards me and let the door swing closed. I wanted to put my hands over my ears; he had always been so adept at talking me out of things and I couldn't let that happen now. I – we – needed to leave him, the house, St Albans and everything that lurked here.

'No,' I said, reaching for the handle of my suitcase and shaking my head so I didn't have to look at him. 'I'm not ready to talk. We're booked into the hotel now and we want to beat the traffic.'

For the first time that I could remember, his clever words – all words – seemed to have deserted him. He handed Stephanie her passport and, silently, picked up our suitcases and carried them to my car. As he loaded them into the boot Stephanie darted into the passenger seat and closed the door. She wound the window down a few short inches and said, 'Bye, Dad,' through the gap before snapping it shut again.

I took one last look around the hallway, a mother's habit to check for things left behind. In the porch Dan put his hand on my wrist. Lines of tension besieged his mouth. 'We'll talk when you get back, won't we? Please, Ros? Don't make any decisions while you're away. It wouldn't be fair.'

I nodded. For a moment the urge to lean into his arms and rest my head on his shoulder tugged at me so hard that I thought I would lose my footing. 'Ring me if there's anything Stephanie and I need to know. About Temperley, I mean.'

Then I was in the car and Dan was shrinking away in the rear-view mirror, his right hand waving. Then he was gone.

THREE DAYS

I woke with a feeling of lightness. The panic that had grown within me for days, sneaking down the dusty corridors of my mind and loosing old fears and dark memories from their chains, had grown weaker. I had a talisman to ward it off, to scare it back into the dark recess where it belonged. As Stephanie showered, I let myself think about the words we had spoken into the pitch darkness of the hotel room as we lay side by side in our twin beds. I had imagined the conversation so many times that, now it had actually happened, its memory had the syrupy texture of déjà vu.

Stephanie had become increasingly tense as we approached Heathrow, checked into our hotel and pushed pasta around big white plates under a shimmering chandelier in the restaurant. The bright lights and shiny flat surfaces of the hotel's interior amplified every sound and sent jagged shadows across the table between us. We barely spoke as we ate and I glimpsed the next two weeks spreading out before us, a marathon of silent dinners and stilted breakfasts. We went to bed after the nine o'clock news but both of us were wound too tightly for sleep. As I lay awake beside Stephanie I breathed deeply and tried to force myself into a state of calm. I remembered reading a magazine article urging mothers to keep their newborns' cots in the same room as they themselves slept to reduce the risk of cot death. Research had shown that a sleeping baby senses its mother's breathing pattern and matches its breaths to hers; by sleeping nearby, a mother gave her baby a template for breathing that made it less likely that the baby would simply stop inhaling oxygen during the night. If I was calm, perhaps Stephanie would breathe in my calmness and anxiety would release its grip on her too.

I used an old trick my mother had taught me for coaxing forth reluctant sleep: I imagined myself walking through the house I had lived in as a child, smelling, hearing and feeling everything around me as I moved from room to room, letting myself sink through layers of memory. I was on the fringes of sleep when Stephanie spoke, her voice a whisper.

'Mum, can I ask you something?'

'Yes. Anything,' I whispered back. I rolled onto my side and tried to make out her shape in the dark. Outside, a plane took off, the roar of its engine reaching a fever pitch before fading into the night.

'Will you promise to be honest? Not to say what you think I want to hear?'

'Yes.'

'Really?'

'I promise.' I said the words slowly, willing myself to mean them, bracing myself for what was to come. It would be Cam, wouldn't it? Cam or Dan. *What's going on?* she would ask. *Why did you marry Dad? Do you want a divorce?*

'Did you ever hate me for what I did with Nate?'

The question and the mention of his name – that vile pet name – were so unexpected that I sat up in bed and forgot to whisper. 'No! I could never hate you. Ever.' I dropped my voice. I had promised honesty. 'I wished you hadn't done it with every fibre of my being. I hated that you had lied to me. I hated knowing that you were able to ring me up and deceive me, knowing that you might never see me again. But I never hated you. There's nothing that could make me hate you and you must never think that.' My throat was constricting, aching to weep.

'But Dad's never forgiven me, has he? And he certainly won't be forgiving me for anything now.'

'There isn't anything to forgive. There wasn't anything to forgive then and there isn't now.'

'He couldn't look at me when I got home. Do you remember? I think it took him two years to look me in the eye. And he couldn't bear to be in a room on his own with me. He'd almost run out of the door.' Once I had pushed Dan – really pushed him – about the way he was with Stephanie and he had snapped at me: *How am I meant to look at her when I know what she did? What am I supposed to say?* Eventually, the way he was with Stephanie had become just another feature of our new normality, like our polite conversations and the way we were all so careful never to raise our voices or to mention love, romance, Scotland, caravans, geography or Nathan Temperley.

'He was angry,' I said. 'Not so much with you as with what happened. He was angry that it happened to his family.'

'To him, you mean.'

'Well, yes. But to you, too. To us.'

'He was always telling you to get over it, wasn't he? But he hadn't got over it at all.'

'I don't think any of us got over it. But never think that anyone hated you because it just isn't true.' I lay back down and pulled the duvet up tight beneath my chin. Stephanie had fallen silent but I knew I wouldn't sleep.

'Ringing you was the worst bit,' she said suddenly. 'I almost couldn't. Nate had to write me a script so I could read it out. That was the only way I could go through with it. As I was reading it I was praying that you would hear a clue in my voice, that you would somehow know and then whatever happened next wouldn't be my decision. All the time we were gone that was the moment I thought about the most.'

I didn't dare to speak. I didn't dare to move.

'I'm sorry, Mum. I'm sorry I made that phone call. I'm sorry I stole your jewellery, too.'

'It wasn't your fault. None of it was your fault.'

'I know what I did to you. To all of you. I don't blame Dad for how he feels. What Nate did was wrong but it was my decision to go with him. He didn't force me to do anything.'

'Stephie, you were just a child. He was an older man, nearly twice your age, in a position of authority over you. He groomed you and manipulated you. You were a victim and he was your abuser. No one has ever blamed you and no one has ever hated you either. Thoughts like that are no help to anyone, darling. Believe me, I know.' I paused. The stirring of old memories had reminded me of something. 'How about you leave all those thoughts here when we take off tomorrow?'

'I wish I could.'

'You can. Close your eyes. Trust me, this helps. People do it all the time. Are they closed?'

'Yes.'

'OK, now you have to imagine a box. Not just any box but a really, really strong one. Mine is like a pirate's treasure chest but yours can be however you want it to be as long as it's got a lid.' I waited a few minutes. She was silent and still. Perhaps she was humouring me or perhaps she had fallen asleep. 'Now. Once you've got your box you need to fill it up. Find each of those thoughts and memories – you know the ones I mean, the ones that race around your head at night, the ones that sneak up and jump out on you to spoil things when you're feeling happy. You need to acknowledge each one, just for a moment, then visualise yourself stuffing it into the box. It might take a while.'

'It might take all night,' she whispered.

'Take as long as you need. But when they're all in there, shut the box – imagine the sound it makes when it slams shut. Then lock it up tight. Mine has a big metal padlock on the front which squeaks when I lock it. Once I've locked it I wrap it up in layers of rusty chains just to be on the safe side.'

'Then what do I do with the box?'

'We don't have enough baggage allowance to take it to Corsica so you'll have to leave it here. You can collect it when we get back if you want to. But I don't think you will.' I picked out the shape of her hair falling across the white of the pillow case. I hoped she was better at leaving her box behind than I was. I hoped it stayed wherever she left it and didn't creep back into her head, rattling its chains and groaning with the weight of its burden until she couldn't help but lift its lid again.

I closed my eyes to let her pack her box in peace. I wondered what she would put in first. I wondered whether her box would need to be even bigger than my own.

I thought she must have fallen asleep when she suddenly said: 'It was me who called the school. I told them I was with him.'

I couldn't stop myself from letting out a single gasp of laughter. I had hoped for this but never dared to believe it. 'But he didn't know it was you?' I wanted to cheer, to lean across the space between our beds and give her a high five.

'No. He didn't know. He couldn't work out how anyone discovered that we were together so quickly. He thought the appendicitis story would give us at least three weeks and by then we would be long gone. He was going to email again and say he had complications from the operation and he needed another two weeks off. He had a forged sick note ready. He planned every tiny detail and when he heard his name on the radio he couldn't understand what had gone wrong. I didn't know anyone could be that angry. It always seems fake in films and on TV when people are red in the face, screaming and shouting, with their eyes bulging out of their heads, but that's what it was like. That's why he hit the policeman, I suppose. All that anger had to go somewhere.'

'Why did you make the call, Stephie? You must have known it would mean you'd get caught. He'd get caught, I mean.'

She was quiet for a minute. 'I don't know.'

'Don't you?'

'I was scared,' she said eventually. 'It was so remote up there and no one except him knew where I was. I thought we'd get caught a long time before we got there. But once we'd been in the caravan for a day I understood what a good hiding place it was. We could have stayed there for months without anyone finding us.'

'Why didn't you say where you were when you rang?' It would have been over in minutes if she had. She would have been home little more than seventy-two hours after I had realised she was missing.

'The police would have turned up right away and he would have known it was me. I just wanted to go home but I couldn't tell him that after everything he'd done for me, for us. He'd taken so many risks and given up everything and there I was crying for my mum like a child.'

'How did you do it without him noticing?'

'He went to Glasgow to see about the fake passports. I'd given all my money to him but I found twenty pence in one of the caravan drawers and I'd seen the telephone box as we drove in. I was so scared he'd come back and find out what I'd done.' She was whispering, as though six years later he might still be listening, hiding in the darkness and waiting to catch her out. 'I just sat there for ages thinking "Do I, don't I, do I, don't I" over and over until I wanted to scream. I tossed the coin in the end: heads I ring, tails I don't. It was tails so it tossed it again. I did best out of three, then best out of seven, then best out of eleven, then twenty-one. My hands were so cold that on the last toss I dropped the coin and it slid under the bed. I thought I'd lost it for good. I panicked then, thinking I'd missed my only chance, that there was no going back. I managed to fish the coin out from under the bed then I ran to the phone box.'

I pictured her rushing alone along a muddy track, a hood pulled low over her face, the wind tugging at her coat and a single twenty pence piece gripped in her hand. It was the bravest act I could imagine; walking on the moon was trivial by comparison. 'Thank you. Thank you for telling me,' I whispered. 'I'm glad it was you. I always thought it must have been Sarah.' As I lay in the darkness I did something I had very rarely allowed myself to do. I imagined them in the caravan. I pictured Temperley pacing the tiny patch of floor, his knuckles bouncing off saucepans, walls, window panes, as he fumed at having been discovered so quickly and his cunning ruse of hospitals and emails being seen through. There is no love in the caravan, just his anger and Stephanie's fear and regret. The air is damp, the ice of the north wind only just kept at bay by the thin walls. They are both balled up in coats and scarves. Stephanie sits on the edge of the bed, her arms wrapped around herself. Her teeth are chattering but he doesn't notice. Raindrops like ball bearings hammer the roof and the windows drip with condensation. He continues to pace and when he turns his back to her she smiles, hugging her secret close. She is no longer hiding; she is waiting to be found.

'I just wanted to go home,' she said, her voice catching on a sob. 'I thought he'd lose his job, maybe get a caution or something. I thought we'd find a way for it all to be OK, stupid little idiot that I was. It was never going to be OK.'

'You weren't stupid, Stephie.'

'He's been locked up for all these years. Because of me.'

'He'd have been caught anyway. You'd never have got out of the country.'

'Do you think that? Really?'

'Yes. The police would have got him. There's no question.' This was something I had always told myself, that everyone had always told me. I had been careful never to question it. Even my darkest thoughts stopped short of the worst case scenario: Stephanie gone, for ever, with him.

'I don't know. No one would even have been looking for him for another two weeks. Sometimes I think about what—'

'No,' I said, more harshly than I meant to. 'Don't say it. It could never have happened. I would have found you.'

'I did love him,' Stephanie said into the darkness just before she fell asleep. 'I really did.'

Stephanie spent so long in the bathroom the next morning that I called through the door and asked her if she was OK.

'Just doing my hair,' she said.

I was washed and dressed, my suitcase zipped and ready. Another ten minutes passed and the bathroom door failed to open. I had a sudden image of Stephanie balancing on the edge of the bathtub, pulling herself towards a window. I shook the thought from my head. If she didn't want to come away with me she could have left by the door. Besides, her phone was still on the bedside table and she wouldn't have left without that. Still, I was uneasy. I kicked off my shoes and crept towards the bathroom, pressed my ear to the wood of the door. For a long minute I heard nothing. Maybe I had been right about the window. I was just about to knock when I heard a sound: something like a coin hitting a tiled floor, followed by a sigh.

I sprang back as the door opened. 'Ready, Mum?' she said. 'Let's go.'

We ate breakfast in the hotel restaurant. I took tiny glances at Stephanie from behind my hair. There was a new sense of calm about her, a sense of resolve.

'Thanks for last night,' she said as we trundled our suitcases through the walkway that led from the hotel to Terminal Five. The sky was blue and clear, the cold winter sun glittering on the frosty ground far below us. 'It was good to tell someone that stuff. And I'm glad we're going away. It's definitely the right decision.'

But her calm was short-lived. The departures board was a kaleidoscope of red cancellations and yellow delays. Outside the terminal's windows, ranks of planes sat patiently beside their gates as figures in orange jumpsuits tended to frozen windscreens and ice-chilled engines. At the check-in desk the attendant told us that our flight would board an hour later than scheduled.

'Oh, for God's sake!' said Stephanie as the attendant took our passports and typed our details into her computer with the click of her long red nails.

'It's only an hour. We'll get through security, buy ourselves some sunglasses and then have a coffee. There's a Gucci shop through there, and Burberry. It'll fly by.'

'But what if the plane can't go? What if we're stuck here?'

'I don't think you need to worry about that,' said the check-in assistant, leaning across the desk and smiling at Stephanie. 'All the cancellations have been due to planes not arriving this morning and yours is already here. It's just the backlog causing delays. We'll get you boarded as soon as we can.'

'See? We'll be fine.' I zipped our boarding passes and passports into my bag.

'Let's go straight through,' said Stephanie. I threaded my arm through hers and led her through the empty maze of queue-control barriers that took us through security. I bit the insides of my cheeks hard and the jagged spark of pain chased away the misplaced guilt I always felt when preparing to go through security checks. I stopped myself from turning my handbag inside out to search for the sachet of cocaine or nugget of Semtex slipped unnoticed into a pocket by a stranger. The rush hour of early morning flights had ended and the only people ahead of us were a couple in their sixties dressed in full safari gear. Stephanie muttered something under her breath as they unloaded armfuls of camera equipment and matching polythene bags wedged full of miniature toiletries into the plastic trays on the conveyor belt. The man had to go through the metal detector three times, divulging new treasures from his waistcoat pockets with every pass, before we could follow him through.

Stephanie flinched, her hand leaping to her throat, when she set the scanner off. She stood rigid while a squat woman in navy ran her hands over legs and arms before stepping aside to let Stephanie pass.

'Right. We're air-side. That means we're officially on holiday.' I drew her into the perfume cloud of the duty free shop. I needed to calm her down, jolly her along until we were safely on the plane. We couldn't afford to be grounded by a panic attack; hers or mine.

'There's no going back now,' she said and leaned into me as though she was afraid of being blown away.

She was OK as long as I kept her busy. We bought a bag full of make-up, testing so many lipsticks and eyeshadows on our hands that we looked as though we had strange, matching skin diseases. We admired handbags and tried on glittery Christmas party shoes. In WHSmiths we chose half a dozen paperbacks and picked up a box of Maltesers for the plane. The sound of the chocolate spheres rolling around in their box reminded me of family holidays to Cornwall, the children high on sugar and straining their eyes for a glimpse of the sea before we had even left Hertfordshire. But if I turned away from her for an instant, or if my attention was caught up with a cashier, I would look back to find her frowning at her watch, poking her phone or scowling at the departures board. She was never still and her fingers pulled at her hair and balled themselves into fists at her sides.

When I had finished paying for our sunglasses – we each chose the same shaped frames, mine in black and hers violet

– I caught her listening to a message on her phone with such despair on her face that it made me shiver.

'What is it, Stephie?' I said when she had lowered the phone from her ear.

'It's nothing, really,' she smiled weakly.

'Jake?'

She nodded.

'You haven't told him where we're going, have you?' I had an image of a young man staggering up to our table at dinner, his breath rank with booze, his face wet with tears.

'No.'

'Why don't you just switch that thing off? As far as anyone knows we're already on the plane. You've got a cast-iron excuse not to speak to anyone. Jake included. Leave him here along with everything else.'

She nodded and did something to the phone. But she must have just switched it to vibrate as a few minutes later I heard the trapped-fly buzz of it vibrating in her pocket.

The boarding time for our plane on the departures boards had crept steadily backwards in five-minute increments. It was already ten thirty and we weren't due to board for another hour. Our energy for shopping exhausted, we found a table in the food court outside Pret A Manger and Stephanie waited with our hand luggage while I queued up and bought two skinny lattes, one with an extra shot of espresso. I wanted the buzz of caffeine to help me through the lingering minutes before our escape was complete. I watched her out of the corner of my eye as I shuffled up the queue and waited for our drinks. She was fidgeting in her seat, tugging strands of her hair over her face and swiping the screen of her little white phone. As I stooped to pick up teaspoons and sugar she gave her phone a final, angry glance before thrusting it deep into her rucksack. She dug through the plastic bags we had gathered on our trip around the shops, eventually surfacing with one of the novels.

'How's the book?' I put the paper cup of coffee in front of her, wincing when a dribble of hot liquid ran over my thumb.

'Good so far. I think I'll enjoy it. I'm just going to the loo,' she said, putting the novel down and getting up from her seat without looking at me. 'I'll be back in a sec.'

I watched her move off into the crowd, her rucksack bobbing on her shoulder, and a memory came back to me. She was eight years old and I knew that something was worrying her as soon as she came out of the classroom door. As she walked towards where Freddy and I waited by the school gate her right hand twirled a strand of her hair into loops. I knelt down and smoothed the hair away from her face but she wasn't ready to tell me what was wrong. On the way home my mind skittered from bullies to anorexia and back again. It wasn't until Freddy had gone to play in the garden that she produced the cause of her troubles from her bag. It was an invitation to a birthday party at an ice skating rink. 'I'm scared of falling over on the ice but I don't want to miss the party,' she whispered. I was so relieved that I had to kick myself in the shin so I didn't laugh. That Saturday I took her to the rink where the party would take place. She had never been ice skating before because I had never been able to bear the thought of sharp blades and tiny fingers; no wonder she was afraid. We got there early, before the crowds arrived. I left her sitting on the edge while I circled the ice a couple of times, finding my balance. I had skated as a child, had loved the liquid sensation of speed, the rush of wind on my face even in the run-down, bumpy council rink near my house. At first I held both of Stephanie's hands. She stood rigid with fear as I pulled her along behind me. She didn't relax until she stumbled and fell, landing on the ice with her fists tightly balled and looking up at me with scared eyes for a second before realising that she was OK, that the worst had happened and it wasn't that bad after all. A few laps later she was holding just one of my hands and skating alongside me. Then she was on her own, streaming ahead of me, her face alight with triumph and her fear sliced to ribbons beneath her feet. I would capture that moment on paper as soon as we got to the hotel, the blue sparkle of the ice, the glint of the skates' blades and the glow of joy in her eyes.

An announcement over the tannoy snapped me back to the airport and the cooling coffee in my hand: 'Passengers flying to Calvi-Sainte-Catherine on delayed Air France flight 6109 may now proceed to gate eighteen where your plane in ready for boarding.'

I whispered a thank you to anyone who might be listening then stood up, craning towards the loos, expecting to see Stephanie walking towards me at any second.

That was how I saw him before he saw me. It was his bright blue jumper that caught my eye. He was five metres away from me, scanning the departures board and twisting a battered passport in his hands.

I snatched up our bags and backed away from him, leaving Stephanie's book open on the table. Sudden movement might have caught his attention so I fought my urge to run. I forced myself to move slowly, to blend in with the gentle ebb of people browsing the sandwich selection in the café. There was a tall stand displaying packets of crisps and popcorn two metres behind me. If I could make it there unseen I could creep around him in a wide circle, hiding behind the knot of passengers gathered around the departures board. I could grab Stephanie the moment she came out of the loo and race with her to the departures gate. We could be on the plane before he caught a glimpse of us.

But Stephanie wasn't in the loo. All of a sudden she had pushed out of the crowd and was standing next to Cam. She smiled at him before uncertainty clouded her face. She drew her arms around herself and took a step away. Then he reached out and put his hand on her arm and I had no choice but to come out of my hiding place.

'Stephie, there you are. We need to go. They're calling our flight.' I didn't look at Cam.

'Ros. I thought I'd missed you. I went to the wrong terminal.' He wasn't even going to pretend this was a chance meeting. I cursed myself for telling him where we were going. I had never suspected that he would do something as stupid as this.

'I don't know what you're doing here but Stephanie and I have a plane to catch. We have to go. Come on, Stephanie.' He started to say something but I raised my hand and motioned for him to stop.

I tugged at Stephanie's sleeve but she didn't move. She looked from me to Cam then back again. 'Why's he here, Mum?'

'That's our plane they're calling. I'll explain later.'

'No. Tell me why he's here.' *I'm very perceptive about things like that.*

'Ros, please. I just want to talk to you. I couldn't let you just leave. I'm sorry I had to come here like this.' He didn't look sorry. There was nothing apologetic in his accusatory glare. 'I rang you twenty times and you didn't ring me back. You didn't even text me. Was I not even worth that?' I had switched my phone off after his second call.

Cam took a step towards me just as Stephanie took a step away. Her face was bone white in the glare from the electric lights. Her lips were quivering. 'After everything you said about Nate, about me. And you've done this with him! Is he being abused too, Mum? Is he a victim too?'

'Don't be ridiculous! He's an adult and I'm not his teacher! And we haven't—'

But she wasn't listening. 'Cam, did you know what you were doing? Did she trick you into it? Take advantage of your innocence?'

'Stephanie—' I started. But then she looked at me, right at me, and I knew my words were empty.

'For God's sake don't tell me it's not what I think!' She shoved my hand off her arm. 'That's exactly what Dad said when I caught him with his little friend. Cam's practically half your age, Mum! I suppose it's not his fault, either. Are you going to put him in a box and shut the lid on him?' The anger in her voice was so intense that it made the words she had spat at Dan on the stairs sound like loving whispers. She looked from me to Cam and the fury on her face turned to something darker. 'Is he why you were so desperate for us to go away? He is, isn't he? Oh my God! It wasn't because of me at all. It was never about me.'

'That's not true! Stephie, I—' But she wasn't listening.

'You're just as bad as Dad, as Nate. All of you are as bad as each other with your lies and your demands and your endless bloody secrets,' she hissed. Then she bolted into the crowd. I started after her but Cam grabbed my arm. His fingers pinched my skin through my coat when I tried to wrench it free.

'Get off me! Let go!' Cam had been gentle smiles and easy laughter. He had been sunlight on a dull day. But now he was hurting me, his face red and his eyes wet with tears.

'No. Ros. No. You can't just toss me aside like this because your husband finally remembered you exist and showed up with a bunch of roses. It's not fair. You promised you'd see me today. You promised.'

'Let go of me!' I twisted my arm in his grip, braced my hand against his shoulder and tried to push him away.

'If I let go now I'll never see you again. Will I?' He shook my arm. 'Will I? Ros? Will I?'

'Oy, back off, mate. Let go of her,' came a deep voice from my right. A thick-set man in a grey tracksuit and denim jacket had advanced on us. He was glaring at Cam, an arm raised towards us, in warning or in preparation to intervene.

'Security! Security! Someone get security!' a tracksuited woman at the man's side screamed at the top of her high-pitched voice. People stopped moving, heads turned, trapping us in a circle of wide-eyed faces. I struggled against Cam's grip. I scratched at his neck with my free hand, twisted and writhed, gasping when my shoulder pulsed with pain.

Cam let go of my arm just as two security guards in black and fluorescent yellow appeared at either side of us. I staggered backwards and thought I would fall until hands reached out to steady me from behind. Stephanie, I thought with a pulse of relief. But it was just another security guard.

'Madam, are you OK?'

'My plane. I have to go.' I didn't wait to see happened to Cam. I heard him shout my name again but I just kept running in the direction Stephanie had gone, calling for her as I ran.

The airport had filled up and I had to weave around knots of people, scanning every face as I ran. I searched the toilets, the cafés, the shops. With every step I expected to see her. With every step I was disappointed.

'Can all passengers flying to Calvi-Sainte-Catherine on delayed Air France flight 6109 please proceed to gate eighteen where your plane in ready for boarding.'

I switched my phone back on and rang her but it went straight to voicemail. Hope sparked. Perhaps she had heard the announcement and gone straight to the gate. Her phone would be off ready for take-off.

A sign told me that gate eighteen was ten minutes' walk away. I ran down corridors and flew across moving walkways, our bags of make-up and books and magazines tangling around my fingers and bouncing off my legs.

'This is the final call for passengers for Flight AF6109 to

Calvi-Sainte-Catherine. Your flight is ready to depart from gate eighteen. Passengers for Calvi-Sainte-Catherine please proceed to gate eighteen immediately.'

Gate 14, Gate 15, Gate 16. Every time I thought I was nearly there the airport's labyrinthine interior would reveal another acre of carpeted hallway to cross, another flight of stairs to climb. I knocked into a woman struggling with a child on her hip, mumbled my apologies but didn't stop to help when she dropped her bag, spilling bottles, dummies and soft toys across the floor.

Gate 17.

'Passengers Rosalind Simm and Stephanie Simm for Flight AF6109 please proceed to gate eighteen immediately where your flight is ready to depart. Passengers Rosalind Simm and Stephanie Simm to gate eighteen immediately.'

The coffee swirled in my stomach and climbed up my throat. A stitch pinched my side but I kept running. She would be standing at the gate, looking for me, waiting.

Gate 19. I heard myself scream with frustration. How could I have missed it? I dropped the plastic bag of books, magazines and Maltesers and left them where they fell. I spun around and retraced my steps.

'This is the last and final call for passengers Rosalind and Stephanie Simm for flight AF6109 to Calvi-Sainte-Catherine. Your flight is ready depart from gate eighteen.'

There it was: Gate 18. I was going to make it. In a few minutes' time I would be sitting on the plane next to Stephanie, catching my breath and trying to find a way to explain about Cam.

The gate was empty apart from a lone man in a navy blue Air France uniform securing a barrier across the door that led to the aeroplane. The monitor at the gate's entrance said CLOSED although I could see the plane below me on the tarmac, still attached to the rubber concertina of its walkway.

'Wait! Wait!' I shouted at the man's back as I ran towards him.

'Rosalind or Stephanie Simm? You've just made it,' he said with a French accent and a smile. He started to retract the barrier. My heart thundered in my ears.

'Stephanie Simm is already on board, isn't she?' I leant on the check-in desk by the door and dug into my bag for my boarding pass, still trying to catch my breath.

'No. I'm afraid she has missed the flight.'

He took my boarding pass from my hand. 'Wait! I can't go without her. Are you absolutely sure she isn't on the plane?' But her passport and boarding pass were in my handbag. She couldn't be.

'Absolutely sure. Madam, I must ask you to board now or we will be forced to remove your baggage from the hold.'

'I can't go without her. Wait just a minute, please. She's my daughter.'

'It's not up to me. We can't delay the plane any further. I'm going to have your checked baggage removed from the aircraft now if you're not going to board.' The more frantic I grew the calmer his voice became.

'No! Wait! This is all your fault. If the plane had taken off on time she would have been on it. This isn't fair! You have to wait!'

He didn't falter; he must have had training for dealing with people like me. 'You'll need to collect it from the baggage reclaim hall. Just ask at the enquiries desk and they will direct you to a carousel.' As he picked up a phone and murmured something into it, I felt the floor shifting beneath me, staggered backwards and landed hard on a plastic chair. My child had gone missing again. I had lost her just when I had dared to think I was finally going to get her back. I sat in that chair and wept with frustration while the attendant sorted pieces of paper into piles and pretended not to notice me. It wouldn't be long before he called security and made me someone else's problem. Or perhaps he would just move on to the next departure and leave me there to become a modern day Miss Havisham, waiting for ever to catch a flight with someone who was never coming back.

The roar of the plane we should have boarded firing up its engines forced me back into the present. It was after one o'clock. Stephanie had been gone for half an hour. I pictured her face when she looked from me to Cam and back again, heard the bitterness in her voice when she said *You're all as bad as each other.* I had been mad to think that she would have boarded the plane. It was more likely that she'd spun off into the crowd, following a trajectory to nowhere, bouncing from place to place until she could marshal control of her shock and anger.

Wherever she was I had to find her.

I rang her phone again but it was still switched off. I sent her a text message: **Please call me xxx**. As I retraced my steps back towards the terminal I forced myself to think about everywhere she could be. I stood still on the moving walkway and shut my eyes. I knew prisoners are always released at seven in the morning. *You still have two and a half days*, I thought. *Sixty-seven hours until you really need to worry.*

I searched the air-side shops, cafés and bars again. I went to the customer service desk and wept until they agreed to broadcast a lost child appeal over the public address system. I waited at that desk for half an hour – veering between hope and despair with the passing of each minute – before I gave up.

I had to explain myself over and over again to be allowed to pass out of the security area and back into the main body of the airport. I asked the grey-haired man who finally led me through a door that opened into the hall of check-in queues and luggage trolleys whether he had seen Stephanie but he had only just come on duty. 'Hope you find her, love,' he said as he closed the door behind me.

Stephanie must have left the airport somehow, by train, tube, coach or taxi. If I was her I would have taken the train into central London, so I followed the signs to the station, pushing my way through ever-thickening throngs of people. The Heathrow Express service into London Paddington had seized up in the cold and the platform was a sea of irritated passengers clutching tickets for a train that was already an hour late. I pushed my way through clots of them, down the length of the platform and back up again, but there was no sign of Stephanie. She must have taken the tube. As I stood at the top of the train station escalators, buffeted by rucksacks and sworn at by executives in suits, I felt her sliding along beneath me, metres below the ground, slipping further away and growing more unreachable as every second passed.

The motorway between Heathrow and West London was an angry snarl of traffic in both directions. I crawled past two cars crunched together by the side of the road, red metal and green metal in a jagged embrace, before creeping slowly onto the A4. By the time I joined the nose-to-tail crawl through Hammersmith and Kensington, it was already dark. I always avoided driving in central London, hating the irrational one-way systems and death-defying cyclists. These roads were unknown to me and the endless honking of horns and revving of engines beneath the street-lamp glare was like the soundtrack of one of my anxiety dreams.

I followed signs for the City and found myself driving up Knightsbridge, slamming on the brakes when a tiny woman laden with green and gold bags and a phone pressed to her ear stepped out in front of me as though the two tonne metal car I was driving towards her was invisible. She put her hand on the bonnet to steady herself then walked on without even looking at me. I followed signs with blind faith, recognising nothing around me until I hit the north bank of the Thames and the bright lights of the bridges danced in my wing mirrors as the snow started to fall again. I leant forward and gripped the wheel as I travelled east, craving the reassurance of each new road sign. Later I would realise how ridiculous my route had been, but as I was driving I didn't let myself think; I just moved forwards as best I could, forcing myself to concentrate on the grip of my hands on the wheel, the pressure of my foot on the accelerator.

It was after seven o'clock by the time I arrived in the little Islington square where Beatrice lived. I had been within metres of it for half an hour but got caught in the one-way system designed to keep me from my goal, then became trapped behind a bus on Upper Street as the driver brought traffic to a standstill by stalling across the Angel junction. The windows of Bea's top floor flat were dark and there was no response to the doorbell. I used the very last gram of charge in my mobile to ring her. She was somewhere loud and fun, shouting to be heard above the music. 'Wait in the Lord Toby. I'm on my way.'

The little Victorian pub in the corner of the square was almost an extension of Beatrice's flat. It was mercifully quiet and so warm after the ice wind that had chased me in from the street that stepping through the door was like a sudden embrace. After a few false starts, my voice quaking and my frigid fingers fumbling to open my purse, I managed to order a double gin and tonic and sat at the bar gulping it until Beatrice arrived.

*   *   *

With the two credible sightings of Temperley and the narrowing focus on Scotland, hope blew through the police investigation like a warm breeze. Combined with Chief Inspector Marwell's assurances about search activities in Oban, it was enough to let Tanya prise out of me my plan to drive up the motorway and hunt for Stephanie. Instead, I tidied her room and made a list of things I would need to buy to replace those I had ruined in my search for clues. I changed the bedsheets and put her toy lobster back on her pillow so its head rested on its claws. The berries on the holly bush at the end of the garden had ripened and I filled a vase with glossy green leaves and bright red fruits and set it on her window sill. When there was no news and nothing left to do the minutes stretched to fill hours. At nightfall I swallowed a sleeping pill to make the time go faster, then I panicked: what if they found her? What if they brought her here under cover of darkness and the door went unanswered as I slept on above? I gulped a pint of water then forced my fingers down my throat until the blue tablet floated intact in the cloudy water at the bottom of the toilet bowl. I poured the rest of the sleeping pills on top of it, popped the tranquillisers from their foil blisters and flushed them all away. I would be here when she came home. All of me. Always.

Marwell and Haskins arrived late the next morning. Dan was on the phone trying – yet again – to convince his parents not to come and 'help' us. He had already spoken to his mother. Now he was dealing with his father who had rung him back to chastise him for making his mother cry. I was surprised they were so keen to see us; I had thought that the shame would have sent them running in the opposite direction, burning family albums and changing their names by deed poll as they fled. 'If they turn up we'll get Tanya to send them away. She can tell them they're impeding the investigation or something,' I whispered to Dan. A shy, remorseful sympathy had grown between us after our row. We had started to seek each other out, to cower in corners and take it in turns to say *It can't be long now* and *They're closing in*.

'Any more sightings?' I asked the chief inspector as Dan finished his phone call.

'Not as yet but we've got teams out in the areas where he was spotted.' Hope dimmed. It occurred to me that perhaps Marwell, with his hard knuckles and weather-beaten face, was standing in my kitchen only to give the illusion of progress in what was now a very high-profile case.

'No new sightings,' I said to Dan as he came to join us around the kitchen table. 'Nothing new at all.'

'Now, Mrs Simm, that's not quite true. I'm confident that we'll have a breakthrough on the car today. We're narrowing it down very quickly. It's a lot easier to find a car than a man these days so getting that number plate is key. Absolutely key.'

'You're not looking for a man, you're looking for Stephanie. For my daughter. My fifteen-year-old daughter.' I was being peevish, I was the child who ran downstairs on Christmas morning and found nothing beneath the tree. A tiny part of me had expected Marwell to arrive with Stephanie in tow. In my post-midnight fantasy he stood in the kitchen door and said, 'Rosalind, there's someone here who wants to see you.' I looked up, my eyes brimming with tears, and she ran towards me, apologies tumbling from her lips, forgiveness from mine.

'Stephanie's our priority. That goes without saying. But it was Nathan Temperley who planned this so he's the key to finding her. I'm sorry we don't have anything more concrete for you this morning but this is how it works, this is the reality of policing. We catch the bastards inch by inch. We don't jump out on them, we creep up on them and then we take them down. Believe me, Rosalind, we're going to get him and when we do we'll bring Stephanie back to you.'

I sat down and covered my mouth with my hand, not trusting myself to speak. Dan put his hand on my shoulder.

'What will happen when you find her?' he said. 'Will she come home straight away?'

'We'll need to ask her some questions. You understand that she's a witness in a criminal investigation?' We nodded. 'But we'll have her home as soon as we can. And you can be there with her for the questions.'

'If she wants you to be,' Inspector Haskins said. She rarely spoke when her boss was in the room. I saw the warning look that the chief inspector shot her. He didn't want her dropping nasty little grains of reality into the picture he was painting for us. But she wasn't willing to be silenced. 'There are things she may not want to talk about in front of her parents.' *Thick fingers, hair dusting the backs of his hands, brown eyes watching her.* I caught Dan's eye, saw his face paralysed with something between rage and shame. 'You should prepare yourselves for that. She's still a teenager in spite of everything that's happened and teenagers can be very private about these things at the best of times.'

'It's OK,' I said. 'We understand. If she's not comfortable with us being there then maybe Tanya could be? I think she'll like Tanya.'

I remember the next two days only as a mosaic of displacement activity. None of us left the house. I suppose we could have but where on earth would we have gone, what would we have done? We could hardly have strolled through the city centre amongst the Christmas shoppers or eaten pizza in a restaurant awash with candlelight and laughter. Beatrice arrived with bags of improbable snack foods: heads of celery, Italian meat selections, olives and bags of mini Mars bars. Tanya went out to buy milk and came back with six pints and a new game for Freddy's console. She stayed with us – with me – most of the time, dropping in 'just quickly' and then not leaving for hours. There were frequent updates from the police: small things that we made much of, stretching their significance out to fill the time. There was a potential sighting in Dunfermline, another in Birmingham and one in Brighton. There was the news that every ferry port and airport was on the lookout just in case. That set my imagination off down a new route and I saw him packing her into a bag, coiling her up and zipping her in then wheeling her down a gangplank and into an echoing metal hold.

Unlike Dan, I avoided reading or watching any news during those long days, turning newspapers over if I happened across them so only their harmless sports pages fell into my line of sight. But that changed when Dan crashed into the dining room where I was sitting with my forehead pressed to the table, trying to remember the words of a folk song I had sung to Stephanie when she was teething.

'That bloody man! I'll kill him! Look at this.' He spread a page of print in front of me. Instinctively, I turned away. 'Look, Ros. It's bloody Pete from number four. He's told this rag everything he knows about us and made up a whole lot of horseshit to go with it.'

What could Pete know about us other than what everyone else saw? He was a busybody and a gossip. He discussed everyone with everyone else, moving through the spaces between the houses on a breeze of speculation. He could have seen me fall over on the drive after I drank too much Pimm's at the Marleys' Independence Day garden party. He could have been watching from his window on the night that Dan was away and I dragged the children out of their beds at midnight and called the police, convinced there was an intruder in the attic. No doubt he noticed the number of occasions on which I left the house only to return minutes later to check that the door was locked, the windows closed or the cooker switched off. I thought of all the times he had fished for an invitation to Sunday lunch or Christmas drinks and regretted never giving him what he wanted.

'It's so bloody intrusive.' He pushed the paper across the table, away from him and towards me. 'Oh, and he says maybe Stephanie felt neglected because you recently got a job. This crappy rag loves guilt-tripping working mothers.'

'Oh.' I didn't think of myself as a working mother. The four hours a day, three days a week that I spent at the gallery was more of a hobby than anything. It helped to fill my days while Stephanie and Freddy were at school. The gallery owner, Margaret, was on the PTA at Stephanie's school. I probably should have been upset when I realised she had employed me for my clothes and my address as much as my passion for art, but I was so grateful for the job that I couldn't find it in me to mind.

Dan paced behind me as I read. NIGHTMARE ON MILLIONAIRE'S MILE: HOW A LOVING FAMILY'S PERFECT LIVES WERE RIPPED APART BY PREDATOR TEACHER, was the headline of the double-page spread. Underneath it was a picture of Temperley. He was wearing a navy blue shirt and smiling at the camera, squinting slightly into the sunlight. His hands were out of shot. Beneath this was a picture of our house, captioned *The Simm family's ultra-desirable million-pound home*. The photographer must have stood in the garden to get the shot without the hedge being in the way. I wondered what we had been doing behind the curtains while he or she stood there, probing us with a long lens.

The article quoted Peter Naylor, *retired insurance broker and resident of exclusive Crispin Avenue*, extensively. In fact, it was easy to see that he was the journalist's only source even though some comments were attributed to 'a neighbour' or 'a fellow Crispin Avenue resident'. We were a lovely family, Pete said. Dan and I lived for our kids although Dan worked long hours in the City; such long hours, in fact, that sometimes he stayed over in London and wasn't seen around the house for days at a time. I was always driving Stephanie and Freddy around and very involved with both of their schools but I had recently taken a job in 'a trendy city-centre art gallery'. 'A neighbour' had suggested that Mrs Simm's recent venture into the world of art had turned family life upside down.

I shoved the paper away. Dan stopped pacing and leant across the table towards me. I hadn't realised the peak that his anger had reached, the effort he was putting into containing it. 'I'm going to go and give him a piece of my mind. He can't go around talking about us like that.'

'Don't. Just think how much these reporters would love a story about you shouting at the neighbours. Imagine the headline – "Schoolgirl's dad in neighbour rage rampage."'

'What, you think we should just let him get away with it? With this?' He pulled the paper off the table and read: '"Of course, Dan works long hours in London so he's not around much." It's bloody spiteful, that's what it is. He's kicking us while we're down.'

'He's treating it like a soap opera. The whole thing is vile, but confronting Pete is just going to make it worse.'

'But—'

'We'll wait, Dan. We'll wait until she's home and then we'll deal with him.' I had decided that Pete would get that Sunday lunch invitation he was always fishing for. I would invite him round, push him down the cellar stairs and then brick the door up behind him so he could never speak to anyone ever again. I wondered how long it would take for him to stop calling for help from the cellar – days? weeks? I would have to remove the remains of the nuclear war survival kit before I pushed him down there, otherwise he could live on for years in the darkness, losing colour and talking to himself like Gollum.

'I'm sick of waiting. They said they'd find her soon and that was two days ago.'

There was a knock at the dining-room door. It opened to reveal Tanya and Inspector Haskins.

'Can we come in?'

'You've found her?' I said, standing up so quickly that I bruised my thighs on the table top.

'No, but we've got the number plate so it's only a matter of time.'

'It really is good news,' said Tanya. 'You'd be stunned by the percentage of criminals we get through their cars.'

Two days after we had been told that progress was imminent, the discovery of the number plate felt meaningless. Progress to me meant Stephanie and nothing less. I felt doubly cheated when it emerged that this breakthrough was the result of luck rather than the cunning 'inch by inch' police work Chief Inspector Marwell had promised. A man from Milton Keynes had come forward to report selling a silver Peugeot 206 to a man calling himself Thomas Smith for fifteen hundred pounds in cash five days before Stephanie disappeared. He had returned from a trek in South America to see Temperley's picture in the paper and recognised Mr Smith.

'Every police force in the country has the licence plate, make and model of the car. As soon as he moves we're going to spot him,' said Haskins.

'Oh, great,' said Dan, every ounce of the dissatisfaction I felt ringing in his voice. 'He's probably ditched it by now.'

'If he's ditched it we'll find it.'

'And you'll be back to square one.'

'Have you looked in Oban?' I said. 'Looked properly? He knew that area. The children studied it.'

'Yes, Mrs Simm. We've had the local police on alert there. They've searched the area and found nothing.' I felt a collective rolling of eyes.

Fourteen hours, each one as long as the one that came before it, followed. The house was stuffy with the close warmth of central heating, unopened doors and broken sleep. My limbs were heavy, my thoughts heavier. At some point, I discovered my jewellery was missing: a pair of diamond stud earrings and the diamond bracelet Dan had given me on our tenth anniversary. I knew Stephanie had stolen them. The police made much of it, but I was just happy to know that she had taken something of mine with her.

Dan and I slept in the sitting room that night, each stretched along a sofa, balancing our heads on cushions. It was the broken rest of a long train journey: I was never asleep but was always waking up, jolting into alertness to see Dan lying opposite me, his eyes wide in the darkness. In the morning I was sluggish and dazed. I tried to remember when I had last showered: yesterday? The day before that? The day before that, even? Freddy, never one to wash without prompting, had probably gone untouched by soap and water for a week. An illicit thought took advantage of my insomnia-dulled mind to sneak into my consciousness: was a child in the hand worth two in the bush? Not when the one in the hand wasn't Stephanie. Nothing was worth Stephanie. I dug my fingernails into my wrist to chase the thought away. I resolved to do better by Freddy from there on in. I would shower then run a bath for him.

As I let the hot water run through my hair and down my back, a man called Gregory Hayne was four hundred miles away, his sharp eyes watching for the coming of the morning light. Thistle Farm Family Camping sat in a sheltered spot behind the town of Oban and accommodated hundreds of tourists every summer. It had a playground, a sandpit and daily activities for children to while away the long summer holidays. But only wind-burned outdoors types who pitch one-man tents on hills camp in Scotland in the winter and the site shut down between October and March. To keep a bit of revenue flowing in, it offered caravan storage out of season. Suburban caravan owners who wanted their vans stowed safely for the winter could tow them to the site and park up for a modest fee. A sturdy perimeter fence and high steel gates fastened with padlocks meant that no one could drive in and no one could drive out. At the end of March, the owners would come to pick up their vans for the start of the caravanning season and stay a couple of nights on the site with its award-winning toilet block and shop selling home-made jam.

It was Gregory's job to check on the site a couple of times a week while his brother, its owner, was away. The cash he received for the easy task was welcome in the winter when the queues of summer tourists were a distant memory and trade in the fish and chip shop he ran depended on a slow trickle of locals. When the morning came, it was a bright one. He decided to walk to the campsite the long way round to make the most of the break in the weather. By lunchtime, dark clouds would have gathered again and the news had warned of the chance of snow. He approached the campsite via a lane used only by his brother's family and the staff who cleaned the toilets and manned the shop in spring and summer. In winter, when Craig and his wife were away and Gregory was the campsite's sole regular visitor, the lane was used only by foxes and the occasional dog walker so he was surprised to see a car parked on the verge. It was tucked in tight under the trees as if someone had tried to hide it. He looked through the windows for any sign of its owner but saw nothing. He tested the door handles and found them locked. There was no good reason he could think of for anyone to park so close to his brother's property.

Gregory made his usual rounds of the caravans, checking that doors and windows were locked. Some caravans were shrouded in canvas covers to protect them from the elements and all had their curtains drawn. He found nothing out of the ordinary amongst the dormant vans and moved on to check the perimeter fence, taking his time and enjoying the crunch of the frosted grass underfoot. His brother's house was visible through the leafless trees at the spot where he noticed something amiss with the three-bar wooden fence that enclosed the site: there were wedges of mud caught on the bottom two slats of wood as though someone had climbed over. His immediate thought was that someone had walked through the site on the way to burgle his brother's house. He climbed over the fence and into the patch of orchard that separated the house from the camp-site. Someone had been there, churning the mud beneath their feet. He ran up to the house and was relieved to find the door safely locked, the burglar alarm still on. He let himself in with his keys and checked every door and window twice. He searched the outhouses but nothing was amiss. The car was still on the verge when he walked back up the lane.

It was a throwaway comment from a customer in the shop at lunchtime that made Gregory wonder. The car and the mysterious fence-climber, the sense of unease he had felt while creeping around his brother's house, had stayed with him and he was anxious to shut up shop and go back to the site before dark. His old classmate Sarah Chapp was picking up fish and chips for her father as she did every Wednesday. She was looking at a copy of the *Daily Mail* as Gregory wrapped a pensioner's portion of chips. 'This teacher off with his pupil is a funny thing, isn't it?' she said. 'It's as if they've vanished into thin air.' When she left, Gregory locked the door behind her and skimmed the article in the paper. Then he rang the police. A few scrapes of mud on a fence wasn't much but the sighting of an abandoned car matching the description of the one being searched for in the hunt for a missing teenager was.

I know all this because I went to see Gregory. I told Dan and the children I was going for a weekend sketching retreat to work on my portfolio ready for my university applications that autumn. I left before dawn and drove all the way to Oban on a Friday morning, walking into the fish and chip shop just as the lunchtime rush came to an end. It was two and a half years after Stephanie had come home. She had still not said a word about what had happened in the days she was missing. I expected Gregory to be reluctant to waste time talking to me about what must have been a minor event in his life but he was desperate to talk, the words bubbling out of him as soon as I explained who I was. He thought he had failed Stephanie by not discovering her hiding place sooner. 'I must have walked right past her when I went up there on the Sunday,' he said, 'and I didn't suspect a thing.' I comforted him over cups of tea in the empty fish and chip shop as his thirteen-year-old son scrubbed down the counter ready for the supper-time fry. Gregory took me to the campsite and I tried to picture it as it would have been that winter, leafless trees, bald earth and mud made hard by frost. But it was full of brightly coloured tents and smiling families. I couldn't see Stephanie there at all. I spent the rest of the weekend filling my sketchbook with imaginings of shrouded caravans, telltale patches of churned mud and bleak winter skies.

One of the caravans stored at the campsite that winter belonged to Temperley's uncle Graham. Graham Temperley and his wife had retired to a bungalow in Ardfern a decade before but his wife had recently passed away. Of course he would tell his nephew where he kept the caravan; Nathan visited him every couple of months and knew all about it. No, he hadn't missed the set of keys from the peg in the kitchen. He hadn't thought about the caravan since he'd dropped it off in Oban, wasn't even sure whether he wanted to keep it now that his Mary was gone.

I didn't know any of this at the time. I just knew that Tanya burst through the door and shouted, 'We've got them! Rosalind, we've got them! She's OK!' There was no thought, just feeling after that. There was a moment of soaring relief when my head was light, my ears ringing. Then there was the crash into fear: the swallowing up of joy in the black hole of all the unknowns that lay ahead. I had felt this sudden flight and fall just once before, on the day that Stephanie was born. After fourteen hours in labour, her heart rate plummeted, doctors circled, lights flashed and alarms sounded. Her first cry was a moment of euphoric relief. Then I touched the tiny curl of her hand and realised that this little human only had one mother and that her mother was me. That was when the fear set in.

* * *

In Beatrice's sitting room, still breathless from rushing up four flights of stairs to reach her flat, I dug my phone charger out of my handbag and plugged it into the first socket I saw. The charger's flex was so short that I had to kneel on the floor to press the buttons that brought the phone back to life. As soon as it found a signal it beeped with a text message. It was from Stephanie: **I need some time on my own. Don't worry about me. I'll get in touch when I'm ready.** That was it. I tried ringing but her phone went straight to voicemail. I wanted to tell her that Cam was nothing more than a flirtation, a mistake, a reaction to Dan's absence, but I couldn't find the words. 'What am I going to do?' I asked Beatrice, holding my phone out to her, still on my knees.

Beatrice read Stephanie's text message, unhooked the phone from its charger and dropped it onto the surface of her sleek sideboard. 'Have a glass of wine and leave her to it. She says she'll be in touch when she's ready.'

I just knelt there, the floor hard beneath my knees. I had thought that Beatrice would understand, would catch hold of the edge of my panic and run along beside me.

'Don't look at me like that, Ros. What else can you do but wait?'

'I can't bear it,' I said. 'It's like she's gone missing all over again but this time it's my fault. We were so close to being on that plane, to getting away from him. If Cam hadn't shown up we'd be hundreds of miles away. She'd be safe. It's my fault that she's not.'

'You couldn't have known Cam would show up like that.'

'But he wouldn't have if I hadn't . . . done what I did with him.'

'You had your reasons. Look, what happened with Temperley was vile and I know you're terrified about what him getting out means for Stephie. He was a monster to do what he did. He's probably still a monster now. But she's not a child any more. She has to find a way to live in the world with Nathan Temperley walking free and so do you. And of course she's upset about Dan and whatever she thinks about Cam. She's going to be angry and confused and you're going to have to work that out between you. But right now you need to listen to what she's saying and give her some time on her own to calm down.'

She sighed and knelt down on the floor in front of me. We had never been the type of friends who hugged all the time or walked through town with our arms linked together – we didn't need to be – so it was a surprise when she put her hands on my shoulders. 'Two days is a long time,' she said. 'You can afford to give her twenty-four hours to calm down.'

'I can't just sit here doing nothing.' My voice faltered and I started to cry, the gin I had drunk on an empty stomach easing the tears from my eyes.

'There's nothing you can do right now. She knows you're there for her. She knows full well that you will do anything for her. You just have to wait for her to come to you.'

'Oh, Bea, it's all his fault. I hate him so much. I'd kill him, you know? I really would. I wouldn't even care about the conse-quences. I would rather be in prison for life than have him anywhere near her.'

'I know, I know.' She squeezed my shoulders again, almost too hard. Beatrice had heard this all before. In the first couple of years after Temperley's arrest she had even joined in. Together we had created elaborate fantasies about his death, killing him over and over again in ever more painful and humiliating ways. But, eventually, she had stopped indulging me. She would listen for five minutes then cut me off, steering the conversation to less violent ground. It was around the time that Dan had told me I should stop spending time with Tanya, that I needed to start letting go. Once or twice, when things had been really bad, I wondered whether Dan was the cause of this change in Beatrice. Perhaps he had emailed her and they had met in a bar near Kings Cross – I knew the one she would choose – and talked about me, keeping their voices low. *Please don't encourage her obsession with Temperley*, Dan would say and with a pang of guilt she would agree. A few times, when the distorting lens of anxiety had turned every thought into a barbed hook of menace, I wondered whether their knees had brushed beneath the table, a second round of drinks had been ordered, his train had been missed. I screwed my eyes shut; I couldn't look at Beatrice with the shadow of that thought in my mind.

'Here's what we're going to do. Stay here tonight. If you haven't heard from her by two o'clock tomorrow afternoon we'll go to her flat. She's most likely there and even if she isn't Sarah's bound to know where she is. Stephie will have had time to think by then and you'll both be in a better place to work things out.'

I nodded. My arms were heavy at my sides, my legs welded to the floor. I didn't have the energy to rub away the tear I could feel poised to drip from my chin. I was a butterfly in a gale, a snowflake in a storm, powerless in the chaos that surrounded me. Would it be so bad to stop fighting it, just for a night? Beatrice took my hands and pulled me up from the floor. She steered me onto the scarlet velvet sofa with its cowhide cushions, and set a wine glass in front of me. As she sat beside me the whole sorry story tumbled out of me, unravelling thread by thread, unspooling across the polished cherry-wood floor in the flat's dim light: the way I had hidden Temperley's release from Stephanie and Dan; the state we had found her in and the way she had started to confide in me since we had brought her home; how my longing for Cam had boiled over; Stephanie shouting about Dan's bit on the side and the way I had lost my grip finger by finger until I was sliding into panic and seeing Temperley in places he couldn't possibly be.

When I had told Beatrice everything, she ushered me into bed in her spare room, layering me with blankets against the draught that sneaked through the sash window.

Beatrice kissed me on the forehead and clicked off the light. Alone in the dark, the wine-soaked corridors of my thoughts echoed with scenes from the day: the blaring airport tannoy, the pain of Cam's fingers digging into my arm, the breathlessness of my run to Gate 18. These moments marched through my consciousness on a loop, slow but insistent. Beneath them I sensed something else – a weak, fragile, half-formed thought fighting for air. I could feel its shape, sense its presence but when I tried to focus on it it disappeared, sinking into the morass of memories of the day. Maybe I was imagining things. Maybe it was just the wine.

TWO DAYS

I woke in darkness, wet with my own sweat. In sleep I had been running through the airport again, the hot air stealing my breath, the bright lights dazzling me and Stephanie constantly shifting out of view. I fought my way out from beneath the pile of blankets and filled my lungs with the room's cold air. I remembered the sense I had had on the edge of sleep of something fighting to be thought or remembered. It was like the feeling I get just before I develop a sore throat: a persistent sensation – not quite an itch, not quite a pain – in the nameless area behind my nose and above my mouth. It was something and nothing at the same time.

There were no new messages on my phone. I rang my voice-mail twice to check. It was only seven twenty-eight and I had agreed with Beatrice that I would give Stephanie another six hours and thirty-two minutes before I hunted her down.

My throat was dry and my stomach fluttered with queasi-ness. We had drunk too much wine and eaten nothing except an elderly bag of parsnip crisps which Beatrice had dug out of a cupboard. Their salt-sweet earthiness clung to my teeth and I wondered whether the suitcase containing my toothbrush was still making slow circles on a baggage carousel deep within Heathrow's bowels. I gulped down the glass of water Beatrice had left by the bed but it wasn't enough. Anything before nine o'clock was hideously early for Bea so I crept down the corridor that led from the two bedrooms to the sitting room without switching on the lights. I opened the sitting room curtains and watched the dregs of night leach out of the sky through the three sash windows that overlooked the square below. More snow had fallen in the night and the garden in the middle of the square was a perfect white oblong splashed with the orange of the still-lit street lamps. I thought about taking the key from its hook in the kitchen and letting myself into the garden. I could push my feet into the undented snow and shiver on one of the little iron benches until my head cleared and the nausea passed. But what if the snow was deeper than it looked? What if my first step into the garden sent me sprawling and I fell into the icy whiteness, down and down until it swallowed me up? I stayed where I was. A man emerged from one of the glossy black doors on the other side of the square and made his way in the direction of Upper Street with the slow, waddling penguin steps of one who fears falling. It was difficult to believe that only two days had passed since I had watched Dan leave the house, striding across the snow as if it wasn't even there. I should have rung him from the airport, or at least as soon as I got to Beatrice's.

I made a cup of tea and stretched out on the sofa. I wanted coffee but I couldn't work out how to use Beatrice's machine. It took up about a third of the worktop space in the kitchen, which made sense for someone who existed on coffee, cigarettes and little pots of tabbouleh and baba ghanoush from Planet Organic. I put the television on for company and watched the news through half-shut eyes. Heathrow was closed today, the runways turned to ice rinks and the planes frozen hard to the ground.

Beatrice spent half an hour on the phone cancelling her plans for the weekend then we walked through Camden Passage, picking our way through the trestle tables of stuffed foxes, costume jewellery and brass candlesticks. Stallholders in finger-less gloves watched us with hopeful eyes as we passed. Out of

'I'm just—'

'We agreed you'd wait until two o'clock.'

I nodded. 'I should ring Dan when we get back. He has a right to know.'

'The eggs Florentine here is good,' said Beatrice.

If only cosmic ordering was as effective as ordering breakfast in a busy Islington café. I had to force myself to dig my fork into the oozing yolk and thick Hollandaise sauce, but once I started eating, the fluttering of nausea subsided. Halfway down my second cup of coffee Bea's calm reassurances started to take effect. Of course Stephanie was upset; Cam turning up at the airport must have convinced her that we were having a full-blown affair. She had been wound so tightly that it was no surprise that she had snapped and spun off into the crowd, but she would calm down. And when she calmed down she would see that there was no comparison to be made between Temperley and me, no comparison at all. She had said it in the heat of the moment, had lashed out at me with the cruellest and most vicious weapon she could lay her hands on. But she didn't mean it, she couldn't. *She's probably ringing me now*, I thought as the café filled up and we reached the bottom of our coffee cups. *Or now. Or now.*

But by two o'clock this fragile optimism had left me. Stephanie's phone was still switched off and she had yet to reply to any of my messages. It was time to go and find her.

I insisted on driving from Beatrice's flat to the one that Stephanie shared with Sarah. It would have been quicker to zip from Highbury and Islington to Finsbury Park on the tube, but I wanted to believe that I would need the car to take Stephanie home. My fingers were numb by the time I had scraped the ice from the windscreen and coaxed the engine out of its sub-zero slumber. I mistrusted the snow beneath my wheels as we crawled out of the square and onto the mercifully snow-less Upper Street. Beatrice thought she knew the way until we found ourselves snared in a one-way system, jostled by a double-decker bus and honked at by a furious obese woman wedged into a tiny pink car, her bare upper arms wobbling as she pounded the horn. My hands were shaking on the wheel by the time I spotted the hulk of the old cinema on Isledon Road that was my landmark for finding Stephanie's street. It had long stopped showing films and now housed a church attended by men in suits and women in brightly patterned dresses. The red letters that had once spelled out film titles bore the message *HE WATCHES OVER ALL HIS CHILDREN*. I thought of Temperley's eyes locked on Stephanie, of his face in the crowd and the person she thought she saw watching the house.

'Ros! Go!' The traffic light had turned green without me noticing. A man with a thick beard, his mouth open in a shout of anger, was already leaning heavily on the horn of his clapped-out van. I pulled into the next side street; we could walk from there. The roads had been cleared of snow but the pavements were packed solid with dingy ice and by the time we climbed the steps of the Victorian villa into the top of which Stephanie and Sarah's flat was squashed, my leather boots were heavy with water. Beatrice stood behind me as I pressed the buzzer and bent my ear to the intercom speaker by the door, waiting to hear Stephanie's voice.

'Hello?'

'Sarah? It's Rosalind.'

There is a pause, a pang of fear that Stephanie has asked Sarah not to let me in, to shield her from me, then: 'Come up.' The intercom buzzed and I pushed open the door, padded across the piles of post for unknown people that always filled the hallway, and up the stairs.

The landing echoed with the memory of picking Stephanie up just nine days earlier. Sarah had been so glad to see me then, had been poised behind the door waiting for my arrival. This time she opened the door slowly and without a smile.

'Sarah. Is she OK? Is she all right?'

'Oh!' Her hand leapt to cover her mouth. 'She's not here. I thought she was on holiday with you?' I wasn't certain that I believed her. I loved this girl but I had never been entirely convinced she had known nothing about Temperley, so there had long been an edge of mistrust in that love. I tried to catch her eyes with my own but they skittered away from me. I was sure she had something to hide.

'She left the airport just before we were supposed to take off. I need to find her. Where is she, Sarah? I know you want to protect her but please just tell me where she is. I just want to see that she's OK. Please?'

'I don't know where she is. I haven't heard from her since yesterday. She texted me from the airport and said she'd send me a postcard.'

'Oh, shit,' said Beatrice behind me. 'Has she been here since yesterday?'

'I don't think so. I was out early and I only got home an hour ago but there's no sign she's been here.' Sarah was still standing in the crack of the partially open door. She was hiding something, I was sure of it.

'I need to see her room,' I said. 'Check if she's taken anything. We've only got until tomorrow to find her before . . .' Before what? Before he hunted her down and wrapped his spider's limbs around her again, snared her in his web?

Sarah nodded. Stephanie must have told her about Temperley's release. She opened the door and stood aside for Beatrice and me to walk in. I led the way to Stephanie's room. The curtains were closed and in the gloom I thought I saw a figure hunched on the bed. I let myself hope that she had sneaked in here quietly and lain down to wait for me. But then Sarah snapped on the light. The sheets had been stripped and the duvet folded in the centre of the bed with the pillows piled on top.

'I cleaned up a bit. The sheets are still in the dryer,' said Sarah. The ash tray, wet towels and empty wine bottles had vanished. I thought of Sarah alone in the flat, on her hands and knees clearing up Stephanie's mess once again. Not for the first time I wondered at the tenacity of their friendship. What had Stephanie ever done for Sarah?

I threw the curtains open. In the light I saw what I had failed to notice last time, when I had seen nothing but my daughter and the state she was in. The room was a blurred counterfeit of her bedroom at home when she was fifteen. A poster of the Golden Gate Bridge, smaller and tattier than the one that had hung in St Albans, covered the wall above the bed. The computer on the desk was a silver laptop and the shelf above it was lined with A4 binder files in purple, blue, maroon, brown and the yellow of a badly stubbed toe. Only the subjects written on the labels had changed. A Kings of Leon CD lay open on top of the stereo and a familiar photo of Sarah and Stephanie aged fourteen and dressed as Alice in Wonderland and the Cheshire Cat – Stephanie as Alice, Sarah as the cat – stood on the shelf.

'I know,' I said to Beatrice when she gasped. She recognised it too. Together we opened the wardrobe and chest of drawers beside it. We found black jeans and purple tops, grey Converse trainers and flat ballet pumps. I didn't even know what I should be looking for. The small suitcase Stephanie used for weekends away and her fleeting trips back to St Albans was stashed under the bed next to the larger case she packed for holidays.

I was stretching up to pull down one of the folders, an eerily familiar dull lavender colour with *Fluid Dynamics II* on its label, when Sarah came into the room behind me and said my name.

I hadn't noticed her leave. As soon as I turned around I knew my instinct that she had been hiding something was right. She was pulling her long dark hair across her face so it covered her left eye and the corner of her mouth. It was a habit that had stayed with her from childhood.

'When I stripped the bed I found these. They were inside the pillow case.' She extended a long arm towards me. The slips of paper in her hand were the colour a child would use to paint the sun. The sight of them snatched the breath from my lungs, made the floor ripple and buck beneath my feet.

Sarah, her eyes wide and bright, didn't hand them to me so I reached out and took them. There were three visitor permits for Prisoner Number NT7909. One was from September and two from October. I wanted to rip them to shreds, to unravel them all the way back through time so they had never existed at all. The trees that would provide the pulp that made the paper would wither as saplings, the carbon that blackened the ink to print them would stay locked beneath the ground.

'I didn't know. I swear I didn't know. She promised me she would never go there.' Sarah was folding in on herself, her long arms wrapping around her ribcage, her shoulders collapsing into her chest. 'I didn't know, Ros. I didn't know.' Her words and the yellow slips of paper nudged something aside within my mind. I waved my hand at Sarah, gesturing for her to be quiet and let me think. I was lying in my hotel bed again, listening to Stephanie's voice in the darkness as she told me about making the phone call to the school. *He didn't know it was me*, she had said, not *he doesn't know*. What if she had told him when she went to see him? What if he had asked her the same question he had asked me on the cold morning I had slipped away from home to visit him in prison? The description of the injuries sustained by the officer who had arrested Temperley shimmered in front of me: *Severe compound rotator cuff fracture consistent with the victim's arm being twisted behind his back with considerable force; broken nose and facial bruising consistent with hard punches delivered with a closed fist, as witnessed by officers in attendance at the scene.* In my worst nightmares I had seen Temperley luring Stephanie back to him; I had seen him bringing to life the choice she had presented us with when she first returned home – to accept their relationship or lose her for ever. I had imagined the two of them arriving for Sunday lunch, him resting his hand on her hip, hot saliva flooding my mouth as they stood on the doorstep in a yin and yang of love and hatred. Would I be forced to kiss him on the cheek? On Christmas Day he would squat at the base of the tree, squeezing the presents in their wrappings and watching me. Dan would carve the turkey, laying aside a pile of gristle and bone for our unwelcome guest. Temperley would let his knife screech across his plate, chew noisily and ask Freddy how he was getting on at school. By three o'clock Dan would be in his study, Freddy would have fled to a friend's house and I would be stickily drunk on champagne, slumped over the arm of the sofa and weeping for everything I had lost. Eventually we would stop inviting him. She wouldn't come alone. She would untether herself from her family and drift away. But what if that wasn't the worst that could happen? What if he didn't want to play out a long-fermented vision of romance, but of revenge-fuelled hate?

'He's going to punish her,' I said. 'He's going to take revenge on her for tipping off the police and thwarting his plan.'

*   *   *

In the first years of Temperley's incarceration, I spent a lot of time picturing him in prison. I had a series of scenes of varying brutality that I visited every time I was reminded of what he had done to Stephanie: when I saw teenage girls in town drinking coffee with their friends while Stephanie was at home alone, when I saw her classmates in sunlit parks chatting up boys, when

I saw Sarah and her mother laughing together outside their house. At these moments I would think of Temperley watching a mesh-caged television in a windowless recreation room, beset by a cacophony of thuggery – men heaving barbells to their chests with grunts and dropping them hard on the floor, a shivering drug addict vomiting noisily in a corner and the endless shouts of 'Paedo!' 'Kiddie-fiddler!' 'Nonce!' Or I would picture him walking along a metal gangway suspended between two rows of cells, men whose sleeveless T-shirts revealed thick arms and smudged tattoos jostling him until he cowered, shrinking into himself and dreading the moment they got him alone in the shower. In the razor-wire-framed exercise yard the other men trip him up; they kick a football into his face so his nose spouts crimson snot; they give him sharp little jabs to the ribs, sly punches in the back of the head; they kick him in the knees so he crumples to the floor. They grind their heels into his toes in the lunch queue and the prison chef pisses on his dinner so he lies awake at night, hungry and afraid. The guards turn the other way, as disgusted by him as everyone else. Sometimes it is not his cell that I see him in but his tiny office at the school, the bunk beds and slop bucket are squeezed in alongside the atlases and maps. My cognitive behavioural therapist had told me I needed to interrupt destructive thought patterns by thinking 'safe' thoughts. What did it say about me that my safe thoughts involved fists beating metal doors, curry laced with urine and blackened nails peeling off broken toes?

Arranging to see Temperley in prison took months. Before I could visit the son I had to visit the father. I went to his house and found him killing himself slowly with whisky and cigarettes. At first I wanted to ask him why he didn't speed things up with a razor blade or a nice pot of pills. Perhaps they were like vampires, these Temperleys, and killing off the creator would turn the son to dust. But after five minutes in that musty house I pitied the man. Two years had passed since we had done the television appeal together, but to look at him it could have been twenty. I watched him try to light a cigarette with one of those long plastic lighters that people used to use to light gas hobs, but even the over-sized ignition button was visibly painful for him to operate with arthritis-snarled fingers. I knelt in front of his chair and lit it for him. He used both hands to pour us stiff measures of Asda own-brand whisky from the litre bottle at his side. It was only ten thirty but I swallowed it in two gulps. With the cheap drink warm in my stomach I asked him to help me visit his son. He agreed without asking why. 'I'm glad that girl of yours doesn't go to the prison, though,' he said. 'She should be looking forwards, a young girl like her. Not waiting around for him.'

Seven weeks later, just as I had given up hope, the yellow visitor slip arrived in the post. After three weeks of looking at it I rang the Visitor Booking Line and took the first slot available. I told Dan I was going to revisit the Impressionists exhibition at Tate Modern. I was surprised by how easy it was to slip out of my life for a whole day; with that one little lie I could be gone from the time the children left for school at eight until they came home again just before four. For more than seven hours no one – except Temperley, of course – would know where I was.

At King's Cross I changed onto the tube and rattled through Central London to Victoria. I could have taken a taxi to the prison but I dreaded the thought of a chatty cabby asking me what took me to that part of town. I also feared the opportunities to open the door and jump out that I would face every time the taxi stopped at a traffic light. At Victoria station there was a fifteen-minute wait until the next train to Wandsworth Common so I bought myself a latte. I forgot to pick up a cardboard sleeve for the cup and by the time the platform number of the next train was announced the pads of my thumbs were throbbing with the coffee's heat.

Wandsworth was uncharted territory for me and I was taken aback to find its pavements thick with oversized pushchairs and scarf-wrapped figures on mini-scooters. Did the parents not realise that only a few metres of brick and barbed wire stood between their precious sons and daughters and a whole prison full of Temperleys? But there was no sign of horror in the faces of the mothers I passed as I skirted the common's expanse of muddy grass and leafless trees. When I reached Heathfield Road I checked my map again; it didn't seem possible that this residential street, with its sweet little cottages and blocks of flats, could be part of the prison's address. But suddenly there it was: a Victorian Gothic horror rising up from the tarmac like a cursed castle in a fairy tale. It was a beast of black slate and grey brick, its face peppered with dark windows, its mouth a wooden door two storeys high and varnished to glimmer in the winter sun. It was gratifyingly grim and I stood still in the middle of the pavement committing it to memory. Better even than its ugly face were the glimpses of what lay behind: tight coils of razor wire-topped brick buildings that spread out from the main prison's bulk like fungus around a tree stump. More than a thousand men lived in those buildings, sharing Temperley's air and waiting for the day they would be set free.

Nestled beneath the prison's left wing was a grubby white hut, perhaps a prefab left over from the war. WANDSWORTH VISITORS CENTRE said a sign beside a narrow blue door. I hadn't known what to expect a prison visitors' centre to look like but it certainly wasn't this. I approached it slowly. Pinned to a noticeboard on the hut's wall was a warning that a ten-year prison term was the price to pay for helping an inmate to escape. I wondered whether there was a price for stopping one from leaving at the end of his sentence, for bricking up the doors and barricading the gates. A skinny woman shivering in a hooded sweatshirt showed something to the person behind the hut's counter then disappeared through the door. For a long minute I didn't think I would be able to follow her. I stood rooted to the spot, watching the hut, until a sharp wolf whistle broke the air.

'Nice arse! Give us a closer look!' I turned to see a shaven-headed man leaning out of the window of a car so clapped out that it seemed to be sinking into the ground. I felt his eyes catching on the denim of my jeans. It was enough to make me put one foot in front of the other, to extend my hand with the yellow visitor slip in it when I was asked to, to submit to a bag search and a pat-down so thorough that I felt the prison guard's fingers graze my left nipple.

The Visitor Room was a wide open space after the dark tunnel where the search and pat-down had taken place. Small windows in the upper reaches of the walls threw light onto rows of tables and chairs, some already occupied by women waiting for their husbands, brothers, lovers, sons. But it was the smell that hit me first. The air was thick with pine-scented bleach as if every surface had been scrubbed with it just moments before I arrived.

I had been told to sit at table seven. I sat still, folded my arms in front of me and looked around the room with furtive glances. Women stared at the walls or picked their nails; those with children held them close. Everyone waited. At table eight a woman my own age crossed and recrossed her legs. Her breasts spilled out of a halter top and onto the table and she kept running her red nails through her hair and touching her fingertips to the pink gloss on her lips. When she wasn't inspecting a part of her body she shot anxious looks at a door in the wall opposite where I had entered the room.

Five minutes passed, then ten. She leaned towards me. 'Always bloody late, aren't they? Seeing me is all my Tony has to look forward to and they can't even let them in on time. What really gets me is that no matter what time they arrive they always get called back in at eleven o'clock on the dot. A forty-minute visit is more like fifteen by the time they get here.' She looked at me expectantly, as though she had asked me a question.

'It's my first visit.'

'Well I'd like to tell you it gets better but it doesn't, not really. You just get used to it. It's my man I feel sorry for and—' A bell sounded. Her head snapped back to the door. She leaned across the table, scanning the line of men in grey tracksuits who filed into the room. As she leapt to her feet and waved, calling out Tony's name, I closed my eyes and forced myself to take lung-fuls of the bitter air.

'Rosalind, how nice to see you.' Suddenly, he was sitting opposite me. I squeezed my eyes closed again and opened them but he was still there. Apart from his clothes he looked exactly as he had the first time I had met him. His dark hair still fell across his eyebrows, except this time I wanted to pull it until his scalp bled rather than brush it back behind his ear. He had shaved and only the slightest shadow of beard dusted his jawline. There were no bags beneath his eyes, no bruises on his face and no sores around his lips from numbing the pain of incarceration with cheap drugs smuggled through the walls inside other people's orifices. None of his front teeth had been knocked out in vicious shower-stall fist fights. My head was suddenly empty of the sniping one-liners I had rehearsed for months.

'Temperley.' I scanned every inch of him visible above the line of the table. It was only when I got to his right hand that I found a single mark of the passage of time: his third finger veered to the left at an unnatural angle so it careered towards his forefinger just above the top joint. He had broken it on the face of the first police officer who had tried to arrest him. Clearly no one had seen fit to set it straight.

'So? How are you?' His voice was bright as though I was a friend he had bumped into unexpectedly on the high street.

I had made a mistake. I looked for the exit. I would just get up and walk out of the room. I would leave him there. But then I would leave with nothing.

'I'm fine,' I said.

'How am I? Surprisingly well. It seems that one can get used to nearly anything if one only tries hard enough. I read a lot and I'm writing a novel. I think it's rather good, actually. Can you guess what it's about?'

'Why did you do it?' I said, the words tumbling out awkwardly so a tiny fleck of spittle fled my mouth and landed on the table between us.

'Do what?' He smiled.

'You know what.'

'Is that what you've come all this way to ask me?'

I nodded. I thought knowing why he had done what he had done would help me to come to terms with it, to move on. A few months had passed since Tanya had broken off our friendship. Dan's willingness to discuss what happened had dwindled to the point that he would walk away, close doors or plug in headphones when I brought it up. Bea had taken a six-month assignment in Dubai. Stephanie was interviewing for places at university. Everyone had moved on. Everyone except me, and Temperley, of course; he couldn't move anywhere.

'I would have thought it was obvious,' he said.

'Not to me.'

He laughed. 'Because I loved Stephanie.' His voice was a mocking sing-song, his smile so wide that I could see the tea stains on his incisors.

'So why not wait until she was sixteen? Until she left school? Why risk this?' I waved my hand around the room, taking in the screaming children, the man with tiny eyes and an anger-red face snarling at a petrified woman, the prison guard already on his way to intervene.

'Where would be the fun in waiting? Anyone can wait.'

'Where's the fun in this? If you'd waited you could be with her now, living free, gambling yourself into oblivion wherever you chose. But you're in here and she's forgotten all about you.' I shouldn't have said that. I should have left Stephanie out of it. I kicked myself hard in the shin to let the pain act as a reminder.

He widened his smile and looked around the room, tilting his head like a man assessing a horse. 'It was a high stakes gamble and I very nearly lucked out. One more day and we would have been gone for good.' He spread his hands wide and shrugged. I wondered if this was how he told the story to the other inmates, the ones that shared his sickness and weren't horrified by what he had done. Maybe they slapped him on the back and offered up their own child abduction triumphs.

'But you didn't luck out. You lost.'

'Only by a whisker. If I'd been left in peace for another twenty-four hours you would never have seen your daughter again. I think about that a lot. There's plenty of time to think in here. It's the best thing about the place.' He said it in the way that a school-gate mother might describe her new home: *The entertaining space is fabulous; it's the best thing about the place.*

'She would have come back.'

'That's not what she said, but perhaps you're right.' He leant forwards and extended his hands across the table as though I might take them in my own. I couldn't even look at them. He dropped his voice to a whisper. 'But has she come back yet, Rosalind? Is she the same girl she was before she left you to come away with me?'

I pinched the skin on the back of my left hand. I needed to remember why I was there, not let him lead me into his games again. 'Why did you do it, Nathan?'

'Does Dan know you're here?'

'That's none of your business.' I twisted the skin harder, felt myself wince. 'Why did you do it?'

'He doesn't! How interesting.' He grinned. 'What about Stephie? Does she know you're here?'

'Why did you do it?'

'Of course she doesn't. You're the Secretive Simms, aren't you? Only most of you aren't as good at keeping those secrets from each other as you think you are. Poor Stephie knew everything – her accidental birth, how you only got married because of her, your panic attacks and all those pills you take, the fact that you and Dan don't even like each other. Is it any wonder she was so keen to get away?'

I stood up. He had tested me and found me weak again. I had been mad to come, insane to expect him to do anything other than bait me for his own amusement.

'Wait, wait, wait! Don't go, Rosalind! I'll tell you whatever you want to know. I promise.'

I stooped down and picked my bag up from the floor.

'Let's make a deal. You ask me a question and I'll ask you one. I'll be honest if you will.' I fought my instinct to leave.

'You go first,' I said, sitting down on the edge of my chair, my bag still cradled in my arms. His question would tell me whether he was winding me up. If he was playing with me, or if he asked me anything about Stephanie, I would walk out without looking back.

There was a pause before he spoke. 'Do you know who made the call to the school, and if not, who do you think it was?' He was leaning back in his chair, trying to look as though his interest was only casual. But his hands were poised on the edge of the table, a pair of spiders tensed to spring.

'I don't know who it was. If I had to guess I would say Sarah. I've never believed that Stephanie could have kept what she was – you were – planning from everyone and if she told anyone it would have been Sarah.'

A burst of irritation flashed across his face, narrowing his eyes and curling his lips into an ugly comma. It was a glimpse of his true face, the face of the man who lured Stephanie away and beat a policeman to a bloody pulp. Then it was gone and the smile was back in place. 'Oh, Rosalind. I would have thought that if you'd learnt just one thing from little Stephanie's big adventure it would be how good she is at not spilling the beans.'

'My question. Why did you do it?' I wanted to leave almost as much as I wanted to hear his answer.

'Because I could. Because I dared to. Because you, she, the school – everyone – let me.'

'Did you love her?'

'You've had your question.' He started to hum a tune to himself. I forced myself to look him in the eyes until a bell sounded. It was the five-minute warning for the end of the visit. When I stood up to leave he didn't try to stop me.

The pine-bleach smell had taken root in my hair and my clothes. It followed me out of the prison and back to the main road where I hailed a taxi and sank into it weeping with frustration. Even after I had washed my hair five times and sent my jeans and sweater to the charity shop I could still smell the harsh plastic pine of that prison.

*　　*　　*

Sarah was sure Stephanie would be with Jake. 'They're always splitting up and getting back together. He takes her back every time,' she said, failing to keep an edge of bitterness out of her voice. She didn't have his phone number but had been to a party at his place and remembered the address. Beatrice would stay at the flat in case Stephanie appeared there. While Sarah put on her shoes and fetched her coat I was beset by images: Stephanie walking across Wandsworth Common in the last of the summer sunshine, the yellow paper slip held tight in her hand; Stephanie standing outside the Visitors' Centre, unsure whether to let her feet carry her inside or not; Stephanie sitting at table seven, waiting for him to take his seat opposite her.

'Ros. Rosalind. Stop it!' Beatrice's hands gripping my arm brought me back to the room. 'Sarah's sure she's at Jake's. Focus on that for now.'

A yellow parking ticket had been pasted over the driver's side of my windscreen and I broke two nails clawing it off the frozen glass. The still-wet glue formed sticky balls beneath my fingernails and stuck my hands to the steering wheel as we joined the stream of traffic on Green Lanes.

'What do you think he'll do when he gets out, Ros?' Sarah asked, crossing and recrossing her legs.

'I used to worry that he'd convince her that she loved him and make her spend the rest of her life with him. Now I'm afraid that he'll hurt her, punish her.' I told her of Stephanie's whispered confession about the phone call, my visit to Temperley and the flash of rage I had seen on his face when I had failed to tell him who made that call.

'But if she's already told him it was her and he's angry about it, she'd know. She'd realise if he meant to harm her, wouldn't she?'

'Not necessarily. He's never had any problem getting her to do what he wants in the past.' *Kiss me. Touch me. Lie to your mother, rob your mother, leave your mother.* 'Apart from that phone call. That was her only little rebellion. She thwarted his plans and I don't think he'll forgive her for that.' Sarah stifled a gasp as I stamped my foot on the accelerator and darted around a double-decker as it pulled out of a bus stop. 'He's a predator and she's vulnerable. That's how I see it.'

'Ros! Ros! Slow down! That was a red light!'

'Sorry.' I eased off the accelerator, tried to stop myself from picturing Temperley's face leering through the windscreen. Sarah

reached over and squeezed my hand. 'Jake will know where she is.'
I wasn't sure whether she really believed what she said or whether
she just wanted me to calm down so I didn't crash the car.

I parked in a side street and followed Sarah towards Crouch
End's main drag. The temperature had dropped further and
the pavements were slick with black ice. My feet felt loose and
untethered, as though they might slide away from under me
at any moment. Jake lived above an antique shop. I remembered Dan's mother telling me about one of her tedious friend's
daughters picking up an unsuitable boyfriend: *He lives above a
shop, you know. A shop!* Good for her, I had thought at the time.

We huddled in the doorway to the right of the plate glass
window displaying drop-leaf tables, a pop-eyed rocking horse
and a pair of ugly grandfather clocks. When Sarah held her
finger on the top button of the intercom it buzzed angrily. She
buzzed again and again but there was no answer.

'They're not here.'

'Where are they then?' I said, pressing the intercom button
myself. 'You must know someone who'd have Jake's number.'

She shook her head. 'He's not my friend.'

'Isn't he on Facebook or something?'

We sat in the window of a café across the road from Jake's flat.
Sarah tapped away at her phone with both thumbs, trying to
track down Jake while I watched his front door, panicking every
time a double-decker bus passed by and blocked it from view.

'I've sent him a message on Facebook and I've asked anyone
who sees Stephie to call me. That's all I can do.'

I had looked away from the door when Sarah had spoken.
When I looked back it was swinging shut. Someone had just
arrived at Jake's flat.

I left the café and ran across the road, weaving through the
queue of traffic and getting yelled at by a cyclist who had to
swerve to avoid me.

'Steph?' came a voice over the intercom a second after I pressed the buzzer.

Sarah had caught up with me and leant over my shoulder to speak. 'Jake, it's Sarah. Stephanie's Sarah. I need to come in.' There was a crackle of interference, a long pause, an intake of breath followed by a rattling beep. Sarah pushed the door open. I followed her inside and up four winding flights of stairs which grew darker the further we climbed. It was difficult to imagine Stephanie here, walking up the stairs, inhaling the dust and mothball smell that seeped into the hallway from the shop below.

As I rounded the last turn in the stairs there was a sudden burst of light in the sooty darkness. I threw a hand over my face and clung to the banister as my foot skidded off the step.

'It's all right, Ros,' said Sarah, grabbing my arm.

Above me in the wedge of light cast by an open door was a young man with a fuzz of golden hair and red-rimmed eyes. His skin was so fair that the light seemed to pass through him. 'Sarah? Where is she? Has something happened?' His words were blurred by their speed.

'We thought she'd be with you.' As though someone had snipped the string that held him up he slumped towards the floor. I felt the same plummeting of hope. He caught himself on the door frame while I gripped the banister more tightly.

'Can we come in, Jake?' said Sarah.

The door opened into an attic flooded with light. It was part office, part studio, part bedroom, part kitchen. It was the essence of my Empty Rooms made real. Intricate charcoal sketches of bridges lined one of the walls. A sleek silver Apple Mac surrounded by sketchbooks lay dormant on a desk. An unmade bed was a tangle of white sheets. The Jake Stephanie had told me about and the one standing in front of me were already peeling apart in my mind.

'I'm Stephanie's mum.' As I spoke I caught sight of something lying on the bed, a cloud of grey marooned on a snowdrift. I walked across the room and picked up the cardigan that Stephanie had been wearing at the airport, the one that looked like a net of dusty cobwebs. Forgetting Jake and Sarah, I pressed it to my cheek. It still smelled of the perfume we had tried on together. 'Where is she?'

'She was here,' said Jake. 'I thought she'd gone away with you. But she turned up here last night.'

'When?'

'About six.' It would have taken her less than two hours to get to Jake's from Heathrow on the tube. Had she been somewhere else first or had she just walked the streets cursing me as the hour of Temperley's release hurtled ever nearer?

'How was she?'

'Upset. Really upset. She told me about that man showing up at the airport.' He looked away. I felt Sarah's eyes on me.

'Where is she now?' I said.

'I don't know. I've been out looking for her. She was OK this morning, she'd calmed down. She said she wanted to stay with me for a while. Then she got a phone call.'

'Who from?'

'It was just a number. A landline, I think, but I only caught a glimpse of it. She didn't answer. She said it was a wrong number but I knew she was lying. She was really shaken up. I didn't think she'd leave, though.'

'What time did she go?'

'Three-ish. A couple of hours after the phone call.' He looked back to me, his eyes full of despair. 'She sneaked out while I was in the shower. She left this.' He reached into his back pocket and pulled out a square of paper. The note was warm in my hands. As I unfolded it a twenty pence piece rolled out and clattered onto the floor.

'That was in with the note,' Jake said, stooping to pick it up. I took it from his hand. I thought of fifteen-year-old Stephanie in the caravan, tossing the coin over and over again to decide whether to ring the school or not, of all the times over the past few days when I had seen her with it in her hands. Had she left it with Jake because she had made a decision, or let it make a decision for her?

> Thank you for being there for me last night. I'm sorry to sneak off without saying goodbye but there is something I need to do. Love S xxx

Stephanie had scrawled in purple ink on the note.

'I don't know what she means. But I bet it's to do with that scumbag in Wandsworth. Nathan Temperley.' He said the name slowly, enunciating every hated syllable. Kinship bubbled between us.

'He's coming out of prison the day after tomorrow,' I said.

'Oh, fuck! Sorry . . . sorry. Does Steph know?'

I nodded. 'Did she talk about him?'

'All the time, especially just before she went away.' His voice wobbled, I thought he might start to cry. 'Sometimes it felt like she only wanted to be with me so she could talk about him. She said no one else would listen.'

'That's not true,' Sarah said.

'She said you wouldn't understand.' He shrugged. 'I hated it. I hate him. She blames herself for him being locked up, but I've read all about it online – all the newspaper reports about when she was missing and the court case and everything – and he was put away for . . . for sex crimes and abduction and what he did to that policeman. He's a violent pervert. What part of that is Steph's fault?'

'But she doesn't see it like that?' I said.

'No. She said they were both to blame for what happened but she was to blame for getting him locked up for so long. You know what she's like, the way she makes everything into an equation? I think she's calculated exactly how much blame they should each take. I bet it's on her computer somewhere – a blame equation all worked out with X equals this and Y equals that.' I wondered whether Stephanie and Temperley were the only ones included in her equation. If N(athan) = 10,000 and S(tephanie) = 0.00001, what does R(osalind) equal, what about D(an)?

'I thought she still loved him,' Jake continued, in his slow, sad voice. 'We rowed about it. But she said it wasn't love, it was guilt. She said she needed him to forgive her.'

'Forgive her?' I spat. 'For what?'

'For ringing the school and setting the police on him. And for the fact that he got all the punishment while she got off scot-free.' Jake saw me shaking my head and shrugged his shoulders. 'I know, it's ridiculous. It's like Stockholm syndrome or some-thing, like whatever sick ideas he planted in her head when she was fourteen or fifteen are still in there. She didn't get off scot-free. She's punished herself every day, every single day for all these years.'

I nodded, swallowed hard. The idea of Stephanie wanting Temperley's forgiveness *was* ridiculous, but it also made a sick-ening sort of sense. *I just want it all to stop*, she had said to me. She blamed herself, thought her father hated her and her mother had let her drift away. Who did she have to turn to to put things right but him? I would have done anything to be able to talk to her then, to put my arms around her and somehow convince her that there was nothing she needed from Nathan Temperley, least of all his forgiveness.

'Did you know about her visiting him?' said Sarah.

Jake nodded. 'I found the visitor slip in her pocket. I think . . . no. I don't know.'

'What?'

'I think she wanted me to find it. It was like a cry for help or something. I tried to talk her out of going. But she said she had to. She said she needed to tell him what she'd done so they could both move on. She said she had to get it off her chest. We argued about it. She stormed off and said she'd never speak to me again. Maybe she'd be here now if I'd just burnt the damn thing.'

'Then what happened?'

'She came back. She came to me right after she'd been to the prison. She still smelled of it, of the prison, like it had infected her. She said it had been a mistake and that she'd never go back there, never wanted to see him again.' He shook his head. 'She was different after that, even harder to reach. That's when the drinking got out of hand.'

'And you had nothing to do with that?' said Sarah, her voice heavy with sarcasm. 'She didn't even smoke before she met you.'

'Maybe you don't know her as well as you think you do. You lived with her and you didn't even see what was going on.'

Sarah flinched but didn't say anything. What could she say? She hadn't seen it, neither had I.

Jake turned away from us and leant on the desk. 'A few weeks later I smelled that prison smell in her hair again. I knew she'd been back there.' I remembered walking across Wandsworth Common, trailed by the sharp stench of pine and chlorine. 'We argued about it. She told me I'd never understand. She stopped speaking to me again. Wouldn't see me, wouldn't talk to me. She came back, eventually. She told me never to let her go to the prison again. But then she went back.'

I would have stopped her, I thought. *I would have locked her up if I had to, if I'd known.*

'What could I have done?' said Jake, as though he had read my mind. He turned to face me, his eyes wet with tears. 'It's like he's still got her on a string and when he pulls she has no choice but to go to him. She doesn't want to but she can't help it. I think that's why she got herself in such a state, so you'd come and get her and take her away and she wouldn't be able to see him again. She was better off in St Albans, wasn't she? I missed her but I wanted her to stay there.' He rubbed his eyes with the back of his hand and looked at Sarah. 'I know I made a fool of myself and that you thought I should leave her alone, but I was just trying to stop her seeing him. I couldn't let her keep hurting herself like that.'

'You were jealous of him,' Sarah said.

He turned to look out of the window again. 'Jealous of him? No. It's because of him that she can't let herself be happy, she can't let herself love anyone.' He blamed Temperley for Stephanie not loving him and he was probably right. Jake's love for her was clear, he was the closest thing to a boyfriend she had ever had, and yet she had treated him like a least favourite pair of shoes, wearing him only when there was muck to be walked through.

'What does he want from her?' I asked.

He shook his head. 'I thought it was just some sick game he was playing to pass the time in prison. But maybe it's more than that if he's about to get out.' Our eyes met and I saw my own fear reflected back at me.

Before we left, Jake typed my telephone number into his phone and rang me so I could save his number.

'I'm going to go and look for her, too,' he said. 'I need to do something.'

'Where?'

He shrugged. 'I'll ask around some friends, look in some places she likes to go. What if . . .' He trailed off.

'What?'

'What if he makes her run away with him again? They had it all worked out last time, didn't they? They would have been living in Thailand or Brazil with new identities if they hadn't been found in time. What if they're going to finish what they started? We might never see her again.'

'I'm not going to let that happen.' On impulse I put my arms around him. His ribcage trembled beneath my hands. Over his shoulder I noticed two sketches pinned to the wall: one in purple ink and one in blue. Both were of Stephanie laughing, her eyes sparkling with a carefree joy I had never seen in them, her hair wild around her head.

'Those are beautiful,' I said.

'They're Steph. Of course they're beautiful.'

As I walked down the stairs I found that my shoulder was damp with his tears.

We retreated to Beatrice's flat, no closer to finding Stephanie than we had been when we left. Her phone was still switched off. I rang Tanya and told her what had happened. I asked her to let me know immediately if she heard from Stephanie. 'You've got thirty-six hours to find her, Ros. Time is on your side,' she said.

'If the worst comes to the worst we'll just have to be there when he's released,' said Beatrice. 'We know where and when it's going to happen. We can be the first faces he sees when he walks out of that door. We'll follow him all the way to his new hole if that's what you want to do.'

It was the best plan we had.

ONE DAY

Dan's anger crackled from my phone's tiny speaker as I stood shivering in my towel, still wet from the shower. I could see him – shoulders hunched to his ears, left hand in a tight fist – pounding empty air as he spoke. 'I just picked up your message. What the hell is going on? Where's Stephanie? I'm in London. Ring me when you get this.'

It was only seven thirty. He must have stayed in London overnight. Perhaps the trains were caught up in the snow again, or perhaps there was more for him here in the city than there was in his empty home. Maybe there was a hotel room with perfect white sheets and lavish trays of room service, teams of staff on hand to take care of his every need. Maybe there was a woman with smooth, scabless lips and uncomplicated demands.

Tanya must have rung while I was listening to Dan's message. Her voicemail arrived with a beep a few minutes later while I was still thinking about what to say to Dan if I rang him back. She sounded panicked and Tanya didn't panic. As soon as I heard her anxious intake of breath I wanted to drop the phone and let it smash into a hundred pieces on the slate tiles of Beatrice's kitchen floor.

Tanya's message was short but I had to listen to it twice before my mind would let the words take root: 'There's been a massive fuck up, Ros. He's already out. He's been out since seven o'clock yesterday morning.'

The phone slipped out of my hand. There was nothing beneath my feet, the ground was rushing up to meet me, the wind pulling at my skin and roaring in my ears.

I must have cried out because when I opened my eyes Beatrice was there, kneeling in front of me where I had slid to the floor by the dishwasher, telling me to breathe. I focused on her hazel irises and the motion of my lungs. She talked me down slowly, pulling me back from panic and into her kitchen again.

'He's already out,' I said as soon as I had the breath to speak.

It was Beatrice who rang Tanya. My fingers were too clumsy, my tongue could not be trusted to shape words. She switched the phone to speaker mode and set it on the floor between us. Tanya answered straight away. She didn't even say hello. 'I've got some more information and it's good news. He's back in St Albans. Don't ask me what I had to do to find this out, but the address he's registered at for parole and the Sex Offenders' Register is Fifteen Brewster Drive. It's—'

'His father's house,' I said.

'Right. And he's due at the station at eight to check in with the parole team. They're tagging him and putting him under curfew. But you didn't hear it from me. Do you understand? I shouldn't be telling you this. I shouldn't even know it myself. The criminal's right to privacy must be protected at all costs, you know.'

I nodded into the phone.

'We understand,' said Beatrice.

'I'm in court with a client this morning but I'll call you when I can.'

'Should I go there? To the house?' I asked. I could feel her slipping away from me. Beatrice loved Stephanie and loathed Temperley, but Tanya was the one who understood. I craved her steady hand, bitter words and wisdom.

'I can't tell you what to do. If you're looking for Stephanie and you think she could be with him . . . Well, you work it out.' She hung up.

'Come on,' said Beatrice. 'Get dressed.'

Beatrice drove while I rang Sarah and Jake. Neither of them had heard anything from Stephanie, although if she had told Jake not to tell me where she was then I was sure he would lie. I left calling Dan until last. He was frothing with anger that I hadn't rung him from the airport. Even my side of the conversation was enough to make Beatrice wince.

'Do what you need to do. I'm going to find our daughter,' I said when I had listened to enough. I clicked the phone onto silent and threw it back in my bag.

'Why didn't you tell him yesterday?'

'Because I knew he'd react like that. He'd blame me and I need to concentrate on Stephanie right now.'

'It's not because of whatever he's been up to? Or Cam?'

'Does it matter?'

'Just remember that he's on your side when it comes to Stephanie even if he does have a funny way of showing it. She has two parents, that's all I'm saying.'

*   *   *

On a good day it takes forty-five minutes to reach St Albans from central London. The day we travelled home after Temperley's sentencing was not a good day. It was early September and the middle of a record-breaking heatwave. We left the court by a side entrance as soon as the sentence was handed down and walked to the car with the sun beating down on our heads and the heat rising from the tarmac and tangling around our ankles.

I sat beside Stephanie in the back of the car. 'I need to lie down, Mum,' she said without turning her head to look at me, so I got into the front.

Even with the air conditioning on the car was so hot that it made me breathless. By the time we had crawled around the North Circular and into Barnet, Dan's face was glazed with sweat. I watched Stephanie's reflection in the windscreen. Her eyes were closed, her face impassive. I thought about dogs dying in cars on hot days until I couldn't help myself from leaning back between the seats and shaking her.

'I'm fine,' she said. It was exactly what she had said to me outside the courtroom door. She had blinked once, long and slow, when the judge read out the sentence. She hadn't taken her eyes off Temperley as two policemen escorted him out of the dock. I gripped her hand and felt her flinch when, a second before he disappeared through the doors that led to his imprisonment, he turned back towards her and shouted, 'It's not over, Stephanie!' The newspapers interpreted this as a protestation of love or an assertion of enduring sexual obsession, the final words of a desperate man to the object of his desire. I interpreted it as a threat. A threat and a promise.

In the street outside, a man with scarlet skin and no shirt smoked a cigarette in a pub garden. A tiny woman, her head wrapped in a shawl, banged on car windows and shook wilted bunches of yellow carnations in drivers' faces. A teenager with heat-mottled arms leant over the handles of a pushchair to deliver a vicious slap to her screaming daughter's bare thigh. We inched forwards in silence.

The nine-year sentence the judge had handed down was as good as we had been able to hope for, its length driven up by the injuries inflicted on the police officer who had been first on the scene. If Temperley had contained his anger and kept his fists to himself, he could have been free in as little as three years once probation was taken into account. Of course, nine years wouldn't be enough, even if he served all of it, which he wouldn't. Eleven eternities wouldn't have been enough. He would never teach again, nor work with children. He would sign the Sex Offenders' Register for a decade after his release and be forced to notify the police of his address. More than that, though, he would carry the banner of his shame with him wherever he went. I would make sure of it because I would be that banner. I had it all planned. Every time he moved to a new house I would print hundreds of flyers and stick them to lamp-posts: *BEWARE OF THIS MAN*. When he got a job I would post letters to his colleagues: *LOCK UP YOUR DAUGHTERS*. If he got a girlfriend I would write to her every day: *A LEOPARD NEVER CHANGES ITS SPOTS*. I would comb his life for glimmers of joy and snap them out wherever I found them. In the run-up to the court case I started to worry about the possibility of him outliving me. I gulped down cod liver oil and Vitamin C, started jogging three times a week, adopted the Mediterranean diet and begged Dr Bashir for statins, HRT, anything that might give me the edge when it came to longevity. I read that the majority of prisoners smoked and hoped he took up the habit. I thought about sending him money to buy extra cigarettes or toxic cell-brewed alcohol that would poison his liver and bore holes in the vessels that carried blood to his black heart. I willed him to take up drugs and inject himself with rusty needles riddled with HIV and hepatitis because I couldn't stand the thought that he might one day walk free of his shame.

Dan saw the story in the *Globe* the next morning. All the papers had reported the sentencing, of course, with the phrase *a female pupil then aged fifteen* replacing Stephanie's name in every report. Her photo was mercifully absent, her identity protected by her age and the nature of his crimes. But the *Globe* had a different headline: SEX SCANDAL SIR GAVE ME TOP MARKS. It was a classic kiss and tell from a woman called Kitty Marks. She had dressed as a caricature of a naughty schoolgirl for the photos splashed across pages four and five of the paper: a white shirt unbuttoned to expose breasts spilling from a red bra, a grey pleated skirt which ended at the top of her thighs, revealing lengths of fishnet stocking. Her face was heavily made-up and her hair dyed a violent shade of orange. At the bottom of page four was a picture of a teenage girl smiling at the camera from beneath a heavy fringe. The resemblance between the two was there in the blue eyes and wide bottom lip. As a teenager, her hair its natural brown, her freckles visible on her make-up-free face, Kitty had had a delicate beauty that her older self lacked. The other photograph, in the top right-hand corner of the page, was of Temperley. It was the one I had seen before, of him standing on a hillside squinting into the sunlight with his arms around a blurred out woman. But the woman had been cropped out of the shot and the image positioned to direct Temperley's squinting eyes at Kitty's breasts.

I didn't need to read the article to know what it would say. The lurching sickness in my stomach and the way that Dan sat rigidly still, his eyes fixed on the table top, told me everything. But I forced myself to read every word, even when my hands shook so much that the print blurred before my eyes.

Pretty Kitty Marks was an innocent fifteen-year-old with dreams of a career in the law when teen-mad teacher Nathan Temperley arrived at her Lincolnshire comprehensive. The day after Temperley was locked up for nine years for abducting and molesting another teen as well as attacking a policeman, Kitty tells the *Globe* how he lured her into his sordid sex fantasies and ruined her life.

'I fell for Mr Temperley the first time I walked into his class-room. He was twenty-four and I had just turned fifteen, but I was very young for my age. While other girls in my year were off getting drunk and meeting boys, I spent all my time in the library or looking after my mum who was ill with ME.

'Before Mr Temperley came along I found geography boring but with him at the blackboard it was my favourite subject! I started making up reasons to stay behind after class so we could be alone together. I was always knocking on his door and following him around the school. I even waited by his car after the last bell so I could say goodbye to him. One day I missed the bus home and he offered me a lift. Let's just say, getting me home wasn't all he had in mind.'

As Nathan Temperley sank his claws ever deeper into the impressionable youngster, the pair spent more time together. 'I would tell Mum I was studying or watching a film with a friend then sneak around to his house for sex. At weekends I'd meet him at the school and we'd do it in his classroom. Once we nearly got caught by the head teacher and I had to hide in a cupboard. He loved sneaking around and the riskier the situation the better as far as he was concerned. He called the head and the other teachers idiots because they couldn't see what he was doing right under their noses. Looking back on it now it sounds sordid, but I was in love with him and I thought he loved me too. I was a bit of a loner and a nobody at school but he made me feel like the most important person in the world.'

But Kitty saw a new side to her teacher lover when she reached sixteen and decided to quit school so they could be together. 'He turned nasty as soon as I stopped going to school. I thought we could be like a normal couple but he said that if I told anyone about our relationship I'd never see him again. He said I was stupid and ugly and that I wasn't good enough for him. Once, he even threw me out of his house in the middle of the night with no coat or shoes. But I loved him and I kept going back.'

Eventually Kitty's mum, Jean, discovered what was happening and threatened to report Temperley to the school unless he left her daughter alone. 'In spite of how he treated me I was devastated when Mum banned us from seeing each other. I snuck out to his house but he wouldn't open the door so I took an over-dose of aspirin. I could have died but he didn't even care. A week later, I heard that he was giving a girl from the year below lifts home. He ruined my life. If it wasn't for him I would have stayed on at school and gone to university. I'd be a barrister now instead of a barmaid.'

Worryingly, Kitty doesn't think that she and the teen from Hertfordshire – who cannot be named for legal reasons – are Temperley's only victims. 'I can't believe that the girl he ran away with is the first schoolgirl he's had a relationship with since me. There have probably been dozens of us by now. Maybe we should get together and form a support group.'

'We have to tell her about this. She'll see it one way or another and it will be better coming from us than someone else.' I took the paper up to Stephanie's room. It was heavy in my hands and I had to stop on the landing to wipe tears of vicarious humili-ation from my eyes. I knocked and opened the door without waiting for her to invite me in.

She was lying on her bed, my copy of *Alice's Adventures in Wonderland* – the one my mother had given me – unopened beside her. I wondered when she had gone into my room and got it. The thing I loved most about the story was precisely the thing that terrified me about it: the way that Alice simply slipped out of one life and into another. One minute she was exactly where she was meant to be, with her sister and Dinah, but a glimpse of a talking rabbit later and all that she knew was gone. For a moment I considered screwing the paper up behind my back, sliding onto the bed and asking Stephanie to read the story to me. We could fall down the rabbit hole together and never come out again.

'Stephanie, there's a story in today's paper that I think you need to know about.'

'I don't want to see it.' She picked up *Alice* and flicked through the pages, ignoring me.

'It's about another girl who says she had a relationship with him. It's not a very nice article, I'm afraid.' I held the paper towards her but she only glanced at it.

'the *Globe*? Nothing they print is even true, is it? That's what Dad always says. It's not fit to wrap our fish and chips.' She mimicked the jut of Dan's chin when he was at his most pompous. I often did the same when I thought no one was looking.

'I think this is true.' I opened the paper to show her the two pages of photos of Kitty. I was about to close the paper and leave when Stephanie sat up and reached for it.

I held my breath as she scanned the article. She let her hair – auburn again now that the dye had grown out – fall across her face. I wished more than ever that I could know what she was thinking. How much of what he had done to Kitty had he done to her? For such a fast reader it took her a long time to look up from the page.

'What a loser. Sounds like she made it all up for a bit of cash. Is that all you wanted?'

'I just thought you should know in case anyone mentions it to you. I didn't want you to be embarrassed. Stephie, I—'

'I've told you I'm not going to talk about it. Give up, Mum.' She lay back on the bed and curled away from me to face the wall.

I bent to scoop the paper up from where she had dropped it onto the floor. I hated the thought of a picture of Temperley being in her bedroom.

'Leave it,' she said.

That night I heard her crying for the first time since she had returned home. I crept into her room and knelt beside her in the darkness. She let me take her hands in mine. I smiled as I stroked her hair; broken hearts could be mended, the memory of betrayal could fade. *Let it all out, Stephie, let it all out and then we can move on.*

She was different after that. She was no less self-contained and she never came close to breaking her vow of silence on the subject of *him*, but over the next few weeks, I caught fleeting glimmers of her as she had been before she disappeared. She still spent nearly all her spare time alone in her room but one warm evening, a month or so later, as she passed through the kitchen, she paused to tease me about my obsession with *The Archers*, dropping her voice into a farmer's brogue and worrying about the price of onions. A few days later I heard laughter from Freddy's room and peered around the door to find her sitting on his bed playing a computer game with him. It wasn't much, it wasn't nearly enough, but it was better than nothing.

I thought about Kitty Marks often. I wondered whether she had sold her story to the *Globe* purely for the money or whether she had seen an opportunity to break her years of silence and take revenge on Temperley. There was a bit of me, too, that wondered whether she had wanted his attention. Either way, I was grateful to her and for a long time, every time I caught sight of Stephanie smiling, I whispered 'Thank you, Kitty' under my breath.

*   *   *

It was Kitty I was thinking about as fields gave way to the first urban smatterings of St Albans.

'Where to first?' said Beatrice. She didn't own a car and was an anxious driver, leaning forward in her seat so her chin almost rested on the steering wheel. She didn't look away from the road to speak to me.

'Home. You get out there and see if she's been back. She might have left a note or something. I'll go on to his father's house.'

Brewster Drive was an ugly little cul-de-sac of squat brown houses built in the seventies. The council had not seen fit to grit the road and my tyres slipped on slush-topped ice. The pavement in front of all but one of the houses had been scraped clear of snow. Of course, that one house was number fifteen with its peeling-paint door and nicotine-yellow curtains. Clearly neighbourliness on Brewster Drive did not extend to an old widower with emphysema and a pervert for a son. As I picked my way to the front door I saw a grey-haired woman in a purple fleece watching me from the house next door. As I drew closer she pulled the net curtain aside to get a better look. A second later she had a mobile phone in her hand.

I rang the doorbell three times. When nothing happened I put my mouth to the letter box and shouted: 'Mr Temperley? Christopher? It's Rosalind Simm. I need to speak to you. It's urgent.' A curtain twitched in the corner of my vision. A bubble of panic – red and throbbing – rose up from my stomach. It set my heart racing and made me press my hands over my mouth to stop myself from screaming. Whoever opened the door – Temperley or his father – was the best chance I had of finding Stephanie. Screaming and trembling on the doorstep wouldn't help, it would only confuse the father and give the son even more power with which to toy with me. I had to breathe. I had to stay calm.

At last I heard movement in the depths of the house. The door opened a crack, then a little wider. A wedge of air thick with cigarette smoke tumbled out.

The four years since I had last seen Christopher Temperley had been cruel to him. Like a dead tree that remains standing in a forest only because of roots and habit, he had withered away so his shirt and trousers hung emptily from him. He was colourless apart from the angry purple of his arthritic hands which gripped a metal walking frame. His left eye had the soupy haze of a cataract.

'Mrs Simm. I'm sorry,' he wheezed. Each word took an entire breath and his lungs made a liquid bubbling as he spoke. I wondered whether he had stopped visiting Temperley in prison, finding the long journey to Wandsworth and back too arduous and making do with gasping into the phone every couple of weeks instead. 'I thought you were that journalist again. He's been here looking for Nate.' He paused, pressed the heel of a hand to his sternum. 'I'm not meant to answer the door or the phone in case he comes back and tries to catch me out.'

'Where's Nathan?'

'He's gone for his appointment with the police. He has to get one of those tags so they can keep track of him.'

'His appointment was at eight. It's after eleven.' We were less than ten minutes from the police station. Surely he should have been back by now.

Christopher Temperley shrugged. 'I'm sure he won't be long.' I wanted to grab him by the thin, sloping shoulders and shake him until he told me where his son was. But that would get me nowhere. He was already easing himself backwards, ready to close the door.

'Was he here yesterday?'

'Yes. He got here about lunchtime. They gave him a train ticket and forty pounds and he walked up from the station. He didn't even have a coat.'

'And did he stay here last night?'

'Oh yes.' He paused to cough wetly. He held a tissue up to his mouth and mopped a thread of brown phlegm from his lower lip. 'He was clattering about all night, rummaging through his old stuff.'

'Where could he be now? Please, Christopher? It's really important that I find him.'

He shook his head then glanced back over his shoulder towards the sitting room. The tinkling theme tune of a television show about amateur property developers drifted towards us. I wasn't sure whether it was the programme or the whisky that was calling to him.

'It's Stephanie, Mr Temperley. My daughter Stephanie. She's gone missing. Has she been here?'

He started to cough, bubbling wheezes at first then great wracking hacks that shook his body and turned his knuckles white on his walking frame. A long minute passed before the coughing fit ended. His eyes were bloodshot and streaming and his chest rattled with every breath. I wondered whether anyone but Nathan Temperley knew or cared how ill he was. 'I've not seen her,' he said.

That didn't mean she wasn't in the house. Christopher Temperley probably passed out drunk most afternoons. Nathan could have ushered or dragged her in, spirited her upstairs. 'Stephanie!' I shouted round his shoulder into the smoky gloom of his home. 'Stephie!'

'She's not here,' Christopher said. But I was already pushing past him, barging into the dark tunnel of the hallway with its hot, moist air and pub-carpet smell. The sitting room was empty, an old-fashioned portable television blaring in the corner. The light bulb in the dining room had blown so I had to fumble my way across the room and pull open the curtains before there was light enough to see that Stephanie was not hiding amongst the broken chairs, stacks of old newspapers and wheel-less bikes that besieged the table. I checked the galley kitchen with its piles of empty tins, peering through the greasy windows to see the snow lying thick and undisturbed in the small garden beyond.

Christopher Temperley stood in the sitting room doorway, his head bowed as I ran up the stairs and into the musty cave of his bedroom. An oxygen cylinder rested against the bed, its metal casing the same shade of grey as the twisted sheets. I looked under the bed, in the wardrobe, behind the curtains, but she wasn't there. The windowless bathroom with its caged animal stench was empty too. The last room had to belong to Nathan. At the time Stephanie went missing he had lived in a flat on a new development a mile out of the city centre. I had never wondered about what happened to the contents of that flat until I saw it all piled up around the single bed in the house on Brewster Drive. Some of the dozen boxes had been opened and their contents strewn around the room: clothes, camping gear, pink Ordnance Survey maps and a nest of nylon climbing ropes strung with karabiners. It was the ropes that made shiver, the thought of Stephanie tied up and gagged that made me rummage through every box – even the small ones – until I was satisfied that there wasn't a shred of possibility she was in the room.

'She's not here,' I said to Christopher Temperley who still stood in the sitting room doorway. 'Can you ring Nathan? Please? And tell him to come back?' *So I can knock him flat in the snow and grind his fingers beneath my heel until he tells me where my daughter is.*

'He's not got a mobile phone. He'll want one but he'll need to get the money together himself. I can't afford to be buying things for him. He's been using my landline enough since he got back as it is. First thing he did when he walked through the door. Not that whoever it was wanted to talk to him.' The coughing fit seemed to have cleared his chest and he spoke without gasping. I was about to interrupt him when he looked straight at me. 'Maybe it was your girl ringing him last night. It was a girl. I answered it.'

'When?'

'Late last night. He rang her then she rang him. There were cross words spoken, that's for sure.'

'Cross words about what?'

'Oh, I don't know,' he wheezed. The little colour he had had before I barged my way into his house had left him and his eyes were wet behind his glasses. 'I'll get him to ring you. Write your number down and he can use the landline.' I dug in my bag for paper and a pen.

As I slid my way back to the car I noticed another set of footprints leading away from the door, across the uncleared pavement and into the street beyond. They must be Temperley's. He had arrived here the day before, coatless and freezing. How bitter his freedom must have felt as he knocked at the door of that mean little house with its closed curtains and walls soggy with misery and booze. It was the house he had grown up in, the place he had escaped from and now he was back: shamed, ruined, broke and alone. He had nothing, really, unless he had Stephanie. He had nothing to lose.

I ran the last few metres to the car, slipping clumsily and knocking my shin hard on the bumper. As I pulled myself upright and reached into my bag for my keys, a shadow fell across the snow in front of me. I raised my eyes from my bag slowly: a pair of men's leather boots, faded black jeans with a rip in the knee.

'Oops! Are you OK?' His chin was rough with stubble. His cheeks were red with the cold. He wore a dark green beanie under the hood of his coat. I had never seen him before in my life.

'I'm fine. Thank you.' I backed away and pressed the button on my key fob to unlock the car. He followed and bent forward as if to open the door for me, then stopped, his hand still resting on the handle.

'Are you a friend of old Mr Temperley's?' he said.

'No.' I reached for the door handle but his hand still rested there.

'You sure about that, Mrs Simm?' There was something phoney in his accent, a dash of the BBC beneath his wide cockney vowels.

'Quite sure. And I'm sure you know all about my daughter's right to anonymity so why don't you just leave me alone?'

'She doesn't have to stay anonymous. She has every right to tell her side of the story and I can help her to do that. She could set the record straight and make herself a chunk of cash at the same time.'

'Is that what the *Globe* did for Kitty Marks? Gave her the opportunity to set the record straight? It didn't look like that to me. It looked like you talked her into making a fool of herself.'

'Kitty came to me wanting to tell her story. I was hardly going to turn her down. And she got a nice little sum for doing it. Stephanie's at uni now, isn't she? She could make all that student debt go away. My editor has a very thick cheque book.'

I pushed my face right up to his, so close that my nose was flooded with the mint of his chewing gum. 'Leave her alone! Do you hear me? You go anywhere near her and I'll have you done for harassment. We don't need your dirty cash.'

He didn't even flinch.

'All right, Mrs Simm. I know how to play the game.' He raised both his hands, palms open in front of him, and took a step away from the car. As I was closing the door, a white business card landed on my lap. I glimpsed the logo of the *Globe*. I looked up to see him mouthing 'Just in case' at me through the glass.

I stopped halfway down the street, ripped the card in two and threw it out of the window. I watched him – Matthew Bonham, Senior Reporter, according to the card – shrug in my rear-view mirror. My hands shook on the steering wheel and I stalled twice before I managed to pull out onto the main road.

I drew into a garage and had started to dial Beatrice's number when an incoming call from Dan arrived. He was at the house with Beatrice. There was no sign of a break-in but his car keys were gone and so was his car. Stephanie. It had to be Stephanie. I felt a fresh rush of fear: the snow was coming down thick and fast now and the road was a patchwork of slippery slush and hidden ice. Dan's car was a flighty little two-seater.

'Where are you, Rosalind?' Dan said. His voice had a familiar forced brightness to it. It was the voice he used to reason with me when he thought I was being unreasonable, a voice one might use with a child on the brink of a tantrum.

'Looking for Stephanie, of course. Temperley's not been home since his probation appointment. We need to find them.'

'You need to calm down. Just because you and Stephanie had a tiff and she ran off at the airport doesn't mean she's with Temperley. She's obviously been here. Bea might have just missed her.' I wanted to reach my hands through the receiver and shake him. I had to grip my phone with both hands to stop myself from throwing it against the windscreen in frustration.

I took a breath, marshalled the last grains of calmness I had left. 'She's been visiting him in prison and he rang her last night. She thinks she owes him something. I'm telling you she's with him now.'

'You don't know that. You can't just go off—'

I interrupted him: 'Our daughter is somewhere in this town with Nathan Temperley *right now*. She's with him, he blames her for sending him to prison and he has absolutely nothing to lose. Do you get that yet? Do you understand?'

'Come back to the house, Ros.'

'Dan. Stephanie's in danger. We need to find her. Now. You have to believe me on this. I'm not having one of my irrational paranoid episodes or whatever it is you call them. Remember what he is. Remember what he did to her. Think about what he did to that policeman – you saw the photos – then tell me I'm being irrational.'

After a pause in which I could hear nothing but my pulse pounding in my temples, he said: 'OK. Assuming she is with him, then where are they? Where would she go?' I don't know if it was the memory of the policeman's bruised face and broken arm, or the sheer force of my insistence that made him believe me. Maybe he was just humouring me.

'That's what I'm trying to work out. They're hardly going to go for a catch-up in Starbucks. Half the town would recognise them and there's already a journalist from the *Globe* hanging around outside Temperley's house.'

'Shit, shit, shit.'

He said something about journalists being the last thing we needed but I had already tuned out his voice. I knew where they would go. She had told me herself it was the perfect place to vanish.

'Go to the police station, tell them what's happening and see if you can catch up with him. Get hold of Inspector Haskins if you can. I think she's still there. Then look in town, the park, the station, anywhere,' I said. Then I ended the call and revved the engine. I would be there in ten minutes if I drove fast.

The lane that led to the car park was a tunnel of snow. Drifts formed banks on either side and surged into the road so my wing mirrors scraped through them as I slid past. The trees above me were weighed down with accumulated flakes and their branches bumped the roof of the car. I lurched down the lane, my need to reach Stephanie pushing my foot onto the accelerator, my fear of losing control forcing me to stamp on the brake. As I took the sharp left turn into the car park, the steering wheel locked in my hands and the engine whinnied over my shout of frustration. I shifted gears and pumped the accelerator until the car leapt forward, jolting the seat belt tight across my chest. I skidded to a halt and got out. Ten metres away, at the bottom of the path that led up the hillside, Dan's blue car glinted beneath half an inch of snow. 'Stephanie!' I shouted as I moved towards it. It was empty but the snowless patch on the bonnet told me that the engine was still warm.

At the top of the hill, Croome House peered out of the falling snow, its battlement-fringed towers and walls piercing the flat grey sky like teeth on skin. The wind bore down on me, catching in my coat and tearing at my hair, hurling sharp little snowflakes into my eyes as though the house was trying to repel me. I put my head down and ran, my feet sinking into the soft pillows of snow. Halfway up the hill my lungs were burning and the muscles of my thighs crying out in pain but I didn't slow down.

I couldn't. I slipped on a patch of iced mud and fell forwards heavily, smacking my right wrist on a stone so blood ran down my hand and my numb fingers tingled with its warmth. Tears blurred my eyes as I pulled myself back to my feet. The snow was falling vertically and horizontally at the same time, it was rising up from the ground and swirling into clouds in front of me. Nothing was still, as though every atom in the universe was moving at once. Even the house itself seemed to shimmer and warp, to be on the brink of teetering off its foundations and making its way down the hill. As I caught my breath a section of the security fence around Croome's perimeter seemed to buckle and lurch forwards. I blinked, shaded my stinging eyes from the wind. Then I understood what I was seeing: not the fence moving, but a person dressed in grey slipping between the steel fence panels. Stephanie. Her grey jeans and coat had camouflaged her against the steel of the security fence and she had the grey scarf we had bought just two days earlier pulled over her hair. I shouted her name but my words were swallowed by the snow.

I was light-headed with breathlessness when I reached the gap in the fence where I had glimpsed Stephanie. I was forced to bend double and suck in great gasps of air before I could find the strength to follow her through the loose panels. Sheltered from the wind, the three metres of space between the security fence and the walls of the house itself were a corridor of calm. The window that Cam and I had sneaked through together was already open. Snow lay scattered on the floor, not yet melted in the relative warmth inside. I crawled through and bent double for a moment to catch my breath.

With nothing to absorb it, sound bounced from wall to ceiling and back again as I ran through Croome's acres of empty corridor. My every footstep was a thunderclap, my every breath the rasp of a hurricane. The old dining room with its circle of chairs beneath the dilapidated painting of the sky was empty. I pushed onwards through a storeroom then a kitchen lined with rusting cookers and fridges, their doors sagging from their frames. How had I ever seen beauty in this creeping decay?

I crashed through another door and into a windowless corridor so thick with darkness that it brought me to a halt. I paused to listen but heard nothing. I forced myself to plunge into the blackness, heading for a lone crack of light to my left and feeling my way along the wall with an outstretched arm. What if I fell here, unnoticed in this dark, abandoned corner? I could hit my head and lie here unfound until the house was bought by a property developer. Builders would find my bones, eventually; the police would use dental records to identify me. And then who would look after Stephanie?

I ran on through a room filled with blocks of lockers and chairs circling a coffee table. A noticeboard on the wall was still pinned with yellow curls of paper. A noise startled me and I froze like a fox beneath a security light. There were footsteps above: slow and purposeful, their sound thudding through the dust-laden air. I imagined him backing her into a corner, advancing on her like a tide, slowly, slowly to give her time to see exactly how she was going to drown. I wanted to swoop up to the ceiling and squeeze between the floorboards into the room above. I would rise up at his feet like a vengeful angel, shielding Stephanie with my wings as I melted his flesh from his bones with my laser eyes.

I plunged back into the pitch blackness of the corridor and out into the light. I took the steps of the grand staircase two at a time, leaping the step on which, in another life or a dream, Cam had kissed me.

At the top of the stairs I paused. What if I burst in and surprised him, triggering his anger and causing him to hurt her? I crept slowly along the corridor towards the old caretaker's room, the one we had drunk tea in the day after Stephanie came home from London. *You could live in here and no one would ever know, would they? It would be as if you'd just vanished off the face of the earth*, she had said.

Stephanie had left the door ajar. They were standing face to face in front of the central window, a ray of cold light reaching through the pane from which the board had fallen and pooling on the floor between them. In the seconds before Stephanie and Temperley noticed me, I saw everything: her tears, the rough stubble that covered his face, the white plastic security tag peeping out from beneath the bottom of his jeans, the bulging rucksack leaning up against the bed.

'Is this all?' Temperley said. A brown envelope thick with banknotes was open in his hand. He had made her bring him money. He wasn't planning to return to his father on Brewster Drive. He wasn't going to report to his parole officer every week or comply with the terms of any curfew. Instead he was going to pick up exactly where he had been when the police had surrounded the caravan in Oban. He was running away. 'We'll need more than this.' He shook the envelope at Stephanie.

'We?' Stephanie said, her voice shaking, pleading. 'I'm not—'

'No!' I heard myself shout. 'You're not taking her with you.' Before I even had time to move he had stepped forward and pushed Stephanie behind him, as though he wanted to protect her. *Him*, protect *her* from me.

'Go away, Rosalind. This is between Stephanie and me. You've had your chance.'

'Stephanie?' I wanted to see her face, to know what she was thinking, but she hunched behind him, hiding herself from view.

'Ignore her, Stephie. She doesn't matter any more.'

'Stephanie. Please come over here.' She peeked at me over his shoulder. There was fear in her eyes and the trembling of her jaw but she didn't move.

'Stay where you are, Stephanie.' He took another step backwards, trapping her between his body and the plywood-covered window. He reached behind him to grip her arm with his left hand. In the moment his fingers met the fabric of her coat I shuddered with nausea, the ground shifted beneath my feet. I had to grip the door frame to hold myself upright.

'Stephanie. Please. You don't have to do anything he says. Not any more. You don't owe him anything.' I started to move towards them.

'Don't listen to her,' he said, never taking his mocking eyes off me. 'She doesn't understand us. She never has. What did you think was going to happen, Rosalind? Did you think you'd all go on merrily pretending none of it happened, pretending I didn't even exist? Did you think she'd leave me at my dad's house with nothing, tagged like a dog and summoned to the police station every two minutes so they can laugh at me and call me names? After what she did to me? Everything I've been through for her?'

'She's done nothing to you. Nothing! Go if you want to. I won't stop you. But leave her here.'

'And why should I do that?' he said. 'Give me one reason. She'll come if I want her to.'

Wasn't knowing your enemy one of the fundamental principles of war? I knew mine. I had studied him for years. He was a greedy man, a vain man, a gambler, a lover of risks, a player of games. This was a game to him; Stephanie was a game. Well, I had a hand to play too. If he wanted to run then I would help him. 'My car's in the car park,' I said. 'It's a black BMW. Five months old. The tank's full and the keys are in the ignition. My purse is on the seat. Leave Stephanie and you can take it.'

I had surprised him and the lure of money and freedom was strong, strong enough for him to drop his grip on Stephanie's wrist and fold his arms in front of him. If I could offer him enough maybe, just maybe, he would leave without the only thing that mattered.

'The PIN for my card is 9754. I'll write it down for you. You can clear my current account out,' I said. 'There's over twelve thousand pounds in there. There's a credit card, too. It's a Gold AmEx. You can withdraw up to five thousand pounds on that. I won't report it missing.'

'I don't believe you.' But I could see his hunger. I was offering him a high stakes gamble and I just needed to convince him of the odds. Stephanie still stood frozen in place behind him. I forced myself to look at him and not her.

'I'll give you a day,' I said. 'Twenty-four hours exactly before I call the police. That's fair, isn't it? You'd be able to get out of the country in that time if you were smart enough.'

'Oh, I'm smart enough, all right,' he said, smirking.

'Really? You got caught last time.' I wasn't sure if I had gone too far but his smirk remained in place. I forced myself to breathe, folded my hands in front of me so he wouldn't see them shake, I had to hold to my nerve.

'I'm smart enough. Believe me. I've got plans,' he said. 'I've had a lot of time to make them.'

'Prove it, then,' I urged. 'This is the only opportunity you'll get. How long do you think it will be before the police will be round at your father's checking up on you? Dan's on his way to the station now. You're running out of time.'

'How do I know you won't call them the minute I leave here? Before I've even got the cash?'

'Why would I?' I forced myself to shrug, to make my voice ring with confidence. He had to think that I believed in this plan. 'I want you gone. I'd buy you a ticket to Australia if you had a passport. I'd fly you there myself if I could. I don't care about the car or the money. It's all Dan's anyway. You can have it. I give you my word that I won't do anything to stop you.' He was tempted; I could sense him adding and subtracting, weighing up my offer, assessing the value of my hatred for him. Behind him, Stephanie had started to move. She was edging away, inch by silent inch, never taking her eyes off him. 'You can take my phone. And Stephanie's. And take her car keys. It will be at least an hour before we can reach a phone box from here,' I added. 'You'll be long gone.'

'You could flag someone down on the main road. A pair of damsels in distress would have all the lorry drivers stopping to help.'

Stephanie was a metre away from him now. I had to come up with something to make him believe that the odds were tipped in his favour. 'Tie me up, then,' I said. 'Tie me to a chair. That will slow me down. Or lock me in here. Don't you understand that I'll do anything to get rid of you? Anything?' I held his gaze even as images of him binding me to a chair filled my mind, even as I pictured him gripping my leg with his hands, twisting and bending until something snapped. 'Break my legs if that's what you need to do.'

He was going to agree to it. I was sure. I took a breath, let my eyes fall from his for a second. Stephanie was two metres away from him. I willed her to melt into the darkness until he was gone.

But when I looked back at him I realised my mistake. He was laughing at me.

'Nice try, Ros,' he said. 'Very nice try. But even if I went I'd come back. I'd come back for Stephanie.' Suddenly he lunged towards her. She flinched away but not fast enough to stop him from grabbing her hand in his and yanking it hard so she stumbled back to his side. 'Unless you're prepared to throw her in as part of the deal I'll have to politely decline.'

'Let go of her. Stop torturing her.'

'I'm not torturing her. I'm just taking what I'm owed.' He pulled her in front of him, winding an arm around her waist, coiling his fingers into her hair. I wanted to fly at him, dig my nails into his face, claw at his vile hands until he let go. But I stood rooted to the spot, too afraid that he would hurt Stephanie if I made a sudden move.

'She doesn't owe you anything. Just take the car and the money and go,' I said.

'Not without Stephanie.'

'Stephie, you don't want to go with him, do you? You don't have to. You don't have to do anything he says.' She wasn't moving. She was drowning in him, in his toxic pool of false love; he was drowning her, dragging her down behind him, further and further from my reach.

'It's no good, Rosalind. You've lost her. You lost her six years ago. Didn't you notice? Or were you too busy worrying about the sky falling in or drowning in the bathtub or the moon crashing to earth and crushing you all in your beds? Or was it nuclear wars or terrorists living in your airing cupboard?'

His taunting words seemed to steal the breath from my lungs and breathe it into Stephanie's. As I froze she came to life. She jerked in his grip, shaking the hair from her face and struggling to free herself. She looked at me with wild, red-ringed eyes as though she had only just realised I was there. 'Let go of me!' she said.

'You're not going to listen to her. You're coming with me.'

'No.' It was almost a whisper. 'No,' she said again, louder.

'What did you say?'

'No. I'm not coming with you. I gave you the money and found you a place to lie low. That's what you said I had to do. You said that would be the end of it. But you always want more. More and more and more! Nothing is ever enough for you and it never will be. You won't stop until there's nothing left of me! Until I'm all used up! Just take Mum's car and go. There's nothing for you here.'

He curled his hand into a fist, strands of her hair still gripped between his fingers. She squeezed her eyes closed as he turned her face towards him.

'You don't know what you're saying. Remember what she is, Stephie. She's a nutcase. She's mad. Remember the trip to Stratford-upon-Avon? Remember Florida? She's just trying to control you.'

But she wasn't listening to him. 'I never said I'd go with you. Not this time. Let go of me. Let go!' She made a sudden twisting lunge to her left, trying to wriggle free of his grip.

That was when he snapped, when his mask fell clean away and he grabbed her roughly by the shoulder and snarled into her face. 'You're coming with me. We have to finish what we started, otherwise they've won. Otherwise it was all for nothing. And I won't lose. I won't lose you. I'd rather die. I'd rather you died too. Then it would all be over, fair and square. We'd all lose together.'

What kind of man grooms a fourteen-year-old schoolgirl and runs off with her three days after her fifteenth birthday? It's easy to say an evil man, a pervert, a freak. But there are plenty of those out there and they don't do what he did; they might *want* to do it but they don't. Instead they prey on the vulnerable, the neglected, the lost, the unloved, the ones who have no voices or no one who will listen. They stay below the radar, their crimes go unseen, hushed up, ignored; their evil grows in darkness, unnoticed and unlooked for. But Nathan Temperley wasn't like them. Stephanie wasn't unloved or lost and his crime was never meant to go unseen: he had whisked her away from right beneath our noses. When I visited him at Wandsworth and asked him why he did what he did, he said *Because I could*. At the time I thought he was just being flippant, taunting me with an answer that was no answer at all. But in Croome House – as I watched fury transform his face, as I saw him reach for

Stephanie just as he had reached for the policeman who had come to arrest him – I realised that he had told me the truth, had laid his character bare before me. In that moment in that cold room in Croome House, I thought I understood Nathan Temperley better than anyone else on earth, perhaps better, even, than he understood himself. He saw himself as a man who could do things others could not, as a winner in a world of losers. It wasn't about Stephanie, it never had been. It was always only about him. What happens if you take a man like that, thwart his greatest enterprise and lock him up for five and a half years with nothing but the memory of the day it all came tumbling down? He doesn't change. He doesn't get better. He doesn't see the error of his ways. He lies in his bunk night after night working out how to get back what he has lost and take revenge on those who thwarted him.

And what do you do when a man like that has his hands on your daughter? When his blunt fingers are digging into her skin, pressing on her bones, crushing the air from her lungs? When you can feel his anger around you, sharp and hot and relentless?

My feet left the floor and I hit him side on, my elbows making contact first and knocking Stephanie free of his grip. Strength and weight were on his side but surprise was on mine. He fell backwards, hard, his head and shoulders connecting with the sheet of mouldy plywood covering the bottom of the room's massive central window. The rotten board crumpled under his weight and with the roar of a tree falling to the ground, the frame gave way and the whole full-length window crashed outwards onto the wide balcony beyond. I had fallen with him, landing hard on his legs and winding myself so that for a moment I could do nothing but fight to draw breath in the frigid outside air.

'Mum!' Stephanie was behind me. Why wasn't she running away?

'Go, Stephanie! Go!' I shouted. The air on the balcony seethed with snow. Tiny pellets of icy sharpness swarmed around me, stinging my face, clogging my eyelashes and burning my tongue as soon as I opened my mouth to speak. The wind tore at my coat, grabbed strands of my hair and plastered them over my face.

Temperley was already freeing himself from beneath me, kicking with both his legs and trying to gain purchase with his hands on the snowy rink of the balcony. I grabbed at him, frantically trying to tether him to the floor, to me, to anything that would slow his progress towards Stephanie. I had hands full of his jeans, his sweatshirt. But he kicked out hard, catching me on the jaw and jarring my head so my vision blurred and I was forced to let go.

He staggered to his feet, slipping and sliding on the icy surface, and leant against the battlement-topped balustrade that ran around the balcony's edge. His hands were bleeding, and for a moment he held them in front of him, palms up. A sudden gust of wind cleared the air of snow and I could see shards of glass from the broken window glittering where they had pierced his skin, and the anger twisting his face.

'You rabid little cow,' he hissed. 'You won't stop me.'

I staggered towards him, my feet slipping, my legs feeling loose and untethered beneath me.

'Mum!' shouted Stephanie from behind me.

He was running towards me, towards the empty window frame and the room beyond it. I launched myself forwards in an awkward rugby tackle, sending us both slithering backwards and tumbling against the battlement. My feet skittered across the ice. The thick stone hit me hard in the side and something within me cracked. He gripped a corner of a crumbling battlement and cried out in pain as the stone drove the glass shards into his flesh. Then I was spinning, or the snow was spinning around me. I was screaming or he was screaming. Then I was falling as I always fell in my nightmares, the air rushing over me and through me. My arms reached into nothing, my hands gripped thin air.

'Mum, it's OK. Mum? Mum? Mum?' Stephanie was shaking me gently, the warmth of her face next to mine. I opened my eyes and saw her leaning over me. Above her was nothing but the sky. I reached out and pressed the palms of my hands into the snow-covered floor of the balcony. Temperley was nowhere to be seen.

TODAY

I like it here. It's warm and white, clean and quiet. Most of all it's still. I'm in a room on my own and nothing moves in here. I have to keep my eyes open, though. If I close them even for a second I see the snow again – billions of flakes in constant motion, gathering around me, filling the air with ever-shifting shapes. I glimpse it every time I blink.

I haven't got long. This narrow wedge of time, the sanctuary of moments in which I can lie here silently in this bed, is already running out. Any minute now someone will come through the door and the questions will start. I'm not sure who will come first. Maybe Dan. Maybe Tanya. Maybe someone else. Most likely, though, it will be a pair of police officers, their handcuffs clipped to their belts, the blank pages of their notebooks waiting to be filled. Robert Lewis warned me they were on their way. A man has died; I suppose they must do their jobs.

Medically, I suspect I don't need to be here. My cracked ribs have already been X-rayed and trussed up. They just need time to heal. But Stephanie won't be discharged until tomorrow so I'm not going anywhere yet. She has suspected concussion because she remembers nothing at all about what happened on the balcony at Croome House. 'It was so icy. I must have slipped and banged my head,' she told the paramedics, Robert Lewis and anyone else who asked as we were driven here, wrapped in blankets and fed hot sweet tea. We didn't talk. We didn't even look at each other, but it wasn't until I was taken away to be X-rayed that she let go of my hand.

I can hear footsteps in the corridor now, not the squeak of the nurses' rubber-soled shoes but the purposeful footfalls of someone coming for me. I could slide out of bed and lock myself in the bathroom or pull the sheet up to my chin and pretend to be asleep, but what would be the point? I know what they want. They want me to reach back in time to that moment in the snowstorm and account for the force that propelled Nathan Temperley over the crumbling battlement and into the empty air beyond. 'What happened up there, Ros, Rosalind, Mum, Mrs Simm?' they will say. As they wait for me to answer they will look at me and wonder: *Would she? Could she? Did she?*

Would she? I've lost count of the number of people I have told that I wish Nathan Temperley were dead, that I would kill him if I had the chance. But what mother wouldn't say the same in my situation? It's just a figure of speech, isn't it?

Could she? Could I? That's harder to answer. I have often wondered whether I could. Over the years I have imagined myself with a gun in my hand, him kneeling in front of me, his head bowed. In my imagination there are no witnesses, no consequences. Could I pull the trigger? I've never been sure that I could.

Did she? Did she push him? they will wonder as they scan my face for answers. I try to remember that moment – the one in which he stopped being on the balcony and started falling to the ground – but it's like trying to see a faint star in the dark night's sky: look slightly to the left or the right of it and it glows palely in the periphery of your vision, but look straight at it and it vanishes from view.

I remember the moment before: Temperley's cry of pain as he struggled to grip the battlement edge with his bleeding hand. I remember the stabbing ache in my ribs and the stuttering passage of air through my lungs, the chill of the snow melting through the knees of my jeans and the pine-bleach prison smell of his hair. I remember how time flexed and distorted to become a gallery of my past: Stephanie smiling at me over Dan's shoulder in the basement flat in Durham; her face on the front of *The Sun* when she had been missing for five days; the way she had looked at Dan when she shouted at him on the stairs; the fear in her eyes when Temperley twisted her hair in his fist.

I remember the moment after, too. I remember opening my eyes and finding Stephanie leaning over me. Together we pulled ourselves up to look over the edge of the battlements. He had fallen into the empty pit of the deep ornamental pond that had been Croome's nod to a moat. He lay still and twisted on the white snow, a crimson halo radiating outwards from the crown of his head. Sometimes, when I remember looking down at him with Stephanie at my side, I think I hear her whispering 'Thank you' but sometimes I don't remember her saying anything at all.

The footsteps are closer now. They're nearly at my door. I wonder if there will be a knock – a tentative tapping from Dan, unsure of his welcome, or the officious *rap-rap-rapping* of a police officer. Time is running out. What will I tell them? What will I say?

In that moment, the one they will want to know about, everything was in motion. He was there beside me, on me, around me, and then he wasn't. There were screams and then there was silence. There was fear – as cold and bright and smothering as the swirling snow – and then that fear was gone. The thing is that the last act of Nathan Temperley's life – whether that was to slip, to fall, to jump or to be pushed – doesn't matter, not when I think about the acts that came before it. What matters is that I can hear Stephanie breathing quietly in her sleep in the room next door. What matters is that the power he held over her has come to an end. He was already disappearing into the blank white landscape as we watched the paramedics look for a pulse and shrug their shoulders when there was nothing to find.

There's someone outside the door of my room now. I hear a breath, the shuffle of a foot, the clearing of a throat. At least one person, maybe two. Perhaps a queue is forming. I watch the handle but it doesn't move. Whoever stands behind the door is hesitating or waiting.

But all of a sudden I am tired of waiting. 'Come in,' I call out.

The handle moves, the door begins to open. I take a deep breath. I know what I am going to say.

ACKNOWLEDGMENTS

Writing *The Daughter's Secret* would not have been possible without the *Good Housekeeping* novel competition and I would like to say an enormous thank you to the teams at *Good Housekeeping* and Orion and to Luigi Bonomi for creating such a fantastic way to inspire and support new writers. Thank you to the competition judges – Lindsay Nicholson, Kate Mills, Kate Mosse, Fern Britton and Luigi – your vote of confidence meant the world to me.

A huge thank you to Laura Gerrard whose super-insightful editing and encouragement helped me to make this story into what I wanted it to be, and to everyone else at Orion who has supported *The Daughter's Secret* along the way.

I am very grateful to my family and friends who have been encouraging me to write fiction for as long as I can remember, especially my mother, and to my grandmother for showing me that it could be done. Most of all I must thank Tim for all the love and laughter and for keeping the world at bay so I could write this story.